WILDERNESS

SAVAGE RENDEZVOUS/ BLOOD FURY

—— DAVID THOMPSON ——

D0638940

LEISURE BOOKS NEW YORK CITY

A LEISURE BOOK®

March 1997

Published by

Dorchester Publishing Co., Inc.
276 Fifth Avenue
New York, NY 10001

SAVAGE RENDEZVOUS copyright © 1991 by David L. Robbins

BLOOD FURY copyright © 1991 by David L. Robbins

Printed in the United States of America.

SAVAGE RENDEZVOUS

Dedicated to
Judy, Joshua, and Shane.
And the Kimmer, Becky, and Crystal—
we can't let you-know-who have all the fun!

Foreword

In the early decades of the nineteenth century America quivered on the brink of a thrilling epoch in her history. East of the mighty Mississippi River lay verdant states rapidly filling with cities and towns as the hardy populace continued its migration from the Atlantic Ocean toward the distant frontier. But west of the Mississippi, with the sole exception of the recently formed state of Missouri, lay the vast domain labeled by one explorer as the Great American Desert.

A vast, virtually uncharted expanse, inhabited by countless wild beasts and potentially fierce Indians, daunted all but the very bravest. To a majority of Americans the foreboding unknown loomed as a terrifying barrier between the U.S. and the Pacific Ocean. Lurid tales were circulated in the press detailing the horrors to be encountered by anyone foolish enough to venture into the inhospitable wasteland.

At first, only a few adventurers and reclusive sorts dared cross the invisible boundary between civilization and the shadowy realm of eternal savagery. Then wearing beaver fur became the height of fashion in Europe and America, and young trappers poured into the wilderness in the hopes of making their fortunes. Few lived to see their dreams realized. In one year alone, 116 men left Santa Fe to spend a season in the Rocky Mountains. Only 16 survived.

Those trappers who did outwit the hostile Indians and escaped unscathed from encounters with grizzlies would become the stuff of legends: Mountain Men.

This is the story of one such youth who was lured into going where few men had gone before in the hope of acquiring riches. Instead, he found adventures galore and wealth of a nobler kind.

Chapter One

The sun shone brilliantly on the verdant land bordering
the Bear River. Rolling hills enclosed the fertile bottoms,
and beyond the hills reared towering mountains capped
with snow even in the month of July. Game abounded.
High in the air wheeled eagles, soaring on the currents
as their keen eyes sought prey far below. Hawks flew over
the fields and forests, alert for a morsel to appease their
hunger. Buffalo, elk, deer, and antelope gorged themselves
on the thick, sweet grasses. Predators were also in
evidence. Solitary cougars prowled the rocky heights.
Packs of wolves trailed the herbivores, patiently waiting
their chance to close in for the kill. Coyotes and foxes
prowled for smaller creatures.

Into this natural paradise rode three figures, two men
and a woman. They came from the southwest, and all three
showed signs of having ridden many miles.

The man in the lead sat loosely in the saddle, flowing
with the rhythm of his white horse. His shoulder-length
hair, beard, and mustache were all the same color as his
animal. Penetrating blue eyes peered out at the world from
under knitted brows. On his head perched a brown beaver
hat, and buckskins adorned his big frame. Cradled in his

arms was a Hawken rifle.

After the oldster came a much younger man, not yet into his twenties, who also wore buckskins and moccasins. Angled across his broad chest were a bullet pouch and powder horn. Two pistols were tucked under his brown leather belt. In a sheath on his left hip nestled a butcher knife with a 12-inch blade. He ran his left hand through his long black hair while retaining a grip on his Hawken with his right, then glanced to the west when his alert green eyes detected movement. A grin creased his lips at the sight of a rabbit bounding off into the brush. "How about stew for supper?" he asked in a distinctive, deep voice.

"All you ever think about is food, Nate," chided the older man. He snickered and glanced back over his shoulder at the third member of their party. "Well, that's not *all* you think about."

Nate bristled. "I won't allow any man to talk about my wife that way," he stated severely. "Not even you, Shakespeare."

The lead rider sighed and shook his head. "I thought we were friends, Nathaniel King."

Surprised by the formality in the other's tone, Nate goaded his mare forward until he rode alongside his companion. "We are. There's no one I consider a better friend than you."

Shakespeare regarded the younger man critically. "Then you should be able to take a joke without reacting like a bobcat defending its mate."

"I didn't mean to hurt your feelings, but you know how I am about Winona."

"I know. Believe me, I know."

Nate saw his friend's face curl in a smile, and he relaxed. "I'm sorry. Ever since I met her I've been acting a little peculiar."

Shakespeare vented a snort that would have done credit to a bull buffalo. "A little? Lord, son, your antics are enough to drive a fellow crazy."

"I haven't been that bad."

"Don't fool yourself. Even my horse commented on it."

Smiling, Nate gazed back at the cause for their conversation, his heart swelling with love and pride at the thought she had consented to be his wife.

Winona was her name, and she was a full-blooded Shoshone. Her long tresses shimmered with vitality, and her brown eyes danced with happiness as she returned his loving look. Prominent cheekbones accented her beautiful features. Clinging loosely to her supple form was a beaded buckskin dress.

Nate beamed and winked.

"Oh, no. Here we go again," Shakespeare groused.

"What are you talking about?"

"Having to put up with the two of you making cow eyes at each other."

"We don't make cow eyes," Nate stated huffily.

"What would you call it?"

"True love."

Shakespeare chuckled good-naturedly. "What do you know about true love?" he queried, and then launched into a quote from his favorite author. "Alas, that love, so gentle in his view, should be so tyrannous and rough in proof!"

"Which play is that from?" Nate inquired.

"*Romeo and Juliet.* You should read it sometime. It describes youthful love perfectly," Shakespeare said, then reached behind him and patted the roll tied behind his saddle. "I'll lend my book to you tonight, if you want."

Nate shook his head, thinking of the huge volume the frontiersman carted everywhere and safeguarded fanatically. "No, thanks. I have other things to do tonight."

"I'm sure."

Sighing in resignation, Nate slowed the mare and waited

for his wife to catch up. He smiled at her, then looked at the three pack animals she led, verifying their provisions were secure.

Winona's hands flew in a series of rapid gestures.

Nate followed her flying fingers closely, knowing if he missed even one gesture the entire meaning could be lost. He'd made great progress in his mastery of sign language since leaving St. Louis over two months ago, but he still had to concentrate intently when others were directing comments at him, and he still made far too many mistakes for his liking.

One of the many surprises connected to his continuing education in the ways of the wilderness had been learning that the Indians employed a universal sign language. No one knew exactly which tribe had started the practice. The origins of sign language, like the origins of many of the tribes, were shrouded in antiquity. But the Comanches, Kiowas, Apaches, Shoshones, Crows, Pawnees, Nez Percés, and many others all used sign talk to communicate when they met because their verbal tongues were so different.

Now Winona concluded her remarks, and Nate reviewed them mentally while preparing his response: She was glad they were almost to the rendezvous; she looked forward to meeting old friends there; she wanted to show off her new husband to certain women she knew; and she hoped the Bad One would not give them any trouble.

The Bad One?

Nate replied that he too looked forward to arriving at the rendezvous and that he would be glad to meet her friends. Then he posed a question using the Shoshone tongue instead of sign, voicing the words haltingly, his pronunciation atrocious. "Who Bad One?"

Winona answered with her hands. "Ask Carcajou."

Nodding, Nate glanced at the mountain man on whom the Indians had bestowed the *voyageurs'* name for the wolverine, a fierce animal famous for its vicious disposition. "Shakespeare, who's the Bad One?"

The frontiersman replied without turning around. "That's the Indian name for Gaston Cleroult. He was a *voyageur* up in Canada for ten years or so. Then he grew tired of working for someone else and struck out on his own. Became a *coureur de bois*."

"A what?" Nate interrupted.

Shakespeare gazed over his shoulder. "I keep forgetting who I'm talking to. Must be a sign of old age." He cackled.

"I know what a *voyageur* is," Nate told him. "Uncle Zeke told me all about them. They're Canadian trappers."

"True. Well, a *coureur de bois* is a trapper who crosses the line between legal and illegal. It's someone who traps without a license. A poacher."

"And this Cleroult poached?"

"Only for a year or so, according to the stories I've heard. Then he made a bigger mistake. He murdered an official who tried to arrest him, and drifted south. The Giant has been roaming the Rockies for seven or eight years now, and I can honestly say he's the most hated man west of the Mississippi."

"The Giant?"

"Yep. That's what everyone hereabouts calls him. Stems from the fact he's six feet, four inches tall and must weigh two hundred and forty pounds."

Nate imagined the tremendous size of the man, and whistled in appreciation. "I've seen few men that size."

"Pray you don't run into him, Nate. He's the Devil incarnate."

"Do you know him personally?"

"We've bumped into each other a few times. It's not an experience I can recommend."

"He's really as bad as all that?"

"Why do you think the Indians named him the Bad

One?'' Shakespeare rejoined.

Nate said nothing. He knew about the significance of names to the Indians. Names were bestowed on babies immediately after birth. Often the infants were named after animals, frequently for an act of nature that occurred the day they were born. If they were born with a physical deformity, their name invariably reflected their condition and they were stuck with it. The women, as a general rule, kept theirs from cradleboard to grave. But the men, the warriors, often took a new name after they counted their first coup, performed some other brave act, or had an exceptionally vivid dream.

If the Indians called this Gaston Cleroult the Bad One, Nate reasoned, then the Giant must indeed be a wicked person. He thought about his own Indian name, Grizzly Killer, given to him by a Cheyenne warrior after a harrowing encounter with a massive grizzly bear. Only by a miracle had he survived. Now, thanks in large part to Shakespeare proclaiming the news to everyone they met, his sobriquet was becoming widely known. Already the Shoshones referred to him exclusively by it.

The Shoshones.

Nate twisted in the saddle and stared at the last hill they had crossed. ''Why did Drags the Rope and the rest of the band decide to camp for the night when we're only an hour and a half from the rendezvous site?''

''Because the Shoshones, like most Indians, are a proud people. They didn't want to ride into the rendezvous looking like something the cat dragged home. After that scrape with the Blackfeet they were in pitiful shape. Look at all the possessions and horses they lost,'' Shakespeare detailed.

''Not to mention the lives,'' Nate added, thinking of Winona's mother and father. Both had perished at the hands of Mad Dog's war party.

''Them too,'' Shakespeare said. ''As you already know,

many of the tribes send groups to the rendezvous to trade, sell their women, and have a grand time. The rendezvous draws them like a magnet draws iron. They can't resist.'' He paused. "It's sort of a neutral territory where everyone is supposed to be on their best behavior.''

"Do they all get along?''

"Sometimes they do, sometimes they don't,'' Shakespeare responded enigmatically. "One thing you can count on for certain. There won't be any Blackfeet there.''

"Thank goodness,'' Nate said.

The brutal Blackfeet were the scourge of the northern Rockies. They relentlessly hounded any whites who ventured into their territory, and they were credited with taking the lives of several dozen trappers. They also constantly waged war on the other tribes, their war parties often traveling hundreds of miles to attack an enemy camp. As with the Comanches and the Kiowas far, far to the south, the Blackfeet were greatly feared and widely despised, particularly by the whites.

"You can count on Drags the Rope and his band to ride into the rendezvous tomorrow morning, all dressed in their best buckskins and mounted on their finest horses,'' Shakespeare said.

"A while ago you told me the rendezvous has already started. How much longer will it last?''

"If we're lucky, about two more weeks. The past two have both broken up about the middle of July.''

"And this is only the third one?''

"Yep. The third of many to come.''

"What makes you say that?''

"Because as long as those dandies and ladies back East are willing to pay good money for prime beaver pelts, there will be trappers roaming the Rockies. At least, until the beaver are gone.''

Nate felt a hand touch his shoulder and glanced at his wife. "What?'' he asked in Shoshone.

Winona pointed at the back of his head.

Puzzled, Nate rested the Hawken between his thighs and the pommel and reached up to gingerly touch his hair. His fingers came into contact with the feather, and he realized it was almost untied.

The feather.

Memories rose unbidden at the contact, memories of the noble Cheyenne warrior named White Eagle, a prominent member of the Bow String Society. In many of the Plains tribes were organizations of their bravest men known as warrior or soldier societies. There might be many such societies in a single tribe, each competing with the others for the honor of being known as the best fighters, a sort of friendly rivalry designed to promote manly excellence. The Cheyennes had six such societies: the Bow String, the Crazy Dogs, the Fox Soldiers, the Red Shields, the Elk Soldiers, and the Dog Soldiers. White Eagle belonged to the Bow String Society and was a top war chief.

Receiving a feather from such a renowned warrior was quite an honor. Nate had been given his after a battle with a Kiowa band, weeks ago, yet only within the past few days had he grown to appreciate its significance. Now he wore it proudly, constantly, tied to his hair with a thin strip of buckskin fringe.

Somehow, the buckskin had come loose.

Nate secured the feather in its proper position again, aligning it to dangle, slanted toward his right shoulder.

Her hands moving rapidly, Winona told him how glad she was to have a husband who had already demonstrated his bravery many times over, a husband who would be a good provider for her and their many children.

Smiling sheepishly, Nate merely nodded. He still could not quite accustom himself to the intimidating frankness of Indian women. Winona entertained no compunctions whatsoever about discussing any subject under the sun, not even sex, and at times her candid references to things that were strictly taboo for the refined, cultured ladies of New York City discomfited him.

And her frankness wasn't the only source of distress.

Nate stared at her left hand. Thin strips of soft hide had been wrapped around the tips of her first two fingers to keep out the dirt and prevent infection.

How could she do such a thing?

To her, Nate realized, such a barbaric act was perfectly normal. She had lost her father and mother to the Blackfeet. Shoshone custom dictated that when a woman lost a member of her family or a dear friend, as a public show of mourning and proof of devotion she had to cut off a finger at the first joint. Nate had seen a few elderly women in the Shoshone camp who were missing the tips of each finger. The males also subscribed to the practice, although not as extensively, but they never sliced the ends off all their fingers for a very practical reason; the first two fingers on the hand they used for drawing a bow were never touched. Even though he knew how devoted the Shoshones were to their customs, Nate still could scarcely believe his wife had actually mutilated herself. Especially after he'd warned her not to do it.

How could she?

Shakespeare unexpectedly reined up. "Let's rest for a bit," he proposed.

"Now?" Nate responded in surprise. "When we are so close to the rendezvous site?"

"Now," the frontiersman stated emphatically. "Fifteen minutes more won't make a difference, will it?"

"No," Nate said rather reluctantly. He was eager to reach their destination, but he'd learned not to question his friend's judgment in such matters.

"The horses can use some water," Shakespeare explained, nodding at the river several hundred yards to the east. "We can brush some of the dust from our clothes and get set for the rendezvous.''

"I'm already ready," Nate said.

Shakespeare stared reproachfully at the younger man. "I wasn't necessarily thinking about you or me.''

Stunned by his own stupidity, Nate looked at his wife. "Oh. I didn't think it would matter to her.''

"In certain respects Indian women are no different from white women. They both like to put on their best dresses from time to time and sashay around for everyone to take a gander. If you want my advice, you'll stop regarding your wife as an Indian and see her as the woman she is.''

"I do regard her as a woman.''

"Perhaps. But you still have a lot of foolish Eastern notions about Indians floating around in that dense skull of yours. Get rid of that nonsense and you'll be much better off.''

"The voice of experience," Nate said, wishing he had a third of his friend's wisdom.

Shakespeare touched the hair hanging over his right ear. "Where do you think I got all this gray from?''

Laughing, Nate signed for Winona to dismount. "I'll take the horses to the river," he offered.

"My old bones thank you," the frontiersman replied, and slipped to the ground.

"Your old bones can run rings around most men a third your age," Nate pointed out.

Inhaling deeply, Shakespeare watched a hawk circle above a stand of pine trees to the south, then gazed at a herd of elk munching in a meadow to the southwest. "Living in the Rockies hardens a man, Nate. Makes him as tough as leather. If I'd spent my whole life in one of those big cities back East, where the only exercise most folks get is walking to their carriages each day, they would have planted me six feet under years ago.''

"You're exaggerating, as usual.''

"Am I? You lived in New York City most of your life.

Did you happen to notice anything peculiar about the air you were breathing?''

"It's common knowledge the air there can be unhealthy at times, particularly on cold winter days when all that coal and wood is being burned. The papers were always full of stories about how bad the situation was, but no one had a solution."

The frontiersman indicated the crystal-clear atmosphere overhead, then motioned at the pristine forest. "This is the solution."

Nate knew better than to argue. Shakespeare's logic could be irrefutable, especially when the topic concerned the relative merits of civilization and the wilderness. Deep down, Nate happened to agree. He'd breathed in the sooty air of New York City on many a day. He'd contended with the widespread carriage congestion. He'd been caught up in the frantic pace of life, in the frenetic drive to amass a fortune no matter what the cost, even if the work itself should be total drudgery. He was intimately familiar with all the dubious benefits of cultured society. And now, after having lived in the admittedly savage wilds and experiencing firsthand the genuine freedom enjoyed by those who had deliberately forsaken civilization's constraints, he tended to regard life in New York City as a veritable prison where men and women had their minds and souls enslaved by greed.

"Are you planning to take the horses today or tomorrow?" Shakespeare asked.

With a start, Nate realized he'd been sitting there reflecting for over a minute. "I'll be right back," he said, and leaned down to take the reins to the white horse from his friend.

"Let the animals drink their full," Shakespeare advised. "They've earned it." He stepped up to the side of his horse and removed some jerked meat.

"Save some for me," Nate said, and turned his mare

so he could collect Winona's animal and the three pack horses. His wife had already taken a seat on a nearby log and was busy running a hairbrush through her long tresses. A porcupine's tail had been used to construct the brush. It had been sewn over a long stick, then the quills trimmed until an inch and a half in length. To cover the seam, beadwork had been applied, resulting in an attractive brush every bit as serviceable as the most expensive variety found at the most fashionable shops.

Winona smiled up at him.

Returning her loving gaze, Nate heard the frontiersman cough loudly, and decided to attend to his task. He headed for the river, five horses in tow, his heart filled to overflowing with happiness. At that moment, there was nowhere else in the world he would rather have been than right where he was. He swung to the left to skirt a dense thicket, humming softly, and had covered ten yards when nature again reminded him that he could not afford to relax his vigilance for a second.

With a mighty growl, a grizzly lumbered from the copse.

Chapter Two

Of all the wild creatures known to exist in the vast tract extending from the Mississippi to the West Coast, absolutely none were more feared than the grizzly bear. Specimens over eight feet in length had been taken, and they were known to weigh up to 1500 pounds. The most unpredictable and dangerous of all the bears, grizzlies were generally given a wide berth by Indians and whites alike. When aroused, the ferocity of the grizzly knew no bounds. They were incredibly strong and powerfully built, and their mouths were filled with huge teeth capable of crunching bone to splinters. And their wicked claws, which could be over four inches in length, could split a man open with a single swipe.

Nate halted, the nape of his neck tingling, the breath caught in his throat. He recalled vividly his previous encounter with a grizzly, at the Republican River, when his left shoulder had been torn open and he'd been fortunate to escape with his life. Dread seized him. He almost employed the Hawken, but he knew the shot might only enrage the beast instead of killing it. Reports were common of grizzlies being shot five, ten, even 15 times with no apparent effect.

The bear had stopped and now stood sniffing the air, not 15 feet off.

Had the beast seen him? Nate wondered. Surely, at such close range, it had. But there was no telling if the bear could distinguish him from his horse. Grizzlies possessed poor vision, which was more than compensated for by their superb sense of smell. He hoped his human scent was disguised by the scent of the six horses.

Grunting, the monster took several ponderous steps forward, its broad head swinging from side to side.

Nate gripped the Hawken so tightly his knuckles hurt. He could call out to Shakespeare for help, but both his mentor and his wife were likely to come running and both would be easy pickings for the bear since they were on foot.

The grizzly, an enormous male with a brownish coat, the tips of the fine hairs tinged by the gray color that gave the species its name, cocked its head and intently regarded the intruders into its domain.

Please let it just go away! Nate prayed. He kept his right thumb on the Hawken's hammer, his right forefinger on the trigger. If the beast charged he would use the rifle first, then bring the pistols into play. When trying to kill grizzlies, the only fairly certain method involved shooting them through the brains. Unfortunately, such a shot wasn't easy. For one thing, there were two large muscles that covered both sides of the bear's forehead, tough muscles difficult for a ball to penetrate. For another thing, the thickness of the cranial bone itself could deflect most shots.

Unexpectedly, the bear started to turn.

A sigh of relief issued from Nate's throat, but it never reached his lips. The tales concerning grizzlies included many in which the monsters would move off at meeting with humans, as if they had no intention of attacking, and then suddenly whirl and rush at their intended victims full-out.

Which was exactly what transpired.

The bear went only five yards before spinning in a surprising display of agility and charging straight at the mare.

It took all of Nate's self-control not to flee pell-mell. He whipped the Hawken to his shoulder, took aim at the center of the beast's skull, and fired. The booming of the rifle produced a small cloud of smoke, but not enough to prevent Nate from seeing his ball smash into the bear above its right eye.

The grizzly stumbled, its front legs buckling, momentarily stunned.

Giving Nate the chance he needed. He wheeled the mare and shouted, driving the other horses off, aware they could hardly afford to lose one. Next to a good gun, the most precious commodity a man possessed was his horse.

A tremendous snarl rent the air to his rear.

Nate urged the mare into a gallop, looking over his right shoulder as he did.

The bear was closing rapidly and would overtake the mare within seconds.

Instantly Nate's left hand streaked to the corresponding pistol and he drew the flintlock, one of a matched set of smoothbore single-shot .55-caliber weapons his Uncle Zeke had purchased for him back in St. Louis. They had limited range, but close in, packed a hefty wallop. He cocked the one in his hand, hastily pointed it at the bear, and fired.

The ball took the bear in the left nostril.

Nate kept riding, his eyes on the beast. He jammed the used pistol under his belt and drew the second.

Slowed by the second hit, the bear vigorously shook its head, spraying blood from its ruptured nose, then faced straight ahead and bore down on its quarry again.

Only one shot left, Nate thought to himself, and gulped as he envisioned those terrible claws tearing into his flesh.

He swung his arm around, taking better aim this time, and waited for the bear to get much closer.

Somewhere, someone was shouting.

The grizzly narrowed the gap swiftly. Although they were not built for long-distance endurance running, they could cover short distances faster than a horse.

Keep coming, you devil!

Nate smiled grimly and held his arm as steady as he could under the circumstances. He tried to take a bead on the bear's right eye, but on a racing horse the feat was akin to shooting a pea from a pod while swinging from a rope.

Almost within striking distance, the grizzly opened its mouth wide, exposing its horrid teeth, elevating its head ever so slightly and inadvertently offering a better view of its eyes.

For a fraction of a second the tip of the barrel and the bear's right eye seemed to be in perfect alignment, and Nate promptly squeezed the trigger.

The ball did the rest. Bursting the right eyeball in a spray of crimson gore, it apparently bored deep into the grizzly's skull, because the very next second the beast crashed to the ground, rolling end over end for a dozen yards before coming to rest on its left side.

Elated, Nate faced forward, about to rein up. In startled shock he realized he was heading straight for a tree, and he hauled on the reins in an effort to turn the mare. A stout limb seemed to leap out at him, catching him squarely across the chest, and he felt his body leave the saddle and sail through the air, his senses swimming. His shoulders hit first, sending waves of agony pounding at his consciousness, and he slid for a few feet, then lay still on his back.

Oh, Lord, it hurt!

"Nate!"

Nate dimly head Shakespeare's cry. He struggled to

remain awake, aware of a great pain in his ribs, feeling as if the tree had fallen on top of him.

What if he was all busted up?

The nearest doctor was over a thousand miles away. Serious wounds and injuries in the wilderness, which might have been successfully treated in civilization, frequently proved fatal. Many a trapper had been shot or mauled and succumbed to infection instead of the wound itself. Indian remedies were highly regarded by the old mountain men, but many involved the use of herbs which very few whites knew how to obtain.

Nate tried to lift his head, and sank down again when assailed by severe dizziness. He thought of his family back in New York City, and wondered if they would grieve when they heard the news. His mother would. But knowing his stern father as well as he did, and knowing how his father could hold a grudge for years, unrelenting and unrepentent, he doubed very much tears would be shed by the King patriarch.

"Nate!"

This time the voice was Winona's. His name had been the first English word she had learned.

"Winona?" Nate croaked, wishing she could be spared the sight of his caved-in chest. He blinked a few times, his vision clearing, and saw her beautiful face appear above his. Her warm fingers touched his cheeks and his neck. "Where's Shakespeare?"

"Right here," came the immediate reply, and the frontiersman knelt next to his friend. "How bad is it?"

"I feel as if all my ribs are broken."

"Let's have a look," Shakespeare proposed, and began gingerly running his rough hands over Nate's chest.

"Is the grizzly dead for certain?" Nate inquired weakly.

"As dead as they come. That was some shooting." Nate grunted and winced.

"Two grizzlies in two months. Not a bad record for

a beginner. I know a fellow by the name of Old Jake who bagged seven grizzlies in two weeks once, but he was an experienced hunter,'' Shakespeare related, increasing the pressure of his hands.

"I don't care if I ever see another grizzly again."

"You will. This country is crawling with them. They won't last long, though, once the white man begins to push west of the Mississippi. For that matter, neither will the buffaloes or the Indians."

Nate would have laughed if he wasn't in so much anguish. "There must be hundreds of thousands of buffalo."

"Millions," Shakespeare corrected him.

"Then how can you say they'll all be killed off? It's impossible."

"Mark my words. The forests in the Eastern states once teemed with deer and elk, yet look at them now. There are very few elk left east of Ohio, and the deer have been drastically reduced in numbers. Give the white man a chance and he'll do the same thing to the buffalo," Shakespeare said, and stopped probing with his fingers. "You can stand up now."

Nate blinked a few times. "Stand? In my condition?'

"All you have are a few bruised ribs. None of them appear to be broken."

Feeling supremely stupid, Nate raised his head and looked down at himself. The pain was still exquisite, but he felt relieved at discovering his chest to be intact.

"Congratulations," Shakespeare said, grinning.

"For what?"

"You're the only man I know who can kill a grizzly and almost kill himself all at the same time."

"Thanks." Nate rose onto his elbows and smiled at his wife. She launched into a string of sentences in the Shoshone language, speaking too swiftly for him to follow her train of thought. His brow knit in perplexity.

The frontiersman noticed. "She says she is happy to have a husband who kills grizzlies so easily," he translated, the corners of his mouth crinkling. "Now she knows why you were named Grizzly Killer, and she can't wait to tell all the Shoshones about your battle."

"I hope she leaves out the part about the tree," Nate said dryly.

Winona abruptly rose and hastened toward the horses, which had stopped 30 feet away, whistling happily.

"Where is she going?" Nate inquired, sitting up slowly, a pang lancing his right side.

"To get her butcher knife. She'll take care of skinning the bear for us."

"Why bother with the bear when we're so close to the rendezvous? Who needs it?"

"We do," the frontiersman said, and gazed at the monster. "That coat is prime, Nate, and will fetch a pretty penny. Bear meat is delicious once you acquire the taste for it, and that one is packing several hundred pounds on his big frame. We'll smoke it and use some for trade. Then there's always the oil."

"Oil?"

Shakespeare looked at the younger man and snorted. "I keep forgetting how much you have to learn yet. A person can get five to eight gallons of oil from a bear, depending on the size of the animal and how much time you're willing to spend boiling it down."

"In New York City I could buy oil at the mercantile," Nate remarked.

"In the big cities you can buy everything nowadays," Shakespeare stated bitterly. "City life is unnatural. A man tends to forget what life is all about if all he has to do is walk into a store and plunk down money for the necessities. That's too easy. Life was meant to be hard, meant to be a struggle from cradle to grave. Hardship breeds character." He stopped and took in the hills and mountains with a sweeping gaze. "Out here you learn the truth. You learn that only the strong survive. Nature has a way of weeding out the weaklings, whether they be rabbits, deer, or men. Cities, on the other hand, are breeding grounds for the weak. If a man wants to *be* a man, he has to get away from the cities."

"Is that one of the reasons you won't ever live in a city again?"

The frontiersman nodded. "I'll be damned if I'm going to trade my freedom for weakness."

"I never thought of it that way before," Nate admitted.

"This land can open your eyes to all sorts of things you never thought about."

"So I'm learning."

"Keep learning, Nate. When you stop learning, you're like a plant that doesn't get any more water. You wither inside and die."

"I think you missed your calling. You should have been a teacher or a preacher."

Shakespeare chuckled. "To tell you the truth, when I was about twelve or thirteen I did give serious consideration to becoming a teacher."

"What stopped you?"

"I knew I didn't have the temperament for the job. I would probably have walloped the first student who got way out of line."

"How does a man know when he's chosen the right life?" Nate mused aloud, and then saw his friend suddenly glance up, past his shoulders, clearly surprised by something. Thinking that the grizzly might still be alive and had risen, he twisted and looked to his rear, discovering the grizzly wasn't the reason.

There were six Indians 25 yards away.

Chapter Three

Nate forgot all about his discomfort and leaped to his feet, his hands automatically straying to his belt. Only then did he remember that the pistol under his belt had been discharged and his other pistol and the rifle had fallen to the ground when the limb knocked him from the saddle.

Shakèspeare also stood, his Hawken in his left hand. "Don't do anything foolish," he cautioned.

"Are they Blackfeet?" Nate queried anxiously.

"If they were, we'd already be dead."

"Which tribe do they belong to then?"

"The Nez Percé."

"Are they friendly?"

"More or less."

Nate abruptly thought about Winona. He looked over his left shoulder and saw her standing still, 20 feet away, a knife in her right hand. He used sign language to direct her not to move, then faced the Nez Percés.

"Let them come to us," Shakespeare said. He smiled and made the sign for "friend," which consisted of holding his right hand at neck height, palm outward, with his index and second fingers held straight up. He then elevated his hand until the tips of his fingers were as high as his head.

"Now it's up to them. If they should attack, I'll hold them off while you grab your guns and reload."

"If anything happens to me, don't let them take Winona," Nate said, nervously fingering the empty flintlock. How long would it take for him to learn his lesson? He already knew not to let a moment go by without having a loaded gun at his side. The previous grizzly attack had taught him the folly of spending even a minute unarmed. Now he was caught in the open, his wife in danger, all because he'd blown a slight rap from a tree limb all out of proporation. He wanted to kick himself.

One of the Nez Percés rode forward cautiously. He was a tall Indian attired in buckskins, a bow in his left hand and a full quiver on his back. His features were composed, radiating confidence. He came to within eight feet and stopped, then addressed them.

Nate listened intently, but the tongue was unknown to him. He almost betrayed his surprise when Shakespeare answered in the same language. His profound ignorance, at times like this, filled him with frustration. There was so much to learn! Hopefully, he'd live long enough to accomplish the learning.

A smile beamed from the Nez Percé warrior's chiseled visage. He stared at the dead grizzly and spoke some more.

Shakespeare responded, using a few sign words to embellish his meaning.

Nodding, the warrior turned his horse and returned to the rest of the band. They began talking among themselves.

"What was that all about?" Nate asked.

"We shared pleasantries. His name is Soaring Raven. I've heard of him. He counted twenty coup before he even turned twenty. All his enemies speak highly of him."

"Is that supposed to be a compliment?"

"Praise from an enemy counts more than praise from a friend, Nate. When a friend gives you a compliment, nine times out of ten they do it because they like you and half of what they say probably isn't even true. But an enemy isn't about to build you up at his expense. His words are sincere. When you've acquired a powerful enemy who speaks highly of you, you'll know you've made your mark in the world.''

Nate shook his head. ''Sometimes your logic escapes me.''

''Anyway, about Soaring Raven. There are over two hundred Nez Percé at the rendezvous. He was out hunting with friends when they heard all the shooting and came to investigate. I accepted an invitation to stop by his lodge in a few days and smoke with him. He wants you to tag along.''

''Why me?''

''Because you're the great Grizzly Killer, the white man who knows no fear, the man who has killed more grizzlies than most ten men kill in a lifetime.''

''Now you're poking fun at me.''

''No. That's exactly what I told him.''

Amazed, Nate stared at the Nez Percés. ''Why would you lie like that?''

''Who says I lied? You *are* known as Grizzly Killer, thanks to White Eagle. And whites east of the Mississippi rarely see a grizzly, let alone kill one. I don't think I stretched the truth at all.''

''But now Soaring Raven will tell his friends, and they'll spread the word among their tribe. At the rate things are going, every Indian in the Rockies will know me by that name.''

''Good.''

Nate glanced at the frontiersman. ''Why good?''

''Because I happen to agree with the Indian philosophy. A name should have special meaning, should stand for the man or woman who has it as a symbol of their true self. That's the reason Indians take so much care in selecting them. They want the name to fit,'' Shakespeare said, and chuckled. "For once old William S. was wrong."

"What do you mean?"

"What's in a name? That which we call a rose by any other name would smell as sweet," Shakespeare quoted, and grinned.

"Let me guess. *Macbeth?*"

"Romeo and Juliet again. You really should borrow my book sometime. Apparently your schooling left a lot to be desired."

A retort was on the tip of Nate's tongue, but the sudden drumming of hooves diverted his attention to the departing Nez Percés, who were riding to the east.

"When we go to visit Soaring Raven, be sure to bring along a small gift," Shakespeare remarked. "Indians like to give and receive gifts. To them, to the honest ones anyway, gift-giving seals a bond of friendship."

"Like smoking a pipe?"

The frontiersman nodded. "But smoking is considered more important."

Nate turned and saw Winona still standing exactly where he'd told her to stay, and he motioned for her to advance. "I'll help Winona skin the bear."

"No, you won't. You'll stretch out by the fire I'm about to start and rest."

"I don't need rest. You told me all I have are a few bruised ribs."

"Which will feel a lot better tomorrow when we ride to the rendezvous if you take it easy today."

"Tomorrow?" Nate repeated, disheartened at the news. "Why not today?"

"We'll need a few hours to skin the grizzly and even longer to boil the hide for the oil. It'll be almost dark by then. So we might as well make camp and ride to the site first thing in the morning."

"If you say so," Nate said sullenly.

"And this way the news about you killing the bear will have time to spread around the rendezvous," Shakespeare added.

"Why are you so determined to build me up as a mighty bear killer, when we both know I'm not?"

"The bears don't matter. I'd build you up as a panther killer if you'd killed a big cat instead. The important thing is that every man at the rendezvous knows about you. You'll have their respect."

"I'd rather get it honestly."

"This is honestly. Or as honest as the circumstances allow. Believe me, Nate. If they label you as green, they can make your life a living hell. I'm trying to spare you from embarrassment, or worse. Trappers live a rough life and they play even harder. For eleven months of the year they break their backs trying to catch beaver, always on the lookout for Indians and wild beasts. Then comes the month or so in the summer when they can sit back and relax, but the truth of the matter is that they don't know how to relax, how to sit still and do nothing. So they gamble and womanize and go wild. Most of them are almost as broke when the rendezvous is over as they were when they got there." Shakespeare stopped and smiled. "You're in for a real treat."

"I suppose," Nate said uncertainly.

Wininoa joined them, leading the horses. She used sign language to inquire about Nate's condition.

The frontiersman answered in Shoshone.

Nate understood almost all the words. He nearly objected when Shakespeare suggested to Winona that she must make him rest at all costs.

Nodding her agreement, Winona hastened to the dead grizzly.

"Between the two of you, it's worse than living at home with my parents," Nate groused.

"Shouldn't you be doing something besides complaining?'' Shakespeare asked.

"I don't feel like resting."

"How do you feel about loading your guns?"

"Almost forgot," Nate muttered, and plucked the empty pistol from his belt. He glanced around, searching the grass and weeds for his other weapons. The Hawken lay directly under the limb he'd hit.

"I'll tend to the horses," Shakespeare said, walking off.

Nate stepped to his rifle and inspected it for damage, relieved at not finding so much as a scratch. Pivoting, he scoured the ground for the second pistol. He recalled holding the gun at the moment of impact, so the flintlock could have sailed over.ten feet in any direction.

Just wonderful.

Before continuing the search, Nate reloaded the two guns he had. First came the rifle. He rested the butt on the ground, poured out the proper amount of black powder from his powder horn and fed the grains down the barrel, then wrapped a ball from his bullet pouch in a patch and inserted both into the end of the muzzle. Using the ramrod, he shoved both all the way down, gazing at his wife and friend as he finished.

On her knees beside the enormous bear, Winona industriously worked her knife under the hide, peeling it off carefully.

Shakespeare, mounted on his white horse, rode toward the Bear River with the rest of the animals in tow.

The Nez Percés were nowhere in sight.

Nate leaned the Hawken against the tree trunk and hastily reloaded his one pistol. With the gun wedged under his belt once more, he reclaimed the rifle and walked in ever-widening circles out from the limb. A minute passed, and he began to wonder if he would ever see the second piece again. A glint of metal drew him to a patch of weeds to his right. There it was, covered except for the hammer. He leaned down, his fingers closing on the barrel, listening to the sounds of the forest, the chirping of the birds and the chittering of squirrels, as the animals found their voices again after falling silent when the guns had blasted. Straightening, he reloaded the second pistol and placed it near its twin.

Now he was ready for anything.

Except another grizzly.

Chuckling, Nate walked toward his wife, intending to assist her in skinning the bear despite Shakespeare's objections. He took only four paces, however, when a strange event occurred.

The forest fell silent again, completely, eerily silent.

Perplexed by the unusual occurrence, and knowing from experience that the wildlife never became quiet without a good reason, Nate halted and rotated, scanning the trees. Were the creatures still jittery over the gunfire or was there another cause? The presence of a large predator might account for the hush.

So would the presence of hostile Indians creeping through the woods.

Nate nervously fingered the Hawken's trigger. He looked at Winona and saw her surveying the surrounding terrain too.

Shakespeare was almost a hundred yards away, making for the water, oblivious to the situation.

An unusual sensation beset Nate, a peculiar feeling that unfriendly eyes were gazing upon him. He probed the shadows, alert for movement, but not so much as a butterfly stirred. Could the Nez Percés have returned? he wondered, and immediately dismissed the notion as nonsense. Soaring Raven had been friendly. The Nez Percés were long gone by now.

Then what was out there?

Nate casually drifted in the direction of his wife. If they were attacked, he wanted to be able to give her protection. An idea struck him, a possibility that worried him greatly.

What if the bear hadn't been alone?

Sometimes, not often but sometimes, grizzlies traveled in pairs. Usually a mother would let a cub stick by her side for a year or so, or until she was ready to give birth again. Then she would drive the youngster off. And more rarely two males would pair together.

Nate held the Hawken at waist height, ready to fire at the first sign of danger. He noticed his wife had stood, telltale anxiety etched in her face.

A second later, as abruptly as it had descended, the silence was broken by the cry of a jay. More birds contributed their distinctive calls, and in short order the forest returned to normal.

But there had been *something* out there. Nate just knew it. He relaxed a little and forced an unconcerned smile as he neared the woman he loved more than life itself. "Want help?" he inquired in his imperfect Shoshone.

"No," Winona answered. "You must rest."

Nate resorted to sign, telling her he felt fit and disliked being treated like a child.

Undaunted, Winona then let him know that if he so much as touched the grizzly, she'd yell for Shakespeare. "You must rest," she stressed, and returned to her task.

Nate signed and turned so he could keep an eye on the woods. "We haven't been married a month," he muttered in English, "and already she's ordering me around. Shakespeare's right. Indian women are no different from white women."

Not comprehending the gist of his statement, Winona looked up at him, smiled contentedly, and spoke three of the first words he'd taught her. "I love you."

Far off to the west a wolf howled.

Chapter Four

The campfire danced and writhed like a thing alive. Crackling and sputtering came from the burning limbs, and tiny sparks wafted high into the cool night air. Nearby the horses were all tied to the jutting branches of a convenient fallen tree, a box elder that had been uprooted recently, probably by a severe thunderstorm, as evidenced by the green leaves still on the branches and the soft earth caking its roots.

Nate sat next to Winona on the north side of the fire, their shoulders touching. The roasted bear meat he'd consumed for supper had been delicious, and now he leaned back and stifled a yawn, overcome by a feeling of lethargy.

"Someone should turn in soon," suggested Shakespeare from the other side of the blaze.

"I don't feel in the mood for sleep, thank you," Nate responded.

"I don't blame you. You're excited about going to your first rendezvous."

"Yes, I am," Nate admitted.

"Just remember to keep your wits about you. As I've told you before, the breed of men who trap in these mountains are a rough and hardy lot. They may take it into their heads to test you. Whatever you do, don't get riled.''

"Test me?''

''Mountaineers are great ones for playing practical jokes. I hope your sense of humor is intact.''

"What kind of test?''

''There's no telling.''

From the southwest, perhaps a half mile away, came the low howling of a wolf. Other wolves joined in, a communal howling that persisted for several minutes and eventually tapered off into a few mournful notes.

''I heard a wolf earlier today,'' Nate mentioned. ''Do they howl often during the day?''

''Not regularly,'' the frontiersman said, his head cocked, listening. ''But they do hunt during daylight hours too. And if one of them becomes separated from the pack, it'll howl until the pack answers.''

''What do you think caused the forest to go quiet?''

''I don't know. From what you've told me, it could have been a panther or even the wolves.''

''Or Indians.''

''Maybe. But the only tribe we need to worry about in this region is the Blackfeet, and I doubt they'd come this close to the rendezvous site,'' Shakespeare said, then shrugged. ''But you never know.''

Nate gazed at the thick book lying next to the frontiersman's left leg. ''So what will it be tonight? *Hamlet? Troilus and Cressida?*''

''Explain something to me, Nate.''

''If I can.''

''Why do you like me to read Shakespeare to you every night, but you won't bother to read the book yourself?''

Nate shrugged. ''You have a knack for reading Shakespeare that makes his words come alive. Myself, I've never much enjoyed reading his works. Too dull for my tastes.

Give me a novel by James Fenimore Cooper any day.''

"Dull?'' the frontiersman repeated in amazement. "Did you have the audacity to call old William S. dull?''

"You must admit some of his work is drudgery to read.''

"I'll admit no such thing,'' Shakespeare stated, and scooped up the volume. He quickly turned the pages until he came to the one he wanted. "All right. I'll show you. See if you think this is dull.'' He paused, licked his lips, and began reading. "Now is the winter of our discontent made glorious summer by this sun of York; and all the clouds that lour'd upon our house in the deep bosom of the ocean buried. . . .''

Although he fully intended to listen intently as he did most every night, Nate found his mind wandering. Lately he had been thinking about New York City a lot, and especially his family and Adeline. There were days when he missed his mother and father terribly, and other days when he remembered how they had attempted to stifle his adventurous spirit and mold him to follow in his father's footsteps. They had been the ones, after all, who'd persuaded him to become an accountant despite his feeble protestations. They'd also arranged for him to meet Adeline, no doubt counting on nature and his normal masculine urges to do the rest.

Sweet Adeline.

A twinge of guilt nagged at Nate as he thought about the lovely woman he'd once regarded as a living angel, the woman he'd planned to marry. He recalled the way her blond hair would shimmer in the lamplight and the sparkle in her blue eyes when she laughed. Any man in the state of New York would have gladly given his right arm for the honor of wedding her. And what had he done?

Turned his back on her.

Turned his back on his family.

All because of Uncle Zeke.

The memory of his dear uncle brought an unconscious

smile to Nate's lips. There was a man who had enjoyed life to the fullest, who had grasped every precious second of existence as if it might be his last. Thanks to Ezekiel King, Nate had left New York City perhaps never to return. His uncle had written a letter, proposing to meet Nate in St. Louis and to share a mysterious "treasure."

Nate should have known better.

Zeke had always been the black sheep in the King clan, always the different one. No one had been too surprised when he'd decided to leave New York, to venture far to the west. And no one had expressed much amazement at later hearing Zeke had built a cabin in the remote Rocky Mountains and taken an Indian woman as his wife.

After that, the subject of Zeke had become taboo in the King household.

But Nate had always retained fond memories of his uncle. When the letter came, he'd been undecided about accepting the offer until he'd realized how much his share of the treasure would mean to his darling Adeline. Accustomed to luxury as she was, Adeline had frankly admitted she expected him to provide for her in the same high fashion. She'd even pressed him to go into the mercantile business with her wealthy father. So with expectations of acquiring the riches Adeline craved, he'd traveled to St. Louis and met his uncle.

Who could have predicted how it would all turn out?

He should have suspected something was amiss when Zeke told him the treasure was at the cabin in the Rockies. He should have balked when Zeke proposed taking him there, taking a year out of his life in the bargain. But he'd gladly gone along, and despite initial reservations related to the slaying of cutthroats and Indians, he'd enjoyed the wilderness experience more than any other in his whole life.

When the double tragedy had occurred, when Zeke had been mortally wounded, and then had revealed there never was a treasure in the sense Nate believed, he could have turned around and headed for civilization. By then, though, he'd come to appreciate the true treasure his uncle had bestowed on him: the priceless gift of genuine freedom.

Who could return to the hectic pace of life in New York City having once tasted the untrammeled richness of life in the Rockies?

Who could adorn himself with the superfluous trappings of civilization having known the naked splendor of the primeval wilderness?

And now look at him. Married to a wonderful Shoshone woman and about to attend his first rendezvous. And look at all that had transpired since leaving St. Louis: He had fought hostile Indians and battled white robbers; he'd participated in a buffalo hunt; he'd shot deer and elk and antelope and fished in crystal-clear streams and lakes; he'd learned to be self-reliant, to live off the land; he'd learned the true meaning of manhood.

But what about the future?

Nate realized he'd given scant consideration to what he would be doing in a week or a month. Did he want to become a trapper? Would he return to Zeke's cabin or build his own home elsewhere? If he did decide to live at the cabin, how would Winona react to being taken so far from the stamping grounds of her tribe? And how long would Shakespeare be willing to hang around, to devote so much of his time and energy to teaching the basics of surviving in the wilds? Troubled by that question, Nate glanced at the frontiersman.

"Dive, thoughts, down to my soul: here Clarence comes," Shakespeare was reciting. "And then Clarence enters, under guard, with Brakenbury."

"Shakespeare?" Nate interrupted.

The mountain man looked up in surprise. "This had better be important."

''When do you have to go back to your cabin?''

Lines formed on the frontiersman's forehead. ''I haven't given it much thought. Are you in a great rush to get rid of me?''

''No. Just the opposite. I'm hoping you'll stay a few more weeks and teach me everything you know.''

Shakespeare chuckled. ''Are you certain it will take that long?''

''You know what I mean.''

''Don't fret yourself, Nate. I'll stay with you until you're ready to strike off on your own. Then one day you'll wake up and I'll be gone.''

Nate leaned forward. ''Will I see you again?''

''I hope so, but nothing is certain in this world of ours. You know the old saying. Here today, gone tomorrow. A man never knows from one day to the next whether he'll greet the dawn, which is the reason we must make the most of every moment the good Lord gives us.''

''You sound like my Uncle Zeke.''

''And who do you think taught him everything he knew?'' Shakespeare said with a twinkle in his eyes.

''I wonder if I'll ever be as skilled as he was,'' Nate mentioned wistfully, gazing into the flickering flames.

''Give yourself time. A tadpole doesn't grow into a frog overnight. First it has to live its alloted time as a tadpole; then it gets to stand on its own legs.''

''Am I still a tadpole, then?''

''Not hardly. I'd say you already have your legs. You're just a mite timid about leaving the waters you know so well.''

Nate nodded, knowing his companion had hit the nail on the head. He glanced at Winona, admiring her loveliness, amazed she could sit still for so long without badgering him for attention. Her patience amazed him, as did her generally even temperament. He'd never known anyone who took everything so calmly, who remained controlled even in the midst of the worst crisis. Her composure was superb, and he often wished he could be half as self-possessed.

"I could go take a stroll if you'd like," Shakespeare remarked.

Nate looked at the frontiersman to see if his friend might be poking fun at him again, but Shakespeare had an earnest expression. "Thank you. It's nice of you to offer. There's no need, though. We'll want a good night's sleep in order to be ready for the rendezvous tomorrow."

"I could use some sleep myself. Must be a sign of my years. When I was younger, I often went two or three days without a wink of sleep and never felt the effects. Nowadays, I can't go twenty four hours without yawning myself silly."

"I don't know how you do it. I'm only a third your age, yet I can't last that long without feeling exhausted."

"That's what comes from being coddled," Shakespeare said.

"I was not," Nate replied, a bit indignantly.

"All children reared in the city are coddled. They have everything provided for them. They never learn how to grow crops, or how to kill game. Most of them can't even fish. Their parents never teach them much of anything worthwhile, and they never learn nature's supreme law."

"Only the hardiest survive," Nate said, recalling his companion's comments from earlier in the day.

"You don't sound convinced," Shakespeare noted.

"To tell you the truth, I'm not."

"Give yourself time, Nate. I just pray you don't learn the lesson the hard way."

From off to the west came the hoot of an owl.

The frontiersman straightened and twisted to scan the inky forest surrounding the clearing in which they had camped. They were half a mile from the Bear River, nestled at the base of a low hill.

"Don't worry about me," Nate said. "I can take care of myself. I've killed two grizzlies, haven't I?"

"Don't let the killing of a couple of bears go to your head," Shakespeare advised.

Again the owl hooted, only closer this time.

Winona raised her eyes from her somber contemplation of the fire and glanced at the woods. She nudged Nate and executed a series of quick signs.

"The owl doesn't sound right?" Nate said. "What does that mean?"

"Exactly what she said," Shakespeare stated. "That owl doesn't quite sound like an owl."

Nate placed his right hand on the rifle by his side. "Indians, you think?"

"Could be. Indians aren't great ones for traveling after dark unless they're going on a raid."

Remembering the eerie silence from before, Nate lifted his Hawken. "Didn't you claim there wouldn't be any hostile Indians this close to the rendezvous?"

The frontiersman shrugged. "I could be wrong."

For several minutes they listened intently, but the call of the owl wasn't repeated.

At length Shakespeare yawned and stretched. "I reckon I'll turn in."

"Do you want me to stand guard?" Nate queried.

"There's no need. I'm a light sleeper."

"I really don't mind standing guard."

"Get some sleep," Shakespeare directed. "My horse will whinny if anything comes with thirty yards of our fire."

"Now that puts my mind at rest," Nate said dryly. He signed for his wife to prepare their bedding and stood, stretching his legs, facing westward. "How long did you say it will take us to reach the rendezvous tomorrow?"

"An hour and a half at the most."

"Good," Nate responded, not bothering to add that the

woods in their vicinity were giving him a bad case of nerves. He couldn't wait to reach the rendezvous where they would be safe from Indians, wild beasts, and whatever caused strange silences.

Winona spread their buffalo hide blankets flat on the ground, placing a heavy hide on the ground for comfort's sake and a thinner one on top. She crawled underneath and said in perfect English, "Come, husband."

Nate obligingly eased himself down beside her, sliding his Hawken under the blanket with him. He reclined on his back, the flintlocks still tucked under his belt.

Turning onto her side, Winona snuggled against him, her lips close to his ear. "I love you," she whispered affectionately.

The soft caress of her breath on his neck gave Nate cause to wish they had erected a makeshift shelter with limbs or else a tent. He resolved to acquire a lodge at the earliest opportunity. Her father's lodge had been lost during the Blackfoot attack, and to replace it he would have to slay several buffaloes and locate sturdy branches of the proper length to make support poles. "Say, Shakespeare?" he queried.

"Hmmmmmm?" The frontiersman drowsily replied.

"Will I be able to buy a lodge at the rendezvous?"

An extended snicker wafted over the fire.

"Did I say something funny?"

"You still have a long ways to go, Nate, before you fully outgrow your city ways. Why do you want to buy a lodge? Are you too lazy to make your own?"

"No," Nate said defensively. "I was thinking of Winona. I'd like her to be comfortable. It might be a few days before we go on a buffalo hunt, unless you know something I don't."

"A point well taken. No, I don't think you'll find many lodges for sale, but you should be able to find someone willing to sell or swap the hides you need. Making the poles will take no time at all.''

"Good. Building a lodge will be my first priority tomorrow. My wife is not going to sleep in the open, on the ground, another night. I won't have it.''

"I don't blame you.''

"You don't?''

"No sirree. Not with all the men who will be there. If I were you, I'd get her an iron chastity belt.''

Nate listened to his friend laughing uproariously, and sighed. In the future he'd remember to keep his big mouth shut. Maybe that way he'd stay out of trouble.

Chapter Five

Bear Lake, which fed into the river of the same name that eventually carried its waters all the way to the Great Salt Lake, had been selected as the site for the 1828 rendezvous for several excellent reasons. First and foremost, the lake was centrally located with respect to the Rockies as a whole, so those trappers ranging far to the north toward Canada and those who were working the southern tributaries of the Green River would have an equal distance to travel. Second, Bear Lake was relatively close to South Pass, the notch in the forbidding wall of the mountains that enabled those daring enough to traverse the Rockies easily. The proximity to South Pass meant the wagons from St. Louis could reach the site without undue delays. Third, the site offered abundant water, ample game, flat land, and was far enough removed from the usual haunts of the Blackfeet to render a conflict with that most aggressive of all tribes a remote possibility.

Sixty miles in circumference, and nestled in a valley surrounded by a high range of snowcapped peaks, Bear Lake had become known by several names. Many of the trappers referred to it as Snake Lake, others called it Black Bear Lake because of the large number of such animals in the land around it, and still others called the body of water Sweet Lake to distinguish it from its brackish cousin to the southwest, the Great Salt Lake.

Nate listened as all of these facts were related by Shakespeare the next morning en route to the rendezvous. They approached the lake from the southwest, following a trail that had been used by game and Indians for decades. "Why don't they settle on just one name and be done with it?" he inquired after the frontiersman mentioned the different designations.

"They will, eventually," Shakespeare said. "Sooner or later someone will get around to making an official map and whatever name they use will become the one the lake will be known by."

"Are there other lakes that have several different names?"

"Not only lakes, but rivers, mountains, and prominent landmarks. It can get downright confusing. But I have a saying that can help you keep it all straight."

"Which is?"

"When in doubt, use the Indian name."

"How does that help?"

"Because an Indian tribe has the common sense not to give five names to the same landmark."

"Do all the tribes use the same name?"

"No. But let's say another trapper wants you to meet him on such and such a date at Ditch Creek. Well, you've never heard of Ditch Creek, but you do know about a Bobcat Creek in the same general vicinity. If it happens that both of you know the Shoshones call it Beaver Creek, then it's a safe bet you're talking about the same one." Shakepeare looked over his shoulder. "Make any sense to you?"

"Sort of."

"Don't worry. After you've lived out here four or five years, you'll know most of the major landmarks fairly well. I doubt you'll become lost more than six or seven times a year.''

"Now there's a comforting thought.''

Shakespeare chuckled and urged his horse up a rise.

Nate looked at Winona and found her probing eyes on him. What was she thinking about? he wondered. He could never tell. To him, women were a source of infinite mystery. Whether they were white or Indian, their thought processes, their outlook on life, and almost every aspect of their temperament were different from those of men, totally foreign in some respects. The mystery of womanhood intrigued him, aroused his curiosity, and at times made him feel woefully inadequate. Adeline, for instance, had been able to wrap him around her little finger. Her slightest wish had been his ardent command.

With Winona, the relationship was not quite the same.

He wanted to please her, of course, and to provide for her to the best of his ability. He loved her passionately, and in moments when she wasn't gazing at him he would surreptitiously stare at her beautiful features, entranced by her loveliness, marveling that she should love him in return and had picked him as her husband. But he didn't adore her in the manner of a puppy adoring its master, as had been the case with Adeline. He didn't set Winona on a pedestal, as he had Miss Van Buren. He regarded Winona more as an equal, a separate and distinct equal, a competent woman who could perform the many tasks required of someone living in the wilderness. She could cook, sew, prepare herbal remedies, skin a buffalo or a bear with admirable precision and dexterity, and keep a lodge clean and tidy.

On top of all those domestic qualities, Winona was a marvelous mate, a woman endowed with a fine sense of humor and a keen zest for life. Perhaps the single trait of hers he most liked was her perpetually sunny disposition, her positive attitude. She took hardships in stride without complaining. She surmounted difficulties instead of whining about them. The deaths of her parents had deeply saddened her, yet she'd recovered and gotten on with her life. She was also affectionate and devoted.

What more could a man ask for?

Smiling, Nate used sign language to convey his intention of buying hides at the rendezvous they could use to build a lodge. He told her the lodge would be small at first, but at the earliest opportunity he would go out after buffalo and acquire the poles needed for a big lodge, a fitting home for the woman he loved.

Winona responded that she was glad they would have their own lodge soon, then pointed out they would need more horses before acquiring a larger dwelling.

Nate wanted to hit himself for not taking that fact into consideration. The bigger the lodge, the more pack horses were required to bear the poles, hides, and other necessary items. An average-sized lodge could be transported adequately by three horses. But any dwelling over 15 feet in height used much heavier support poles, and many more of them, not to mention larger and thicker hides. The greatest lodge he knew of had been 30 feet tall, braced by 30 poles, and transported on the backs of 15 horses.

Apparently sensing his thoughts, Winona told him that a small lodge would serve their needs for the immediate future, at least until such time as they had their first child.

Curious, Nate asked her how soon she wanted to start their family.

Smiling, Winona pointed at him and said in English, "When you want."

How soon should they? Nate reflected. First he must decide where they were going to live, which brought to mind Zeke's cabin far to the south. He broached the subject, making the proper signs competently and fluidly.

Winona's brow furrowed and she stared at the ground.

What if she refused to travel such a distance? Nate

watched her expectantly. If she did, if she wanted to stay closer to her tribe, he'd need to ask Shakespeare's advice on how to proceed.

After a minute Winona glanced at him and responded. She admitted to being scared at the notion of traveling away from the land she knew so well and being separated from her many friends and relatives. But she respected his judgment. If he truly believed they would be happy at the cabin, she would try her best to adapt. There was a condition, however. She would be very grateful if he would agree to journeying to visit the Shoshone tribe at least once a year. Twice a year would please her even more.

Relieved and not a little grateful at her agreement, Nate made signs assuring her that she would indeed be happy at the cabin. He offered to give her a year or so to make up her mind. If they stayed there that length of time and she wasn't content, they would then decide where else they might like to live.

Winona readily assented and let him know she was fortunate to have a husband who possessed such wisdom.

As usual, Nate felt uncomfortable being the recipient of her affectionate compliments. He smiled self-consciously and praised her for being an understanding wife.

For several minutes they rode along in contented silence.

"Teach more words," Winona prompted in English.

Nate nodded, then proceeded to point out various objects they passed and repeated the names for them while Winona did her best to reproduce the designations. He marveled at how readily she picked up the language and wished he would learn her tongue even half as fast.

Engrossed in the lesson, they lost all track of time.

The land around them rose gradually. They followed the natural contours of the lowlands between the mountains, surrounded by abundant wildlife, breathing crisp, invigorating mountain air. They were thousands of feet above sea level and climbing steadily higher.

When Shakespeare came over a rise and reined up, his young companions were enjoying a chuckle over the word "chipmunk," which Winona found delightfully amusing.

"Why did you stop?" Nate inquired. He gazed at the valley stretching for miles to the north and discovered the reason for himself.

They had arrived at the rendezvous site.

"Take a gander," Shakespeare said. "This is what the average trapper lives for. Eleven months of the year a mountaineer fights nature, Indians, and beasts just so he can collect enough pelts to make decent money, then he comes here and spends most of his earnings in three or four weeks." He paused. "The rendezvous is the biggest get-together of white men west of the Mississippi. It sort of reminds me of St. Louis back in the old days."

Nate had visited St. Louis not two months ago, and he wouldn't go so far as to compare the bustling city to the sight he now beheld, but for a man who had seen no other large gathering of humanity for many weeks, whose last contact with a group of any size had been a modest band of Shoshones, the sprawling, swirling mass of living souls spread before his wondering gaze prompted a ripple of excitement to tingle his spine. "I didn't know there would be so many."

"Frankly, neither did I," Shakespeare said. "The affair keeps growing bigger and bigger every year."

The south shore of Bear Lake had been transformed into the setting for a wild assembly the likes of which not more than five hundred white men had ever laid amazed eyes on. Nearest the lake were the habitations of the trappers, consisting of tents and crude, makeshift shelters, principally lean-tos and shacks that looked as if they would topple over if someone sneezed too hard in their immediate vicinity. Since the trappers knew they would only be in the area for several weeks, they hadn't bothered erecting permanent dwellings. Most of them simply slept out under the canopy of stars.

Also near the lake were the booths set up by the operators of the supply caravan, 40 in all, for trading purposes. Around them were clustered scores of eager buyers, except for the booths belonging to the fur buyers. Lined up in front of those were anxious trappers with their bundles of furs, each hoping to command the highest price possible for his goods.

There were also Indians present, thousands of them. To the west were 300 lodges of Shoshones. North of them another 200 lodges belonging to the Bannocks, who were close friends to the Shoshones. Slightly northwest of both were 90 lodges belonging to the Nez Percés.

Shakespeare pointed out the location of the different tribes as they rode toward Bear Lake. Between them and the water stood even more lodges, 80 or so.

"Which tribe is this?" Nate inquired, nodding at the nearest encampment.

"The Flatheads. Next to the Shoshones, they're about the most friendly tribe around. They always treat whites fairly, and they've never taken a white scalp as far as I know."

"Didn't you once tell me that you married a Flathead woman long ago?" Nate asked.

"Yep. Pretty near twenty years ago." Shakespeare bowed his head and sighed. "Sometimes it feels like only yesterday. She was as beautiful as the dawn and the best damn wife a man ever had. If the rotten Blackfeet hadn't killed her, I'd probably still be with her."

Nate stared at the Indians in the Flathead camp. "Should we go around them?"

"Whatever for?" The frontiersman glanced up, grinning.

"Is it considered polite to ride through an Indian camp without permission?"

"Why this concern all of a sudden?"

"You're the one who is always telling me to be careful not to violate an Indian code of conduct or I'll antagonize them."

"True," Shakespeare admitted, and chuckled. "You're learning, Nate. And yes, it's all right for us to ride on through. If we came on their camp way out in the middle of nowhere, then we'd do things differently. We'd approach them slowly, let them see us coming, and smile the whole time to show them we were friendly. But this is the rendezvous. Tribes travel hundreds of miles to trade with the whites. And as I told you before, this is considered sort of neutral territory. Anyone can come and go as he pleases."

Nate noticed several Flathead warriors gazing in their direction and positioned his mare alongside Winona's horse. He idly placed his right hand on the rifle slanted across his thighs. "I have a question for you."

The frontiersman laughed.

"What struck you as funny?"

"Nothing. What's your question?"

"You mentioned the earnings the trappers make. How much can the average trapper bring in?"

"Varies quite a bit. Depends on how many furs they have to sell and the quality of the pelts. On average, though, I'd say between one and two thousand dollars."

Nate's eyebrows arched. Two thousand dollars was a lot of money. A typical carpenter, by comparison, made only five or six hundred dollars in an entire *year*.

"Most of those men will have little of it left by the time the rendezvous is over," Shakespeare said.

"How can they spend so much money in three or four weeks?" Nate responded skeptically.

"Because they're fleeced by the fine gentlemen from

St. Louis,'' Shakespeare stated, his tone tinged with bitter scorn.

"Explain."

"Do you happen to know how much whiskey costs in St. Louis?"

"About thirty cents as gallon, I believe."

"Here it costs three dollars a pint. And the whiskey they sell is so watered down it takes ten gallons just to make a man feel good."

"What?" Nate declared in disbelief.

"That's not all. How much does coffee cost in St. Louis?"

"Ten cents a pound."

"Here it's two dollars a pound."

"That's outrageous."

"It gets worse. Gunpowder, which costs about seven cents a pound back in St. Louis, goes for over two dollars a pound here. The same with lead, which only cost six cents a pound back East."

"Why, a man could go broke in no time."

"You don't know the half of it. Sugar goes for two dollars a pint. Blankets can cost from fifteen to twenty dollars apiece. Cotton shirts are five dollars each. And tobacco is two dollars a pound."

Nate stared at the wagons and shook his head. "That amounts to robbery. Why do the trappers tolerate it? They should refuse to buy goods at such inflated prices."

"Where else would they go to buy the things they need?"

Nate pondered for a moment and realized the obvious. "There is nowhere else they can go."

"Exactly. They must buy from the agents of the St. Louis suppliers at the rendezvous or do without for another year, unless they aim to make the long trip back to St. Louis. In that case they'd lose months of time they could have spent trapping."

"Something should be done to change it."

"Nothing can be done," Shakespeare said. "And you haven't heard the half of it."

"Why?"

"Not only are the trappers at the mercy of the sellers when they buy goods, but they're also at the mercy of the buyers when they sell their furs."

"Do they get a fair price?"

"The top price paid for pelts is four to five dollars a pound."

"Sounds like a lot," Nate commented.

"Not when you consider the same pelts are resold in St. Louis for up to eight dollars a pound."

"No one told me about this aspect of the trapping trade."

Shakespeare shrugged. "There's nothing anyone can do about it. A trapper has to make as best he can. The R.M.F. and the other fur companys have total control."

"The R.M.F.?"

"Sorry. The Rocky Mountain Fur Company. They're the main outfit in this part of the Rockies. They hire men to trap for them, set the date for the rendezvous, and bring the pack train and the wagons out from St. Louis."

"You mentioned other fur companies."

"Yep. The Hudson's Bay Company operates to the north, mainly in Canada. But they've been working farther south more and more. Then there's the American Fur Company."

"I've heard of it," Nate interjected. So had everyone who could read. The newspapers carried regular stories on the American Fur Company and the man who had founded the firm, John Jacob Astor. Astor had moved to America from Germany when he was twenty years old. He entered the fur trade in 1787, and was successful enough to launch his own company in 1808. He eventually became a millioniare, and in recent years had been described as the richest man in the country.

"They used to do most of their trapping around the Great Lakes, and I imagine you know about the big plans Astor had for his Columbia River enterprise. Anyway, the American Fur Company trappers are moving into this territory and taking a lot of business away from the R.M.F."

"Is there bad blood between them?"

"They don't shoot at each other, if that's what you mean. But there is sort of a friendly rivalry."

"If you were trapping for a living, which company would you hire on with?"

"None of them."

"Then how would you make any money?"

"Nate, all the fur companies are hungry for pelts. Their agents are more than happy to buy furs from anyone. Even though a company might have up to two hundred men out trapping streams at any one time, they'll take pelts from Indians and any free-trapper who has some to sell."

"I seem to recall hearing about free-trappers."

"A free-trapper is a man who doesn't have a contract with any of the fur companies. He traps when he pleases, then sells his furs to whichever company he thinks will pay him the best price."

"Is a free-trapper paid the same rate as the company men?"

"Usually. Sometimes a little less. On occasion, if the furs are all prime, the company will pay a little bit extra."

"Then that's the way I'd like to live," Nate declared. "As a free-trapper."

"It's no work for weaklings," Shakespeare remarked.

They were almost upon the Flathead village. Many of the warriors, women, and children stopped whatever they were doing to stare. Several members of the tribe shouted friendly greetings to the frontiersman, who responded good-naturedly.

Nate noticed that Winona held her chin high and rode gazing straight ahead.

A few dozen yards to the north were three men on horseback. They were engaged in earnest conversation with a Flathead warrior. One of the trio abruptly looked up and straightened, a wily grin creasing his thin visage.

Nate instinctively disliked the strangers. An indefinable air of latent menace seemed to radiate from them, particularly the thin rider, a man of weasel-like proportions and demeanor. All three wore smoked-skin moccasins, leggings, and fringed shirts. The weasel wore a blue cap adorned with a fox tail. Each one had a rifle.

"All your guns are loaded, I trust?" Shakespeare unexpectedly inquired.

"Certainly. Why?"

The frontiersman nodded at the trio. "You may need them in a minute."

Chapter Six

The weasel addressed his two comrades, and together they rode not more than 15 feet and reined up, waiting.

"I knew it," Shakespeare said, and scowled.

"What?" Nate asked.

"They're going to give us some trouble."

"Do you know them?"

"Just the one wearing the blue cap. His name is Laclede. He's a Frenchman. Never turn your back on him."

"Why do you expect trouble?"

"Two years ago at the rendezvous I came across Laclede whipping a Nez Percé woman. Seems he bought her, then wasn't satisfied with the purchase."

"What happened?"

"I beat him with his own whip."

Nate glanced at the frontiersman. "Didn't you once tell me not to butt into the personal affairs of others?"

"The Good Lord gave us common sense so we can tell the difference between things like private matters and unjustified brutal behavior. He was whipping the poor woman out in the open. Her face and back were all bloody. She pleaded for him to stop and he wouldn't. I took all I could stand, then tore the whip from him. The bastard tried to knife me in the back when I turned away. Made me a bit angry, so I gave him a taste of his own treatment.''

Nate studied the three men. "How can they cause trouble? Isn't the rendezvous supposed to be neutral territory, as you put it, where no fights take place?''

"I never claimed fights don't occur. The neutral part applies to the whites and the Indians. Almost any tribe can come here to trade without fear of being attacked. There are exceptions, of course, like the Blackfeet. But fights take place every single day. Some of them result in killing," Shakespeare detailed. "So stay alert at all times and remember the advice I've given you.''

They drew nearer to the trio. Laclede said something to his friends that elicited bawdy laughter.

An intuitive feeling that something would indeed happen gripped Nate, and his visage hardened. He'd traveled to the rendezvous to enjoy himself, learning about the trapping trade, and mingle with the men of the mountains, not to spend his time brawling. Back in New York City he'd rarely been compelled to defend himself. His size alone deterred potential assailants. At six feet, two inches tall he possessed a naturally powerful physique that had been tempered by the elements and the arduous events of the past couple of months. His face had been bronzed by the sun and his long hair resembled a dark mane.

"Well, what have we here?'' the weasel declared loudly in a distinct accent. "Are my eyes deceiving me, or is this the great Carcajou?''

Shakespeare halted six feet from the three men. "Still haven't learned to curb that tongue of yours, have you, Laclede?'' he said harshly. His right hand rested on his rifle.

Laclede smiled and extended both his arms in an exaggerated gesture of pure innocence. "I meant no disrespect, *mon ami.*"

"I'm not your friend and I never will be."

"*Vraiment*? And how do you know? No one can predict the future, eh?"

"There are some things a man can predict with certainty. For instance,I know I'll never eat buffalo droppings. In the same way I know I'll never think of you as a friend."

"Are you perhaps comparing me to buffalo droppings?"

A patently fake smile curled the frontiersman's lips. "Would I do such a thing?"

For a fleeting instant transparent hostility flickered across Laclede's countenance. He recovered quickly, though, and his smile returned. "No, of course you wouldn't." His gaze drifted to Nate and Winona. "And who might your companions be?"

"Nathaniel King, the man the Indians call Grizzly Killer, and his wife."

"So˙ you are the Grizzly Killer?" Laclede said, regarding Nate intently.

"I am."

"There was talk around the camp last night that you killed one of the mighty beasts not far from here."

"Yesterday."

"Tell me. How does one so young become so skilled at killing grizzlies?"

"Practice," Nate said, and noticed Shakespeare grin.

"I have slain a few of them myself," Laclede said. "They die hard."

Nate didn't bother to respond. He strongly disliked the man and saw no reason to pretend otherwise. One of the other men, he realized, was staring at Winona with a scarcely concealed lecherous expression.

"Will you be staying through the rest of the rendezvous?"

The frontiersman answered before Nate could reply. "Maybe we will, maybe we won't."

"It is a good gathering this year. They say over four hundred white men are present. *Magnifique,* eh?"

"I suppose," Shakespeare said noncommittally. "We'd like to go see for ourselves. Why don't you move aside and let us pass?"

"Certainment, mon ami." Laclede moved his horse to the left while the others moved theirs to the right.

Shakespeare rode forward between them.

His left hand holding the reins, his right on the Hawken, Nate slowly did likewise. He waited until he came abreast of the man with the lewd aspect, then suddenly leaned to the right and swung the heavy Hawken in a vicious arc.

None of the three men anticipated the move. The man smirking at Winona awakened to his peril too late. He grunted when the barrel slammed into his mouth, splitting his lips and jarring his teeth, and catapulted to the ground, his rifle flying. An audible thud sounded when he landed hard on his back. For a moment he lay there, dazed, then tried to rise. He froze when he saw the rifle pointed at his head.

"Not so much as a twitch," Nate warned. He glanced around and saw Shakespeare covering Laclede, then focused on the man he'd hit.

Astonishment had been replaced by fury, and the lecher's face was now a crimson hue. Blood trickled from his lips. "Why the hell did you strike me?" he demanded, and began to rise.

Nate cocked the Hawken, causing the lecher to freeze. "I won't tell you again. Don't move unless you want to die."

"*Fou*! You're crazy!"

"I've never been more serious."

"What did I do, bastard?"

"You know damn well what you did," Nate said, the words clipped and low.

"I do not," the man protested.

"Hey, Grizzly Killer," Laclede interjected. "Around here men do not take kindly to being treated like a mongrel."

"And I don't take kindly to any man who looks at my wife the way your friend just did," Nate responded.

"Maybe you imagined it, eh?"

Nate looked at the weasel. "Are you calling me a liar?"

Laclede seemed about to give a sarcastic retort until he gazed into the younger man's eyes and changed his mind. "No," he said. "I would not call you a liar. If you say Henri showed disrespect to your wife, then he did."

"What?" Henri exploded. "Whose side are you on?"

"Be quiet or I'll shoot you myself," Laclede stated. "Everyone knows you have a fiery passion for the ladies. Too often your eyes roam where they shouldn't roam."

The man named Henri gingerly touched his lips and glared at Nate. "You have the advantage for now, *monsieur.*"

"Is that a threat?"

"I never threaten a man who is aiming a rifle at me," Henri stated.

"Let's go, Nate," Shakespeare said.

Reluctantly, still angered by the man's effrontery, Nate motioned for Winona to precede him, and once she had ridden past with the pack animals in tow he urged the mare after her, keeping his gaze on the trio all the while.

The frontiersman angled his white horse closer and rode to the left of the mare.

None of the three men so much as moved for a full 15

seconds. Then the injured lecher stood and commenced arguing with Laclede.

"You've made an enemy there," Shakespeare mentioned softly, looking over his left shoulder. "Maybe three enemies."

"Did I handle myself properly?"

"Yes, and no."

"Explain," Nate prompted, also watching the trio.

"Well, you did right by defending Winona's honor. I saw how he stared at her and I almost taught him some manners myself. But you did wrong by leaving him alive."

"Are you saying I should have shot him?"

"You'd have saved yourself a lot of aggravation if you had. Mark my words. That man won't rest until he's taken revenge. You'd be wise to keep one eye over your shoulder at all times. Any way he can cause you misery, he will."

"I couldn't just up and shoot him, no matter how much he deserved it."

"True. But you could have goaded him into trying to shoot you, then killed him in self-defense. That's what I would have done."

Nate looked back one last time. The lecher and Laclede were still quarreling. He hoped the frontiersman was wrong about future trouble, but realistically he knew Shakespeare was speaking the truth. Already his first rendezvous had been tainted by the prospect of impending violence. For that matter, life in the wild seemed to be an unending chain of one violent incident after another. As if having to worry about Indians and beasts wasn't enough, he also had to be on his guard with other white men.

"Thank you, husband," Winona interrupted his reflection, using proper English.

Employing sign language, Nate let her know he'd simply done as any husband would do.

Winona's hands flew as she praised him for having the courage to defend her honor. There were some men, she maintained, who would not stand up for their wives no matter what.

"She's right," Shakespeare chimed in. "Some men don't know the meaning of the word backbone. They're weak in more ways than one. Sometimes it's not their fault, though. They're bred that way by parents who spoil them when they're young, who spare the rod and spoil the child. Too much kindness can be as bad as too little."

Nate recalled many sermons he'd listened to at church. "But what about turning the other cheek?"

"The Good Book says to turn the other cheek if someone slaps you on the face. It doesn't say to lay down and let the other fellow stomp you to death."

"I never thought of it that way," Nate said, and chuckled. He abruptly remembered the Hawken and eased down the hammer. "Have you read the Bible, Shakespeare?"

"Yep. Once."

"Do you believe in all you read?"

"Let's just say I believe in more than I practice."

"Did you understand all that you read?"

The frontiersman glanced at his friend, noticing the earnest expression cast his way. "Any man who claims to understand every word in the Bible is a fraud."

"What makes you say that?"

"Because no one man can claim to know all there is to know. Haven't you ever wondered why there are so many religions? It's because a dozen men will read the Bible and come up with a dozen different ideas about what it means. Oh, they'll all agree on the essentials. But they'll find enough to argue about so that they wind up at each other's throats instead of loving one another like the Good Book tells us to do."

"I've never read the whole Bible," Nate said. "But my parents took me to church once a week whether I wanted to go or not. I have all the Commandments memorized. One of them seems to have no meaning whatsoever for men living out here, and that bothers me."

"Thou shalt not kill?" Shakespeare said.

"How did you know?"

"Because you take after your Uncle Zeke. When he first came West, he was bothered by the same thing. After living all his life in New York City, where a person can go a whole lifetime and never have to kill a soul, it took some time for him to adjust to the conditions out here. He asked me about all the killing once, and I'll tell you the same thing I told him," Shakespeare stated. "First of all, the Indians know nothing about the Ten Commandments. Where an enemy is concerned, a warrior knows just one law. Kill or be killed. And in the case of the Blackfeet, they generally kill almost everyone else because they regard everyone else as enemies. They hate white men in particular."

"Why is that?" Nate interrupted.

"Some folks attribute their hatred to the Lewis and Clark expedition, although I'm inclined to doubt that was the cause."

"What did Lewis and Clark do?"

"Lewis, not Clark. In 1806, on their way back from the Pacific Ocean, they separated for a while so Lewis and a few other men could explore the Maria's River country. A band of Blackfeet tried to steal the guns and horses of Lewis's party, and Lewis was forced to shoot one of them in the belly. Another man stabbed a Blackfoot to death. Ever since, the Blackfeet have been out for white blood."

"Why do you doubt that incident is the reason the Blackfeet hate all whites?"

"Because the Blackfeet were a contrary tribe long before Lewis met up with them. They love to make war, plain and simple."

Nate pondered the disclosure and stared to the north. They were almost past the last of the Flathead lodges. Before them lay a wide field packed with trappers and Indians engaged in various activities. Some were merely talking. Others were taking part in horse races. Mainly the trappers were also engaged in foot races, wrestling matches, hopping contests, tossing a ball, and sundry sports. "Is there another reason a man should accept all the killing and the violence as just the way of life for those living in the wilderness?"

"Yes. The best one of all."

"Which is?"

"You can go to sleep at night with a clear conscience."

The frontiersman's irrefutable logic made a profound impression on Nate. When he'd slain his first man the feat had bothered him for days. He'd been unable to sleep and eat. And he still hadn't fully reconciled himself to the need to shed blood now and then. In New York City, as Shakespeare had noted, citizens were rarely compelled to slay other people. Apparently there were benefits to civilization, after all.

A raucous din filled the air, the whoops, cheers, and oaths of the participants.

"Does this go on throughout the entire rendezvous?" Nate inquired, having to raise his voice to be heard.

Shakespeare nodded. "Doesn't let up for a minute until the last day."

"They must need eleven months to rest up for the next one," Nate joked.

Just then a piercing shriek arose from a lean man astride a black stallion. Attired in buckskins, a big wool cap on his head, the man waved a rifle overhead and galloped straight at them. "Shakespeare McNair, you mangy son of a bitch!" he bellowed. "I'm going to skin you like the polecat you are!"

Chapter Seven

The frontiersman suddenly goaded his white horse toward the man, voicing a wild whoop and wagging his own rifle.

Bewildered by the unexpected development and thinking that Shakespeare was being attacked, Nate raised the Hawken to his shoulder and took a bead on the man in the wool cap. He hesitated, not wanting to commit a rash act, and felt a hand grip his arm.

"No, husband," Winona said.

Nate glanced at her. "Why?"

"Friend," Winona answered. "Much friend."

"He is?" Nate responded skeptically, lowering the rifle. He saw the two men race to within yards of each other, then both abruptly hauled on the reins and stopped with their mounts nearly touching shoulders.

"Shakespeare!" the other rider shouted, smiling broadly.

"You crazy bastard!" the frontiersman replied.

The two men hugged heartily, pounding one another on the back in the bargain, both laughing uproariously as if they'd just heard the funniest joke in the world.

"If they're not friends, then they're the strangest pair

of enemies I've ever laid eyes on," Nate commented, and made for them.

"Not understand," Winona said.

Using sign language, Nate attempted to translate the statement. The fact that she didn't so much as crack a smile indicated he'd not quite succeeded. He idly gazed to the east and saw a half-dozen men involved in horse racing. The race was already under way and an Indian on a brown horse had a substantial lead. About 20 spectators were cheering on their respective champions, and many of the onlookers held liquor flasks or bottles.

"Here's a fine-looking couple! Not too plump and not too thin. I bet they'd be delicious with the proper seasoning."'

Nate faced forward to find the grinning thin man regarding him intently. "Are you a cannibal?" he inquired in jest.

"Maybe I am," answered the thin man, and cackled crazily. "I've been called worse."

Shakespeare turned his animal so he could see them all without having to bend his neck. "Allow me to introduce everyone." He nodded at the character in the cap. "This is Crazy George. He and I go back a long ways."

"Yep," agreed the thin man. "We shared the same cradle until I got tired of him stealing my diapers."

Nate offered his right hand, leaning over the pommel. "I'm Nathaniel King. Pleased to make your acquaintance."

Crazy George looked at the hand for a moment, then cast an accusatory gaze at Nate. "Do you realize, young man, that you have dirt under your fingernails?"

"I do?" Nate said, and withdrew his arm to inspect his hand.

"Green as grass," Crazy George stated, and laughed.

"He's not as green as you think," Shakespeare said,

coming to his protégé's defense. "And I don't want you to spread any tales around to the contrary."

"Who, me?" Crazy George retorted. "I'm hurt, kind sir, to hear you make such an unflattering mockery of my noble name."

"Noble?" Shakespeare repeated, and erupted in unrestrained mirth.

"Pay no attention to him," Crazy George said to Nate. "He's a bit touched in the head."

"Me?" the frontiersman declared. "You're the one known far and wide as the loon of the Rockies."

Grinning at their antics, Nate extended his right arm again. "I'm still pleased to meet you, loon or not."

"Then it's a fair shake I'll give you," the thin man stated, and did so vigorously. "Did you teach this young man his manners?"

"I can't take the credit. His parents gave him a proper upbringing back in New York City."

"That den of iniquity?" Crazy George said, grimacing. "It's Sodom and Gomorrah combined, a vile nest of vipers where rats breed like rabbits."

"I seldom saw a rat in New York City," Nate mentioned.

"I was referring to the two-legged variety."

"Shakespeare shares your estimation of big cities," Nate noted. "He wouldn't live in one for all the money in the country."

Crazy George nodded. "McNair is a wise man, sir. You'd be well advised to head his words of sage advice. Next to me, he's the smartest man in the Rockies."

"Listen to him. You'd think he was the only man to ever win a debate in the Rocky Mountain College," the frontiersman said.

Nate had heard the term before. An unknown trapper had invented the title less than two years ago. It applied to the arguments, debates, and general yarn-spinning conducted during those long winter evenings when the frigid weather prevented the trappers from plying their trade, confining them to their cozy cabins or lodges. They would stay up until the wee hours of the morning engaged in earnest philosophical dialogue every bit as lofty as the debates held at prestigious universities back East.

Crazy George looked at Winona and politely doffed his cap. "Since this handsome maiden is too young for a grizzled old coot like McNair, she must be your wife, Nathaniel."

"Call me Nate. And yes, Winona is my wife."

"Keep a close eye on her, son."

"I always do."

The thin man's dark eyes darted to the left and the right, and he lowered his voice conspiratorially. "I'm serious, Nate. There are those who might try to take her from you."

"Who?"

"I can't say," Crazy George whispered. "Maybe later."

Nate smiled at Winona, then stared somberly at George. "I'd like to see anyone try to take her. I'll put a ball in their brain for their effort."

"Now there's an attitude I admire."

"We should find a spot to make camp," Shakespeare interjected, glancing to the north. "We want to get settled before we make the rounds."

"It just so happens there's a nice spot near my camp," Crazy George revealed. "It's right on the south shore of the lake. You'd have all the water you need at your fingertips, and there's a stand of cottonwoods not far off where you can gather all the wood you need."

"Why isn't such a choice site already taken?" Nate inquired absently.

"I'll tell you why," Shakespeare replied. "The other men tend to give George a wide berth. They don't want to be too near him if he's been drinking."

"Why not?"

"Because he becomes as belligerent as a female grizzly with cubs," Shakespeare said, and looked at the thin man. "I want your word that you won't cause us any trouble if we camp next to you."

Crazy George squared his slim shoulders. "You have my promise I'll behave myself."

"I hope so," Shakespeare said. "I heard how you shot two toes off Frank six months ago. If you try any of your antics on my friends, I'll be obliged to shoot you myself."

"Understood."

Nate studied George as the man replaced his cap. "Was Frank an enemy of yours?"

"No. He's one of my best friends."

"And you shot his toes off?"

Crazy George shrugged. "So he claims. But I was drunk at the time and don't remember doing it. For all I know, he accidentally shot his own toes off and then had the audacity to blame me."

"If he's your friend, as you say, why would he blame you for something you didn't do?"

"As a practical joke."

"In that case, your friend must have a strange sense of humor."

"He sure does," Crazy George said. "Frank isn't the sensible type, like me." At that he threw back his head and cackled on and on.

Shakespeare sighed and gestured for them to resume their ride to the north.

"You certainly have some unusual acquaintances," Nate remarked with a smirk.

"Just remember that you're one of them."

Chuckling, Nate observed the activities taking place all around them. Of special interest was a dance off to the left. A husky man wearing Scottish attire, including a kilt, provided a lively tune on bagpipes to which over a dozen men were whirling about and stomping their legs with all the enthusiasm of cavorting youngsters and all the gracefulness of a gaggle of geese. Half the dancers were paired off and had their elbows hooked, spinning just as fast as they could go.

Shakespeare glanced at Nate. "Do you know how to dance?"

"Never had much practice. I'm fair at slow dancing, though. Adeline used to compliment me all the time on my waltzing."

"You won't find much waltzing done here. Just hope no one picks you as a dancing partner."

Crazy George came up from behind and rode on the frontiersman's left. "Say, I've been meaning to ask you. Where the hell is Zeke?"

A cloud seemed to descend on Shakespeare's face. "Dead."

"No! How?"

"A Kiowa warrior did him in."

"Damn! There was a fine man, the salt of the earth," George stated. "I'm proud to have known Zeke King." He suddenly blinked a few times, then stared at Nate. "King. King. Didn't you tell me your name is King?"

"Zeke was my uncle."

"Were you with him when the end came?"

Nate simply nodded.

"How did he die?"

"What does it matter? He's gone and that's all that counts," Nate said gruffly.

The thin man recoiled as if struck. "Sorry, young fellow. I didn't mean to rub a nerve."

"Let's not talk about it."

"Fair enough. But first tell me this. Did the Kiowa bastard get away?"

"No."

"Zeke got him?" Crazy George smiled. "That would be just like Zeke. Full of fire to the very end."

"Zeke didn't kill the Kiowa. I did."

"Oh."

"I'll show you his scalp later, if you want."

"Would you? Thanks," George said, then gazed around them, his expression furtive. "Speaking of scalps, have you gentlemen heard the news?"

"What news?" Shakespeare queried.

"About the killings?"

"What are you talking about?"

George lowered his voice when he said, "The killing of the three trappers here at the rendezvous. Each one lost his hair."

Twisting in his saddle, Shakespeare regarded the thin man skeptically. "Is this another of your wild stories?"

"When have I ever told wild stories?" Crazy George rejoined.

"At least once a day."

"Name one."

"How about the time you claimed you went all the way out to California with three Frenchmen?"

"I did. I did," George said, bobbing his chin.

"And you claimed you saw a new type of tree out there. What were they called again?"

"The Spanish had a funny name for them. I called them stone trees because the wood was just like rock. You couldn't cut it if you tried."

"Stone trees," Shakespeare stated sarcastically. "And if I recall correctly, you told us there were stone birds in those trees, and those birds laid stone eggs."

George adopted a sheepish countenance. "Well, I may have exaggerated a bit to make the story more interesting."

"You never went to California and you know it."

"I did so," George declared angrily. "I'll take you there to prove it."

"I might get out there one day yet," Shakespeare said. "But I'll be damned if a man who is touched in the head is going to lead me."

"You've hurt my feelings, McNair," the thin man responded, sounding genuinely distressed.

"Excuse me," Nate said, interrupting them. "I'd like to hear about the three trappers."

"Will you believe me if I tell you?" George asked.

"Every word."

"Really?"

"But stick to the facts."

"I will. The first man, Kevin Hughes, was found dead the second day of the rendezvous. Someone slit his throat from ear to ear, then lifted his hair," George detailed. "And that wasn't all. Hughes had sold four hundred ten pelts the day before, but there wasn't any trace of the money on him or with his belongings."

"The killer must have taken it," Nate speculated.

"Most likely."

"Could Indians have been responsible?"

It was Shakespeare who answered, his interest now fully aroused. "No. Not if, as I take it, Hughes's personal effects weren't touched."

"They weren't," Crazy George confirmed. "His guns, blankets, horses, and everything else was right where he left them."

"No Indian would ever pass up plunder like that," Shakespeare said thoughtfully. "Horses and blankets mean more to an Indian than a handful of money. They have no appreciation of money's value. They're traders by nature. When they want something from white men, they trade for it.''

"What about the other two trappers?" Nate inquired.

"They were killed a few days ago," George related. "Like Hughes, they'd just sold their furs and had close to two thousand dollars apiece."

"Who were they?" Shakespeare wanted to know.

"Aaron Hersch and Jimmy O'Connor."

"Damn. I knew O'Connor. He was an old hand and as decent as they come," the frontiersman said.

"Were their throats also slit?" Nate questioned.

"No. O'Connor took a knife in the back, and Hersch had his neck broken."

"It must take a strong man to break another person's neck," Nate commented.

"Not really," Shakespeare said. "All it takes is one good twist if you know how to apply the pressure." He paused, looking at Crazy George. "No one found a clue to the killer's identity?"

"Not so much as a hair. Of course, it's easy for a man to hide his tracks if he's of a mind. Some of the trappers are of the opinion that Hersch put up a bit of a struggle before his neck snapped."

"Didn't anyone hear the fight?" Nate asked.

"Not a soul. But then, they'd gone off a ways by themselves. Pitched camp in some trees near the Bannock lodges. Someone told me they were planning to buy a couple of Bannock women and celebrate their earnings," George disclosed, and frowned. "Poor devils."

Nate looked at Shakespeare. "Has anything like this ever happened before?"

"Not to my knowledge."

"All of the trappers are on edge," Crazy George mentioned. "The main topic of conversation is the murders. No one goes anywhere without a loaded gun. And you don't want to walk up behind anyone without letting them know you're there, or you'll wind up with a ball in your brains.''

Raucous laughter erupted from a group of trappers off to the left.

''They don't seem very concerned about the murders at the moment,'' Nate observed.

''Of course not, young fellow. It's daylight,'' George responded. ''Besides, most of the men here are accustomed to life in the wild. I'd say the majority have lived in the Rocky Mountain region for at least a year, and quite a few have been out here for two or three. They deal with Indians and animals all the time, so they're not the kind to scare easily.''

''What if the killer strikes again?''

George shrugged. ''What if he does?''

''Has anyone thought to post guards at night? Maybe all the trappers should sleep in the same general area. That way the killer would find it harder to attack his victims.''

''Got it all figured out, have you?'' Crazy George said, and laughed.

''The trappers would never agree to such an arrangement, Nate,'' Shakespeare stated. ''They're too independent-minded. They'd rather take their chances than do anything that might give the impression they're afraid.''

''Doesn't make sense to me,'' Nate said, and turned to the thin man. ''You told us two trappers were killed near the Bannock camp. Where was the third man slain?''

A mischievous grin curled George's mouth. ''At his camp, right on the south shore of the lake, not far from a stand of cottonwoods.''

Nate and Shakespeare exchanged glances.

''It wouldn't happen to be the same spot where you want us to pitch camp, would it?'' the frontiersman inquired.

"As a matter of fact, it would," Crazy George answered. "But don't worry. All of the blood has seeped into the ground by now." So saying, he tossed back his head and roared.

Chapter Eight

Against Nate's better judgment he allowed Shakespeare to persuade him to avail themselves of the site near the water. The ground was flat and grassy, ideal for the horses. Their nearest "neighbors" were two Irishmen located 30 yards to the east, three men from Pennsylvania about the same distance to the west, and Crazy George approximately 40 yards to the south.

Several hours were spent in arranging the camp to their satisfaction. Winona tended to the animals, unpacking them and letting the horses drink from the lake before hobbling their legs so they couldn't stray far. She also gathered wood and proceeded to get a fire going on the exact spot where the slain trapper had had his.

Nate decided not to tell Winona about the murderer stalking the rendezvous. He saw no reason to alarm her needlessly. The killer was obviously after men who had recently sold furs, and since neither Shakespeare nor he had any to sell, he doubted they were in any danger.

The frontiersman went with him to the Shoshone encampment, and they tried to find a warrior willing to part with the buffalo hides needed to construct a small lodge. Only one Shoshone had a teepee cover he could spare, but it was old and torn and would have fallen apart at the first heavy rain.

"I wish we could have found one for Winona's sake," Nate commented as they rode back toward the lake.

"Face facts. You'll just have to kill a few buffaloes and chop down the saplings you'll need for the poles."

"Can we do it today?"

"There's no rush. And I'd like to mingle, visit the booths and such."

"So would I," Nate said. Earlier they had skirted the crowds flocking around the booths so they could reach the lake that much sooner. Now his eagerness to mingle and see the sights fought with his sense of duty to his wife, and he came to the conclusion that an extra night or two spent sleeping on the ground wasn't too great of an inconvenience. "We'll go with you. I can always hunt buffalo tomorrow."

They were passing the stand of trees to the west of their camp. Ahead were the horses and possessions belonging to the trio from Pennsylvania, none of whom were around. Nate smiled as his gaze roved over the items, marveling that they had been left right out in the open. Back in New York City such an act would be the equivalent of sheer stupidity; the possessions would be gone before the owners returned. Out in the West, though, things were different. The people subscribed to a personal code of honor, a morality that prevented them from stooping to petty robbery.

Well, almost all the people.

There were always exceptions like the killer.

"What the hell!" Shakespeare unexpectedly exclaimed, and galloped eastward.

Nate took one look and did the same, his pulse quickening, the Hawken clutched in his right hand. There were four riders at the camp. He recognized one of them right away.

Laclede!

What were the weasel and his cohorts doing there? Nate wondered. As he drew rapidly closer his gaze was drawn to the largest of the quartet, a veritable giant of a man on a brown stallion. Well over six feet tall, the man was endowed with a bronzed, muscular physique. This giant wore no shirt. Deerskin moccasins covered his feet, and he wore leggings constructed from the hide of the same animal. He also wore a breechcloth, Indian fashion, on the outside of the leggings. Tucked under the belt girding his waist was a tomahawk, and resting across his huge thighs was a rifle.

Crazy George stood facing the four men. Behind him, near the fire, squatted Winona.

Alarmed for his wife's safety, Nate urged the mare forward and caught up with Shakespeare. The frontiersman had a grim visage, grimmer than Nate could ever remember seeing. In less than ten seconds they closed the gap and reined up hard.

"What the hell do you want?" Shakespeare gruffly demanded.

The big man had calmly watched their approach. He nodded and said in a deep voice, "Allo, Carcajou."

"You didn't answer my question, Cleroult."

"I don't know if I like your attitude, McNair."

Shakespeare turned his mount so the barrel of his rifle was angled in the direction of the four men without actually pointing at any of them. "I didn't invite you to our camp. Since the last time we met we nearly came to blows, I know this isn't a social visit."

"There's where you're wrong," Cleroult stated smugly. "I came to pay my respects and welcome you to the rendezvous. If I don't show you there are no hard feelings now, *mon ami,* I may never have the opportunity. A man your age might not make it to the next gathering.''

"Don't you worry about my age. And I'll tell you the same thing I told Laclede. I'm not your friend and I don't want you spreading it around that I am."

Cleroult's eyes narrowed. "You always were too touchy for your own good, Carcajou."

Crazy George stepped closer to Shakespeare's horse. "He told me he came here to see Nate."

"Is that a fact?" the frontiersman said.

Nate suddenly found himself the object of the quartet's attention. He returned Cleroult's gaze without flinching. "Why were you looking for me?"

"I understand you had a disagreement with my good friends here," the big man said, an edge to his tone.

For a moment Nate hesitated. He noticed Shakespeare and Crazy George both glance at him, and he reasoned that a lot rode on his response, that Cleroult was trying to intimidate him into displaying a trace of fear. He saw Laclede smirking, and the one he had struck, the lecher named Henri, was grinning broadly despite his split lips. Adopting an air of casual indifference, he spoke calmly, yet firmly. "Disagreement, hell. They came close to being planted in the ground. You should pick your friends more carefully."

Gaston Cleroult squared his shoulders, his lips twitching. "Do you know who I am?"

"I've heard of you," Nate admitted. "The Giant, I believe you're called."

"*Oui.*"

"And the Indians refer to you as the Bad One."

"*Oui,*" Cleroult said again, grinning.

"Which isn't a compliment, in my estimation," Nate stated, and was gratified to see the Giant's countenance harden.

"The Indians have a tendency to exaggerate."

"And here I thought they're basically honest."

Cleroult looked down at his rifle, then at Shakespeare and George, before settling his gaze on Nate again. "You smashed Henri in the mouth."

"He's lucky I didn't shoot him. No one takes liberties with my wife, not even with their eyes."

"You can't stop a man from thinking."

"What he thinks is his business. It's when he shows it that I object."

The giant stared at Winona for several seconds. "Shoshone, isn't she?"

Nate merely nodded.

"I had a Shoshone wife for about six months once. She couldn't cook worth a damn. Sleeping under the same blanket with her was like sleeping with a log," Cleroult said, and glanced at Nate. "I hear all Soshone women are the same way."

The obvious attempt to provoke him almost prompted Nate to laugh. Instead, he kept his voice level as he said, "I wouldn't know. I've never slept with a log."

Cleroult glowered for a moment. "You have much to learn, Chipmunk Killer."

"That's Grizzly Killer."

"Whatever," the Giant said. He turned his horse and started off, glancing back as he did. "*Je ne vous oublierai pas.*"

Laclede, Henri, and the third trapper wheeled their animals and trailed Cleroult to the south.

"What were his last words to me?" Nate inquired when they were out of earshot.

"He said he won't forget you," Crazy George translated, and tittered. "He must be in love."

"You did well, Nate," Shakespeare said. "I couldn't have handled him better myself."

"I'm surprised he left without trying to thrash me within an inch of my life."

"If he caught you alone, he would have," Shakespeare declared. "He just didn't like the odds."

"That big bastard won't leave you alone now," George mentioned. "He doesn't back down for any man, and he'll figure he owes you something. You'd better watch your back all the time."

Sighing, Nate dismounted. "I thought one of the best things about coming to a rendezvous was making new friends?"

"It is," Shakespeare said.

"You could have fooled me. All I seem to make are enemies."

The frontiersman beamed and slid down from his own animal. "We'll worry about Cleroult when the time comes. Right now we should take a stroll over to the booths."

"I'm for that," Nate concurred. He walked over to Winona and used sign language to explain about the fruitless search for the hides and poles necessary to build a lodge.

Winona responded that she was in no great hurry. She would be content to wait until things worked out.

Reassured, Nate proceeded to strip his saddle from the mare and tied her near the other horses. Taking Winona's hand, he joined Shakespeare and Crazy George and together they strolled toward the heart of the rendezvous. The air was filled with shouts and oaths, laughter and music, plus the periodic retorts of guns.

Crazy George took a deep breath. "Ahhhh, this is the life, gentlemen. A man feels so alive at a time like this."

"Except the three men who have been murdered," Shakespeare noted.

"Why spoil everything by bringing them up?" George

asked testily. "This is a day to frolic and do what comes naturally."

"Just remember my warning about having too much to drink," the frontiersman said.

"I remember. But surely you won't begrudge me a drink or two?"

"No."

"Or three or four," George declared, grinning.

"Just so you behave."

They passed other campsites. Few were occupied. At one of them, off to the west, a Scotsman called out to Shakespeare and invited all of them to visit him that evening. The frontiersman replied that they would try.

"Who was he?" Nate inquired as they continued onward.

"Sir William Drummond Stewart," Shakespeare said. "He's a Scottish gent who came last year as a lark. Evidently he liked it so much he came back again."

Soon they reached the booths. Swarms of people were everywhere: trappers, traders, Indians, and half-breeds. On display, for sale or barter, were the goods brought all the way from St. Louis. There were clothes, tobacco, coffee, sugar, rifles and pistols, knives and axes, gunpowder, trade items for the Indians such as calico, blankets, pans, and beads, and much more.

Nate took Winona from booth to booth. They inspected the wares and discussed possible purchases. He saw her eyes light up at the sight of a red blanket, and although the trader had overpriced it by five dollars, he splurged and bought the thing for her. The affection her eyes radiated afterward more than compensated for the expense.

The time went by swiftly.

The booths where whiskey was being sold enjoyed the most business. There were always long lines, and men who barely were able to stand erect would stagger up to the counter for more.

Nate had just passed one such booth, and had halted to survey the activities taking place on the field beyond, when a firm hand clamped onto his left shoulder and he was rudely spun around, losing his grip on Winona.

There stood a stocky man attired in buckskins, a pistol wedged under his belt, a bottle in his left hand. A brown beard, moist around his thick lips, jutted from his chin. "Hello, friend," he declared in a clipped accent.

Nate jerked his shoulder free. The man's breath would inebriate a horse, he reflected. He plastered a friendly smile on his face. "I don't believe we've been introduced, friend."

"My mates call me Eddy. Edward Mulhare is my given name."

"Having a grand time, are you?" Nate politely inquired, surveying the crowd. He realized Shakepeare and Crazy George were nowhere in sight.

"I'm having the best time of my life. We never had an affair like this back in England."

"Is that where you're from?"

"Yes. I came to America about fifteen years ago. Been on the move ever since."

"Well, my name is Nate King and I'm pleased to meet you."

"Share a drink with me, Nate King," Mulhare said.

"Perhaps some other time," Nate suggested.

"Why not now?"

"My wife and I are making the rounds."

"That's no reason," Mulhare stated testily, and shoved the bottle under Nate's nose. "You insult a man when you refuse to drink with him. So come on. Share a sip or two."

.

Annoyed, but not wanting to anger the Englishman and provoke a fight, Nate reluctantly took the whiskey and swallowed. The burning liquid scorched a path down his throat and seemed to hit his stomach with the force of an exploding keg of gunpowder. He grimaced and returned the bottle to its owner. "Thanks. We'll be moving on."

"Have another drink."

"Not now," Nate responded firmly.

"I take that as an insult."

Nate sighed and looked around for Shakespeare. The last thing he wanted was to make another enemy. He decided to be tactful and prevent trouble. "All right. One more drink."

The Englishman grinned and handed the bottle back. "Have a go, mate."

Again Nate swallowed, and this time the whiskey didn't bother him as much. He wiped his mouth on his sleeve and extended his arm. "Thanks. I really must be going."

"Have another drink."

An uneasy feeling seized Nate, a feeling that there was more to the Englishman than met the eye. Although the fellow's breath reeked, there was nothing in the man's manner to indicate he was drunk.

"Have another drink," Mulhare said yet again.

"No."

"I insist."

"I refuse," Nate countered, and hefted the Hawken. "Find someone else to drink with."

"I want to drink with you," Mulhare declared, and took a stride backward. "So take a sip or else."

"This is foolish."

"Foolish, am I?" Mulhare responded loudly, much louder than necessary. He cast the bottle to the ground and raised his clenched fists. "Let's see how much of man you are, mate. Put down that bloody long gun so I can crack your skull.''

"No."

"Suit yourself," Mulhare said, and lowered his head and attacked.

Chapter Nine

Nate was unprepared for the charge. He barely had time to let go of the Hawken before the Englishman plowed into him, catching him about the waist and knocking him to the ground. Unexpectedly his foe released him. Nate rolled and stood, acutely conscious of the converging spectators who were eager to witness the fight.

Edward Mulhare had regained his footing and now adopted a boxing posture. He smirked and cried out, for all to hear, "This man has insulted me. I intend to teach him a lesson."

"I did not insult you!" Nate countered.

"And I say you did. Now defend yourself, mate." Mulhare abruptly waded in, his arms flying.

Once more Nate was taken off guard. He managed to block two swift punches, but then a third connected with his left temple and a fourth slammed him on the chin. He staggered and went down to his knees, dazed, aware of murmuring voices on all sides but unable to distinguish the words. Slowly his senses returned to normal and he saw the Englishman five feet away, waiting patiently for him to recover.

"Ready?" Mulhare asked sarcastically.

Nate struggled to his feet and imitated his foe, lifting his arms to protect his face and his midriff.

"Good," Mulhare said. "You'll provide a bit of sport after all."

"Teach the pup a lesson!" bellowed someone in the crowd.

The voice sounded familiar. Nate looked and spied Gaston Cleroult, Laclede, and the other two not two feet away. All four were clearly delighted by his predicament. But where was Winona? Concerned for her safety, he failed to watch the Englishman, and a moment later paid for his mistake. A fist rammed into his stomach, doubling him over, and another pounded him on the top of his head. He fell like a rock, sprawling on his stomach, flattened and stunned.

"Give him another one, Eddy!" shouted a bystander.

Nate inhaled and shook his head, striving to regain control of his limbs, confused and angry. This had all happened so fast! One minute he'd been minding his own business, and the next a fool Englishman wanted to beat him into the ground. And all because he had declined a third drink?

"Get up, Nate!"

The prompting came from the one man at the rendezvous Nate could truly call a friend. He blinked and gazed to his left, elated to behold Shakespeare, Winona, and Crazy George. His wife held his rifle.

"Stand, Grizzly Killer!" George yelled. "Show this upstart how you earned your name!"

Placing his palms on the grass, Nate shoved erect and glared at Mulhare. "Care to try that again?"

"Gladly."

Instead of staying rooted to the spot, Nate retreated when the Englishman came at him, deflecting a series of punches. He skipped lightly to the left, blocking more blows, impressed by Mulhare's ability. He wondered if the Englishman had had any professional training at bare-knuckle fighting, and recalled reading an item in the paper about a certain boxing school in London that had opened in 1719 and produced a number of top fighters. His reflection almost cost him dearly, however, as the English-man came at him with renewed vigor and almost landed a crushing punch to the mouth that would have rendered him unconscious if it had connected.

Shouts arose from the onlooking trappers. Partisans cheered on their respective champions. Most of the enthusiastic yells were directed at Mulhare.

Nate held his own with extreme difficulty. He'd experienced his share of childhood fights, but he'd never engaged in a bare-knuckle bout as an adult. His only hope, as he saw it, was to constantly keep moving, to make himself an impossible target to hit. But to do so he was compelled to constantly shuffle his legs, and after so many weeks of sitting astride a saddle his leg muscles were sorely out of condition.

The Englishman became chagrined at his failure to down the younger man quickly. The longer they fought, the angrier he grew. His swings were wider, his jabs less focused. He began muttering curses under his breath.

So engrossed was Nate in simply evading Mulhare's fists that he failed to keep track of his position. He didn't realize he was in any danger until a leg lashed out from the sidelines and tripped him, sending him to his hands and knees. He glimpsed the Giant standing nearby and knew who to blame. At the moment, though, he had more pressing concerns.

Mulhare stepped in close and directed a devastating kick at his opponent's head.

Nate ducked under the Englishman's moccasin, flipped onto his side, and seized Mulhare's other leg. He wrenched with all of his might, upending the stocky man, then surged erect. For the first time since the fight began he landed two solid blows of his own, smashing a right and a left to the Englishman's face and knocking his foe flat.

"Well done, Nate!" Shakespeare shouted.

"Now bite his nose off!" Crazy George added.

Tempted as he was to plant a kick while the Englishman was down, Nate resisted the temptation and moved to the right, letting Mulhare rise.

"You'll bloody well pay for that!"

"You were the one who started this," Nate pointed out. "I intend to finish it."

"You're dreaming, boy."

The last word, dripping with scorn, provoked Nate into a reckless flurry. He succeeded in hitting the Englishman twice, but neither blow was effective, and he received a gut-wrenching fist to the abdomen for his efforts. Another punch arced at his mouth and he dodged to the right and straightened, ignoring the agony in his stomach.

"Damn you! Stand still and trade blows like a man!"

"Maybe you'd prefer to have me tied down?" Nate taunted.

Mulhare threw all caution to the wind and closed again, his stout arms pumping, a sneer contorting his features, sweat beading his brow.

Nimbly Nate backed away, using his forearms to counter and hoping for an opening he could exploit. Seconds later the Englishman threw a right, his left held near his waist, leaving his chin unprotected. Nate moved in and drove a right hook to Mulhare's chin, throwing his entire body into the swing.

The force of the punch lifted the Englishman off his feet and sent him sailing for over a yard to crash down on his back.

The spectators were in a frenzy.

Nate clenched his fists so tightly the knuckles ached and edged nearer to his opponent.

Blood trickling from the corners of his mouth, Mulhare

sat up, groaning, clearly dazed. He gave a little growl and pushed himself from the ground, shaking his head.

Someone was bellowing a string of words in French.

Eager to finish the battle, Nate feinted with his left, then delivered a right that jarred the Englishman and made the man stagger rearward. He pressed his advantage, trying to break through Mulhare's guard, elated that the man's movements were much slower than previously.

A wild look came into the Englishman's eyes, a look of haunted desperation. He sensed he was losing and he fought frantically.

The insight gave Nate added confidence. He gritted his teeth, let his fury fuel his limbs, and battered Mulhare's arms aside. A fleeting expression of panic etched the stocky man's visage an instant before Nate swung his right fist into Mulhare's nose.

The Englishman's knees buckled, but he somehow kept his footing although his arms sagged and he weaved from side to side. "No," he mumbled weakly.

"Yes," Nate stated, and delivered another right to the face. He followed through with a left, then a right. Left, right, left, right; he pounded and pounded, only vaguely aware of the blood splattering onto his clothes and the sudden silence that had descended on the onlookers. Not until Mulhare abruptly dropped did he desist, and even then he stood there waiting for the Englishman to rise once more.

"It's over!"

Was that Shakespeare? Nate wondered, regaining control of his emotions. Slowly the scarlet haze dissipated and he stared down at Mulhare's bloody, mashed face in disbelief that he could have accomplished such a feat.

"Nate?"

Almost reluctantly Nate lowered his weary arms and turned.

Shakespeare and Winona were a yard away, both

regarding him with commingled concern and esteem.

"Are you all right?" the frontiersman asked.

"Fine," Nate muttered, and looked down at Mulhare. "Better than him, anyway."

"No one has ever beaten that rascal at fistfighting," Shakespeare mentioned. "He finally received his due."

A pervading fatigue filled Nate's body. He licked his lips, feeling sore all over and wishing he could sleep for a week. His hands, in particular, were throbbing.

"I heard tell that Mulhare did some fighting over in England years ago," Shakespeare said. "Almost killed a man once, I believe. When he's been drinking, he's a regular terror."

Winona stepped forward and tenderly placed her right hand on Nate's cheek. The affection in her eyes conveyed a world of meaning.

Suddenly they were surrounded by loud, laughing trappers, many of whom clapped Nate on the back and offered their hearty congratulations.

"Well done, Grizzly Killer!" declared a bearded man of the woods. "You're everything they say you are. As quick as a cat and as tough as they come."

"Yep," chimed in another. "Thanks to you I just won forty dollars."

"My name is Swenson," said a third. "Feel free to visit my camp anytime. I'd like to hear about the bears you've killed."

The compliments continued for a couple of minutes. Nate smiled and nodded and mumbled responses, bewildered by all the attention. He'd finally made friends, dozens of them, but at what a cost! When the crowd began to disperse he spotted his wife and best friend standing off to one side, both grinning, their expressions reflecting their pride.

"You'll be the talk of the rendezvous tonight," Shakespeare predicted, coming over.

"Lucky me," Nate said. He looked around and saw Edward Mulhare being supported by the Giant and Laclede, heading to the west.

The frontiersman gazed in the same direction. "It didn't take Cleroult long."

"What do you mean?"

"You don't think the fight you just had took place by mere chance, do you? It was no accident."

"It wasn't?" Nate said, his fatigue affecting his mental sharpness, making him lethargic.

"Of course not. Mulhare and the Giant are good friends. Cleroult undoubtedly persuaded the Englishman to goad you into fighting," Shakespeare said grimly. "I'll say this for the Giant. He doesn't waste time in getting revenge on those he despises."

The entire incident now made sense, and Nate's lips compressed in simmering anger. "I'll pay Cleroult back."

"He'll get his due in good time," Shakespeare said, and studied the younger man for a moment. "We'd better get you back to the camp. Winona can tend to those bruises and that nasty cut on your chin."

Nate reached up and touched his jaw, surprised to discover one of Mulhare's blows had split the skin and blood was trickling down his neck. He wiped the blood on his hand.

"Let's go," Shakespeare suggested, motioning for them to start moving.

"Where's Crazy George?" Nate inquired, walking northward. Winona fell in on his right.

"Who knows?" the frontiersman said.

"Tell me. What was that business about the man who won forty dollars?"

"He bet on you."

"Bet?"

Shakespeare nodded. "A lot of the trappers like to place wagers on the outcomes of the horse races, wrestling matches, jumping contests, and the like.''

"Does a lot of money change hands?''

"Oh, I wouldn't describe it as a lot. They're usually friendly wagers. Twenty dollars here. Maybe fifty there. Every now and then a couple of heavy drinkers will go overboard and bet a few hundred.''

Nate glanced to the right and left, noticing the looks cast toward him by many of the trappers, noticing their hushed conversations. He wasn't sure if he liked all the attention. Once the story about the fight spread, he'd be widely regarded as a tough mountaineer, a man not to be trifled with. Knowing the trappers' propensity for telling tall tales, the story would be exaggerated out of all proportion. And once the rendezvous broke up, the trappers would travel to the far ends of the Rockies and elsewhere, and the story would undoubtedly be related around many a campfire for months to come. He just might wind up with a reputation the equal of Jim Bowie's. The thought caused him to smile.

What was wrong with that?

"I wonder when Cleroult will try again,'' Shakespeare remarked.

"You think he will?''

"Of course. The Giant and those vultures that hang around with him want you to suffer.''

"Is there anything I can do to prevent it?''

"You could get on your knees in front of the Giant and beg for forgiveness,'' the frontiersman said, and chuckled.

"I'd rather not.''

"Figures as much. Then your best option is to kill them.''

Nate halted. "Are you serious?''

"Never more so. Turn the tables on them. Provoke Cleroult and his bunch into a fight and slay them.''

"Just like that, huh?''

Shakespeare snapped his fingers. "Just like that.''

"Need I point out there are five of them, if you count the Englishman?"

"I'll help you."

"Five to two. I still don't like the odds."

"But you like the idea?" Shakespeare probed, intently scrutinizing Nate's features.

"I'll be honest. I do."

"Then there's hope for you after all," Shakespeare said, beaming.

They returned to their camp by the lake. Winona gathered cool water in a pan to use in tending Nate, then ministered to his minor wounds while Shakespeare went fishing for their supper.

Seated on a blanket, idly observing the sun on its westward descent and admiring the majestic scenery, Nate manfully resisted the urge to grimace when Winona's cloth touched his bruises. Despite the fight, he felt supremely content and relaxed. The wilderness life appealed to him, had a fascinating allure he found irresistible. He even had to admit to himself that the ever-present element of danger added a certain spice to living. Not once since he'd ventured west of the Mississippi River had he experienced the boredom that typically beset him in New York City.

Winona finished tending him and sat down. Her hands moved gracefully as she described her feelings during the fight. She expressed her happiness at his victory, and also her fear that the Bad One would make more trouble for them. She wondered if it might not be wiser to move their camp.

To where? Nate signed.

To the Shoshone encampment, Winona replied, where they would be safer.

Nate informed her he wasn't about to run from the trouble. To do so would only delay the inevitable. Sooner or later the Bad One would strike, and he would rather it occurred when he was prepared.

Reluctantly, Winona acceded to his wishes.

An hour later Shakespeare strolled back, a string of large bass and perch dangling from his left hand, whistling happily. "I'll do the honors tonight," he offered. "You haven't tasted delicious fish until you've eaten mine."

"My mother can cook tasty fish too," Nate mentioned.

The frontiersman snorted and deposited his rifle on his saddle. "Let me give you some advice. If you intend to stay out here, you'd better learn to cook for yourself."

"I can cook," Nate said defensively.

"Oh, you roast venison well enough. But I'm talking about really cooking, about learning to season your food with herbs and salt when they're available, about turning your meals into feasts fit for a king." Shakespeare paused, then laughed at his inadvertent pun.

The rest of the afternoon and early evening was spent in leisurely fashion. True to his word, Shakespeare prepared a savory meal that would have done justice to the finest cook in the States.

Nate took his first bite and let the soft meat rest on his tongue, relishing the taste.

"Well?" the frontiersman queried impatiently. "What's your verdict?"

"Not bad."

"Not bad!" Shakespeare exclaimed. "Why, you wouldn't know flavorful food if it jumped up and bit you."

Laughing, Nate dug into his meal in earnest.

Gradually the light diminished and stars dotted the firmament. All around were campfires, scores and scores of them, and the aroma of burning wood wafted on the breeze.

Winona arranged the bedding a few feet from the fire.

"I'm surprised George didn't pay us a visit," Nate commented.

"I'm not," Shakespeare said. "He's probably indulging in his favorite pastime. He'll wander into his own camp about midnight, drunk as can be.''

"If you dislike his drinking so much, why do you tolerate him as a friend?''

"You've got it backwards. Because he is a friend I tolerate his drinking. A few bad habits don't make a man bad. And George didn't always drink so much. At one time he was the most sober man around. Then his wife lost her life in a flood. Ever since he's been trying to drink himself to death without much success.''

"I didn't know,'' Nate said lamely.

"Judging other people is another dangerous habit. No one else can quite measure up to our own standards of right and wrong.''

"Never gave the matter much thought,'' Nate confessed.

"Most don't,'' Shakespeare said. "More's the pity.''

The soothing sounds of a bagpipe drifted from the south, a slow, almost melancholy song that rose and reduced in volume like waves lapping against a seashore, a haunting melody that seemed in keeping with the natural setting, with the immense, glassy lake and the ring of towering peaks.

Nate listened and felt his soul stirred. He asked Winona if she was ready to retire, and she responded that the events of the day had put her in the perfect mood for sleep. They got under their blanket and Nate lay on his back so Winona could rest her head on his chest. He draped an arm around her and gazed up at the stars. Never, ever, had he felt so happy.

After a while Shakespeare turned in. The entire countryside became quiet, the voices and the music tapering off as the men of the mountains took their nightly repose.

Nate had difficulty sleeping. He thought of the confrontations with Laclede and the Giant, and reviewed in his mind's eye the fight with the Englishman. The day had been eventful from dawn to dusk, but then every day in the wild was the same, filled with new experiences and never a boring moment. His eyes began to droop and he felt himself on the verge of slumber, when suddenly a sharp snap came from somewhere off to the south.

What was that?

Nate came abruptly awake, straining to catch the faintest noise. The snap had sounded like the breaking of a twig, which meant someone must be moving about.

Who?

And why so late at night?

He twisted his neck and stared into the night. Most of the campfires were already out or little better than flickering embers. Even their own fire produced few flames.

An inky figure moved from east to west, perhaps 20 yards away.

Nate was all attention. Whoever it was, the person had to be between their camp and Crazy George's. He watched with baited breath, perplexed by the figure's stealthy movements.

What if it was the killer?

The shadowy wraith moved steadily toward the camp of the three Pennsylvanians.

Alarmed, Nate gently eased Winona from his chest and slid out from under the buffalo hide, his right hand closing on his rifle. He crouched, uncertain of what to do.

It might just be a trapper returning to camp.

A dreadful, intuitive sensation came over him, a belief that it wasn't a trapper. He rose, bending at the waist, and tiptoed for a good ten feet to avoid waking Winona and Shakespeare. If the figure should turn out to be an innocent trapper, he'd feel like a fool if he'd needlessly awakened them. Once he had gone far enough so they wouldn't hear his steps, he broke into a run and hastened in pursuit.

The nocturnal prowler had disappeared.

Nate increased his speed, covering 20 yards, over half the distance to the Pennsylvanians' camp.

From up ahead a shrill scream pierced the darkness.

Chapter Ten

Nate straightened and ran all out. The feeble sparkle of a dying fire pinpointed the exact location of the trio from Pennsylvania, and in the dim glow he detected a struggle taking place, two men locked in mortal combat.

Shouts arose to the east and south. Men were calling out, demanding to know who had screamed.

To the rear a deep voice bellowed, "Nate? Where are you?"

"Here!" Nate cried. "This way!" He hoped he would be in time to aid the three men, but a glittering hint of metal and a horrified wail indicated he might not be. He deliberately yelled again, thinking that the attacker might flee. "Shakespeare! There's someone in the Pennsylvanians' camp! Hurry!"

More trappers were now adding to the clamor.

Nate had ten yards to go when he spotted someone slinking off to the southwest. "Halt!" he ordered, but the person paid no attention. He whipped the rifle to his shoulder, then hesitated.

What if it wasn't the killer?

Annoyed at himself, he sprinted to the camp and stopped, aghast at the grisly sight. Two of the Pennsylvanians were dead in their blankets, their throats slit, blood pouring down their necks. The third had resisted their attacker. He lay near the fire, on his back, a butcher knife jutting from his chest.

Dear Lord!

Nate took four strides, probing the night. He spied someone moving quickly away, almost at the limits of his vision, and he impulsively raised the Hawken, sighted, and fired.

The next moment the figure vanished.

Had he hit him? Nate swiftly reloaded, listening to the shouts of the aroused trappers.

"Who the hell fired a gun?"

"What's going on?"

"Someone said it's the Pennsylvanians' camp!"

"Where the hell are they?"

"By the south shore of the lake."

Men were converging rapidly, many bearing torches, dozens of them from the west, south, and east.

Nate heard heavy footsteps just as he finished reloading, and spun, relieved to see Shakespeare on the other side of the fire.

"Was that you doing the shooting?" the frontiersman asked, gazing at the corpses.

"Yes. I saw the killer." Nate walked over.

"Did you hit him?"

"I don't know."

Trappers arrived from all directions, with more right behind them. They stared in shock at the three dead men. One trapper placed his hand over his mouth and ran off.

"Son of a bitch!" a tall man exclaimed.

"Not again!" declared another.

"Did anyone see who did this?" asked a third.

"I did," Nate volunteered. "A glimpse of him, anyway."

"And who might you be?" demanded one of the crowd.

"Nate King."

"Never heard of you."

"Some people call me Grizzly Killer."

"Oh."

A commotion ensued as several men shoved their way to the forefront of the trappers. One of the new arrivals towered over everyone else.

"What have we here?" snapped Gaston Cleroult. On his left stood Laclede. On his right, glaring at Nate, was Edward Mulhare.

"The killer has struck again," a trapper said.

"So I see," the Giant responded. "It's getting so a man can't close his eyes at night. Did anyone see the killer?"

"Grizzly Killer did," someone mentioned.

"Is that a fact?" the Giant said, and regarded Nate coldly. "You *claim* you saw the bastard?"

"I don't claim nothing," Nate retorted. "I was the first one here, and I did see him. Just a glimpse, but I know it was the one."

"How convenient, eh?"

"What are you implying?"

"That maybe you didn't see the killer at all. That maybe you are lying to protect yourself. That maybe you're the killer."

Nate took a step toward the Giant. "That's ridiculous!"

"Is it?" Cleroult replied. "You admit that you were the first one on the scene. How do we know you didn't kill them, then simply stayed here until the rest of us came?"

"How dare you accuse me," Nate said angrily. He hefted his rifle, about to smash the stock into the Giant's face.

"You don't know what you're talking about, Cleroult," Shakespeare interjected. "As usual."

A number of trappers laughed lightly.

The Giant, surprisingly, didn't take offense at the remark. "I would expect you to vouch for the boy, McNair. He's your friend, after all."

"Indeed, *mon ami,*" Laclede joined in. "Perhaps you are lying to protect him."

Before anyone quite knew what was happening,

Shakespeare had taken two long strides and rammed his rifle barrel into Laclede's abdomen, doubling the man over.

The Giant made a move as if to grab the frontiersman and suddenly found himself looking down the same barrel.

"Go ahead," Shakespeare said. "Make me happy."

None of the trappers moved. All eyes were on the mountain man.

"No one calls me a liar," Shakespeare stated in a flat, menacing tone, his gaze locked on Laclede. "Either you own up to it or get set to eat crow."

"I didn't call you a liar," Laclede said weakly, inhaling raggedly. "I said perhaps you lied."

The rifle barrel swung in a short arc, slamming the weasel in the temple and dropping him to his knees.

"That's the same thing," Shakespeare said, and backed away a pace. "Whenever you're ready."

At that moment another commotion occurred as more men arrived and made their way through the assembled trappers. One of them tapped the Giant on the shoulder and said politely, "Excuse me."

"Who the hell," Cleroult declared testily, and glanced over his shoulder.

Nate expected the *voyageur* to tear into the newcomer. Instead, to his amazement, the Giant quickly moved aside.

"Bridger! I didn't know it was you."

The object of such unexpected civil treatment unconsciously projected an air of indisputable authority. Six feet in height and muscularly proportioned, he wore a flannel shirt, brown pants, a buckskin jacket, and a wide-brimmed black hat. His grave expression was accented by high cheekbones, an aquiline nose, and a high forehead. He glanced at Laclede, then faced forward. "Hello, Shakespeare."

"Hello, Gabe."

"Having a bit of trouble?"

"You know how these two are."

"What now?"

"Laclede saw fit to call me a liar. And they're both trying to accuse my friend here of being a killer," Shakespeare said, nodding at Nate.

"And who might your friend be?"

"Where are my manners?" Shakespeare commented with a grin. He gestured at each of them in turn. "Nate King, I'd like you to meet Jim Bridger, a big man in the Rocky Mountain Fur Company and the most honorable man in the Rockies."

"Mr. Bridger," Nate said dutifully.

"Call me Gabe," the man in the black hat responded. He stepped forward and knelt to examine the Pennsylvanian who had taken a knife in his chest. "Not again," he remarked grimly, then stared at Clerbult. "You've made a serious accusation against Shakespeare's friend. Do you have any proof?"

"He was the first one here," the Giant answered defensively. "Even admitted as much."

"Which hardly constitutes proof," Bridger stated. He motioned at the dead men. "I think you'll agree they were all killed with a knife." He looked at Nate. "Do you have a butcher knife?"

"Right here." Nate handed the implement over.

Bridger held the knife aloft so the light from the torches reflected off the blade. "Not a trace of blood," he said.

"That doesn't prove a thing," the Giant said. "He could have carried two knives and used the spare to do the murdering. When everyone showed up before he could sneak off, he left the spare in that poor bastard's ribs."

Sighing, Bridger straightened and returned the knife to Nate. "How long have you been at the rendezvous?" he inquired.

"We got here today."

"We?"

"Shakespeare, my wife, and myself."

"Just got here today," Bridger repeated, as if to himself, and pivoted, looking at Shakespeare. "So none of you were here when the first killings took place."

"We were with the Shoshones. Find Drags the Rope. He'll verify we were with his band."

"I don't need to talk to Drags the Rope," Bridger said, and glanced at Laclede. "Only a fool would try to label you a liar. Every trapper knows you're as good as your word." He shifted his attention to the Giant. "And since they weren't here when the first killings took place, it's highly unlikely that Nate King is responsible for these."

"He could have done it," Cleroult stubbornly persisted.

"*I* don't think so," Bridger stated in a manner that signified the subject was closed.

The Giant appeared about to dispute the issue until Mulhare nudged him. He glanced down at the Englishman, who jerked his thumb to the rear. Cleroult twisted to find scores of openly hostile faces fixed on him. "It would appear most everyone agrees with you, Bridger."

"Have you anything else to add?"

"No," the Giant snapped, and assisted Laclede to stand. "I know better than to buck you." He cast a hateful gaze at Shakespeare. "This isn't finished yet. Not by a long shot, Monsieur McNair."

"Anytime."

Cleroult, Laclede, and Mulhare departed, shoving through the crowd, eliciting curses in their wake.

"Thanks for backing us, Gabe," Shakespeare said.

"I wouldn't have backed you if I didn't believe your friend is innocent," Bridger replied. He moved to another of the dead Pennsylvanians. "Has anyone checked to see if they were robbed?"

"No," said one of the trappers.

"I doubt the killer had time," Nate mentioned. "I chased him off and took a shot at him."

"Did you miss?"

"I don't know," Nate said. He pointed to the southwest. "He was heading that way. I could barely make him out when I fired."

Bridger glanced at a burly trapper. "Williams, take a dozen men and scour the area. Check the ground for blood."

The burly man nodded, quickly selected the others, and together they hastened off.

"These men sold some prime furs a few days ago," Bridger divulged as he knelt and began to examine one of the bodies. "Between them they were probably carrying five or six thousand dollars."

"This sort of senseless violence is common in the big cities," Shakespeare said. "I never expected it to happen here."

"Whoever is responsible should be skinned alive," suggested one of the trappers.

"If we catch the son of a bitch, he'll be sorry," vowed another.

Jim Bridger held his left hand up, displaying a brown leather pouch. "What have we here?" He lifted the flap and peered inside. "Money. I'd estimate close to two thousand. So thanks to Nate, the killer didn't get what he was after."

"Which means he'll likely be bound and determined to try again," Shakespeare speculated.

Bridger stood and walked to a tall man in buckskins. "Dan, I'd like you to take care of the bodies. Collect all their personal effects, and give them a proper burial. See if you can find addresses of relatives back in the States so we can send the money and the belongings to them."

"Will do, Gabe."

Turning, Bridger smiled at Shakespeare. "Why don't I walk your friend and you back to your camp?"

"We don't mind helping out here," the frontiersman said.

"I'd prefer to walk," Bridger stated with a forceful emphasis.

"Whatever you want, Gabe," Shakespeare responded, his eyes narrowing.

Nate fell in behind the two men as they departed. The trappers moved aside to let them pass, and once they were beyond hearing range Bridger clasped his hands behind his back and spoke softly.

"I was fixing to pay you a visit tomorrow morning, but I might as well warn you now."

"Warn me about what?" Shakespeare asked.

"About the Giant and his friends."

The frontiersman chuckled. "I know they're out to get Nate and me. I'll keep my eyes open. Don't worry."

Bridger looked at the aged mountain man. "Cleroult isn't a man to be trifled with."

"So long as I don't turn my back on him I'll be all right."

"No, you won't. That's my whole point. The Giant and his bunch have been spreading stories around about how they're going to get even for the way you've treated them. They've been telling anyone who will listen that you're crazier than Crazy George and twice as dangerous. They're also trying to convince everyone that Nate is a cold-blooded troublemaker. They claim he started the fight with Mulhare."

"That's a damn lie!" Nate snapped. "I did everything I could to avoid the fight."

"Figured as much," Bridger said.

"Why are you so concerned about Cleroult, Gabe?" Shakespeare inquired. "We've both handled bullies like him before. You know how cautious I am. I won't take unnecessary chances."

"I know. But from what I've heard, the Giant has something particularly nasty planned for Nate and you. A friend overheard a couple of acquaintances of Cleroult's talking. They were drunk and joking about how the Giant is going to set a trap for you using special bait."

"Special bait?"

"Those were their exact words. My friend didn't learn the details. I'm convinced Cleroult has a clever scheme up his sleeve. He won't take you lightly. Whatever he has planned will be well thought out.''

They walked in silence for several yards.

"Thanks for the warning," Shakespeare said. "We'll take extra precautions from now on."

"Why don't you move your camp? I'd welcome the company."

The frontiersman smiled. "Thanks again, but this is our affair. We'll see it through to the end."

Bridger placed his hand on Shakespeare's shoulder. "Just make sure the end isn't your own."

Chapter Eleven

Nate slept fitfully, shifting from side to side, repeatedly awakening with a start and gazing at the glittering vista of stars overhead in anxious expectation, his heart pounding, certain that someone was about to plunge a knife into him. Once he heard Shakespeare snoring lightly and marveled at the frontiersman's ability to take everything in stride. Toward dawn he dozed off yet again, and he would have sworn he'd only been asleep a few minutes when an object touched the tip of his nose. He absently swatted at it, thinking a fly or mosquito to be the culprit. His fingers smacked something hard, something smooth.

Someone tittered.

Jolted rudely awake, Nate's eyes snapped open and he found himself staring down the barrel of a rifle. For a moment dread engulfed him and he believed he was about to be shot. Then his gaze drifted to the face looming above the barrel, to the grinning countenance of Crazy George, and anger supplanted the dread. "You dunderhead!" he exclaimed, and swatted the rifle away.

The trapper cackled.

"How dare you!" Nate declared, rising, his fists clenched. "I should knock a few of your teeth out for that idiocy!"

"Be my guest," Crazy George said, slapping his thigh in mirth. "I'm already missing four. What's a few more?"

Furious at the trapper, Nate gave George a shove, his right palm hitting the man's left shoulder. He didn't use all of his strength, and he expected George to stagger backward a few feet, not even fazed by the blow.

Instead, Crazy George clutched at his shoulder and doubled over, grimacing in pain. "Damn!" he snapped. "There was no call to do that!"

"What's the matter? I hardly touched you."

"Some months back I fell off my horse and busted my shoulder. It healed okay, but it's been sore as the dickens ever since," George explained.

"You fell off your horse?"

"Yep. I was a bit intoxicated at the time." Crazy George straightened and abruptly walked off, heading toward his camp. "I'll see you later," he said, and glanced down. "Morning, Shakespeare."

Nate saw the frontiersman sitting up.

"Let me have a look at your shoulder," Shakespeare said.

"That's not necessary. I'll be as good as new in a little while," Crazy George said, hurrying off.

Shakespeare stared at the retreating back of the trapper for a moment, then faced Nate. "I didn't know he'd broken his shoulder. He's one of the most secretive gents around when it comes to his personal affairs."

"I didn't mean to hurt him," Nate stated apologetically. "I'm afraid I lost my temper."

"It wasn't your fault. I woke up just as you were knocking his gun aside. The fool should never play stupid tricks like that."

"One of these days he'll get himself shot," Nate predicted. He turned to check on Winona and found her already up, standing silently not a foot from him. She beamed.

"Good morning, husband."

"Good morning, beloved."

A protracted sigh came from Shakespeare. "No wonder I keep having this urge to read *Romeo and Juliet.*"

The three of them began the new day by rolling up their blankets, then washing their faces and hands in the cold lake water. Shakespeare attended to rekindling the fire while Winona prepared a meal of dried venison strips supplemented by tasty roots she had collected several days before.

"What do you have in mind for today?" Nate asked the frontiersman as he chewed heartily on a bite of venison.

"I thought we'd spend the morning buying the supplies we need, then use the afternoon to visit with friends of mine."

"Sounds fine to me."

"One thing, though. Until the rendezvous is over, you and I should stick together for protection."

"Are you worried about the Giant and the others?"

"Not worried so much as I am realistic. I know they'll try something sooner or later, and it makes good sense for us to cover our backs. Look at what happened to you yesterday with Mulhare."

Nate nodded and touched a bruise on his cheek. "Okay. Where you go, I go."

"Except when nature calls," Shakespeare said, grinning.

Winona suddenly pointed to the southwest and spoke in the Shoshone tongue.

Several men were approaching. In the lead, distinguished by his black hat, walked Jim Bridger.

"A bit early for a visit, isn't it?" Shakespeare called out good-naturedly.

Bridger waited until he came within ten feet before replying. "It's only early if you've been to bed."

"You haven't?"

"No." Bridger stepped over to the fire and held out his hands, warming them, his gaze on the tranquil surface of Bear Lake. The two men with him stood nearby.

"Why don't you sit awhile?" Shakespeare suggested. "I'll make some coffee. We have a little left."

"I wish I could," Bridger responded. "It's been a long night and it promises to be a longer day." He paused and looked down. "Actually, I came to give you the news."

"What news?"

Bridger nodded at Nate. "Apparently Grizzly Killer is a good shot. We think the killer is wounded."

Shakespeare stiffened. "You found blood?"

"Not much, but enough to have us believe the ball probably nicked him."

"Serves the bastard right. Too bad Nate didn't drive a ball into his head."

"We found addresses for relatives of the Pennsylvanians, and I found someone trustworthy who will take the money and the belongings to St. Louis. From there they'll be mailed to the families."

"Good," Shakespeare said, studying his friend. "But I get the impression something else is bothering you."

"You always did have the eyes of a hawk," Bridger said dryly. "As if we didn't have enough to be concerned about, what with the killer still on the loose and reports of hostile Indians in the area—"

"Hostile Indians?" Nate said, interrupting. "I thought they stayed away from the rendezvous."

"A few like to prove how brave they are. Five days ago a Frenchman was attacked by a band northeast of here."

"Blackfeet?" Shakespeare guessed.

"He wasn't able to identify them. The incident took place twelve miles from the lake."

"That's a little too close for comfort."

"I know," Bridger said. "And now a man who went out two days ago to hunt is missing."

"Who?"

"McClinden. Know him?"

"Believe we've met once or twice."

"He told his friends he'd only be gone for six hours or so. We're organizing search parties now. Care to join one?"

"Sure," Shakespeare said.

"We're sending out three groups this morning, then three more this afternoon. If you're willing, Nate and you can ride with one of the later search parties."

"Fine. Just let us know when they're leaving. We'll be all set to go."

"I knew I could count on you," Bridger said. He nodded at Winona, then turned and walked in the direction of the booths. "I'll send a man around to tell you when and where to meet the others," he told them over his shoulder. The two men with him kept pace on his right.

"First a killer, now a war party," Shakespeare remarked. "This rendezvous is turning out to be more memorable than the last couple of get-togethers."

"I know I'll never forget it," Nate commented.

They finished eating and ambled to the south, Winona staying so close to Nate that she bumped into him now and then. There was no sign of Crazy George at his camp, and they continued on until they reached the booths. Although it was still early, many of the traders were already open for business, eager to reap the hefty profits they garnered every day of the rendezvous.

Shakespeare took Nate and Winona to booths managed by traders he knew personally, men who out of the kindness of their hearts would reduce the price of their goods a few cents. They purchased coffee, sugar, ammunition, trinkets and blankets to use for trading with Indians, and varioius other items.

The sun had almost reached its zenith by the time they concluded their transactions and returned to their site by the lake.

Declaring that he could make the best cup of coffee on the North American continent, Shakespeare proceeded to make good on his boast.

Nate sat a yard from the fire and inhaled the delectable aroma. He draped his right arm around Winona's shoulders and gazed at her lovely features. Using sign language, he told her all about the missing trapper and the band of unfriendly Indians believed to be responsible for the man's disappearance. He explained about the search parties and advised her not to expect Shakespeare and him back until nightfall, possibly later.

Winona tenderly touched his cheek, then responded that she had complete confidence in his ability and wouldn't worry in the least while he was gone. She asked if it would be all right for her to visit friends in the Shoshone camp to the west of the lake.

Not feeling very pleased at the prospect of leaving her alone, Nate gladly urged her to visit her friends and encouraged her to stay there as long as she liked.

Smiling, Winona thanked him and promised to have their evening meal prepared by the time they came back.

All the while they conversed, Shakespeare rested and stared to the south, his brow creased, deep in thought.

"What's on your mind?" Nate inquired when he concluded his chat with his wife.

"Nothing much."

"You don't fool me. I know that look by now. What is it?"

"I'd rather not say yet."

"Why are you being so secretive?" Nate pressed him.

The frontiersman sighed and plucked at a blade of grass. "Very well. If you must know, I've been pondering the nature of madness."

Nate almost laughed until he noticed the serious expression his friend wore. "I don't understand."

"And I don't expect you to know what I'm talking about," Shakespeare said. "Read *Hamlet* sometime. Then you will."

"What does *Hamlet* have to do with anything?"

"Everything," Shakespeare responded, and launched into a quote from his favorite author. "That he is mad, 'tis true: 'tis true 'tis pity, and pity 'tis 'tis true: a foolish figure; but farewell it, for I will use no art."

Shaking his head in bewilderment, Nate leaned back on his palms. "Have you gone mad, then?" he joked.

"Though this be madness, yet there is method in it," Shakespeare quoted again.

"If your're an example of the effect reading Shakespeare has on a man, I'll stick to James Fenimore Cooper," Nate said, grinning.

"There's the rub," the frontiersman stated, and laughed.

Nate gazed idly to the southwest and spied four men approaching on horseback. "We have company coming," he announced, and stood.

Shakespeare took a sip, then rose slowly. "I don't know any of them," he said.

The quartet came closer and reined up. All four wore buckskins. One man, the tallest, nodded and smiled. "You two must be Shakespeare McNair and Grizzly Killer."

"That's us," Nate replied.

"Gabe sends his compliments. He was going to have someone ride over and tell you where to meet us, but I figured we'd save time by coming ourselves. Hope you don't mind."

"Not at all," Shakespeare said. "And who might you be?"

"The name is Bannon."

"Give us a minute to saddle up and we'll be all set to go."

"I'd like to make a request first."

"Oh?"

"I know a lot about you, McNair. You know this country better than I do. I've only been out here five years. All of us already talked it over and we'd like you to lead this search party," Bannon proposed.

"I have no objections," Shakespeare stated.

"Good. Then we're ready when you are."

Nate and the frontiersman quickly saddled their respective mounts. Winona gave them both dried venison to take along, then stood back and waved as they rode off to the east.

"Don't look so miserable," Shakespeare told his young companion. "You'll see her again."

"I know. I just feel . . . strange."

"Can you be more precise?"

"I wish I could."

Bannon and the others were a few yards behind them. The tall man raised his voice. "The trapper who has been missing was last seen riding to the northeast."

"Wasn't that Frenchman attacked northeast of here?" Nate queried.

"Sure was," Bannon confirmed.

The uneasiness Nate felt intensified as he gazed across Bear Lake at the mountains beyond. Why was he so apprehensive? he wondered. Simply because he would be separated from Winona for seven or eight hours? Or was his intuiton trying to warn him about impending danger? If so, from what source? The Blackfeet? He chided himself for being needlessly anxious and squared his shoulders. There was a job to do and he intended to see it through.

Come what may.

Chapter Twelve

They rode along the shore, maintaining a steady gallop, until they reached a point northeast of the lake. With a wave of his right hand Shakespeare led them across a narrow field and into the forest beyond. As a precaution should they be attacked, they strung out in single file. Mounted men were easy enough targets as it was; bunched together they were sitting ducks. Shakespeare took the lead, his keen eyes roving over the terrain, sitting relaxed in the saddle yet as alert as a panther on the prowl.

Nate rode second in line, his Hawken cradled in his right arm. He saw squirrels and birds and a few deer during the early going, but nothing out of the ordinary.

None of the men spoke. Except for the thudding of the hooves and an occasional snort from a horse, their passage through the forest was conducted in prudent silence.

The ground sloped gradually upward. A few elk spotted them and fled. They crossed a series of progressively higher hills, drawing ever nearer to the towering peaks glistening with snow.

Nate absently swatted at a pesky fly and wiped his hand across his brow. He glimpsed a raven soaring far overhead, then focused on the rough ground ahead. His mare was her usual perky, energetic self, and he had to hold the reins tightly to prevent her from moving up alongside Shakespeare's animal.

The miles went by quickly. They entered a broken, rugged region where there were fewer trees. Large boulders dotted the landscape.

Nate detected movement on a mountain off to the east and stared at the slope just below the snow line. Dozens of white forms were moving nimbly about on the sheer rock face, displaying extraordinary agility. He recognized them as mountain sheep, or bighorns as some of the trappers referred to them. The animals appeared to be fearless. They stood on tiny rock outcroppings thousands of feet above the ground with the same casual air of a man sitting on a log. And they could leap incredible distances from outcropping to outcropping, their hooves landing on a patch of rock no more than several inches square, their balance and coordination superb.

Soon the search party came to a stream and Shakespeare called a brief halt to water the horses and refresh the riders.

Standing on the bank, holding the mare's reins in his left hand, Nate saw a large fish swim past. "If I live to be a hundred, I'll never get over the beauty of the wilderness," he commented.

"You too?" Bannon said. "I originally came out here intending to stay a year. There's a quality about living in harmony with nature that gets into a man's blood. I could no more go back to live in the States than I could stop breathing."

"Me neither," Nate said, and the revelation startled him. In the back of his mind he'd always believed he would be going back to New York City one day. Was he serious? Did he really prefer to live in the wild, to live the life of an Indian?

"Most men feel the same way after they've been out here a while," Shakespeare mentioned. "If you want to know the truth, I believe this type of life is the kind God intended for us. He put Adam and Eve in a garden, didn't he? There must have been a good reason. I think that somewhere along the line mankind lost track of the things that really matter. Those people who live in the cities would rather be comfortable than truly free. They'd rather be secure than independent.''

"Is that wrong?'' Nate asked.

"I'm not the one to judge. I guess every person has to decide for themself how they want to live. And in the long run they'll have to answer for their decision to their Maker.''

Bannon chuckled. "Gabe told us you were a thinker, but I had no idea.''

"You ought to know by now that living in the wild makes a man think about the important things in life.''

"Why's that?'' asked one of the other men.

"Because out here we're face to face with death every day of the week. Out here we have eternity staring us right in the face, so to speak. When a man knows he's standing on the brink, he just naturally wants to find out the meaning of it all,'' Shakespeare said. "Then too, all those long winter days and nights have to be spent doing something.''

A skinny trapper laughed. "Why do you think I just bought me a Bannock woman? I know how I plan to spend my winter.''

General mirth ensued.

"Okay. Let's mount up,'' the frontiersman directed, and did so.

Nate climbed onto the mare, and in a few seconds he was following Shakepeare along the west bank of the stream. He spied an eagle soaring on the air currents and grinned, feeling at home.

For two more hours they scoured the area for some sign of the missing man. They were skirting the base of a mountain range when they reached a small lake. To the east reared a stark peak. To the north were a few hills. Off to the west, one hundred yards at the most, lay an expanse of verdant forest.

Shakespeare rode his white horse up to the water and was about to dismount when he tensed, his eyes narrowing. ''Hold on,'' he said.

''What is it?'' Bannon inquired.

''Tracks,'' the frontiersman replied, and slid down. He knelt and gingerly touched his fingers to the soft earth. ''Other horses have been here. Indian horses would be my guess.''

Nate leaned down but could barely distinguish the faint impressions in the soil. ''How long ago?''

''Nine or ten days, maybe.''

Bannon rode closer. ''Then they're nothing for us to worry about. The Indians who made them are probably miles away by this time.''

''You hope,'' said the skinny trapper.

Shakespeare straightened, stared westward for a moment, then swung into the saddle and rode hard for a stand of cottonwoods 20 yards to the northwest. ''Quickly!'' he urged them. ''Take cover.''

Startled, Nate obeyed. He gazed at the forest and saw no indication of the reason for the haste, but he trusted the frontiersman implicitly.

Bannon and the others were doing the same.

In seconds they darted in among the trees and reined up. Shakespeare moved to the west side of the stand, staying far enough back so as not to be visible from afar, and peered at the distant tree line.

''What did you see?'' Bannon queried nervously.

''A jay.''

''A jay?'' Bannon repeated quizzically.

''Yep. Flapping into the air as if its tail feathers were on fire.''

The skinny trapper snorted. ''You got us all excited over a dumb bird?''

''Nature has its rhythms, friend, and the truly dumb one is the person who ignores them. These mountain jays are normally quite friendly. They like to stay close to our camps in the hope of getting a bite to eat. Takes a lot to spook one, and the jay I saw was definitely spooked.''

"I'm not arguing with that. But the bird could have been frightened by a fox or a bobcat. It's foolish for us to be hiding like this.''

"Is it?'' Shakespeare responded, and the certainty in his tone prompted every man to gaze to the west.

Nate felt the back of his neck tingle. He grasped the Hawken with both hands and hunched over the pommel.

"I'll be damned!'' exclaimed the skinny trapper.

A large body of Indians were emerging from the trees. There were dozens of them, all on foot. Most wore scant clothing. And all were armed, either with war clubs, fusees, bows and arrows, or tomahawks. They headed directly toward the small lake.

"Are they Blackfeet?'' Bannon whispered.

"No.''

"Really?'' Bannon said, louder this time, transparently relieved by the news.

"No, they're not Blackfeet,'' Shakespeare reiterated. "Those are Bloods.''

"Dear God!'' one of the men declared.

"If they catch us, we're dead men,'' added another.

Nate stared at the Indians, then at the frontiersman. "Who are these Bloods? They sound worse than the Blackfeet.''

"In a way they are. I told you once before that the Blackfeet not only constantly make war on the whites, they also attack almost every other tribe in the Rockies. They're on friendly terms with only two others, the Piegans and the Bloods. Between the three of them they control most of the land from the Saskatchewan River to the upper Missouri.''

"If that lost fellow ran into this war party, he's never coming back,'' the skinny trapper said.

"What do we do?'' Bannon wanted to know. "Should we make a run for it? We have horses. It will be impossible for them to overtake us.''

Nate gazed back the way they had come. There was no cover for hundreds of yards, which would expose them to a hail of arrows. The nearest shelter consisted of a cluster of boulders located 900 feet to the southeast. He started to shift his attention to the west again when, to his sudden consternation, an Indian came in view around the south side of the boulders, then another and another and another. The warrior in the lead had his gaze fixed on the ground, as if tracking, and it abruptly occurred to him just who the band must be following. "Shakespeare!" he declared, and pointed.

The frontiersman and the rest of the men looked. Several of the trappers uttered oaths.

"More Bloods," Shakespeare said. "And they're right on our trail."

"We can't stay here," Bannon declared. "They'll find us for sure." He hefted his rifle. "What do you say, McNair?"

Nate didn't envy the frontiersman. He didn't know what he would do if he had to make the decision. Fleeing to the west and the south was out of the question. Going due east was impossible due to the rocky peak. To the southwest lay Bear Lake, but if they rode in that direction they would pass between the two groups of Indians and expose themselves to a lethal volley. Going northward along the lake shore and to the hills beyond seemed to be their safest option. A moment later he received confirmation.

"We'll go north," Shakespeare said. "Move slowly to the north edge of these cottonwoods, then ride hard when I give the word."

Together they turned their animals and complied, each man doing his best to keep his animal quiet and to stay in the shadows. They were all aware of the consequences should they be discovered.

Shouting broke out behind them. The band coming from

the southeast, which numbered about 20, spotted the other Bloods approaching from the west. Several warriors were yelling at once.

"What are they saying?" Nate asked.

"The smaller band is telling the large band about the fresh tracks they've been following. One of the warriors is certain there must be white men nearby," Shakespeare translated.

More shouting ensued.

"Just our luck," the frontiersman muttered. "The Bloods have several parties out hunting for whites."

Nate patted his mare, hoping she wouldn't whinny, and stopped when the others did. Ahead lay a field, perhaps 200 yards in length, then the hills. At the very end of the field rose a long, low knoll.

"Everyone ready?" Shakespeare asked.

"Let's just get the hell out of here," Bannon stated.

"I'm ready," the skinny trapper said. "Last one to those hills is a pincushion."

One of the men foolishly laughed.

Shakespeare abruptly urged his horse forward. "Ride for your lives, men!"

Ride they did, bursting from the cottonwoods at a full gallop and racing toward the knoll. The skinny trapper, astride a fine brown stallion, took an early lead.

Piercing war whoops and yells of rage erupted to their rear, a commingled savage chorus that echoed off the nearby mountain and added impetus to the flight of the six whites.

Nate glanced over his left shoulder and saw the large party of Bloods sprinting in pursuit. He marveled at their speed. Although afoot, the Indians were as fleet as deer, covering the ground in great leaping strides, their arms and legs pumping. He knew his mare could outrun them, yet he still felt a twinge of dread at the thought of being overtaken. He'd heard countless stories about the atrocities committed by Indians, about the brutal beatings and grueling tortures they inflicted. He remembered a tale Shakespeare once told about a Blackfoot warrior captured by the Crows. They had held their captive down while one of them sliced open the Blackfoot's stomach and ripped out the intestines. According to Shakespeare, the Blackfoot had not so much as whimpered. Nate doubted he would be as brave if the same thing happened to him.

The skinny trapper had pulled out a good 20 feet in front of his companions, and he was furiously striving to goad his stallion to go even faster.

A hasty look to the right revealed the smaller band was also in frenzied pursuit, and Nate kept low in the saddle in case the Bloods cut loose with their bows and guns.

It was well he did.

An instant later an arrow whizzed past and smacked into the earth not a yard from his left leg.

Nate focused on the knoll and concentrated on reaching it to the exclusion of all else. His body flowed with the swaying of the mare, his left hand gripping the reins while his right held the Hawken. He stayed close to Shakespeare. The other trappers had fanned out a bit to his right and left, all except for the skinny one, who was now 30 feet ahead of everyone else.

Whooping wildly, the Bloods were running for all they were worth but still falling behind.

Confidence welled in Nate. Once the trappers were over the knoll, the danger would be past. More arrows were descending. So far, undoubtedly due to the fact the warriors were shooting on the run, none had scored a hit. The fusees opened up, trade guns the Indians received from the Hudson's Bay Company and others, smooth-bored flintlocks that were generally quite inferior to the typical rifles used by the trappers.

The horses covered the ground swiftly. Fewer and fewer arrows landed around the men.

"Those savages will never take our hair!" Bannon shouted when they had gone 150 yards.

"Don't count your chickens until they're hatched," Shakespeare advised.

"What can go wrong now?" Bannon retorted, and laughed in elation.

Nate smiled himself. Back in the cottonwoods he'd felt the chill of impending death. Now he experienced the warmth of the sun on his back and the flush of triumph at their narrow escape. Life seemed sweeter. He thrilled to the sensation of simply being alive, of knowing he would see Winona again and hold her in his arms.

The skinny trapper was gazing back at the Bloods and cackling, mocking them, letting his stallion gallop at full speed. He reached the gently sloping knoll well before his comrades, and he was still chortling when his mount came to the crest.

Both of them abruptly disappeared.

Nate blinked, not quite believing his own eyes. One second the trapper and the stallion had been there; the next they were gone. He exchanged puzzled glances with several of the others, and all of them slowed, riding up the knoll cautiously. Not until they came to the rim did Nate comprehend, and suddenly his feelings of imminent doom returned.

Below them lay a ravine 40 feet deep and 30 feet wide. At the bottom, lying in disjointed heaps in the midst of scattered boulders, were the skinny trapper and his stallion. Neither so much as twitched. Both were splattered with blood.

Nate took one look, then glanced to the rear at the Bloods. The Indians had spread out across the field and were charging with renewed vigor, as if they knew all about the ravine.

As if they knew the white men were trapped.

Chapter Thirteen

"Give them a volley to slow them down!" Shakespeare bellowed, wheeling his white horse. He took quick aim and fired, his rifle booming and billowing smoke.

A Blood warrior carrying a bow jerked backwards and toppled to the grass.

Nate spun the mare, raised the Hawken to his right shoulder, took a bead on a strapping Blood armed with a fusee, held his breath to steady the barrel, and added his shot to those of his companions.

The warrior with the fusee dropped the gun, clutched at his chest, and fell.

Other Bloods were also on the ground.

"Ride to the west!" Shakespeare directed, and goaded his mount in that direction.

"What about Yates?" Bannon yelled.

"There's nothing we can do for him now," Shakespeare replied. "We've got to save our own hides."

They rode at a breakneck pace along the rim, heading for the forest where they could lose themselves in the trees.

Nate stared at the Bloods, who had stopped and were attending those who had fallen. The respite would be all too brief. Already several warriors were gesturing and urging the others to continue the pursuit.

Shakespeare had taken the lead, riding superbly, seemingly a part of the animal under him, his long gray hair flying.

Could they do it? Nate wondered. Could they reach the sanctuary of the woods before the Indians cut them off? He thought of poor Yates and the brown stallion lying at the bottom of the ravine, and frowned. He disliked leaving the man there, possibly still alive and badly injured, but the frontiersman had been right. Under the circumstances, what else could they do?

The Bloods nearest the treeline sprinted to the northwest, attempting to intercept the trappers. One warrior in particular, a tall Blood with long legs, easily outdistanced the other members of the war party and closed rapidly.

Nate wished he could take the time to reload his Hawken. Because the Bloods to the west were closer to the trees and were running at an angle, the Indians had a shorter space to cover than the horses. Even though the animals were faster, having more ground to cover made the life-and-death race much too close. Thank goodness he had both pistols tucked under his belt!

Arrows rained down again, a few at first and then an increasing number as the warriors found the range.

One of the trappers screamed.

Nate looked over his shoulder and saw the last man in line tumble from the saddle, a shaft inbedded in his head. He recalled an Indian trick he had learned and employed it, swinging down on the far side of the mare while hooking his left leg over the saddle and his arm around the pommel. Now he was almost impossible to hit. But the Indians could always go for the horse.

For dreadful, tense seconds—each one an eternity it itself—the desperate race went on.

The ravine narrowed near the trees to only 15 feet in width. The sides were too steep to negotiate. Boulders lay strewn all along the bottom, apparently dislodged by heavy rains.

Nate stared at the point where the ravine and the forest met. The chasm might have been formed by an ancient earthquake or a flash flood, and the rift had neatly divided the woodland into two separate tracks. The trees bordered the very edges, rendering passage along the crest impossible.

Shakespeare was almost there.

The tall Blood had drawn uncomfortably close, within 20 yards of the fissure. He carried a slender bow in his left hand, which he whipped up and extended as his right hand closed on an arrow, and he halted to take better aim.

Nate peered around the mare's neck and saw the warrior drawing the string back.

One of the other trappers pulled a pistol and fired a wild shot that missed.

Methodically, almost leisurely, the Blood sighted along the shaft.

With a start, Nate perceived the warrior was aiming at his mare! If the animal should be hit, both of them might topple into the ravine and be dashed to broken bits on the boulders. He couldn't hang there and do nothing! Instantly he swung upright again, grabbed the reins with his right hand, and clawed at a pistol with his left. Even as he did, he realized he was too late.

The warrior let the arrow fly.

Nate saw the shaft streaking toward him. He instinctively went to remove himself from its path by sliding over the side of the mare again, but in his haste and excitement he committed a grave blunder. His right hand tightened and jerked on the reins, and the mare reacted as she always did; she promptly obeyed. Before he awoke to his mistake, the damage had been done.

The horse obediently swerved, right over the edge of the ravine.

In a shocking flash of insight, Nate comprehended the awful truth and straightened. Below them lay certain death. He envisioned himself being crushed to a pulp, and gulped.

For her part, the mare extended her front legs and locked her knees at the same time she sank onto her haunches, her rear legs bent to support her weight. With her head tossed back and her spine arched, she slid down the precipitous incline on her buttocks, raising a cloud of dust in her wake.

Nate expected the animal to pitch forward at any second. He arched his own back, hauling on the reins for all he was worth, doing his best to slow their momentum. The mare's wide eyes told him she was as frightened as him, and he felt sorry that his stupidity might cost them their lives.

A huge boulder loomed almost directly under them.

Turn! Nate's mind screamed. Turn! He violently yanked on the reins, attempting to angle the mare to the left, but the animal had very little control over her direction and rate of descent. Gravity dictated both. He braced his moccasins in the stirrups to prevent from tumbling to the earth and offered a silent, sincere prayer for deliverance.

From somewhere up above came ferocious shouting.

The tall Blood! Nate had forgotten all about the Indian in the exigency of the moment. He was thankful for the billowing dust. If the warrior had a clear shot, he'd undoubtedly receive an arrow in the back. The Blood might fire a shaft anyway, and the prospect filled him with apprehension. He yearned to reach the bottom.

In a shower of loose dirt and sandy powder, the mare finally did.

Nate tugged on the reins with all his might and managed to force the horse to the left as she surged to her feet. They missed the boulder by inches. He slapped his legs against her sides, goading her into a run, and glanced up at the southern rim.

There stood the tall warrior and four others. They gestured at him and yelled excitedly.

Bending low over the mare's neck, Nate threaded a course among the boulders and other obstructions such as mounds of dirt and an occasional log.

An arrow lanced down from above and sank into the soil almost under the horse's pounding hooves. Then another struck the ground, and another.

Ignore them! Nate told himself. Pay attention to the route ahead and nothing else. A single misstep could result in tragedy. The mare had to be skillfully guided at all times.

Something sharp bit into his right shoulder and glanced off.

Nate raced onward. The perilous course required all of his horsemanship to negotiate. He lost all track of time and distance, riding hard for his very life, skirting boulder after boulder, glimpsing the towering walls on both sides, feeling hemmed in and vulnerable. For minutes he rode westward, and only when he happened to gaze up and saw trees lining both rims did he abruptly stop.

The mare was breathing deeply, her nostrils flaring.

Where were the Bloods?

Twisting in the saddle, Nate looked back, and was delighted and surprised to see he had gone several hundred yards into the forest and outdistanced the war party. He breathed as heavily as his mount, his blood pounding in his temples. The elation at escaping temporarily eclipsed an important consideration.

Now what?

He scrutinized the north and south crests, his forehead creasing in perplexity. His predicament wasn't much better than before. Although he might, with supreme difficulty, be able to climb out by himself, he'd never abandon the mare. He was hemmed in with only two options, either going due east or due west. To go back the way he came constituted certain suicide, so he rode to the west, taking his time, conserving the mare's energy and intently studying the ravine for a means out of the earth prison.

Where were Shakespeare and the two surviving trappers?

Nate speculated that his companions must be in the forest to the south, probably hiding from the Bloods. He doubted the frontiersman would leave the general vicinity until verifying his fate. If he fired a few shots to attract their attention, he'd also draw the Bloods to him like wolves to a helpless buck.

The trees on the rim cast long shadows into the ravine, and the high walls served to insulate the bottom from normal woodland noises. An eerie hush enshrouded the landscape.

Fidgeting nervously, Nate eagerly sought a way to reach the crest. Either crest. The clopping of the mare's hooves only aggravated his anxiety. He tried to calm his jangled nerves, but inadvertently started when a rabbit scrambled from behind a boulder ahead and bounded to the west.

A rabbit?

Nate rode faster, trying to keep the long-eared bouncing ball of fur in sight. How had it gotten down there? Fallen? Jumped? Or was there a trail to the top, a trail to freedom?

The rabbit went around a log, then vanished.

Urging the mare forward, Nate hurried to the log and reined up. To the west were more boulders, and the ravine would in a serpentine fashion for as far as he could see. There was no trace of the rabbit.

And no trail.

Annoyed, Nate resumed riding, searching every corner, scouring the walls. He thought of the Bloods, then suddenly remembered the Hawken wasn't loaded.

How careless could he be!

Halting yet again, Nate slid down and took a minute to reload. As he was wrapping the ball in a patch he happened to glance to the rear and detected movement along the southern crest. He froze, watching intently, and distinguished the running form of a lone Indian.

The tall Blood.

Jolted into feverish action, Nate quickly finished reloading, swung into the saddle, and cut out to the west. He looked back, estimating the warrior must be 50 or 60 yards away, and brought the mare to a trot. If he could stay ahead of the Indian until a way out presented itself, he'd be all right. But what if there wasn't a way out?

What if the ravine went on indefinitely?

The Blood suddenly uttered a harsh cry.

Nate glanced around and saw the warrior moving faster. He'd been spotted! The temptation to shoot was nearly irresistible. At such a range, and with so many convenient trees for the warrior to take cover behind, he'd likely wind up wasting the ball. He decided to refrain, to save the shot for when it would really be needed.

The ravine curved to the right.

With a last look at the Blood, Nate rode around the bend. In 20 feet the course changed again, bearing to the west for a short span before winding to the south. The sinuous chasm became more difficult to negotiate and the width tapered to ten feet.

An enormous downed tree almost blocked the bottom.

Nate swung to the right to skirt the obstacle. The limbs still bore green leaves, which indicated the tree had recently fallen into the ravine. He brushed at the longest branches with his left arm. Most were shattered or had been partly broken by the fall, and at ground level a twisted mass of foliage obscured the lower portion of the trunk.

Just then, from under the mass, issued a distinctive rattling, a sound made by only one type of creature in all creation.

Rattlesnake! The sound caused an involuntary ripple of fear to run along Nate's spine. He glanced down, trying to spot the reptile, and took hold of the Hawken with both hands in case he needed to fire.

The mare suddenly reared, instinctively terrified by the noise.

Taken unawares, his grip on the reins slack, Nate completely lost his grasp and toppled backward. He landed hard on his shoulders and rolled to the right to avoid having his head caved in by a pounding hoof.

Uttering a fearful whinny, the horse took off, galloping westward.

Nate swept to his feet and saw the mare vanish around a turn, then glanced down at the foliage and glimpsed the rattler slithering under the trunk. He ran after his mount and covered 15 yards before the futility of his pursuit brought him up short. The mare wasn't likely to slow down until her fright subsided, which might take minutes. He couldn't hope to catch her until then, so prudence dictated he should conserve his energy and do his best to stay ahead of the Blood.

A stinging sensation in his right shoulder reminded Nate of his wound, and he took a moment to examine a two-inch tear in the buckskin. The flesh underneath had been sliced open. Fortunately, the wound wasn't very deep and the blood loss had been minimal. After he made it back to the rendezvous he'd ask Winona to bandage the shoulder.

The clattering of falling rocks arose to the east.

Nate looked, and was astounded to see the tall warrior sliding down the wall of the ravine. He hoped the Blood would slip and plummet to the boulders below, but the man was endowed with extraordinary balance and reflexes.

The Blood slid on his buttocks and used his hands to retard his descent. He shoved away from the side when still ten feet above the ground and dropped next to a waist-high boulder, landing lightly with his knees bent. Voicing a shout of triumph while unslinging his bow from across his back, he turned and charged.

Chapter Fourteen

Nate snapped the rifle to his shoulder and took aim, but before he could fire the Blood ducked for cover behind a cluster of boulders 30 yards away. He recollected the many tales Shakespeare had told about the incredible feats of marksmanship Indians performed with bows and arrows, and he realized the Hawken didn't give him that much of an advantage.

The tall warrior hadn't shown himself yet.

Spinning, Nate ran as fast as his legs would carry him, weaving among rocks, boulders, and logs, repeatedly glancing over his shoulders. His moccasins crunched on the gravel and rocks underfoot. He came to the first turn and paused to study the ground he'd covered. There was still no sign of the Blood.

The warrior must be stalking him, Nate deduced, and raced around the turn. A straight stretch relatively clear of obstructions afforded him an opportunity to increase his lead on the Indian, and he ran the 50 feet to the next bend. A brief glance confirmed he'd left his adversary far behind.

Nate smiled and continued. Sweat caked his sides, legs, and back as he sprinted to the next turn, then the one after that. The mare's tracks were imprinted in the soil here and there, inspiring him with the hope he could find his horse and escape before the Blood overtook him.

The sun climbed higher in the blue vault of the sky, casting more light and heat into the ravine.

Nate began to feel as if he was trapped in an oven. Perspiration coated his forehead and he licked his dry lips again and again. The Hawken, which was heavier than most other rifles anyway, felt even heavier. He checked to his rear every ten feet or so, mystified by the warrior's absence.

What was the Blood up to?

After five minutes and two more bends, Nate stopped to catch his breath. He faced east and rested his hands on his thighs, inhaling deeply. A shadow flitted past his legs, and he tilted his head to discover a hawk circling over the north rim. He envied the bird its wings.

Not the slightest sound betrayed his foe.

So much for resting, Nate decided, and hurried to the next turn. He took this one slowly, grimacing at the discomfort in his lower legs, and halted in midstride at the sight of the mare, her reins caught in the barren branches of a dead tree that had succumbed to the elements and toppled into the ravine, many of its dried roots exposed up near the crest.

Overjoyed, Nate hurried to her side, soothing her by talking about how much he missed her and couldn't wait to ride her again. She reacted skittishly for a bit, then calmed down. He gripped the reins and untangled them, then swung into the saddle.

So much for the Blood.

Brimming with self-confidence, Nate started to ride. The instant he turned, there came the soft patter of onrushing feet behind him. He tried to swing around and bring the rifle into play, sensing he was already too late. Strong hands gripped his buckskin shirt and he was hurled from the saddle, wincing in agony when he crashed into the tree and a limb gouged him in the ribs.

The warrior laughed.

Enraged, still clutching the rifle, Nate whirled and leveled the barrel. But the Indian had closed, a cruel smirk destorting his features, and he batted the Hawken aside, then sprang. The momentum propelled Nate backwards onto the trunk, jarring his spine, and the rifle was torn from his hands.

The Blood contemptuously tossed the gun aside and spoke a few words in his own tongue.

Nate barely heard. Panic flooded his mind and he surged upward, wildly swinging his fists. He clipped the warrior on the chin and delivered a left to the abdomen.

Unaccustomed to fisticuffs, the Indian was caught by surprise and doubled over. He recovered instantly, voiced an incensed bellow, and pounced.

Nate managed to land another solid blow to the face before the Blood rammed into him and drove him against the tree. The warrior pinned his arms to his sides, then picked him up bodily and threw him to the earth. He started to shove erect when a stout arm looped around his neck while a hand seized the back of his shirt and held him fast. Certain he was about to be strangled, Nate struggled in a frenzy, kicking and tugging on the arm clamped on his throat.

Strangely, nothing happened.

Bewildered, Nate ceased resisting. What was going on? Why hadn't the warrior tried to choke him? For that matter, why had the Blood taken him alive when it would have been easier to slay him? The Indian had passed up a perfect opportunity to plant an arrow in his back, and yet—

Taken him alive!

Suddenly Nate perceived the ghastly reason. The warrior intended to take him to the Blood village! He knew about the horrible tortures the Indians inflicted on one another and on any captured whites, and he could well imagine the fate in store for him if he fell into their hands. He must escape!

But how?

The obvious occurred to him, and he felt a twinge of embarrassment that he'd let the panic eclipse his reason. He chided himself for his loss of control and let his hands fall to his sides. The Indian abruptly sent him sprawling to the ground on his stomach. Twisting, he looked up.

Grinning broadly, his face a malicious mask, the Blood gestured for his prisoner to stand. He exuded arrogance. Apparently believing he'd already subdued his quarry, the warrior exhibited rash overconfidence.

Nate set a resigned expression on his face and began to rise, keeping his back to the Indian, his right hand groping for a pistol. He glanced at the warrior, who was pulling a knife, then whipped his arm out and around and fired at point-blank range.

The ball took the Blood squarely in the forehead. He staggered backwards, then keeled over, the knife slipping from his limp fingers.

For a full ten seconds Nate simply stood there with his empty pistol pointed at the dead warrior. He involuntarily trembled, thinking of how close he had come to meeting his Maker. If the Blood hadn't been so careless, his fate would have been sealed. He gazed down at himself and realized his buckskin shirt had hitched higher during the struggle, and a few folds of the material had then sagged over his pistols, partly concealing both. Perhaps, in the flush of combat, the Indian hadn't noticed them.

Sighing in relief, Nate reclaimed his rifle. The mare had only gone a dozen feet and was calmly staring at him. He took the time to reload the Hawken and the pistol, then mounted and gazed at the corpse.

What about the scalp?

The Indians and many of the whites regarded the taking of the enemy's hair as a prestigious act. A scalp was a symbol of bravery and manliness, and a collection of ten or 20 wasn't all that uncommon. Many warriors, in particular, took great pride in displaying the scalps they'd obtained; one Bannock chief was known to have fringed his shirt, leggings, and buffalo robe with the hair of his foes.

Nate shook his head and rode to the west. He'd lifted a few scalps himself, but he found the practice repugnant. No one had seen him slay the Blood, so no one could criticize him for failing to take the Indian's hair. Maybe other Bloods would find the body and take it back to their village. If not, the wildlife would dispose of the corpse soon enough.

He rode hard, pushing the mare, eager to find a way out of the ravine and hoping to do so sooner rather than later. A mile went by, then two. The walls narrowed to six feet apart, and on several occasions he was compelled to dismount and move limbs and small logs out of the way. Just when he began to think there really might not be an avenue of escape, he rounded a bend and discovered two surprises.

The north side of the ravine went on for another hundred yards, ending at a wall of solid rock, but the south side had buckled at some point in the past. The earth had caved in, resulting in an easily negotiated incline from the bottom to the rim.

And perched on that rim were three familiar figures, one of whom called out happily, "Nate!"

"Shakespeare!" Nate cried in delight, and galloped up the incline to rejoin his friend, Bannon, and the other trapper.

The frontiersman beamed and moved his horse next to the mare so he could reach over and clasp Nate's arm. "Thank the Lord you're safe! I've been worried to death about you.''

''I've been worried to death about me too,'' Nate said, and grinned.

''We heard a shot awhile ago. Was that you?''

''Yep. One of the Bloods caught up with me.''

Bannon peered down into the fissure. ''What happened to him?''

''He won't attack any more trappers,'' Nate stated with finality, then looked at Shakespeare. ''But what about you? How did you get here?''

''We've been searching for a way down in there ever since Bannon told me you'd gone over the edge. I didn't see you fall in or we would have started looking sooner. As it was, we rode a couple of miles from that field where the Bloods swarmed after us before I stopped and discovered you were missing. Then we circled around to the west, figuring to avoid the Bloods if they were still on our trail, and doubled back in this direction. Just a minute ago we found this way down, and we were debating whether all of us should go or only me when you showed up,'' the frontiersman related.

''What now?'' Nate asked. ''Do we keep looking for the missing trapper?''

''With a war party of Bloods in the area?'' Shakespeare shook his head. ''Besides, we couldn't do much more searching before dark. Let's head back to the rendezvous and report to Gabe.''

''I'm for that,'' Bannon concurred, and glanced at Nate. ''How the hell did you do it?''

''Do what?''

Bannon nodded at the ravine. ''Survive falling in there. Either you're the best horseman who ever lived, or the luckiest son of a bitch alive.''

Shakespeare winked at Nate, then turned to the trappers. ''Didn't you know? Grizzly Killer leads a charmed life. He's also one of the toughest men in the Rockies. Why do you think the Indians respect him so highly?''

Bannon shook his head and chuckled. "I'm beginning to believe the stories I've heard are true."

"They are," Shakespeare stated, and wheeled his horse. "I'd suggest we move before the Bloods find us."

"I'm all for that," chimed in the other trapper.

"Then let's ride," the frontiersman proposed, and headed to the south.

Nate followed as closely as the trees and the press of undergrowth would allow. He thought of Winona and longed to hold her in his arms. After the harrowing ordeal in the ravine, he was happy to be alive and thankful for the blessings life had to offer. Once again an essential fact about the wilderness had been impressed upon him. A man never knew from one day to the next whether he'd be alive to greet the dawn, so he might as well live each moment to the fullest.

"Say, McNair?" Bannon spoke up.

"Yes?"

"What about Yates?"

"What about him?"

Bannon gestured to the east. "Shouldn't we go back and check? He could still be alive."

"You saw the blood. It looked as if every bone in his body was busted. I doubt very much that he's still alive."

"Don't we owe it to him to make sure?" Bannon persisted. "He's a friend of mine. I feel bad about just leaving him there."

The frontiersman reined up. "All right. But since the Bloods are probably still in the area, we should take a vote on it. Nate, what do you say?"

"I vote we take the risk."

The other trapper shook his head vigorously. "You can count me out. I'm not about to go back there, and anyone who does is asking for an arrow in the back."

"I thought you liked Yates, Hopper," Bannon said.

"You shared a drink with him many a time."

Hopper nodded. "Sharing a drink with a man is one thing. Dying for him is another. Besides, Yates is already dead."

"We don't know if he is or not."

"I'm not going," Hopper declared, "and that's final."

Shakespeare turned his horse. "Then you can ride back to the rendezvous by yourself."

"What?" Hopper responded, blinking a few times. "By myself?"

"You certainly can't expect us to come all the way back here after we check on Yates. We'll be making a beeline for Bear Lake."

"You can't leave me alone. There are Bloods all over the place," Hopper stated anxiously.

"Either you go it alone or you ride with us," Shakespeare said. "Take your pick."

Nate saw fear flicker in Hopper's dark eyes, and he felt a measure of disgust. He couldn't fault anyone for not wanting to die, but the trapper's blatant cowardice repulsed him. Being afraid was a normal reaction to danger. The true test of manhood lay in conquering such fear instead of letting terror gain the upper hand.

"Let's go," Shakespeare said, and rode to the east.

Nate did likewise, Bannon on his right, and glanced over his shoulder. He wasn't at all surprised a few seconds later when Hopper elected to go with them.

"I've decided to come along," the trapper announced. "You might need my help if you run into the savages."

"Sure we will," Bannon said flatly.

The four of them rode steadily in the direction of the field where the Bloods had attacked them. They proceeded cautiously, the frontiersman in the lead, their rifles at the ready. Squirrels chittered at them or scampered higher into the trees. Birds regarded them with aloof indifference. Once a mule deer, a magnificent buck, burst from a thicket, snorting belligerently, and bounded away to the northwest.

Nate became increasingly tense as they neared the vicinity of the attack. He began to doubt the wisdom of returning. His eyes darted from shadow to shadow, probing the underbrush for an ambush. Before he knew it, they reached their destination.

Halting near the tree line, Shakespeare peered at the field. He studied the stand of cottonwoods and the small lake beyond. "I believe they're gone," he declared.

"Then let's go," Bannon said, starting forward.

"Wait," the frontiersman advised.

"Why?"

"I could be wrong. It's not smart for all of us to ride into the open. Only one of us should go to the ravine."

"Don't expect me to do it," Hopper said.

"I don't," Shakespeare said. "I'll go."

Nate thought of the consequences should his friend ride into a trap, and shook his head. "No. I'm going."

"Why you?"

"I'm the one with the charmed life, remember?" Nate replied, grinning, and moved from cover before the frontiersman could protest. He goaded the mare to a gallop, eager to be done with the task. He tried to recall the exact point where Yates had plunged over the rim and slanted toward it.

Not a creature stirred anywhere in sight.

The Bloods must have gone on their bloodthirsty way, Nate reasoned. There was no reason for them to stay. Still, he couldn't suppress a certain degree of anxiety. Indians were remarkably clever at concealing themselves; the Bloods could be sighting on him at that very moment. He gazed to the northwest, where the other trapper had taken an arrow in the head. The body was gone.

Nate slowed as he neared the ravine, constantly twisting in the saddle to scrutinize the cottonwoods and the forest.

When he came to the crest he discovered he'd missed the exact spot by 15 yards, but there wasn't any need to move closer. From where he sat he could see the brown stallion, its tongue protruding, its eyes wide and lifeless, covered with blood. The carcass was in the same position as before.

Yates, however, had moved.

Or been moved.

The skinny trapper lay on his back on a flat rock, his arms outstretched. He'd been stripped, mutilated, and scalped.

Nate felt queasy at the grisly sight. Somehow, incredibly, the Bloods had climbed down the sheer wall and scaled it again with their trophy. He hoped Yates had been dead when they went to work. Jerking on the reins, Nate turned and made for the trees. His desire to be with Winona had intensified. At least back at the rendezvous he could enjoy some peace and quiet.

He'd had enough of killing for one day.

Chapter Fifteen

A myriad of stars glimmered in the heavens and a stiff, cool breeze was blowing from the north when Nate and Shakespeare finally made their way toward their campsite after reporting to Jim Bridger.

"He took the news about Yates and the other trapper hard," Nate commented, arching his back to relieve stiffness at the base of his spine.

"Gabe's a good man, Nate. He's not in the trapping business just for the money. He likes this sort of life, and he cares about the men," Shakespeare said. "Tomorrow he'll have the word spread around the rendezvous for everyone to stay away from the country where the war party is on the prowl."

Nate gazed at the south end of the lake, trying to pinpoint the fire Winona undoubtedly had going. They were still 200 yards off, and it was difficult to ascertain precise distances in the dark. "I can't wait to taste some of my wife's cooking. She promised to have a hot meal all ready for us."

"She's quite a cook," Shakespeare said. "Almost in the same class as me."

Chuckling, Nate glanced at his companion. "I never

met a man so fond of his own cooking as you are.''

"It's not the cooking I'm fond of," Shakespeare said, correcting him. "It's the eating."

They rode nearer to Bear Lake, passing several camps en route. The frontiersman hailed a few trappers he knew and exchanged bawdy pleasantries.

Nate thought about his late uncle's cabin high in the Rockies, far to the southeast, where Winona and he would begin their married life in earnest. He idly imagined the happy existence they would lead, and grinned in contemplation of the many, many hours they would spend in each other's arms. He tried to envision what it would be like to have children, and decided rearing a child wouldn't be any more difficult than having a horse or a dog to look after. They all required feeding, pampering, and maybe a scolding now and then. It wouldn't be too hard.

Would it?

Shakespeare abruptly reined up.

"What is it?" Nate asked, stopping.

"There are no fires."

"Where?" Nate inquired, staring at the south shore of the lake.

"There isn't a fire at our campsite and there isn't one at Crazy George's."

"He could be off drinking," Nate said, incipient anxiety gnawing at his mind. "But Winona should have one started by now."

"She doesn't," Shakespeare said, and goaded his white horse forward.

Puzzled, Nate followed, his right hand on the Hawken. There must be a perfectly logical reason for the absense of a fire, he told himself. Perhaps Winona was still visiting her friends at the Shoshone encampment and she'd lost all track of time. Perhaps she'd started a fire earlier, then dozed off, and the fire had gone out. She had to be safe. Had to be.

They came to Crazy George's campsite and found his gear piled around the ring of rocks he'd used to enclose his fire. The trapper was nowhere to be found.

Nate hurried northward, probing the night, hoping he would see Winona curled up on the ground. He drew close enough to distinguish their stack of supplies and the flat ground around the spot where they'd build their fire. She wasn't there. "Winona?" he called out, halting. "Winona? Where are you?"

"She's not here," Shakespeare stated, coming up on the mare's left.

"She could be taking a stroll along the lake," Nate suggested halfheartedly.

"With her horse?"

Nate swung around and spied their hobbled pack animals 30 feet away, but the animal Winona regularly rode was gone. "Then she must be out for a ride," he said, nodding in relief at the obvious explanation.

"It's not safe to go riding at night unless it's absolutely necessary," the frontiersman stated. "You know that and so does she."

"Then she's with the Shoshones."

A new voice addressed them from the darkness. "No, she ain't."

Nate whipped to the right, elevating the Hawken, and saw a figure approaching.

"Don't shoot! It's just me! Crazy George!"

"Where's my wife?" Nate demanded as the lean man walked up to them.

George took off his wool cap and hung his head. "I've got bad news for you, son."

Shakepeare leaned toward his longtime friend. "What happened?"

"The Giant took her."

Nate was off his horse in a rush. He grabbed the front of George's shirt. "What? When? Where did they go?"

"Calm down!"

"Where is she?" Nate snapped, overwhelmed by anger and apprehension, shaking the trapper. "Why'd they take her?"

Crazy George tried to pry the younger man's fingers from his buckskin. "Let go of me and I'll tell you!"

Startled, suddenly aware of what he was doing, Nate let go and stepped back. "Sorry," he mumbled.

"I don't blame you none," George said, smoothing his shirt. "I'd be the same way if those bastards took my woman."

"When did this happen?" Shakespeare inquired, dismounting.

"About an hour ago. I was coming back from sharing a few with Old Lewis when I saw a bunch of fellows at your camp. It was too far for me to make out who they were, but something didn't feel right so I came over. That's when I found Cleroult and his bunch. They were forcing Winona to saddle her animal at gunpoint."

A chilling rage seized Nate and he clenched his rifle until his knuckles hurt. "If it's the last thing I ever do, I'll kill every one of them!"

"That's the spirit," Crazy George exclaimed.

"Did Cleroult see you?" Shakespeare queried.

"Hell, I spoke to him."

"You saw him abducting Winona and he let you live?"

"Yep. He wanted me to give the two of you a message," George said. "I marched right up to him and demanded to know what he was doing. He told me that he was glad I stopped by. It saved him the trouble of leaving a note."

"What's the message?" Nate asked, his tone hard and low.

"The Giant says he'll be waiting for both of you at Coyote Rock. He says you'd better show if you want to see your wife again."

"So he took Winona as part of his plan to get revenge

on us,'' Shakespeare said.

"He sure did. He's using her as bait to draw you into his trap."

Nate turned and took hold of the mare's reins. "He'll get his wish sooner than he expects."

"Hold up," Shakespeare advised. "Don't go rushing off half-cocked. We should tell Gabe and get some help. With your wife's life in the balance, we can't afford to take chances."

"And you can't tell Gabe," Crazy George interjected.

"Why not?" the frontiersman responded.

"He wants just the two of you. He'll have men watching the trail, and if anyone else is with you, then Winona will be dead by the time you reach Coyote Rock."

"How many are with him?"

"Four," George said. "There's Laclede, of course, and the one Nate hit with his rifle, Henri. There's also a man by the name of Peterson." He paused. "Oh, yeah. And that English boxer, Mulhare."

"That's a nasty crowd," Shakespeare remarked.

"And Winona is in their clutches," Nate declared. He mounted his horse and looked down at the frontiersman. "Are you coming or not?"

"Do you need to ask?" Shakespeare rejoined, and climbed into the saddle. His white horse fidgeted a bit, then quieted down.

"Don't forget about me," Crazy George told them. "Give me a minute to fetch my animal."

"We can't take you. Cleroult only wants us, remember?" Nate reminded him. "If you should be spotted, Winona will be murdered. You stay put."

"But I can help. I'll swing around Coyote Rock and sneak up on them. They'll never know I'm there."

"No," Nate stated.

"You can use an extra gun."

"No," Nate reiterated, "and if I catch you following

us, I'll shoot you myself."

"I'm only trying to help."

"Thanks anyway."

Shakespeare turned to the southeast. "It'll take about three hours of hard riding to reach Coyote Rock. I've passed by it a half-dozen times or so, but never at night. The trail can be dangerous even in broad daylight. There aren't many who would try it after dark."

"Isn't there anything I can do?" Crazy George persisted.

"You can let Gabe know what's happening," Shakespeare said.

"But you heard—" George began.

"I know," the frontiersman said, cutting him off. "But I want you to wait an hour and a half, then inform Gabe."

"What good will that do? He won't be able to reach Coyote Rock in time to help you."

Shakespeare shrugged. "No, but if he finds us dead he can track the Giant down and turn Cleroult over to the soldiers at Fort Leavenworth. You can be a witness."

"Me in a court of law?" Crazy George cackled. "I'd rather pluck my toenails out one by one than have anything to do with civilization."

"Do it as a favor to me."

George sighed and nodded. "For you I'll do it. But you'll owe me a favor." He paused. "Though, to tell you the truth, I doubt it'll get that far. Gabe will probably turn the Giant over to the Crows instead. They'd love to get their hands on him. I bet they could make twenty pouches from his skin, maybe more."

"I don't care what Gabe does, just so Cleroult pays for his deeds."

"Enough talk," Nate said impatiently. "Let's get going."

"Stay right behind me," Shakespeare advised, and started off.

Nate dutifully followed.

Crazy George watched them until they were lost in the night. He threw back his head and laughed in delight, then danced a frenzied jig, chortling all the while, his arms flapping and his legs skipping in time to an inner beat, lending him the aspect of an ungainly bird. After a minute he halted and gazed to the southeast. "I know something you don't know!" he whispered conspiratorially, and launched into the jig again, repeating the same statement again and again. "I know something you don't know! I know something you don't know . . . ."

The half-moon overhead provided scant illumination. Nate was hard pressed to stay directly behind the frontiersman once they entered the forest southeast of the rendezvous. Limbs constantly tore at his clothing, and once a branch gouged his left cheek and drew blood. He barely noticed. All he could think about was Winona in the clutches of those sons of bitches. The most exquisite rage he'd ever known fueled him with a fire for revenge.

He thought about the callous audacity of the Giant in taking Winona under the very noses of the other trappers and Indians. Cleroult must have threatened to kill her, Nate reasoned, which explained why she hadn't called out for help. He envisioned his hands on the Giant's throat, squeezing until the flesh discolored, and he smiled in grim satisfaction.

They wound through a series of hills. Around them the murky forest was alive with sounds: the distant howling of wolves, the occasional hoot of an owl, and the even rarer scream of a panther.

Nate held the Hawken in his right hand, the barrel slanted across his saddle, and stared at the frontiersman's back. "Tell me something."

"If I can."

"Why is this place we're going to called Coyote Rock?"

"A Mexican gave it the name a few years ago. He said the shape reminded him of the head of a coyote."

"But what's a coyote?"

"Oh. Sorry. Coyote is the word he used for the animals we call a prairie wolf and the Indians know as the medicine wolf."

"Why do they call it by that name?"

"Because Indians are the most superstitious people you'll ever meet, and many of them happen to believe the medicine wolf can predict the future or give them warning of an approaching enemy."

"Predict the future?" Nate repeated in disbelief, glad for the conversation, for the chance to take his mind off Winona.

"Yep. Some tribes believe that when a medicine wolf comes near their village and barks, it means someone will soon die. Other tribes claim the barking means enemies are close at hand. I've been in villages when a prairie wolf's barking has caused all the warriors to put on their war paint and grab their weapons in preparation for an attack. The women all scurry for cover and the old ones wail their death chants. It's quite a sight."

Nate said nothing. He was thinking about the Indian superstition that medicine wolves, or coyotes, were harbingers of death, and he wondered if Coyote Rock would be the site of his own.

Chapter Sixteen

After two and a half hours of arduous travel, pushing their mounts as fast as they dared, Nate and Shakespeare emerged from a stretch of woodland onto a plain sparsely dotted with stands of trees and clusters of huge boulders. Rearing above the center of the plain, hundreds of feet into the crisp night air, was an imposing bluff.

"Are we near Coyote Rock yet?" Nate asked.

The frontiersman pointed at the bluff. "Only four miles to go. You can't tell it from here, but the top is solid rock."

Nate studied the contours of the black silhouette. He failed to discern any resemblance to a prairie wolf, but he did spot a flickering point of light on the crown. "Is that a fire?"

"Appears to be," Shakespeare confirmed. "There's a flat area at the summit. The Giant must be waiting for us there."

"Let's not disappoint him," Nate stated harshly.

They rode onward, moving side by side, for over two miles before either man spoke.

"The tricky part is coming up," Shakespeare informed his companion. "The trail to the top winds back and forth across the face of the bluff. One slip and you'll fall to your death.'' He paused. "It would be easier if we could use torches, but the Giant would spot us if we did. As it is, I expect he'll post someone between the bottom and the top to give us a proper reception.''

"Is there another way to scale the bluff? What if we went around to the far side?"

"Too steep. There's just the one way up.''

Nate fixed his gaze on the fire. Was Winona next to it right at that moment? Was she bound? Had the bastards molested her? He couldn't wait to get the Giant in his sights. For the first time in his life he keenly relished the prospect of killing another human being. He wanted to taste the sweet nectar of revenge, to see Cleroult's blood pumping onto the ground, to know the man would never pose a threat to Winona or him again. And to Shakespeare, of course. He glanced at the frontiersman he'd grown to care for more than anyone except his wife, and frowned at the thought of the men awaiting them on the bluff. "Say, I've been thinking.''

"About what?''

"Since the Giant took Winona, I should be the one who confronts him.''

"How do you figure?''

"She's my wife.''

"He wants both of us to show up, remember?''

"Then why don't you let me go on ahead. You come on if you hear any shooting.''

Shakespeare snorted. "That's the dumbest idea you've ever had. I guess it's true that too much thinking wears out the brain.''

"What's wrong with it?''

"For one thing, you'd never make it to the top of the bluff by yourself. I doubt you'd even get halfway. For another, Cleroult might be the meanest son of a bitch in the Rockies, but he's not stupid. If you show up alone, he'll suspect a trick and kill Winona and you both before you can get off your horse."

The older man's logic was irrefutable. "I just wish there was another way," Nate said.

"You're not the only one."

They drew nearer to the bluff and lost sight of the campfire. Shakespeare angled toward the northwest corner of the base, his rifle cradled in his arms. He led the way past a row of trees, then rode slowly to an incline running horizontally across the precipitous face.

Nate craned his neck to look at the top, which gave the illusion of reaching the very heavens, and almost didn't notice when his friend stopped.

"This is it," Shakespeare whispered. "From here on out make as little noise as possible. Keep your mare behind my horse at all times. Above all, don't look down once we're up there unless you're not afraid of high places."

"I'm ready."

The frontiersman began the ascent, proceeding carefully, leaning over the pommel so he could better see the way.

Nate sat rigid in the saddle, tense with expectation. The first stage of the climb turned out to be easy and gradual, with the trail five feet wide. After going 40 yards he relaxed, thinking the difficulty had been exaggerated, and almost immediately the trail turned sharply to the left, cutting back on itself, and narrowed to three feet. The slant became steeper, much steeper, and he had to tense his thighs to keep himself from falling, fighting the pull of gravity.

Less than 50 feet farther on, the trail reversed itself again and became a mere two and a half feet wide. Jagged rocks jutted from the cliff. Bumping into any one of them could send horse and rider plunging over the edge.

The mare picked her way carefully, placing one hoof after the other, taking short strides. Whenever she drew abreast of a rock she brushed past it cautiously.

Nate's mouth went completely dry. He tried not to think

about the danger, not to think about the consequences should his horse slip. His life depended on her performance. He stroked her neck every now and then and spoke softly, soothingly, to reassure her.

The climb became more treacherous. They slowed, picking their passage, the cool breeze chilling their sweat.

Nate lost all track of the time it was taking them. He'd assumed they'd only been climbing for ten or 15 minutes when he glanced down at the plain and was shocked at how high they were. The trees below resembled bushes. He licked his lips and supressed an involuntary shudder. Dwell on Winona, he told himself, on Winona and nothing else.

Winona. Winona. Winona.

They were two-thirds of the way up the bluff and rounding a curve when Shakespeare unexpectedly halted.

Nate quickly reined up to avert a collision. He saw the frontiersman gazing at something above them, and he strained his eyes to discover the reason.

The cliff concealed its secrets well.

Frustrated at seeing only the rock wall, Nate glanced at Shakespeare, and was about to whisper a question when his friend resumed their climb.

Twice again the trail reversed itself, and after the second bend it widened, becoming much like the section at the bottom.

Nate breathed a sigh of relief, then realized the frontiersman had stopped again. He glanced up in alarm.

"Do like I do," Shakespeare directed, and without any warning whatsoever he broke into a gallop.

Stunned, Nate obeyed, his heart beating faster. Past experience had taught him to rely on Shakespeare's judgment. If the mountain man wanted him to ride like a bat out of hell, he would. The mare responded superbly, staying close to the sheer face.

A rifle blast shattered the night.

Nate glanced to his left and saw a vague figure perched on what appeared to be a ledge situated just below the rim. He snapped off a return shot, not expecting to hit the rifleman, but the discharge of the Hawken was greeted with a piercing scream and the figure toppled from view. Seconds later the mare swung from the trail onto the bluff proper, and Nate realized with a start they had made it. They were on top of Coyote Rock!

Shakespeare stopped and slid from the saddle. "Get down," he declared.

Well aware of the tempting target he made on the mare, Nate dropped to the ground and crouched.

"Reload," Shakespeare instructed him.

Nate did so, relying more on feel than sight, approximating the amount of powder as best he could.

They were near the western rim of the bluff. Before them was a flat area, dozens of yards in circumference. To the north were enormous boulders; to the south a low rise that obscured whatever lay beyond it, although the faint light dancing above the rise indicated the campfire was on the far side.

Squatting and peering into the darkness, Shakespeare cocked his rifle. "I think we should split up," he said quietly.

"Why?"

"Because they're expecting us and they're probably spread out to catch us in a cross fire. If we go in together, it'll be easier for them to pick us off."

Nate finished reloading and gazed at the rise. He didn't like the idea of being separated, but he knew better than to argue.

"You go that way," Shakespeare said, and pointed to the east. "I'll work my way along the rim. Stay low at all times, and under no circumstances go near the fire."

"Will do."

The frontiersman rose, bent over at the waist, and moved

off. "Take care of yourself, Nate."

"You too."

In seconds the night swallowed the older man.

Imitating Shakespeare's posture, Nate headed to the east along the bottom of the rise. Solid rock was underfoot, enabling him to pad silently. He stopped every 20 feet to listen and survey the terrain. The wind picked up, stirring his long hair and whistling across the top of the bluff.

Nothing moved within the radius of his vision.

Nate came close to the east end of the stony rise and eased his hands and knees, then flattened and crawled to a point where he could see the stretch of bluff in the vicinity of the fire. He saw a single person seated near the blaze, the figure's back toward him, but he couldn't make out who it was.

A faint scratching noise wafted to his ears from the darkness behind him.

Moving slowly so as not to betray his presence, Nate inched his head down and twisted. He looked toward the boulders and immediately spied an inky form moving among them. Since Shakespeare had gone along the west rim, it couldn't be him.

The man headed straight for the rise.

Indecision gnawed at Nate's mind. Should he shoot or try to take the man alive? The abduction of Winona justified killing in cold blood, but he couldn't bring himself to point a rifle and fire. Despite the provocation, he wasn't a callous murderer. He watched the person approach, calculating he would pass a few feet to his right, and came to a decision.

Walking stealthily, the man crossed the flat area.

Nate waited until the man was a mere yard away, anticipating a sharp cry of discovery at any second. But lying in the deepest blackness as he was, he remained safe from detection.

The man abruptly halted and looked over his shoulder.

Now! Nate thought, and leaped to his feet. He started to point the Hawken at the other's chest and declared prematurely, "Don't move!"

But the man did move, with astounding speed, whipping around and batting the Hawken aside with his own rifle barrel, then sliding in close and swinging the stock.

Nate took the blow on the point of his chin, and he stumbled backward against the rise, the Hawken slanting uselessly to the right. An instant later he found himself staring down the menacing barrel of the man's rifle.

"Don't you move!" his captor hissed.

Obediently, Nate froze. He recognized his captor as the trapper he'd struck, the lecher named Henri.

"You're not such a big man now, Grizzly Killer!" the trapper stated contemptuously.

Nate said nothing. He still held the Hawken in his right hand. If only he could bring it into play.

"Where's Carcajou?" Henri demanded, glancing around.

Even with the gun in his face, Nate almost sprang. He tensed to leap, then changed his mind when he spotted someone else running toward them from the northwest.

"Laclede!" Henri declared. "I've caught the pup."

"I know," the weasel responded angrily. "I heard you clear over by the rim. Why don't you shout it out at the top of your lungs, you idiot!"

"Why are you mad at me?" Henri asked. "I caught him, didn't I?"

Laclede halted and stared at Nate. "So we meet again, *mon ami.*" He came around behind Henri and took the Hawken. "You won't be needing this. Nor these," he added, and snatched the pistols and knife.

"Where's my wife?" Nate snapped. "What have you done with her?"

"How touching, yes?" Laclede said to his companion,

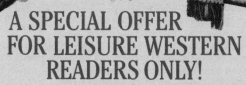

and they both snickered. "If you want to see your woman, we'll take you to her." He motioned with his right arm. "Lead the way, please. Head for the fire, and no sudden moves unless you want to die."

"You plan to kill me anyway," Nate noted resentfully as he started to go around the rise.

Laclede laughed. "True enough. But would you rather die now or later?"

The solitary figure still sat near the campfire. Nate hoped it was Winona and increased his pace.

"I haven't seen the old man," Henri said. "He must be on top of the bluff too."

"So? McNair won't try anything now that we have his protégé. Cleroult will be very pleased."

"Where's Peterson? I heard shooting a while ago," Henri mentioned. "I was coming to investigate when the pup tried to capture me."

"Peterson is dead."

"You're sure?"

"I'm sure. I found his body lying behind rocks on the ledge. Someone put a ball through his head."

Nate grinned at the news.

"Cleroult will not be so pleased about that," Henri observed. "I think I'll let you tell him. You know how he is when his temper is aroused."

"I do."

The fire was only ten feet off. Nate couldn't take the suspense any longer. He thought he detected Winona's raven tresses, but the flickering shadows caused by the wind-whipped flames prevented him from being certain. He ran the final distance and stepped in front of the person, his heart soaring with joy as he laid eyes on the woman he loved. "Winona!" he exclaimed in relief.

She gazed up at him, her eyes conveying the depths of her affection, her mouth unable to convey anything because she'd been securely gagged with a thick strip of cloth. Her wrists had been bound, and her arms tied to her bent legs just above the ankles.

Nate glared at the two men. "Cut her loose!"

"We can't do that, *mon ami,*" Laclede said condescendingly.

"That's right. We wouldn't want her to go running around in the dark and maybe fall off the bluff," Henri chimed in, smirking.

Nate's burning emotions almost seethed out of control. He took a stride toward them, his fists clenched. "If you didn't have the upper hand, I'd shove those words down your throat!"

"Have a care, pup," Henri responded, wagging his rifle. "Cleroult wants you alive, but he didn't forbid me from putting a ball into your leg if you give us trouble."

Spinning, Nate crouched next to Winona and tenderly squeezed her shoulder. "It will be all right," he assured her. "We'll get out of this fix."

She looked at him quizzically.

Nate was about to repeat his statements using sign language when a deep voice addressed him from the right.

"Don't delude yourself, Grizzly Killer. You're not leaving Coyote Rock alive."

Straightening slowly, his features hardening into a mask of fury, Nate pivoted and saw Gaston Cleroult and Edward Mulhare walking toward him, along with one other. The sight of that third person transformed his fury into a state of absolute shock. "It can't be!" he blurted out.

"But it is, you stupid son of a bitch," Crazy George retorted, and cackled insanely.

Chapter Seventeen

In a daze, as if he'd just been clubbed on the head and his brain no longer functioned, Nate gasped at the thin man in the big wool cap, at the man he considered to be a friend, the man Shakespeare cared for so deeply.

Crazy George pointed at him, still chortling. "Look at the great Grizzly Killer. He's trying to catch moths in his mouth!"

The other men, except for the Giant, all laughed.

"I told you I wouldn't forget you," Cleroult stated, his face agleam with an elemental wickedness, his baleful features accented unnaturally by the glow from the crackling fire. "No man insults me or those who ride with me and walks off to brag about it. We've had a debt to pay to McNair for years, ever since he stopped Laclede from giving an Indian bitch the treatment she deserved. But he's crafty, that McNair, and dangerous. Very dangerous. So we've bided our time until the right opportunity should come along." He grinned broadly. "And here you are."

Nate absently listened to the words, his gaze still on Crazy George. "But you!" he declared. "How do you fit into their scheme?"

"Me?" George glanced at the rest and sniggered. "Why, I started riding with Cleroult about a year ago. Found out we have a lot in common. He's a man after my own heart."

"What are you talking about?"

"Well, it's like this, son. When you've been in the wilderness as long as I have, when you've survived burning deserts and frigid winters where your spit can freeze in midair, when you've lived like an Indian, and at times like an animal, when you've known the way of life nature intends for us to lead, it changes you."

"I don't understand," Nate said, his bewilderment impairing his reasoning.

"Out here ain't like back in the East. Out here the only law is survival. But maybe you know that already. Maybe you know that, as those naturalist fellows are fond of saying, everything eats everything else. The big animals eat the medium-sized animals, and the medium-sized animals eat the little animals."

Nate listened in perplexity, wondering if George was raving about nonsense. He knew of the many naturalists who had ventured into the unchartered West to collect specimens and compile information on new species. The newspapers in New York had regularly carried details of the fascinating discoveries made by the intrepid botanists and zoologists. But the connection to Crazy George and Cleroult eluded him.

"I learned the hard truth about all this a number of years ago," George was saying. "I'd bought an Indian woman, a Flathead, and we settled into this valley high up in the Rockies. Winter came on, the worst winter in fifty years. A blizzard buried our valley. I couldn't find game anywhere, and before too long we used up all our food."

Suddenly Nate saw the connection and stark horror seized his soul.

Crazy George stared into the flames. "I resisted

temptation for as long as I could. It was either both of us, or her, and I damn sure didn't want to die.'' He sighed. ''That's when I developed the taste for it. Better than buffalo meat, actually.''

''Dear Lord!'' Nate breathed.

''There have been six or seven others since. One night, a year or so ago, I was treating myself when Gaston came into my camp. I hadn't had time to bury the remains, and he figured out what I was doing right away.'' George grinned. ''Didn't bother him none, though. Said it was my business. I never expected him to be so sensible about it. Been riding with him off and on ever since.''

''Which reminds me,'' the Giant stated. ''When are you going to turn over our share of the money you took from those trappers?''

''Money?'' Nate repeated quizzically, another insight dawning. ''Then you were the one who murdered those men!''

''Yep. I grew tired of just barely making ends meet all the time. I'm getting on in years, son. Gaston showed me there are more ways to make a living than by busting my back.''

Flabbergasted, Nate said nothing. Total revulsion generated a shudder, and his countenance mirrored his disgust.

''What about our money?'' Cleroult asked again.

''Is our deal still on?'' George responded.

The Giant nodded. ''Half of what you took for the Shoshone. I'd say that's fair.''

George looked at Winona, then licked his lips. ''I'm getting a bargain. I've wanted her ever since I spied on their camp a couple of days ago.''

''That was you in the woods!'' Nate exclaimed, remembering when the forest had gone strangely silent.

''Sure was.''

A deep sense of betrayal added to Nate's swirling

emotions. He'd been manipulated and played for a fool. He'd trusted when he shouldn't have trusted. And he should have killed Cleroult when he had the chance.

"Everything has gone according to my plan," the Giant boasted.

"Thanks to me," Crazy George said. "I was the one who persuaded Winona to ride straight into your arms." He snickered. "I told her McNair and King wanted her to meet them on the first hill southeast of Bear Lake, and she believed me!"

"Now that we have these two, capturing McNair will be easy," Laclede predicted.

At that moment, from the surrounding darkness, cracked a hard-edged command. "Drop your weapons!"

Cleroult and the others tensed and swung around, searching for the frontiersman.

"I think not!" the Giant retorted. "We have the advantage, do we not? If you fire at us, we will kill Grizzly Killer and his woman."

"Come on out, Shakespeare," Crazy George called out. "I promise you that you won't be made to suffer."

No response came from the encircling night.

"Did you hear us?" the Giant bellowed. "Come out where we can see you or we'll shoot your friends."

This time the reply was immediate. "Go ahead."

The Giant and Crazy George exchanged glances.

"I don't think you understood," Cleroult stated. "If you don't come out in the open, we'll shoot Chipmunk Killer and his woman."

"Shoot them."

Nate noticed that each time Shakespeare spoke, the voice emanated from a slightly different direction. He pinpointed the frontiersman's position as south of the campfire and deduced Shakespeare was constantly moving from west to east.

"You want their deaths on your conscience?" Cleroult

asked in surprise.

"It won't bother me," Shakespeare declared. "You'll be the one pulling the trigger."

What was the frontiersman doing? Nate wondered. There must be a purpose behind the uncharacteristic baiting.

The Giant took a stride and angrily wagged his rifle. "Do you think I won't? If so, you don't know me very well. I'll ram my barrel down their throats and shoot them one at a time. So help me God I will."

"You'll try, but you'll be dead before you fire."

"You can't get all of us!"

"Probably not, but I'll shoot at least one of you." There was a pause. "Which of you wants to be the first to die?"

Only then, when all five men had their backs to him as they tensely scanned the bluff, did Nate perceive his friend's strategy and realize the part he must play. He gauged the distance to Laclede, who still held the Hawken, pistols, and knife cradled in the crook of his left elbow, and tensed. Should he do it now or wait? Maybe Shakespeare would give him a clue when to spring into action.

"You're bluffing, McNair!" the Giant shouted. "You won't shoot with your friends in danger!"

"Do you think I won't?" the frontiersman responded, mimicking Cleroult. "Then I guess I'll have to prove I'm not bluffing."

Crazy George glanced at the Giant and spoke in a whisper. "He'll shoot, Gaston. Take my word for it."

"He wouldn't dare."

From out of the darkness came the cue Nate had been waiting for, the words spoken quickly and sharply. "Tell me when, Nate."

"Now!" Nate cried, and pounced, grabbing Laclede around the upper thighs and bearing the trapper to the ground. He vaguely heard several of the band vent yells of alarm, then the retort of a rifle from somewhere off to the southeast.

Someone shrieked.

Nate grappled with Laclede, who had released all the weapons in order to try to break free. Above them and nearby, more rifles blasted, but Nate paid scant attention. He had his hands full preventing Laclede from strangling him. The rogue had twisted and clamped iron fingers on Nate's throat. They thrashed and rolled from side to side, glaring into each other's eyes, their features set in grim masks.

"You're dead, bastard!" Laclede hissed.

Nate didn't bother to reply. He tugged and yanked on his enemy's wrists, attempting to wrench those choking fingers from his neck, but nothing seemed to work. All the while they were rolling, and he lost all track of which direction they were going. Seconds later he found out when, to his utter consternation, they rolled into the fire.

Laclede, who wound up on the bottom, cursed and arched his spine, releasing his grip, more concerned with saving himself from being gravely burnt than with achieving victory. He squirmed and flopped, struggling to get clear of the flames.

Which suited Nate perfectly. He flipped away from the fire, surged to his knees, and spotted his weapons lying not eight feet away. Instantly he rose and sped to the pistols, retrieving them just as footsteps pounded directly behind him. He whirled, bringing the guns up just in time.

Laclede had already gotten out of the fire and now charged, brandishing a butcher knife.

Instinctively, Nate cut loose with both pistols, the twin shots catching the weasel high in the chest and catapulting him rearward. Without waiting to see the results of his handiwork, Nate let the guns drop and reclaimed his Hawken. He crouched, surveying his surroundings, prepared to battle to the death. But there was no one to battle. Winona sat in her original spot, firmly bound and gagged. A few feet to the east of her lay Henri, the lecher, who had taken Shakespeare's unerringly aimed ball in the right eye. He'd never ogle another woman.

Was he the one who had shrieked?

Nate saw no sign of anyone else. The Giant, Mulhare, and Crazy George were all gone, vanished into the night. They'd undoubtedly fled out of the radius of light so Shakespeare couldn't pick them off.

Where was the frontiersman?

As his gaze alighted on Winona again, Nate scooted to her side and furiously assaulted her restraints. He had to remove her from the vicinity of the fire before it occurred to one of the missing three men that they could pick her off at their leisure. The ropes were hopelessly knotted, thwarting his efforts. He ran to the spot where his knife lay and scooped it into his left hand.

More footsteps pounded.

Nate rotated, drawing the knife back for an overhand throw. He checked the swing, though, when he saw it who it was. "Shakespeare!"

"Hurry and get her out of here," the frontiersman directed. "I'll cover you."

They hastened to Winona's side, and Nate swiftly cut the bindings and removed the gag.

"Husband!" Winona exclaimed happily.

"There's no time! Come!" Nate urged, and helped her to rise. Together they moved to the south until they were shrouded in gloom.

"This is far enough," Shakespeare said.

"What now?" Nate asked.

"We hunt them down. I traded shots with the bastards and hit Henri, but the other three ran off. I doubt they'll try to race down the bluff at night. The way I figure, they'll hide out until daybreak and then try to escape."

"So they could be anywhere on top of Coyote Rock."

"There aren't that many places to hide."

Nate kissed Winona on the cheek and said, "Stay here. Don't move until we come back. Understand?"

"Yes," she replied. "Take much care."

"I will," Nate promised, and glanced toward the fire. "I'll need my pistols."

"Then let's go," Shakespeare stated.

Side by side they raced close to the fire once more. Nate recovered both pistols and straightened, the short hairs at the nape of his neck tingling, feeling exposed and at the mercy of the killers. He silently voiced a prayer for deliverence: Please don't let them shoot! Please! Please!

One of them did.

Nate and the frontiersman went only five yards when the shot rent the night. For a second Nate believed the killer had missed, until Shakespeare unexpectedly sank to his knees and groaned.

"They got me."

"Hold on," Nate told him, and looped his left arm under his friend's shoulder. Straining every muscle, moving rapidly before the man lurking out there could fire again, he brought Shakespeare to relative safety, rejoining Winona.

"Carcajou hit bad?"

"I don't know," Nate said softly, and lowered the frontiersman carefully.

Shakespeare doubled over and grunted. "It's a scratch. Give me a few minutes and I'll be raring to go."

"You'll stay put," Nate instructed him. He began to reload the pistols.

"You can't face them alone. The odds are three to one."

"I don't have much choice. We can't sit here and do nothing while they creep up on us," Nate said. "Besides, don't worry about me. I don't intend to die," he added lightheartedly to cover his anxiety.

"Who ever does?"

Nate ignored the rejoinder. He finished reloading, stuck the pistols under his belt, double-checked to make certain his knife was snug in its sheath, then grabbed the Hawken and rose. "I'll be back," he informed them, and moved to the west.

"Stay low," Shakespeare reiterated.

Like a panther stalked by hunters, Nate stealthily moved toward the rim. He planned to work along it to the north until he reached the area where the boulders were located, the most logical place to start looking if only because the trio would need some sort of cover.

But what if they had split up?

If so, Nate reasoned, it reduced the odds against him. He stood a much better chance of surviving by fighting them singly instead of all at once.

Something moved at the periphery of his vision, on the right. Nate crouched and concentrated on the inky shape gliding southward almost at the very edge of the bluff. He realized that someone else had had the same idea he did, only in reverse. His enemies were trying a flanking maneuver.

The man creeping ever nearer halted.

Nate tensed, his finger on the rifle's hammer, dreading that he might have been spotted. After several tense seconds, however, the figure began moving again. He estimated the silent stalker to be 15 feet away. Inching his right arm upward, he pressed the stock tightly against his shoulder and waited.

Just a few more steps, you bastard!

As if the man sensed he wasn't alone, he stopped again.

Nate could only hope the cutthroat mistook him for a boulder or a hump in the rocky surface. He held his breath, the sweat trickling down his back and sides. He wanted the man to be directly in front of him when he fired to minimize the risk of missing.

The figure took another stride.

And one more.

Holding the Hawken steady, Nate let the ball fly. The booming crack of the shot sounded like thunder. He saw the man stagger backward, then topple out of sight. Sweeping erect, Nate ran to the rim and gazed over the edge.

Already dozens of feet below, thudding against the cliff face and bouncing outward in a deceptively graceful arc, the body plunged toward the murky base of the bluff.

Nate smiled in triumph. He'd done it! Shakespeare would be proud of him. And it was too bad his Uncle Zeke wasn't alive to see how well he'd learned his lessons about surviving in the wilderness. He could shoot better than most men and knew how to use stealth when necessary. He could live off the land and could hold his own against Indians and wild beasts. What else had Zeke stressed? Oh, yes. To always watch his back.

Incredibly strong arms suddenly looped around Nate from behind, pinning his own arms to his sides, and a gruff voice spoke maliciously in his left ear.

"I'm going to kill you slowly, Chipmunk Killer."

The Giant! Nate struggled to break free, bucking and kicking to no avail. He envisioned being hurled to his death and gaped at the ground so very far below.

"Drop your rifle!" Cleroult directed.

Nate stopped resisting for a moment. The Hawken was of little use to him empty. He tossed the gun to the side and heard it clatter on the ground, grateful it hadn't gone over the crest.

"Very good, Chipmunk Killer," Cleroult stated scornfully. "Get set. I'm about to teach you the reason the Indians call me the Bad One."

Whipping his head back, Nate struck the Giant in the chin. He clawed at his pistols, but before he could grasp them firmly he was swung around and flung to the hard earth, landing on his left side. He tried to rise. A heavy foot slammed into his stomach, doubling him over and whooshing the air from his lungs. He felt rough hands at his belt, and both pistols were yanked out.

"Now it will be man to man, *enfant*," Cleroult stated, and chuckled.

A second kick caught Nate in the left side of the head and sent him sailing. He jarred his right elbow when he crashed down, and for a few seconds the stars spun and Coyote Rock seemed to shake as if from an earthquake.

"You're not so tough, Chipmunk Killer."

Nate inhaled raggedly and endeavored to focus. If he didn't do something, *anything,* and do it soon, the Giant would beat him to death.

"This will be too easy," Cleroult bragged. "Perhaps I should tie one hand behind my back to make our fight fair, eh?"

The stars abruptly ceased revolving. Nate could see a pair of moccasins walking toward his head, and he resisted the temptation to look up. The Giant must believe he was totally helpless. He bunched his hands into fists and gritted his teeth in determination.

Cleroult's right foot swept rearward, the prelude to yet another kick.

Nate finally went on the offensive, rolling straight at the Giant and ramming into the killer's right shin. The leg started to buckle, and Nate clamped both arms just below the knee and heaved with all his might.

Taken unawares by the tactic, Cleroult vented an oath in French as he fell onto his back.

Releasing his hold, Nate shoved to his feet and closed in swinging, planting his right fist on the Giant's nostrils and his left on the former *voyageur*'s mouth. He skipped to the side, evading a swipe at his face, and darted in to box the Giant on the ear.

"Damn you!" Cleroult roared, and rose in a fury.

Nate wasn't about to let his foe get the upper hand again.

What he lacked in size, he more than made up in speed and agility. He employed both to their fullest, stepping in and feinting, lancing a left at the Giant's eyes that was promptly blocked, then delivering his main blow, a right below the belt.

Cleroult uttered a strangled gasp and covered himself.

Not slowing for an instant, Nate drove his right moccasin into the Bad One's left knee and heard a distinct snap. He rained a series of punches to Cleroult's head, and when the Giant raised his hands in reflex, he hammered his knuckles into the groin area.

Wheezing and tottering, Cleroult turned. Off balance, he stumbled a few yards, then righted himself.

Nate kept on attacking, striking the killer in the spine. A backhanded swing struck him on the cheek and knocked him to the right.

The Giant twisted his torso, keeping his groin well out of Nate's reach. "I underestimated you," he said, and took a deep breath. "I won't make the same mistake twice."

Heedless of the threat, Nate waded in again. This time his adversary was braced, and an iron fist clubbed Nate on the crown, precipitating more dizziness. Fingers seized his shirt and he was lifted bodily into the air, then thrown head over heels. The jarring impact stunned him. He wound up on his stomach, his face bruised and bleeding, his right hand touching a long, slender object.

The Hawken!

Nate gripped the barrel and rolled onto his left side. Lumbering toward him like a gigantic monster out of his most horrid nightmares came Gaston Cleroult. Nate placed his other hand firmly on the cool metal, bunched his shoulders, and rose in a rush, swinging as he did. The heavy stock smashed into the Giant's face, rocking the man on his heels. Nate swung again and again and again, a primal ferocity lending savage strength to his limbs. On the fourth blow Cleroult pitched to the side, toward the ground.

Only there wasn't any ground.

In silent amazement Nate watched the Giant go over the rim. In the heat of their combat he'd lost all track of the edge of the cliff. He lowered the Hawken, overcome with fatigue.

"Well done, son."

Nate whirled.

Six feet away stood Crazy George, his rifle leveled. "I wouldn't believe it if I hadn't seen you do it with my own eyes. No one has ever beaten Cleroult."

"What now?" Nate asked, stalling, girding his legs for a last, desperate lunge.

"You know," George said softly. "In a way, I regret you must die. I sort of like you."

Nate said nothing.

"First I'll dispose of you, then Shakespeare. Where is he, by the way?"

From out of the darkness two words were pronounced with fiery passion. "Right here."

Crazy George didn't move. Oddly, he laughed lightly and responded in a calm, affectionate tone. "I'm glad it will be you. I'd hate to have a stranger be the one."

"We don't need to go through with this. Drop your rifle."

"Please, McNair, don't insult my intelligence. Not after all we've been through together."

"Please, George."

"I'm truly sorry."

Nate saw the demented mountain man start to pivot. The that followed echoed from the bluff and wafted out over the plain beyond, heralding the demise of a noble soul who long ago had fought the wilderness on its own terms, and lost.

Epilogue

Nate stood on the south shore of Bear Lake, his right arm around Winona's shoulders, staring thoughtfully out over the glassy surface. The lake, he reflected, possessed a quality in common with certain people; there was no telling what lurked underneath. He heard footsteps and turned.

"Well, tomorrow is the last day of the rendezvous," Shakespeare mentioned idly.

"How's your side?" Nate inquired.

The frontiersman gingerly touched his left hand to the tender area just below his ribs. "Coming along fine. In another month I should be all healed."

"Have you made up your mind yet?"

Shakepeare adopted a puzzled expression and scratched his chin. "About what?"

"You know damn well about what."

"Oh. Your offer." Shakespeare grinned and gazed at the distant mountains. "You wouldn't want me hanging around your cabin."

"If I didn't, I wouldn't have asked you to come with us."

"Aren't you forgetting something?"

''What?''

''You haven't had any real time to yourselves since you were married. You might like some.''

Now it was Nate's turn to grin. ''I've already thought of that. We'll set up a lean-to behind the cabin. When we want you to leave, you can sleep out there.''

''Good Lord. I'll be sleeping there the whole time.''

Nate raised his head and laughed his joy to the heavens.

BLOOD FURY

*Dedicated to
Judy, Joshua, and Shane.
And to Sign Talking Eagle,
who recorded it all for posterity.*

Chapter One

Nathaniel King heard a twig snap, and froze. All around him was the majestic scenery typical of the Rocky Mountains in the month of August. Caps of gleaming snow crowned the towering peaks that ringed the valley in which he was hunting. Cottonwoods, aspens, and pine trees grew in profusion along the banks of the narrow stream meandering from north to south. Ink-black ravens soared lazily high above his head. Sparrows chirped in a thicket to his left. And somewhere directly ahead, hidden in the undergrowth, was the black-tailed buck he'd been stalking for the better part of two hours.

The strapping 19-year-old crouched and scanned the densest vegetation for his quarry. If he was right, if he'd learned the lessons taught by his grizzled mentor properly, then the buck should be there. Deer usually spent a hot afternoon hidden in the shade, where they could rest safe from predators until they ventured out in the cool of the evening to forage in earnest.

Nate's gaze strayed to the stream, which gurgled not more than a yard to his right, and he caught a glimpse of his reflection. His buckskins fit his broad shoulders and muscular frame loosely, allowing for adequate ventilation and unrestricted movement. An eagle feather bestowed on him by a noted Cheyenne warrior was tied securely to his long black hair, the quill pointing skyward. Slanted across his chest was a powder horn and a bullet pouch, and tucked under his brown leather belt were two flintlock pistols, one on each side of the buckle. On his left hip, nestled snug in its sheath, was his butcher knife.

A crackling sound issued from the brush in front of him.

Nate's green eyes narrowed as he probed for movement. Always look for a hint of motion against the backdrop of plant life, Shakespeare had instructed him. Now he put the teaching to good use, and spied something 20 feet away moving from east to west.

He raised the rifle clasped firmly in his hands, the heavy Hawken he'd obtained in St. Louis from the brothers of the same name who were just beginning to earn a reputation as makers of superb guns, and sighted on the vague form. He saw a flash of brown, but couldn't identify the game as the buck he sought, and he certainly didn't want to shoot something else by mistake. Especially a grizzly bear.

The animal halted and snorted.

Nate had heard such sounds before, and always from deer or elk. He was confident he'd found the buck, and he took a bead on a small opening in the undergrowth located a few yards from it. If he made the shot, he'd be able to transport enough meat to the cabin to last for two weeks, even allowing for the fact there were three mouths to feed counting his. He thought of how easy acquiring food had been back in New York; all it took was the correct amount of money and a person could eat whatever they desired. But in the wilderness the difference between a full stomach and starvation often hinged on the squeeze of a trigger or the twang of a bowstring. Since his wife and best friend were eagerly awaiting his return with fresh meat, he didn't intend to miss.

For the longest time nothing happened. The creature stayed put, apparently in no great hurry to get anywhere. A pair of robins flew into a tree above it.

The strain of holding the Hawken steady produced moderate pain in Nate's shoulders. He estimated five minutes had gone by before the thing finally stepped closer to the opening. Just a little bit farther, he mentally noted, and his patience would be rewarded.

Tentatively, as if sensing an element in the forest was amiss, the animal edged westward.

At last Nate had an unobstructed view, and there stood a magnificent buck sporting a 12-point rack. He held his breath and aimed between its eyes, which were locked on him, then squeezed the trigger.

The rifle didn't fire.

Baffled, Nate glanced down at his rifle to discover he had failed to cock it in his excitement. He hastily remedied the mistake, and looked up to find the buck on the move. Alarmed that he was about to lose such choice meat, he discarded all caution and plunged into the underbrush in pursuit.

The deer darted deeper into the timber.

Nate ran at his top speed, battering limbs aside with his arms and making enough noise to spook an entire herd of buffalo. He came to the opening and paused to survey the forest. Elation coursed through him when he spied the black-tail 60-feet away in the middle of a clearing, gazing over its shoulder in his direction, apparently more curious than afraid. Instantly he whipped the Hawken up, took a fraction of a second to line up the shot, and squeezed the trigger.

At the loud retort the buck started to turn, but the ball caught the animal in the left eye before it could take a stride. The impact jerked its head forward and the animal stumbled to its knees, tottered, and fell on its right side.

Nate was already running toward his prize. There was always the chance the deer might rise and bolt, and the last thing he wanted to do was chase the buck for miles and miles until it dropped for good. He drew his right pistol as he closed. When still 15 feet away he realized another shot wouldn't be necessary after all.

A dark crimson pool formed a halo around the buck's head and antlers. A neat hole now existed where its left eyeball had been, and its tongue protruded from between its lips.

Smiling in satisfaction at his marksmanship, Nate wedged the pistol under his belt and halted. He'd left his horse and the pack animal several hundred yards to the north in a stand of pines, so his first priority should be to reclaim them before any wandering Indians came by.

Pivoting, Nate hastened off. He returned to the bank of the stream and paused to enjoy a refreshing sip off cold water, then straightened and was about to continue when his oversight checked him in midstep.

Would he never learn?

He grinned as he reloaded the Hawken, wondering how long it would be before he automatically did so after every shot. Although he'd been on the frontier for almost five months, he still neglected on occasion to reload immediately. One day, he mentally noted, the mistake could cost him his life.

From deep in the woods came the hoot of an owl.

After replacing the ramrod, he trekked briskly northward, invigorated as much by the crisp mountain air as by his success at hunting. Feeling supremely happy, he began humming the tune to "Home, Sweet Home," a song written by John Howard Payne.

A large yellow and black butterfly flew past his face.

Nate gazed at the nearest peaks, thinking of his wife and the joy they had shared during the month and a half they'd been married. He'd learned more about women in that brief span than in all the years before the wedding. The thought made him laugh. How would he refer to a short Shoshone ceremony presided over by his wife's father as a wedding? All he'd done was promise to protect her, to treat her kindly, and to stay with her in good times and bad, and just like that they were united in matrimony.

Well, not quite.

There had been a little matter of giving her father a horse. In effect, as he saw it, he'd bought her, and the idea still rankled him. He knew that many trappers bought Indian women for a season or longer. He also knew Indian warriors customarily offered horses and other valued possessions to the fathers of the brides-to-be. In his estimation such a practice rated as a notch above outright slavery, and he disliked both.

Winona didn't mind, though.

That aspect of the practice amazed him. Indian women actually *wanted* to be purchased. They considered it to be a great honor. If a man wanted a woman for his wife and didn't offer to pay, she'd be insulted.

Nate shook his head and chuckled. How strange and wonderful life in the wild could be! If he ever returned to civilization, perhaps he would write a book on his adventures as so many of those who'd ventured West had done.

He soon reached his horses, and proceeded to lead them back to the clearing. His mare, a frisky animal he'd purchased in New York City, became skittish as they neared the spot where the buck lay. Not until he came within sight of his prize did he discover the reason, and the sight filled him with consternation. He halted, uncertain whether he should fire or flee.

A panther was astride the black-tail.

Nate had never seen one of the big cats up close. Ordinarily they took great pains to avoid humans, and would run at the first glimpse of a man or woman. They were also deathly afraid of fire. Their other habits were generally unknown to the majority of trappers because they were so reclusive. Some Indians believed seeing one was a good omen.

This one appeared to have no intention of leaving. Light brown in color, it measured six feet from the tip of its nose to the end of its twitching tail. Its rounded head was fairly small for its size, but the teeth displayed when the cat growled definitely weren't.

Nate raised the rifle. He reasoned the panther must be either very hungry or very old, or both, and decided to avoid killing it if at all possible. His mentor, Shakespeare McNair, had impressed upon him the Indian view of staying wildlife: Never kill any animal unless it was absolutely necessary.

The fierce cat snarled and swiped a paw at the intruder.

"Go away!" Nate shouted. "That's my meat!"

A feral hiss was the response.

Nate took a few paces, seeking to frighten it off, but both horses halted and refused to budge despite firm tugs on his part. Frustrated, he led them off to the east and securely tied both to the jutting branches on an enormous log. "That should hold you," he said, and cautiously made for the clearing once more.

The panther was still there. It had taken a bite out of the buck's neck, and now greedily lapped at the blood flowing onto the ground.

Resolved to recover the deer at all costs, Nate advanced steadily. As before, the cat glared at him and growled. Nate trained the Hawken on its head, never breaking stride.

For a few moments the cat held firm, its lips curled back to expose all of its wicked, tapered teeth, its eyes flashing a raging hatred. Then it rose and swiftly sped to the southwest in prodigious bounds stretching 15 feet or more. The vegetation swallowed the cat, leaving an unnatural stillness in the air.

Nate beamed and walked to the carcass. He'd saved the meat! Wait until he related the story to Winona and Shakespeare. To be on the safe side, he waited several minutes before attending to the skinning, his eyes surveying the woods in case the panther should think twice about leaving the meal.

Not so much as a leaf stirred.

The owl vented another hoot, closer this time.

Satisfied he was out of danger, Nate pulled his knife and squatted. He placed his rifle behind him, rolled the buck onto its back, and set about skinning it. Since the cat had already torn the neck open, he didn't bother with bleeding the carcass. Instead, he first cut a slit from the anus to the head, beginning between its rear legs and slicing upward. He wisely avoided puncturing the stomach and intestines.

Next, to prevent the contents of the esophagus, if any, from contaminating the meat, he tied a string around it. He did the same with the anus. His hands were coated with blood and gore, so he sat down and wiped them on the grass while admiring his handiwork. Shakespeare had taught him well.

Nate gazed at the sky, calculating the amount of time required to complete the job. By all rights, after he removed the heart, liver, and other organs, he should hang the deer from a stout limb to let the blood drain completely and give the air a chance to cool the body. He figured there were eight hours of daylight remaining, at least. If he let the buck hang for a couple of hours, he would be able to leave the valley and clear the ridge to the east before nightfall. Since he was a full day's ride from the cabin, the sooner he started, the better he would like it.

The owl hooted a third time.

Rising to his knees, Nate leaned over the blacktail, then remembered a fact Shakespeare had taught him about owls. They were nocturnal birds of prey and rarely were abroad during the day. How odd that one should be flying about in the early afternoon.

Then it hit him.

What if the cries were being made by something else?

Or, more precisely, *someone* else?

Intuition tingled the hairs at the nape of his neck and he spun, reaching for the Hawken, already too late because at the east edge of the clearing stood an Indian warrior armed with a bow, an arrow set to fly.

Chapter Two

Nate instantly threw himself to the right, holding the rifle next to his chest as he rolled over and over. Amazingly, the shaft never struck him, and he surged to his feet, bringing the Hawken up, prepared to return fire.

Only the Indian hadn't released the arrow.

The warrior nodded and spoke a few words in an unknown tongue.

Perplexed, Nate shook his head to indicate he didn't understand. He didn't know what to make of the situation. If the Indian had wanted to kill him, he'd most certainly be dead. But if the warrior had friendly intentions, why point the shaft at him?

Again the man tried to communicate, speaking longer this time.

Nate didn't know enough yet about the various tribes to be able to determine which ones individuals belonged to at a mere glance, as Shakespeare could do. He had no idea if the man in front of him was a Shoshone, Crow, Cheyenne, or Arapaho. The warrior wore leggings and moccasins and had a knife on his right hip. There were no distinguished marks, such as paint, on his face or body, and his hair was unadorned.

Of one fact Nate could be certain. The Indian wasn't a Blackfoot or Ute. Any member of either tribe would have shot him on sight. Of all the Indians inhabiting the Rockies and the Plains to the east, none caused more trouble for the trappers. Both tribes hated all whites.

The warrior glanced at the buck, then at Nate. He slowly let up on the bowstring, easing the tension, then lowered the bow to his side. A tentative smile creased his thin lips.

Reassured by the man's behavior, Nate likewise let the rifle fall to his waist, although he kept a finger on the trigger. "Who are you?" he asked. "Do you speak English?"

Now it was the Indian's turn to shake his head.

Nate didn't give up hope. Winona had taught him enough Shoshone to enable him to engage in a conversation without fear of being misunderstood. He tried that language now, but the effort proved unavailing. At last he resorted to sign language, letting his hands do the talking, and saw the warrior smile.

Almost all of the tribes relied on the silent language that had been passed down from generation to generation from their ancestors in the distant past. The origins of sign were lost in antiquity, and no one knew how the language had become so universal in extent, but its effectiveness was indisputable. Sign language enabled Indians from different tribes, who might live hundreds of miles apart and have virtually no customs in common, to establish an immediate rapport.

Of all Nate's accomplishments since heading west, he was most proud of his grasp of sign. He'd spent countless hours learning the proper movements of the hands and fingers, first under the tutelage of his late Uncle Zeke, then under Shakespeare and Winona. Just a few days ago the frontiersman had complimented him on his ability. He now told the warrior that he came in peace, that he was hunting for meat for the table and nothing more.

The Indian slid the arrow into a quiver on his back, then responded by revealing his name to be Sitting Bear.

"From which tribe do you come?" Nate asked with his hands.

"I am Crow."

Nate breathed a sigh of relief. The Crows and the Shoshones were two of the friendliest tribes in the entire territory. They befriended whites regularly and were implacable enemies of the Blackfeet and the Utes.

Sitting Bear's fingers flew. "What is your name?"

There were no Indians signs that would adequately translate his English name, so Nate disclosed the Indian name bestowed on him by the same Cheyenne who had given him the eagle feather. "I am Grizzly Killer."

The Crow blinked. "Are you the same Grizzly Killer who was at the big gathering of whites during the last Blood Moon?"

Blood Moon was the Indian way of referring to July. "I am," Nate responded.

Sitting Bear seemed impressed. "And are you the same Grizzly Killer who killed the Bad One?"

"Yes," Nate admitted, wondering how the warrior knew about the incident at the rendezvous involving a rogue trapper and his band of cutthroats.

"I am happy to meet you," Sitting Bear said with his hand. "I camped with a band of Bannocks nine days ago. They were at the big gathering and told me all that happened."

So that was it, Nate thought. "I am happy to meet you," he dutifully stated. "But why did you point an arrow at me?"

"For that I am most sorry. I did not know if you would be a friend or an enemy. Some whites believe all Indians are enemies and shoot us without warning."

"I only shoot Indians if they try to shoot me," Nate assured him.

Sitting Bear came closer and pointed at the black-tail. "I heard a shot and came to see who it was." He admired the deer for a moment. "You will have much meat."

Remembering the many lessons Shakespeare had imparted on Indian etiquette, Nate knew what he had to do. "I would be pleased to share some of the meat with you."

"I could not accept," Sitting Bear signed, although his expression betrayed his interest. "Even though my family has not tasted deer meat in three moons."

Nate smiled and walked over to the warrior. "I insist you take some of the meat. There is more than I can possibly use."

The Crow considered the offer for a few seconds, then looked up. "I will accept your kindness if you will agree to share my lodge tonight."

"How far is your lodge?"

Sitting Bear pointed to the south. "A mile from here on the west bank of the stream."

Nate hesitated. He wouldn't be able to make

it back to the cabin tonight anyway, so why not accept? If he rode out at first light, he'd be home shortly after dark tomorrow. "I would be happy to," he signed. "I'll stay at your lodge tonight, but I must leave in the morning."

"You honor me," Sitting Beat said solemnly. "My friends will not believe that so great a warrior has stayed with my family."

The compliment made Nate feel uncomfortable. He had yet to accustom himself to the frank manner in which Indians discussed everything. They were invariably direct and to the point, and they never practiced idle flattery. Evidently the news of his encounter with the Bad One was spreading rapidly by word of mouth around the campfires of the whites and the Indians. At the rate things were going, soon he'd be as widely respected and feared as Shakespeare. "How many members of your tribes are here?" he asked to change the subject.

"My wife, my two sons, and my daughter."

"Your family is here alone?" Nate inquired in surprise. The Central Rockies were the hunting grounds of the Utes, and for any Crow to travel into the region was extremely dangerous.

"Yes."

"What about the Utes?"

Sitting Bear shrugged. "We had to come. There was no choice."

Nate looked around. "Do you have a horse?"

"No."

"I must go get mine. Would you watch my buck while I am gone?"

"Yes. I will guard it as if it was my own."

Gripping the Hawken by the barrel, Nate hurried toward his animals. It was his understanding that only the poorest of Indians didn't own horses, and he wondered why Sitting Bear hadn't simply stolen a mount from another tribe. Horse stealing was a common pastime. Special raids were frequently conducted expressly for that purpose, and those warriors who succeeded were esteemed as brave men. Not to mention rich. Horses, to Indians, were conspicuous evidence of affluence.

He found the mare and pack animal munching contentedly on grass, and in no time at all he was back at the clearing and standing over the buck. "Will you give me a hand hanging this up?" he asked. "I have rope in one of my packs."

"We can take the buck to my lodge," Sitting Bear suggested. "My wife has made berry juice, and my sons will take care of your horses."

Nate liked the idea. This was his first contact with the Crows, and he was curious to learn more about them, to see how they differed from the Shoshones. "Let us go," he said with his hands.

Together they lifted the buck onto the pack animal and strapped it down tightly. Nate swung into the saddle, took the lead in his left hand, and nodded for his newfound friend to show him the way.

"Is it true you are close to Carcajou?" Sitting Bear queried, glancing over his shoulder to catch the reply.

"Yes," Nate sighed. Carcajou was the name by which Shakespeare was known far and wide among the various tribes. The word itself was French, Nate believed, and referred to the fierce animal otherwise called the wolverine.

Sitting Bear used his hands as he walked, the bow slung over his left shoulder. "I met him once years ago. He is a white man whose word can be trusted."

Nate started to respond, but he realized the warrior wasn't looking at him. He focused on the surrounding trees, searching for the panther or any other threats. The likelihood of the big cat returning was slim, but in the forest it never paid to take chances.

For ten minutes they wound southward. Sitting Bear demonstrated an uncanny knack for finding passages through the thickest brush, usually by following the narrowest of animal trails. The trees thinned out, and ahead appeared a clear strip adjacent to the stream.

Nate rode to the edge of the water. Across the stream, nestled at the edge of the woods on the far side of the field, sat Sitting Bear's lodge. Smoke curled lazily upward from the ventilation opening at the top. A woman and a young girl were seated outside the lodge, working on a buffalo robe. Two boys, both in their teens, were honing their skill with bows and arrows near the trees.

Sitting Bear raised his right arm and hailed them in his native tongue, then glanced at Nate. "Come," his hands stated. "Meet my loved ones."

Nate waited for the warrior to enter the water, then urged the mare forward. The stream had a depth of two feet at its deepest points and was only five feet in width. He crossed easily and reined up on the far bank.

The family ran out to meet him. All four halted a few yards off and regarded Nate with amazement and, in the case of the mother, a trace of fear.

Sitting Bear indicated their guest and launched into an extended speech in Crow. The quartet listened attentively, with repeated stares directed at Nate.

For his part, Nate was amused by their reaction but tactfully maintained a solemn face. He noticed the boys were keenly interested in his rifle. The little girl, who wasn't any older than ten, smiled at him the whole time.

At length Sitting Bear concluded and turned. His hands and arms did the talking as he explained his comments to Nate. "I told them about our meeting and let them know you are the great Grizzly Killer. I told them you have kindly offered to share your meat with us, and that they must all be on their best behavior."

Nate faced them and addressed them in sign language. "I am most happy to meet all of you."

The woman nodded nervously, the girl giggled, and the boys couldn't seem to take their eyes off the Hawken.

"Let me introduce them," Sitting Bear said, coming around in front of the mare. He touched each member of his family as he went from one to the other. "My wife is Evening Star. Our daughter is Laughing Eyes."

"Hello," Nate said aloud.

The Crow paused, his features reflecting his pride. "And these are my sons, Strong Wolf and Red Hawk."

Both boys grinned self-consciously. The taller of the pair, Strong Wolf, said something to his father in their own language.

"He wants to know if you will allow him to shoot your rifle," Sitting Bear disclosed. "But he is too shy to ask you himself."

"I would be happy to have him fire it," Nate replied, and was about to compliment his host on having such a fine family when the mother suddenly pointed to the east and cried out in alarm. Twisting in the saddle, he discovered the reason.

A herd of 25 or 30 buffalo had crested a rise seven hundred yards distant and were pounding directly toward the camp.

Chapter Three

Nate turned the mare, then used sign language to explain his purpose to Sitting Bear. "Hold my pack horse and I will turn the herd," he proposed.

"Be careful," the Crow replied, taking the proffered lead.

The small herd raised tendrils of dust behind it as the huge beasts drew closer.

About to ride off, Nate paused when an idea occurred to him. He glanced at his host. "Would your family like a buffalo or two?"

The suggestion brought a wide smile to the warrior's face. "We would be much in your debt," he responded.

"Have Evening Star sharpen her knives," Nate advised, and goaded the mare into the stream again. He crossed quickly and rode to intercept the bison.

Although the majority of the great brutes migrated from the high country to the Plains early in the spring, there were always those hardy animals who seemingly preferred the higher elevations and stayed in the mountains the year round. They grew as large as their counterparts below, with the males standing over six feet high at the shoulders and weighing upwards of two thousand pounds, and were similar in every other respect except for the fact their coats were shaggier.

Few animals were as numerous as the buffalo. On the Plains their numbers were estimated to be in the millions. A single herd could take days to pass a specific point. And of all the wildlife existing west of the Mississippi River, the bison were most essential to the Indian way of life.

Every tribe utilized the buffalo to some extent. Hides were used for clothing. Robes, moccasins, leggings, shirts, dresses, belts, and even underclothes all came from treated skins. Lodge furnishings, riding gear such as saddle blankets, hackamores, and hobbles, and various tools and utensils were constructed from various parts of the beasts. Knife sheaths and shields were manufactured from rawhide. Bowstrings were made from bull sinew. Even the buffalo's dung came in handy; chips were burnt as fuel.

Nate had encountered bison before, and he held them in great respect. With their broad, massive heads sporting horn spreads of up to three feet, and the fiery temperament of the bulls when aroused, they were formidable game. They were also hard to kill unless the person doing the hunting knew exactly where to hit them. He'd heard about trappers who'd put 15 balls into a single bull, yet the animal had refused to drop.

And here he was trying to turn a herd of 30. Shaking his head in astonishment at his own audacity, Nate pondered how he could best achieve his goal. Riding straight at them in the hope of diverting them to either side would be an exercise in futility as well as certain suicide. A shot might do the job, but he must time it perfectly and hope the lead bull wasn't in a belligerent mood.

The thundering hooves of the onrushing bison became louder and louder.

Nate spied a mammoth male at the head of the herd and made toward it. The mare responded superbly; she'd participated in a buffalo hunt with him once before and wasn't fearful. He held the rifle and the reins in his right hand, then drew a pistol with his left.

Already the brutes had covered two hundred yards.

Almost as an afterthought, Nate speculated on what could have spooked them. Buffalo were notorious for standing their ground against their natural enemies such as wolves and panthers. Normally, they even refused to flee at the sight of men, Indian or whites. If Nature had given them the intelligence and ferocity of the grizzly, the buffalo would have long since driven all two-legged creatures from their domain.

The flat land worked in Nate's favor. He had plenty of room to maneuver and could outrun them if the need arose. To the north lay the forest; to the south a level field. He didn't particularly care which way they went, just so they turned aside from Sitting Bear's camp.

On they came, the largest animals in North America, their bulky bodies rising and falling rhythmically as they ran.

Nate extended the pistol, counting off the yards separating him from those tapered horns. He waited until there were only 50, and fired.

For a few seconds the buffaloes acted as if they hadn't heard, and then they started to swing to the south.

Elated at his success, Nate went to rein up when the mare suddenly stumbled and went down, throwing him from the saddle. He thrust his hands out to brace the impact, and winced when a searing pain lanced up his right arm. Tumbling end over end, he wound up flat on his back, dazed, staring at a cloud overhead.

What in the world had happened?

He rose onto his elbows and saw his horse rising. Behind her were a series of holes with openings a foot wide. Badger burrows. Concerned the mare might have broken a leg, he shoved to his feet and grabbed the reins.

From his rear arose the drumming of the buffaloes.

Nate glanced over his right shoulder and was stunned to discover the herd had resumed its original course and was a mere 20 yards distant. His guns had flown from his hands when he fell, and he frantically searched the high grass around him.

The Hawken lay not four feet away.

Hauling the mare after him, Nate lunged and scooped up the rifle. He swung toward the herd, cocked the hammer, and prayed the weapon wouldn't misfire. In an instant he sighted on the lead bull and pulled trigger.

For a heart-thumping second the herd came on rapidly, a living wall of tough sinew and iron determination, their nostrils flaring, their humped shoulders bouncing.

Nate recoiled, expecting to be trampled and gored, and seized the mare's mane in a desperate bid to escape. He saw the foremost bull go down in a disjointed jumble of flashing legs and whipping tail, sliding to a stop within inches of his moccasins, and the rest of the herd split into two groups, half bearing to the left, half bearing to the right. The pungent scent of them filled his nose, and dust obscured everything. He held onto the mare with all his might and listened to the rumbling din as the beasts passed him by. The very ground shook.

In moments the herd had left him behind.

Coughing and waving his left hand to dispel the choking dust, Nate took several strides to the west. Had he done it? Or were the bison still bearing down on the lodge? He scarcely breathed until he glimpsed the herd, reunited and racing to the southwest, well clear of the camp.

Relief washed over him and he voiced a cry of triumph. His temples still pounded, and when he held his arm out his fingers trembled. But he was alive! Fully, wonderfully, alive, tingling in every fiber of his being. He spun in a circle, laughing heartily, then walked to the dead bull and stared down at its huge head and dark eyes. "You almost got me, big fellow," he said by way of a compliment.

Shouts rent the air from the direction of the lodge.

Turning, Nate saw the Crows running toward him, the mother carrying the girl in her arms. He grinned and indicated his trophy.

Sitting Bear reached him first. He uttered a whoop and began prancing around the buffalo, waving his bow overhead.

Nate chuckled, tempted to join the warrior.

Strong Wolf and Red Hawk were next, and they promptly joined their father in the victory dance, yelping like coyotes as they leaped and whirled.

Girlish laughter announced the arrival of Evening Star and Laughing Eyes. They stood to one side, observing happily, and the mother gave Nate a friendly look.

Proud of his accomplishment, Nate hefted the Hawken. If not for the rifle, he'd be dead. The reliable weapon had saved his skin once again, and the thought prompted a decision. There were some frontiersmen who took to calling their rifles by pet names. He'd always considered the practice rather foolish until that very moment. Old Reliable was a fitting name for a rifle, and from that day on he would refer to his Hawken as exactly that: Old Reliable. He couldn't wait to tell Shakespeare the news.

The Crows were still celebrating wildly.

Nate lowered the rifle, his right wrist brushing against the pistol wedged under his belt. He abruptly recalled his other flintlock and turned, scanning the field. It had to be there somewhere. But what if the flailing hooves of the buffaloes had pounded it to bits?

Sitting Bear stopped dancing and walked over. He said a sentence in Crow, then resorted to sign language. "Every word they say about you is true. You are the bravest man I have ever met."

"Thank you," Nate replied, still scouring the grass.

"My family will always treasure this day, and the story of your deed will be passed on to my grandchildren and my great-grandchildren. I will also record the events on a hide for all future generations to see."

Nate stopped looking and smiled at the Crow. "You honor me too much. I only did what I had to do to stay alive."

"You are still young. You do not yet realize the

gift the Great Mystery has given you."

"What gift?"

"The gift of courage."

Nate had never regarded himself as exception-ally brave. He smiled and gestured at the trampled field. "I need your help."

"Anything we can do for you, we will."

"I lost one of my pistols," Nate began to explain, and the warrior cut him off.

Sitting Bear barked instructions to his family, and every one of them immediately devoted themselves to searching for the missing flintlock.

Nate resumed hunting, thinking of how close-knit Indian families were, how they stuck together and were supremely devoted to one another. He'd yet to witness or hear about a single instance of a child disobeying a parent. By comparsion, many of the families in the cities had succumbed to the severe stress of city living and were rife with animosities. Many children treated their fathers and mothers with outright disrespect. There were some who claimed the crime in the cities was due to the breakdown of discipline and parental guidance. Perhaps they were right.

Strong Wolf gave a yell and raised his left arm.

Nate beamed when he laid eyes on the flint-lock. He hurried to the youth's side and took the gun in his hand, inspecting it carefully. The pistol wasn't damaged. He guessed that the grass and weeds had cushioned it from the hooves, and he chuckled at his good fortune as he slid the barrel underneath his belt.

"Is it broken?" Sitting Bear inquired.

"No." Nate glanced at the eldest son. "Thank you for finding it."

The boy pointed at the bull. "You have given us enough meat to last a month. I am glad to help you."

Sitting Bear squinted up at the sun. "We must get busy if we are to finish by nightfall. Now we have a buffalo and a buck to skin and strip."

"I am ready when you are," Nate offered.

"We will take care of both," Sitting Bear stated. "You can rest while we work."

"We will work together," Nate insisted.

"As you wish. We will go get all the knives, rope, and utensils we need."

"I will stay here."

The Crows hastened toward their camp, chatting excitedly among themselves.

A sensation of extreme fatigue seized Nate, a belated reaction to his brush with death, and he wished he could curl up on the ground and take a nap. To keep busy, he methodically went about reloading the Hawken and the flintlock.

The mare took to nibbling on the sweet grass.

He idly gazed at the lodge, and saw the family bustling about in the vicinity of the lodge. They were decent people, those Crows, and he was glad he'd met them. He hoped he could prevail on Sitting Bear to travel to his cabin. Winona would be grateful for the company, and Shakespeare genuinely liked making new acquaintances.

Nate stretched and stared at a lofty peak to the south. What were his parents and brothers doing at that very moment? he mused. Did they miss him? Were they still mad that he'd departed New York City so unexpectedly? Or had they forgiven him and wanted him to return?

His peripheral vision registered movement.

Nate shifted to the east, looking toward the rise over which the buffaloes had appeared, and there, seated on a brown stallion, was an Indian warrior.

Chapter Four

For a moment Nate stood still, recovering from his surprise. The man had on a buckskin shirt and leggings and carried a lance. He couldn't determine if the warrior was a Crow or from another tribe, and he wondered how long the Indian had been watching him. A glance over his shoulder confirmed that Sitting Bear had yet to start in his direction. He faced the warrior and waved.

The Indian didn't move.

Puzzled and curious, Nate stepped to the mare and vaulted into the saddle. He gripped the reins tightly and galloped toward the figure.

Immediately the warrior wheeled his horse and disappeared over the crest.

Nate rode hard until he came to the rise, then reined up. Below was a gradual slope and a wide meadow hemmed in by dense forest. The Indian was nowhere in sight. Mystified, he leaned on the pommel and surveyed the woods. Why had the man run off? Was the warrior friendly or hostile?

He waited several minutes, hoping the Indian would show himself.

The woods were quiet, the meadow serene.

So much for trying to establish contact, Nate reflected, and rode back toward the bull. Although the man hadn't made any threatening gestures, Nate was bothered by his presence. He'd learned to regard everyone he encountered in the wilderness as a potential enemy until they demonstrated otherwise.

Joking and laughing, the Crows were finally returning.

Nate reached the buffalo first and dismounted. He debated whether to inform them and decided withholding the news might prove disastrous later.

"Where did you go?" Sitting Bear signed when he was still a dozen feet off.

"I saw a warrior on horseback."

The disclosure brought a worried expression to the Crow's face. He gazed eastward, then swept the south and north horizons. "Do you know which tribe he was from?"

"No."

Evening Star was clearly troubled. She addressed her husband apprehensively.

Sitting Bear responded softly, his forehead creased, in deep thought.

"If you are worried, I can help you move your camp," Nate offered.

"What good would it do? A competent tracker would find us in no time. I say we stay where we are until morning, then we shall move," Sitting Bear stated. "We cannot leave until we are done with the butchering anyway, which will not be until after dark."

"If you are sure," Nate said.

Sitting Bear nodded.

They set about skinning the buffalo. Nate marveled at the skill and efficiency of the Crows. Both Sitting Bear and Evening Star wielded their knives with expert precision, knowing exactly where to cut to speed the process along. They only stopped once, after an incision was made in the abdomen.

Nate watched in fascination as the warrior laid his bloody knife on the ground, then reached into the abdominal cavity and pulled out a handful of intestines.

"Would you like some?" Evening Star queried.

"'No, thank you," Nate answered, his stomach churning, slightly nauseated by the grisly, pulpy mess of entrails.

The Crows each took a portion and began eating ravenously, chewing and smacking their tongues, their chins dripping wet. The little girl giggled as she ate.

Nate pretended to be interested in a distant mountain. He'd been told by Shakespeare that Indians usually ate buffalo intestines and the brains at the site of a kill because neither could be preserved, but the foreknowledge hadn't braced him for the reality.

Far above the mountain a bald eagle soared.

After five minutes the family concluded their snack and resumed skinning the shaggy brute.

Nate noticed Laughing Eyes grinning up at him, her cherubic features caked with gore, and he thought about the child Winona and he planned to have at the first opportunity. He realized that his wife undoubtedly would teach the youngster to partake of intestines too, and he nearly burst into laughter envisioning how his parents would react to such a scene.

Compared to life in the Rockies, New York City was an alien world.

The flickering red and orange flames cast dancing shadows on the interior of the warm lodge. Curling wisps of smoke wafted up and out the ventilation flap, and the aroma of the cooking food permeated the air.

Nate gazed at the pot in which the venison stew boiled. Constructed from the buffalo's paunch, it was supported next to the fire by four thick, straight limbs lashed together at the top to form a peak.

Evening Star monitored the progress of the meal attentively. She kept the stew heated by regularly dropping in heated stones taken from around the fire, and stirring vigorously. Earlier she had added wild onions and turnips to the concoction.

Nate couldn't wait to tear into the food. Butchering the bull and the black-tail had been hard work, and combined with the other events of the busy day had left him fatigued and famished. He glanced at Laughing Eyes, who stood beside her mother, then at the boys, who were seated across from him on Sitting Bear's right.

The lodge inside was typical of those Nate had seen. A brightly painted inner lining covered the lower third of the sides. Hanging at various points on the sides were three bows and quivers, a shield, a medicine bag, and parfleches— rawhide bags used to hold everything from food to herbs. The bedding was rolled up at the rear, and other possessions were scattered along the base.

"We can never thank you enough for the gift

of the buffalo," Sitting Bear reiterated yet again.

"I only wish I could have shot another one for you," Nate said.

"Will you consider staying with us tomorrow?"

"I would like to stay, but I must take the deer meat home," Nate explained.

The warrior shrugged. "I understand."

"May I ask you a question?"

"Of course."

"What are you doing here by yourself? Where is the rest of your tribe?"

"North of here three days' travel. I will rejoin them after I collect the feathers."

"What feathers?"

"Those of the eagle."

Nate reached up and touched his own. "Do you shoot them to bring them down?"

Sitting Bear blinked. "Who would kill a bird to get just its feathers?"

Acutely self-conscious of having demonstrated his ignorance of Indian customs, Nate quickly tried another query. "Do you take the feathers from nests?"

"No, I take them from the eagles."

Nate grinned. "And what are the eagles doing while you are removing their feathers?"

"They try to esape, but cannot."

"Do you catch them in traps?"

"No, with my bare hands."

"How is such a feat possible? Surely the eagles try to claw you."

The warrior nodded. He held out his left arm and tapped a two-inch scar above the wrist. "An eagle did this when I was fourteen."

Nate looked at Strong Wolf and Red Hawk. "Do your sons help you?"

"No. They are not old enough. Soon Strong

Wolf will accompany me, and I will teach him the way that was handed down to me by my father."

"But you still have not explained the reason your family is here alone. It would have been safer to bring friends along, other families who could help out in times of need."

"The shame is mine, so I must do this alone. My family came with me because they love me."

Shame? Nate almost requested an elaboration until he recollected the advice his mentor had given concerning the private affairs of others: Never pry.

"Would you care to hear my story?" Sitting Bear asked.

"Yes."

"Very well." The warrior sighed. "Two moons ago I was one of the happiest men in the Crow nation. I had counted twenty-seven coup and owned fourteen horses. All the young men respected me, and the chief asked my opinion in our councils. My family never went hungry. The Great Mystery smiled on my life."

Nate leaned forward, hanging on every word.

"And then the tragedy occurred," Sitting Bear signed. "One day a hunter reported seeing signs of an Arapaho raiding party near our village. The chief believed the Arapaho were there to steal our horses, and he decided to post guards at night to protect them. I was chosen to stand guard on the second night."

Strong Wolf and Red Hawk both frowned.

"I had worked hard that day," the Crow went on. "I foolishly let myself become tired, and that night I could barely keep my eyes open. For as long as I could I tried to stay awake, but eventually I fell asleep. The Arapahos must have been watching, because as soon as I closed my eyes, they struck. I was hit on the back of the head, and the next thing I knew, one of my friends was shaking my shoulder and shouting at me for letting the Arapahos get the better of us."

Nate looked at Evening Star and noticed her sad countenance.

"The raiders got away with thirty-nine of our horses," Sitting Bear related. "Not only that, but one of those fish-eaters, probably the same one who knocked me out, took the five feathers I had in my hair."

"Fish-eaters?"

"My people never eat the creatures of the rivers and lakes."

Nate nodded his understanding. By calling the Arapahos fish-eaters, Sitting Bear had handed them the ultimate insult.

"I was ashamed in front of my whole tribe," the warrior related. "It was bad enough I let the horses be taken, but the Arapahos added to the insult by leaving me alive. They were letting everyone know of their contempt for my people."

It took Nate a few seconds to grasp the warrior's meaning. By not killing Sitting Bear, the Arapahos had shown they viewed all Crows as less than men. The raiders were saying, in effect, that they weren't worried in the least about the fighting prowess of the Crow warriors and didn't dream the Crows worthy of counting coup on.

"I could not hold my head up anymore," Sitting Bear said. "The younger men mocked me. The chief no longer wanted me at the councils. I made amends as best I could by giving away all of my horses to some of those who lost animals in the raid, but it was not enough to restore my honor."

Now Nate understood the reason the family didn't possess horses. He also comprehended the significance of the quest for new eagle feathers. "So you plan to replace the feathers that were stolen?"

"Yes, and then I will wage war on the Arapahos and recover the same number of horses that were taken."

"All by yourself?"

"Yes."

The forceful sincerity of the reply impressed Nate. "But you will not stand a chance alone."

"I lost them alone. I will recover them alone."

"You will be killed."

Sitting Bear squared his shoulders. "At least I will die with honor and my family will not be shunned by my people."

Nate knew all about the importance of honor and proper behavior to an Indian. Insults must always be redressed and taboos must never be violated. But the task Sitting Bear had set for himself was impossible.

"Tomorrow I will start on the road to reclaiming my manhood," the warrior vowed.

Just then Evening Star walked over bearing bowls of stew. She dutifully distributed one to each of the men, then brought on cakes and a previously boiled flour pudding to which dried fruit had been added to give it a delicious taste.

Nate ate with relish, savoring every morsel. Few words were spoken by anyone; they were all too famished. Except for the noises they made while eating and the crackling of the thin branches fueling the fire, the only other sound was the whispering of the northwesterly breeze against the lodge. So it was that midway through the meal they all distinctly heard the patter of heavy pads from outside followed by the guttural growl of a large bear.

Chapter Five

Strong Wolf and Red Hawk were up and to their bows in a flash. They each grabbed arrows from one of the quivers and turned.

Sitting Bear addressed them sternly while slowly rising. He walked to the side and retrieved his own bow and an entire quiver, then stepped toward the front flap.

Although the very notion of tangling with another bear bothered Nate, he grabbed his rifle and stood. He'd already experienced harrowing encounters with two grizzlies, and if he never saw another bear as long as he lived he'd be happy.

The mother said a few words in Crow.

Silence reigned outdoors. The bear had ceased growling and moving about.

Nate cocked the Hawken and halted to the right of the flap, which was closed but not tied. He caught the warriors' attention and made the sign for "Now?"

"Wait," Sitting Bear said, listening with his left

ear pressed to the liner.

The sound of loud sniffing filtered inside, and part of a paw appeared underneath the flap.

Instinctively, Nate crouched and pointed the barrel at the center of the flap. If the bruin came through the doorway, they'd be trapped. There wasn't another way out.

Sitting Bear motioned with his right arm, signifying not to fire. He crouched and drew his hunting knife.

Perplexed, Nate watched in fascination. The bear paw eased further inside, revealing black hair and claws over an inch long, and he expelled his breath in relief. It was a black bear, not a grizzly! Even though the former were dangerous when cornered, they weren't in the same class with their fierce cousins, the mightiest carnivores on the continent and the scourge of Indians and whites alike.

Grinning at a private joke, Sitting Bear reversed his grip on the knife, holding the weapon by the blunt edge of the blade, and raised it overhead. He waited until the full foreleg of the bear poked within, then brought the hilt down with a resounding thump.

A bestial bellow erupted from the startled black bear and the paw was yanked from view.

Nate laughed as he heard the bruin beating a rapid retreat into the forest at the rear of the lodge. It crashed through the underbrush like a bull gone amok.

"Perhaps I should have invited the bear for supper," Sitting Bear signed, and his entire family joined in a chorus of general mirth.

Chuckling, Nate eased the hammer down and returned to his seat. He resumed eating, and in no time at all had finished the meal. No sooner had he swallowed the last morsel than Evening Star brought seconds of everything. Despite being almost full, he tackled the second portions with as much enthusiasm as he had the first, knowing that it was considered an insult for a guest not to eat every bit of food that was offered.

After the meal the family sat around and discussed every topic under the sun, from the habits of the wildlife to the state of affairs among the Crows and the rest of the tribes inhabiting the Rocky Mountains and the Plains.

Nate learned a great deal about their customs and beliefs. He learned there were approximately seven thousand members of the Crows nation, and that about four thousand were women. Due to the high mortality rate of the men, who daily risked their lives while hunting, on raids, or in defense of their villages, there was a chronic shortage of suitable husbands. The same state of affairs existed in other tribes as well.

Some of their customs were quite intriguing. He discovered it was a serious breach of conduct, punishable by the harshest of penalties, for a parent to strike a male child. Children were taught the correct way of doing things, and then received constant encouragement to always do good and obey all tribal laws. Rarely did the Crows have problems with their offspring.

The subject of chiefs came up, and Nate posed a question when he heard Sitting Bear mention one by the name of Long Hair. "Why does he have such a name when all Crows have long hair?"

"Because none have hair as long as his. When last I knew, it was twice as long as you are tall."

Nate knew better than to doubt the statement, even though he was skeptical. "Does he tie it around his waist so he can walk?" he asked.

"No. He wears it folded at the back of his head. They say his hair has never been cut, never trimmed, since he was a baby. I have talked with him a few times, and I can tell you I have never seen such hair as his. It is the color of fresh snow and as soft as the best robes."

The topic drifted to the subject of buffalo and beaver. Sitting Bear mentioned that he'd noticed declining numbers of both in recent years and attributed the drop to the presence of white men.

Nate grinned and shook his head. "How can you blame us? First of all, there are not more than a few hundred whites in the whole territory. Second, the Indians kill far more of both than the trappers and the hunters."

"All I know is that before the whites came, there were many beaver in all the streams. Now there are fewer, although there are still a lot. As for the buffalo, once every valley in the mountains was home to small herds. Now a person can ride for hours without seeing a single one."

"I would not worry about it," Nate commented. "There are enough beaver to last for a hundred years, and the buffalo will never die out."

The warrior adopted a solemn air. "I pray not. If the buffalo ever die, then all the Indians will fade away too. The Crows, the Arapahos, the Cheyenne, the Sioux, and the Kiowa will all become as dead grass and blow away on the wind."

"You forgot about the Blackfeet and the Utes."

"They will never die off."

"Why not?"

"They are too mean to die."

Nate laughed, and they went on to discuss the benefits the white man had bestowed on the

Indians, such as guns, better knives, and tin pots and pans. Toward midnight the conversataion finally wound down. The children and Evening Star were already asleep under buffalo blankets when Nate turned in. He positioned his blankets close to the door in case he had to relieve himself.

Slowly the fire died down until only the embers were sparkling and gave off occasional sparks.

Lying on his back with his head resting on his hands, Nate gazed at the conical ceiling and mused on the bizarre twists and turns of outrageous Fate. If anyone back in New York City had ever told him he'd one day share a meal with a family of Crows and enjoy every minute of their company, he'd have thought the person to be insane. He looked forward to prevailing on Sitting Bear to visit his cabin. The idea of staying over another day to observe how the warrior obtained the eagle feathers appealed to him, but the obligation of getting meat to his wife and friend took precedence.

Eventually Nate dozed off. He dreamed of lovely Winona, of her dark tresses and unfathomable brown eyes, and imagined he felt the warmth of her pliant body next to his. Then he also imagined he heard soft footsteps and assumed she had gone outside to attend to the call of Nature. Sluggishly, filled with drowsiness from his head to his toes, he imagined that he opened his eyes and gazed at the entrance.

The cruel visage gazing in at him was not his wife's.

Instantly the face vanished, and Nate grinned at the foolishness of his dream. Then he heard Sitting Bear snoring, and he suddenly realized he wasn't asleep. The face had been really there! Shocked, he sat up and seized the Hawken, swiveling to cover the flap.

The hide hung motionless.

Nate shook his head vigorously, striving to wake up. He blinked and glanced at the sleeping Crows, then at the vestige of the fire that scarcely illuminated the interior. None of them had so much as stirred. If there had been someone at the door, one of them was bound to have heard. He decided he must have imagined the incident, after all, and was about to lay back down when his ears registered the muffled tread of a solitary footfall.

Shoving to his feet, Nate inched to the flap and waited for the noise to be repeated. He wondered if he was all excited for no reason. Maybe the bear had returned, and in his dreamy state he'd envisioned the bear's head as that of a human. It was the middle of the night, after all, and few men, even Indians, were abroad after the sun set.

There were no other sounds for over a minute.

Nate pursed his lips, debating whether to retire or investigate. He was tempted to inform Sitting Bear, but refrained because he'd feel like an idiot if there was no one out there. If he had any brains, he reasoned, he'd simply secure the flap and go back to bed. But he couldn't.

A cool breeze caressed his left cheek as Nate emerged into the enveloping darkness. He moved to the right and squatted to prevent anyone who might be lurking out there from taking a bead on his silhouette against the background of the lighter lodge.

From off to the southeast an owl hooted.

Nate was reminded of the hoots he'd heard earlier. He'd forgotten to ask Sitting Bear if the Crow had made the calls. Inching forward, he eased onto his elbows, then flattened, searching in all directions for the nocturnal prowler.

The leaves in the woods rustled from the breeze, and in the west a coyote howled.

Oblivious to the passage of time, Nate stayed immobile. He couldn't go back to sleep until he knew for sure. The prospect of having his throat slit while he slumbered was a tremendous incentive to stay alert. He heard insects, and the faint, hideous scream of a panther, but no more footsteps and there was no hint of movement in the forest.

He twisted and focused on the field. A quarter moon on high cast a feeble radiance on the landscape. He could see the mare and the pack horse, hobbled 30 feet away, moving slowly along while they ate.

Think! Nate chided himself. If there was an Indian spying on the camp, the man must be nearby. He recalled the warrior he'd observed on the rise, and speculated that the same Indian must be the culprit. After five more minutes elapsed and the night refused to yield its secrets, he opted to crawl to the south. If he hid in the high grass, he might be able to catch the warrior in the act.

A bug flew out of nowhere and hit him in the left cheek.

Nate recoiled, then grinned grimly. If he wasn't careful, he'd give himself away. In ten yards he reached a patch of waist-high vegetation and slid into concealment. He turned, his movements methodical, trying to shake the grass as little as possible, and faced the lodge.

Now all he had to do was wait.

Fatigue gnawed at his consciousness, dulling his awareness despite his best effort to remain fully awake. He placed his forearms on the hard earth and propped his chin on top. Something crawled over his left hand, but he ignored it.

The moon arched higher on its westward passage.

Nate's eyelids drooped. He wondered if he was being foolish, if the whole incident might not be the product of his overactive imagination. Those comfortable blankets awaiting him in the lodge were more and more tempting as each minute went by. Sighing, he put his palms on the grass and tensed to rise.

There was brief motion to the west.

All drowsiness evaporated. Nate gripped the rifle and squinted, his eyes riveted to the front of the lodge. The only way someone could get to the Crows was through the entrance. All he had to do was keep watching the flap, and sooner or later the person would appear.

Seconds later someone did.

Nate distinguished a hunched-over figure gliding toward the doorway. He warily pressed the rifle to his right shoulder, then hesitated. Should he fire, when there was a remote possibility the nighttime stalker could be friendly, or issue a challenge?

The figure drew tentatively nearer to the flap.

There wasn't much time to decide. Nate reflected on what Shakespeare McNair would do in the same situation, and cocked the Hawken once more.

Unexpectedly, a second figure materialized, treading on the heels of the first. Then a third and a fourth came into view, all strung out in a line as they crept around the lodge.

There was no doubt the Crows were about to be attacked. Four against one weren't the best odds, but Nate couldn't let those men get inside.

He rose to his knees at the same moment the leading form moved next to the flap, and with the profound hope his wife wasn't about to become a widow he aimed as best he could and squeezed the trigger.

Chapter Six

The sharp retort of the Hawken was punctuated by a shrill screech, and the figure near the flap toppled backwards. Nate crouched and drew his right pistol, and the motion saved his life.

One of the attackers returned fire.

Nate heard the ball whiz past overhead even as he extended the pistol and shot at the second form. The target staggered against the lodge, then straightened and bolted for the sanctuary of the forest.

The other pair also fled.

"Damn you!" Nate bellowed, and burst from cover. He slipped the discharged flintlock under his belt and pulled out its mate, but there was no sense in trying another shot.

All three figures reached the trees and dashed into the dense undergrowth.

Nate was tempted to loose a parting shot anyway. The folly of wasting his last ball disuaded him, and he turned to the one he'd shot.

Shouts arose in the lodge. Sitting Bear snapped

commands, and Laughing Eyes cried.

Exercising extreme caution, Nate stepped over to the man on the ground. As he'd suspected, it was an Indian. He nudged the warrior with his right toe and received no response.

Suddenly the flap swung open and out barged Sitting Bear, an arrow notched to his bow. He almost tripped over the body, halting in amazement.

"They're gone," Nate said, knowing his friend wouldn't comprehend the words but hoping the message would get across. For added emphasis he gestured forcefully at the woods.

The Crow nodded, then knelt and examined the casualty. He muttered a sentence in his own tongue that ended with a familiar term. "Ute."

Nate stiffened and swung around to cover the trees. Where there were four Utes, there might be more. He deliberated whether to pursue them, but the matter was taken from his hands before he could make a decision.

Strong Wolf and Red Hawk emerged. Their father spoke to the eldest and pointed to the west. Without a word they sprinted off.

Nate wanted to ask a question, yet had to refrain because the darkness would obscure his hand movements. He saw his host seize the Ute and start dragging the man inside. As the flap parted, light played over the two Indians. He guessed that Evening Star had rekindled the fire.

Not a sound came from the forest.

Should he stay out and guard the lodge or join Sitting Bear? Nate wondered, and chose the latter. Squatting, he darted inside, and stopped short at finding the Ute blocking his path.

The enemy warrior would never stalk another foe. The ball had hit him squarely in the forehead between the eyes and burst out the rear of his cranium. His dark eyes were wide and lifeless. He wore leggings and moccasins, but no shirt, and a knife was tucked into the top of his pants. Amazingly, his left hand still clutched a tomahawk.

"This is a Ute," Sitting Bear disclosed in sign language.

"I know," Nate said. "There were three more. I think I hit one of them." He paused. "Perhaps you should call your sons back before they run into those three."

"No. My sons must learn the art of war and there is no better teacher than experience."

"They could be killed."

"Life is but the pathway to death."

The profoundly philosophical response wasn't the answer Nate anticipated. He tried another tack. "But they're just boys."

"True. Boys who are eager to become men, and among my people manhood is attained only after coup has been counted for the first time."

Nate glanced at the mother, thinking she might give him moral support, but she hadn't been paying attention. Her gaze rested on the Ute. Her arms were around Laughing Eyes, who had stopped crying.

"We were fortunate there were only four of the skunk-eaters," Sitting Bear stated, and looked at Nate. "And once again you have done my family a great service. How did you know they were out there?"

"They woke me up."

"Truly you have the senses of a wildcat," Sitting Bear remarked. "When we return to my village, I will tell all of my people about the greatest white man I have ever met."

Nate didn't know what to say. He appreciated the compliment, although the blatant exaggeration bothered him. If things kept going the way they were, soon he'd have reputation to match Jim Bridger's.

Evening Star spoke for a minute, pointing repeatedly at the body.

"She says she does not want the Ute left in here all night to soil the air," Sitting Bear translated. "I must haul him out after you are done."

"Me?"

"Yes," the Crow said. "You killed him, so by all rights his hair is yours."

Nate looked at the body. Revulsion filled him at the thought of slicing the warrior's scalp off. He'd done the horrid deed before, but it became more difficult to do each time.

"Is something wrong?" Sitting Bear asked.

"I grow weary of taking scalps," Nate confessed.

"You have that many?"

"More than I will ever need."

Sitting Bear shook his head in amazement. "I have known one other man who had more scalps than he needed, and he was an old chief who had counted at least one coup for every one of his seventy-two years."

"That is a lot," Nate agreed, placing his hand on the hilt of his knife. He wished there was a way he could avoid scalping the Ute, and he grinned at an idea that popped into his mind. "May I ask you a question?"

"Certainly."

"Please bear with me, because I do not yet know all the ways of the Crows. In return for the kindness you have shown me, I would like to give you a gift."

"You have already given us the buffalo."

"I know. But the bull was for your whole family. This would be a personal gift from me to you."

"What is this gift?"

"The Ute's scalp."

The warrior's mouth fell open. "I have never heard of such a thing."

"Would you accept such a gift?"

Sitting Bear assumed an intently thoughtful expression. He reached out and touched the Ute's hair, then glanced to his right at the string of 14 scalps already adorning the teepee. "You are very kind in making such an offer, but I cannot accept. The Ute's hair is yours. You must be the one to scalp him."

"I was afraid you'd say that," Nate said in English, and knelt beside the dead man's head. He leaned the Hawken against the side and slowly pulled his knife out.

Evening Star spoke to Laughing Eyes in a stern manner, emphasizing her point with firm gestures.

Stalling, his stomach slightly queasy, Nate looked at the warrior. "What does your wife say?"

"She is explaining that Laughing Eyes must never again cry in times of danger. Did you hear her?"

"Yes."

The Crow frowned. "Such behavior is not tolerated. Women, as well as men, must learn to be brave. Are white women brave?"

Caught off guard by the question, Nate had to think of all the white women he knew. "In their own way they are as brave as the men, although very few of them have ever taken part in war or been in fights."

"Our women do not fight either, unless the village is being attacked. Then they all become as fierce as rabid wolves."

Nate girded himself for the task at hand.

"The Utes do, though," Sitting Bear said.

"Do what?"

"Let their women fight. That is because they are less than animals and have no knowledge of the proper ways of men and women. Some women even go on raids."

The revelation startled Nate. What if the other one he'd shot had been a woman?

"I have a friend who killed a Ute woman in battle," Sitting Bear went on. "He said she fought as well as any man and he was sorry to have to take her life. Now her hair is one of his prized scalps and he would not part with it for a dozen horses."

"How nice," Nate commented, and gripped the top of the dead Indian's hair. He inserted the tip of his knife into the skin at the hairline and proceeded to neatly remove the grisly trophy.

"Well done," Sitting Bear stated when the job was done. "I have not met many whites who know how to take hair, but you do."

"Thank you."

"Would you like my wife to wash it for you?"

"If she would be so kind," Nate sighed, and gladly handed over the hair when Evening Star came over in response to her husband's instructions.

The patter of rushing feet arose outside, and a moment later Strong Wolf and Red Hawk dashed excitedly into the lodge. Both talked at once. Sitting Bear held his right arm aloft, quieting them, then posed a series of questions that they dutifully answered.

"What happened?" Nate asked when the warrior paused.

"The Utes are up to their old tricks. There were four horses hidden west of here and they made good their escape."

"What will you do now?"

"Stay."

"But they might return."

"I cannot leave until I have five feathers to replace those that were stolen," Sitting Bear declared.

"Are five feathers worth the lives of your loved ones?"

"My mind is made up," the Crow stated obstinately.

Nate reclaimed his rifle and moved to one side as the boys attended to stripping the corpse and then dragged it from the lodge. He moved close to the fire and held his hands over the flames, enjoying the warmth. Sometime ago Shakespeare had explained to him the concept of Indian honor, and detailed how in some tribes a man would do anything to regain prestige once he had fallen from social grace. In a way Nate felt sorry for Sitting Bear. The disgrace of having let the precious horses be stolen was more than the poor man could bear, and now the Crow was willing to sacrifice his family rather than endure the disgrace.

What should he do? Nate asked himself. Stay and assist the warrior or head on home? He wanted to return to Winona quickly, but he couldn't bring himself to desert Sitting Bear in the man's hour of need.

The Crow came over. "I apologize if my words seem hard. My family and I have discussed this issue and we are all of one mind."

"I understand."

"Since you will probably leave early tomorrow, I thought I should tell you again that we are grateful for all you have done."

"Who said I am leaving?" Nate responded.

"You plan to stay?"

"I would like to see how you catch eagles with your bare hands."

The warrior's eyes narrowed. "Is that the only reason?"

"Yes."

"You are not obligated to us in any way."

"I know," Nate said, and remembered the question he had to ask. "Was that you today hooting like an owl?"

"About the time you shot the black-tail?"

"Yes."

"That was me. When I heard your shot, I believed you might be a Crow so I called to you as an owl would. We often call to each other by imitating the owl. When there was no answer, I knew you were either a stranger or an enemy. That is why I approached you with my arrow ready to fly."

"Perhaps you can teach me the call sometime."

"Gladly." Sitting Bear turned to walk off. "We should get sleep. Tomorrow will be a busy day."

"Should I take the first watch?"

"What?"

"We should take turns doing guard duty until daylight," Nate proposed. "I will go first."

The Crow grinned. "There is no need. The Utes will not be back tonight."

"How do you know?"

"I know," Sitting Bear stated enigmatically, and moved to the bedding he shared with his wife.

The boys returned bearing the clothing, weapons, and other personal effects belonging to the slain Ute. They deposited the items in front of Nate.

"Give these to your father," Nate told them. "I have no need of them." He reluctantly walked to his blanket and lay down, listening to the family discuss his gifts, and positioned the rifle next to his side. With a hostile band of Utes roaming the area, he wasn't about to go to sleep. Instead, he rolled on his back, propped his head in his cupped hands, and reflected on the whims of Fate. Here he was, about to participate in an eagle hunt, when if he possessed any intelligence whatsoever he'd ride out at first light. As the Crow had said, tomorrow would undoubtedly be a busy day.

Just so it wasn't his last.

Chapter Seven

Whispered conversation brought Nate awake, and he opened his eyes to find golden rays of sunlight streaming in the open flap. Startled, he sat up and clutched the Hawken. He couldn't believe he'd fallen asleep! Outside the lodge were Strong Wolf and Red Hawk, both engaged in sharpening arrows. He looked behind him and saw Sitting Bear, Evening Star, and the little girl by the fire.

"The new day has begun," the warrior signed.

Nate numbly nodded and ran his left hand through his hair. He had no idea when he'd finally dozed off, but he felt as if he'd only slept for an hour or so.

"We have tried to be quiet so as not to wake you," Sitting Bear disclosed. "I did not know you are such a late riser."

Late? Nate peered through the doorway again and saw the tip of the sun peeking above the eastern horizon. What did the Crow consider to be early? he wondered, and rose sluggishly. He went outside, smiled at the boys, and walked into the forest to relieve his bladder. The crisp morning air invigorated him, and he swung his arms back and forth to get his circulation going. Birds chirped lustily on all sides, greeting the dawn in their own inimitable manner. The avian choir assured him there were no Utes in the area. He propped the rifle against a tree, attended to business, and returned to the lodge.

Strong Wolf glanced up and his hands flew. "My father has told us you are going with him today. It is good. He is a brave man, but he should not be out there alone."

"I agree," Nate concurred, and entered.

Evening Star beckoned him. In her right hand she held several small, round cakes.

"Would you like to eat before you leave?" Sitting Bear queried.

"Yes," Nate said, joining them. He took a seat and gratefully accepted the cakes.

"We have a two-hour trip to the eagle peak," Sitting Bear revealed. "If all goes well, we can be back here by midday."

Nate placed the cakes in his lap to pose a question. "Is that two hours on foot?"

"Yes."

"Then I suggest we ride to save time."

"We could save a little, perhaps," the Crow said, "but most of the journey is uphill over very steep terrain. The horses would only slow us down and we would be forced to leave them a mile from our destination. While I thank you for the offer, your animals would be safer if we left them with my family."

"Whatever is best," Nate stated, and dug into his breakfast. In five minutes he consumed the cakes and enjoyed a cup of blackberry juice Evening Star provided.

Sitting Bear spoke to his wife, then slung a leather pouch over his left arm, grabbed his bow, aligned his quiver on his back, and started for the flap. "I am ready if you are," he announced.

"Wait," Nate said, and quickly checked the rifle and both pistols to ensure they were loaded. Once done, he walked to the entrance and grinned. "Lead the way."

They exited, the warrior in the lead. He took the time to speak to both of his sons, then gestured and led the way to the northwest.

Nate stayed a few yards behind the Crow, moving as silently as he could, his eyes constantly roving from side to side as he alertly scanned the undergrowth. His host set a rapid pace that he easily matched, and they covered several miles without incident.

The forest eventually ended at the base of a sparsely covered hill, which they negotiated. Then they started up a high mountain. On the craggy heights above were bighorn sheep, white dots against the brown of the cliffs the animals frequented.

Nate saw Sitting Bear slow and peer intently at a thicket to their right. He halted when the Crow did, and he was all set to inquire about the reason for the delay when the warrior stooped and lifted a fair-sized stone. Puzzled, Nate kept silent.

Sitting Bear suddenly hurled the stone into the middle of the brush, and out darted a large rabbit. It picked up speed swiftly. In a fluid, practiced motion the Crow whipped an arrow from the quiver, notched the shaft, elevated the bow, and took a fraction of a second to aim.

Nate watched in fascination. The rabbit bounded all out, and he didn't see how anyone could hit such a streaking target. He heard the humming vibration as the string was released, and glimpsed the flashing arrow. To his amazement, the rabbit abruptly tumbled end over end, dead before it came to a stop, the shaft jutting from its twitching body.

The warrior hastened to recover the animal and came back grinning happily. He slung the bow over his right shoulder and nodded at the peak far above them.

"Why did you kill it?" Nate asked.

Sitting Bear stuck the exposed portion of the shaft under his left arm and answered with his hands. "To use as bait. Come. We have a long way to climb."

They did exactly that, going steadily upward. The slope, at first, was gradual and dotted with trees and patches of shrubs.

Nate tilted his head and spied a solitary eagle soaring on the currents to the south. The distance was too great to determine if it was a golden eagle or a bald eagle. Both were numerous in the Rockies, as were many varieties of hawks.

The climb became more arduous the higher they ascended. Fields of enormous boulders had to be traversed and occasional crevices skirted. Sheer cliffs were bypassed. The sun rose steadily, warming even the rarefied air at the upper elevations.

A layer of sweat caked Nate's skin by the time they came to an incline spanning a hundred yards in length and twice that distance in width. Short alpine grass covered the ground.

Sitting Bear stopped and turned. "We are here."

Nate gazed uncertainly at the grassy stretch. "This is where you will catch the eagles?"

"Yes." The Crow headed for the center of the tract.

Perplexed, Nate followed. He scanned the heavens for eagles, but saw none. On another mountain to the north, near the summit, was a large herd of elk making for the lower regions.

Slowing, Sitting Bear studied the area ahead. He .voiced an exclamation in Crow and walked to a shallow depression, where he knelt and began feeling the surface with his fingers extended.

Nate placed the rifle stock on the ground and simply observed, at a loss to explain the Indian's behavior. He thought about Winona, and passionately wished he was with her instead of on a forlorn peak many miles away. In all fairness, he mentally noted, he had only himself to blame. He was the one who had craved deer meat when there were other types to choose from. The lake near his cabin abounded in fish. There was also plenty of elk and small game in the neighborhood of his homestead. Even a small herd of buffalo. If he'd settled for a continued diet of fish or a different game animal, he'd be snug and warm in his own home where he belonged.

The warrior chuckled and began tugging at something. Moments later he succeeded in lifting a three-foot-square latticework constructed from thin limbs.

Amazed, Nate stepped nearer. The limbs had been woven tightly together to form a sturdy platform on which there rested an inch or two of soil topped with grass. Perfect camouflage, he realized, and grinned at the ingenuity displayed. Under the covering was a circular pit, its sides braced by a layer of flat stones.

Sitting Bear shoved the latticework to the left and looked at Nate. "This pit was dug by my father's father. There is another over there," he revealed, and pointed at another slight depression ten feet off. "Conceal yourself within. Soon an eagle will come. If I am fast enough, I can get all five feathers I require from one bird. If not, we will be here a while."

"Is there anything I can do to help?"

"Just do not make any noise. Not even a sneeze. And whatever you do, be sure not to bump the covering. Eagles have great eyesight and can see a blade of grass tremble from a mile up."

Nate knew that to be an exaggeration, but he refrained from debating the point. He moved to the spot indicated and succeeded in removing the cover to a second pit. A glance back disclosed his companion positioning the bait at the edge of the trap by jamming the bloody tip of the arrow that transfixed the rabbit into the soil. Nate eased down onto his buttocks, pleased to find there was enough room to sit up. The rifle went between his legs. By poking his fingers into the lattice-work, he grasped the cover and slid it over him, leaving an inch gap on the side facing the Crow's hiding place so he could view whatever transpired next.

Sitting Bear dropped into the first pit and covered himself. He aligned the top to leave a gap for his arms next to the rabbit.

The simplicity of the technique appealed to Nate, and he marveled yet again at the adaptability of the Indians to their environment. They had met Nature on less than equal terms and bested her. Whether they were hunting buffalo or obtaining feathers, whether they were selecting medicinal herbs or edible plants, they demonstrated an affinity for the wild that the whites couldn't hope to match. Oh, there were a few white men who had lived among the Indians long enough to be their equals, but in general the Indians had learned to live in harmony with the wilderness while the white race sought to conquer it.

Time went by slowly.

Nate made himself as comfortable as he could. A layer of gravel covered the bottom, and he was tempted to lift the covers and tear out some grass by the roots to use as cushioning. To do so would spoil the trap, however, so he bore the minor irritation in resignation. He leaned against the side, his eyes on the rabbit, his mind adrift in reflections of his childhood in New York City. Sometimes, especially in periods of inactivity, he missed his family and civilization.

He dwelled on the lovely woman he'd planned to marry, Adeline Van Buren, and hoped she'd secured another eligible beau, someone her father would approve of. No doubt she had. With her natural beauty, wit, and charm, she could take her pick of any man in New York. He'd never quite understand what she'd seen in him. In his eyes, she'd been a goddess and he her supplicant.

Who would ever have thought that he would give up a Venus like Adeline to marry an unaffected Indian woman who was as far removed in her manners and customs from the ways of polite society as the sun from the earth? Truly the whims of circumstance and design were beyond comprehension.

Nate began to feel sleepy, and he struggled to keep his eyes open. He didn't want to miss the moment when an eagle first took the bait. Try as he might, though, the lack of rest took its toll and his leaden eyelids closed.

A peculiar fluttering sound reached his ears.

Instantly Nate's eyes snapped open. A loud swishing filled the air, and out of the blue plummeted a diving bald eagle, its terrible talons pointed downward, its wings held erect as it dived for the kill. With bated breath he saw the mighty bird grab hold of its prey, and at that very moment a pair of sturdy arms surged from under the adjacent latticework and firm hands seized its legs.

The eagle promptly strained upward, its wings beating powerfully, voicing an unusually weak chittering cry from so magnificent a creature.

Sitting Bear straightened, the covering on his shoulders, his sinews rippling as he fought to restrain the bird. He managed to grip both its legs in his left hand and plucked at its white tail feather with his right.

At last the eagle understood what was happening and twisted, trying to peck the Indian in the head and neck. Its own wings prevented the bird from craning its neck far enough.

Nate stood, tossing the covering to his pit aside, and scooped up his rifle. He wanted to assist his friend but had no idea what to do.

The Crow managed to tear out four feathers and was working on the fifth. His left hand slipped, and the eagle turned even further and snapped at his left shoulder. He ducked to avoid the bird's wicked beak, then wrapped his fingers around a fifth white plume.

Enraged to the point of being berserk, the eagle flailed and thrashed savagely, its wings striking the warrior again and again. It was able to tear its left leg free, and like a striking rattlesnake it lanced one of the biggest beaks in the bird kingdom, a beak that could shred the toughest of flesh, at its tormentor.

Nate gazed in horror as the eagle tore into Sitting Bear's face.

Chapter Eight

Nate surged out of the pit and raced toward the Crow. "Sitting Bear!" he cried out, unable to fire because of the proximity of the bird.

Voicing a shrill shriek, the eagle suddenly took wing, speeding skyward with the dead rabbit still clutched in its steely talons.

The warrior pressed his left hand to his face. Blood trickled over his fingers as he gazed at the departing creature, a wry smile on his lips.

"Are you all right?" Nate inquired urgently in English, temporarily forgetting himself. He quickly rephrased the query in sign language.

Sitting Bear nodded absently, his eyes brimming with triumph. He lowered the hand to reveal a nasty cut three inches long, from just under his left eye down to his chin.

"That eagle almost took your eye out," Nate declared. "What do you have to be so happy about?"

Smiling wider, Sitting Bear extended his right arm and slowly unfolded his right hand. Resting in his palm was the fifth feather.

"You did it!" Nate gestured excitedly. "Now you have all the feathers you need."

The warrior collected all five plumes and climbed onto the grass. He stared up at the eagle, still visible but receding rapidly, and spoke in the Crow tongue.

Nate was delighted at the success of their quest, for more reasons than one. Now they could return to the lodge, and before too long he would be on his way home. If it wasn't for the threat of the Utes, all would be well.

"I thanked the eagle for the gift of its feathers," Sitting Bear explained after a minute. "My first task is done. Next I will recover the horses stolen by the Arapahos."

"Are there other warriors who will go with you?"

"No. Until I reclaim my honor, my friends shun me."

"They do not behave like friends."

Sitting Bear shrugged. "It is the Crow way." He gingerly ran a finger along the slash he'd sustained. "I will have a scar," he commented proudly.

"We should wash it at the first opportunity or it might become infected," Nate noted.

"Evening Star will apply herbal medicine. She is a skilled healer."

Nate tilted his neck and spied the dwindling form of the great bird. "I learned an important lesson today."

"What lesson?"

"I would rather have a feather given to me than pluck one myself."

The Crow laughed heartily.

After covering the pits, they commenced the

descent, the flush of triumph and the pull of gravity conspiring to hasten their pace so that they reached the bottom in much less time than the climb had taken.

"I have an idea," Nate signed as they were crossing the hill side by side. "Why not bring your family to my cabin and spend time with us? My wife will be delighted, and I know your wife would not mind."

"True. Women are more social than men. But I must think on it."

"Why?"

"Because if we visit you, my quest to restore my standing in my tribe will be delayed."

"What harm can a few days do? Besides, I have another friend staying with me whom you might like to meet."

"What is the name of this friend?"

Nate grinned. "Carcajou."

The warrior pondered the news. "Yes, I would like to see Carcajou again. Perhaps we will come with you. But we have a problem."

"What?"

"We travel very slowly without horses to pull our lodge. My sons and I must do the hauling while Evening Star carries our daughter and parfleches. You would be delayed getting back."

Nate stared straight ahead, debating whether to offer his animals to transport the lodge. He abruptly halted when he spotted figures moving in the trees below. There were men on horseback riding toward the hill. He grabbed the Crow and yanked him flat.

"What is it?" Sitting Bear signed.

Nate simply pointed. He recognized the riders as two Indians. The foremost warrior appeared to be inordinately interested in the ground. A tracker, Nate realized, and the man was smack dab on their trail.

"Utes," Sitting Bear said.

"Two of those from last night," Nate speculated. What could have happened to the third? Had his ball eventually killed the man?

"They have not seen us yet."

Twisting, Nate scoured the slope for a place to take cover. There were a few trees off to the left, and a low cluster of brush to the right. Neither was ideal, but under the circumstances there was no alternative. He nudged the Crow and indicated the three trees. "We should make our stand there."

"Lead the way."

Nate turned, placed the rifle in the crooks of his elbows, and crawled rapidly southward. He glanced repeatedly at the forest, marking the progress of the Utes. The pair rode out of the woods at the same time he reached the trees, whose trunks were no thicker than his thigh and afforded scant protection, and rose to his knees.

Sitting Bear crouched behind the next tree and drew an arrow from his quiver as he unslung his bow.

Advancing at a surprisingly leisurely rate, the Utes ascended the hill. The one at the rear was talking animatedly.

"They believe we are hours in front of them," Sitting Bear related. "Once the tracker sees our return tracks, they will know we are here."

Nate estimated the duo would pass within 20 yards of their position, and started to state as much when he remembered there was no sign motion for the word "yard." He modified his statement. "They will come within twenty paces of us. I will take the first man if you will slay the second."

"When you fire, I will."

Easing onto his stomach, Nate braced the barrel on the bole and waited. The lead Ute carried a lance, while the second warrior held a bow. Since Indian men could hurl a spear or shoot an arrow with uncanny speed and accuracy, he took slight comfort from the edge his rifle gave him. If he missed, there wouldn't be an opportunity to reload it; the flintlocks would be his last resort.

Onward came the warriors, the lead rider leaning over his animal's neck to better see the soil.

Nate took a bead on the first Ute's chest, his pulse quickening. He glanced at the slope, estimating the point where their return tracks had ended when they crawled to the trees, and decided to fire when the warriors were at least 15 feet from the spot.

The second Ute fell silent and idly surveyed the countryside. He stared at the mountain to the west, the mountain to the northwest, and then at the trees.

Nate's breath caught in his throat. The Utes were 40 yards off, too far to guarantee both would be killed at the outset of the impending fight. They must come closer! He remained still, well aware of the keen eyesight Indians possessed.

Displaying no alarm, the Ute strayed his gaze farther south.

Relieved, Nate grinned and adjusted the position of his left elbow.

The second Ute's head unexpectedly snapped toward the trees again and he reined up, calling out to the first man, who also stopped.

Dread welled within Nate like a bitter bile, and he cocked the Hawken in anticipation of what would happen next. Nor was he disappointed.

Gesturing excitedly, the second Ute abruptly whooped, hefted his bow, and charged. A second afterward the lead rider followed suit.

Casting caution to the wind, Nate stood and aimed at the first man. He delayed firing for several seconds, wanting to be sure, then squeezed the trigger.

Simultaneous with the cracking discharge the foremost Ute performed a remarkable maneuver. He swung down on the off side of his animal, using his left forearm and his left foot to retain his hold on the horse, minimizing the target he presented.

Nate knew the ploy firsthand, knew it would take an exceptional shot to dislodge the Indian from his perch. He lowered the rifle and drew both pistols.

Thirty yards out the second Ute was in the act of drawing his bowstring to his cheek when Sitting Bear's arrow took him high on the left side of his chest. He jerked backwards and tumbled from his mount, landing on his side, then pushed erect with the shaft jutting from his torso.

Sitting Bear stepped into the open, another arrow nocked, intent on making his next shaft the final one. He totally ignored the first Ute.

Since the tree afforded some protection, Nate stayed where he was. He lifted both flintlocks, trying for a clear shot at the leader, unwilling to shoot unless he was certain of scoring.

The tracker was only 20 yards away, his horse bearing down on the trees at full gallop, his foot and forearm the only parts of him in view.

Knowing he shouldn't let the Indian get any closer, Nate dashed from his marginal cover, racing to the west, trying for a better angle. He had managed four strides when the Ute suddenly straightened and hurled the lance. Instinctively, he ducked, thinking the warrior had thrown the weapon at him. But he was wrong.

Standing tall, exposed and unsuspecting, Sitting Bear let his arrow flash forward. With his gaze riveted on the wounded man, he never saw the slim spear that arced through the air and struck him just above the right hip. The impact spun him around. He dropped his bow and fell to his knees, his face distorted in agony, clutching at the lance.

The fury that dominated Nate's mind caused him to take a reckless gamble. Already the lead rider was swinging from sight again, and only his head and shoulders were above the horse. Nate rashly pointed both pistols and fired them together.

Twin balls bored into the Ute's forehead, and he uttered a short scream as his arms flung outward and he toppled to the hard earth.

Nate pivoted, concerned about the second enemy, but Sitting Bear's arrow had pierced the center of the man's chest and laid him out flat. Sitting Bear! He ran to his friend, who was doubled over and trembling, and squatted next to him.

The Crow looked up, grimacing, beads of sweat on his brow. He hissed a few words in his language and nodded at the Utes.

Nate placed the flintlocks down and examined the wound. The lance had transfixed Sitting Bear, with about half its length sticking out his back. Blood flowed copiously, covering his thigh and leg in red.

Gasping with the effort, the warrior moved his

hands to say two words. "Pull it."

Nodding, Nate licked his lips and moved around in front of the warrior. He knelt, seized the bloody spear in both hands, and looked into Sitting Bear's eyes. "This will hurt like hell," he stated.

Although he hadn't understood a word, Sitting Bear bobbed his chin and gulped.

Nate tensed his arms and legs, then tugged on the lance with all of his strength. To his amazement, the shaft came out easily, so easily he lost his balance and fell onto his buttocks. He flung the spear to the ground, then wiped his blood-soaked hands on the grass.

Sitting Bear was in terrible torment. He grunted, closed his eyes, and bent in half.

Drawing his knife, Nate stood and ran to the Ute he'd shot. The man wore leggings, and Nate swiftly cut strips of buckskin to use for bandages. Holding them in his left hand, he raced back to his friend and frantically attempted to stop Sitting Bear's life fluid from gushing forth. All his efforts were unavailing. The buckskin strips became drenched. Nate stood, about to go cut more, when the drumming of hooves arose to his rear. Whirling, he was stunned to discover another Ute bearing down on them—a Ute armed with a fusee.

Chapter Nine

Fifty feet separated Nate from the onrushing Indian. All three of his firearms were empty, and the knife he held was no match for the warrior's gun.

Fusees were smooth-bored flintlocks the Indians received in trade with the fur companies, particularly the Hudson's Bay firm. The barrels were invariably shortened to accommodate ease of handling on horseback. All fusees were notoriously inferior to the rifles of the trappers and mountain men, both in range and accuracy. At under 25 yards, though, they were formidable weapons.

Nate was surprised the Indian hadn't fired already. He saw the man weave as if drunk, and noticed a crimson stain on the warrior's buckskin shirt. In a flash of insight he perceived it must be the one he'd shot outside the lodge.

The Ute slowed and tried to level the fusee.

Desperately casting about for anything he could employ to defend himself, Nate saw Sitting

Bear's bow lying in the grass. He dropped the knife and scooped it up, then slid an arrow from the Crow's quiver. A hasty glance showed him the Ute had stopped and was taking aim.

During his early teens Nate had taken an interest in archery and learned the basics. He'd spent many an idle hour practicing, and learned the proper way to draw the string and sight along an arrow. After the first several months he'd been consistently able to score a hit within two or three inches of the center of the target.

Now he notched a slender shaft constructed from ash to a bowstring composed of buffalo sinews, elevated the bow, and pulled. To his consternation, the string barely moved. He looked at his adversary and saw the Ute slumped forward, the fusee pointed at the grass. Again he endeavored to pull the string back, straining his muscles to their utmost, and succeeded in drawing the sinews to his chin.

The Ute was straightening.

Nate's left arm trembled as he tried to hold the bow steady. He attempted to aim, but the tip of the shaft kept moving up and down.

Scowling in sheer hatred, the Ute lifted the fusee to his shoulder once more.

A sensation of impending doom spurred Nate to make a last, herculean effort. He brought the string all the way to his ear, held his breath for a second, and let the arrow fly.

A blurred bolt of wooden lightning leaped from the bow to the Ute. The shaft struck the Indian below his left ribs and twisted him around. He grabbed the arrow, teetered precariously, and pitched over.

Nate grasped another arrow and raced toward the warrior. He had to be sure before he could attend to Sitting Bear. As much as he disliked finishing off a helpless foe, he had no choice.

Exhibiting remarkable endurance, the Ute rose to his knees. He'd dropped the fusee as he fell, and it lay a yard to his right. With the shaft protruding from his body, he moved slowly toward the gun.

Despite himself, Nate admired the tenacity of the Indian. He nocked the second arrow as he ran, and when he came within eight feet of the Ute he halted and whipped the bow up.

Apparently hearing the footsteps, the warrior glanced at the white man. He stared at the razor point fixed on his chest and uttered a defiant challenge in his own language, shaking his left fist in anger.

Nate let the bow do his talking. This time the shaft pierced the Ute high on the right side of the chest, and the man fell without voicing another sound. Satisfied by his victory, but disturbed by the deed, Nate returned to Sitting Bear.

The Crow was almost unconscious. His eyelids fluttered like the wings of a hummingbird, and he breathed in loud, ragged gulps. Blood continued to gush from the wound.

In a frenzy of anxiety, Nate racked his brain for something he could do. If the bleeding didn't cease soon, Sitting Bear would assuredly die. Since bandages hadn't worked, he must try something else. But what?

Inspiration hit him when his eyes strayed to the trees. He tossed the bow to the earth, retrieved his knife, and sprinted to the source of the Crow's salvation. Working furiously, he hacked off and collected an armful of thin limbs, raced to Sitting Bear's side, and proceeded to make a fire. He tore out handfuls of dry grass to use as tinder, then turned to the blaze itself. Since the flint he normally used was in a pack back at the lodge, he restorted to a trick he'd seen performed by a trapper at the rendezvous. He quickly reloaded one of the pistols and held the gun at ground level, next to the limbs.

Nate cocked the flintlock, then packed kindling all around it. He hesitated before squeezing the trigger, afraid the tactic wouldn't work. A groan from Sitting Bear reminded him of the necessity, and he fired into the ground. Thankfully, stray sparks ignited the dry grass on the first shot. Elated, he bent down and nursed the initial pinpoints of flame by blowing lightly on the tinder.

It took several minutes of sustained effort, but Nate succeeded in getting the fire going. He stuck the pistol under his belt.

Sitting Bear was on his right side, unconscious, his leggings drenched.

Nate waited until the fire crackled before selecting a branch that would suit his purpose. He gripped the outer end and slowly turned it over and over, letting the flames char the opposite tip. Not until it glowed bright red did he lift the branch and turn to his companion. He rolled the Crow over, exposed the hole, and began cauterizing the wound, inserting the scorching tip as far as it would go.

The grisly operation seemed to take forever. Nate repeatedly reheated the tip. Each time the branch touched Sitting Bear's flesh, there would be a loud sizzling and a pungent smell. He came close to gagging twice. Eventually the bleeding stopped. By then the rims of the entry and exit holes had been burnt a crisp black.

There was no rest for the weary. Nate gathered all of his weapons, reloaded his guns, and walked toward the horse belonging to the third Ute. The animal, a fine black stallion, had moved less than 40 feet from the spot where its rider had been slain. It nibbled at the grass, and glanced up once as Nate approached. He moved carefully so as not to spook the steed.

True to Indian custom, the horse had a war bridle attached to its lower jaw with a lark's-head knot. The rope reins dangled from its neck.

Nate slowed to a snail's pace when a yard from the stallion. "Be a good boy," he said softly. "Don't run off."

The horse paid him no attention.

Tentatively extending his right hand, Nate succeeded in grasping the reins. He patted the animal's neck to reassure it, then swung up onto the bare back. Happily, the stallion didn't resist. "Just don't buck me off," he said, and goaded the steed forward, finding the horse easy to control. Swinging in a loop, he rode back to his friend.

One of the other Ute mounts was 60 feet to the north. The last animal had strayed to the west a good 40 yards.

Nate stared at Sitting Bear, then at the horses. He thought about the sacrifice the man had made to atone for the Arapaho raid and came to a decision. Wheeling the stallion, he rounded up the others.

Only then did Nate try to revive the Crow, but without water his efforts were unavailing. He slung the bow over his left arm, then carefully lifted Sitting Bear onto the horse and held him up while climbing on behind him. Gripping the warrior around the waist, Nate headed out. He wished he could carry the weapons belonging to the dead Utes, but his arms were full as it was.

So began the long ride to the lodge. Nate was

compelled to travel slowly for fear of jarring Sitting Bear and starting the hole bleeding again. He constantly scoured the forest for additional enemies. Fortunately, none appeared.

The golden orb dominating the heavens climbed steadily higher. Low gray clouds filtered in from the west, then bigger and darker ones. The breeze intensified, becoming a brisk wind.

Nate looked over his shoulder and frowned at the sight of the blackened horizon. Roiling harbingers of Nature's elemental fury were bearing down on the woodland, and he estimated they would overtake them before he covered another mile.

As was often the case at the higher elevations in the Rocky Mountains, the storm raged across the landscape with astounding rapidity. The trappers and the Indians often remarked about the incredibly swift changes that occurred. One minute the sky could be sunny and clear; the next minute the atmosphere could be in intense turmoil. Many a hunter had found himself taken unawares by a freak hailstorm or snow shower in the middle of the summer, to say nothing of the fierce thunderstorms that shook the very earth and gave the impression the world was coming to an end.

Nate saw numerous lightning flashes, and heard the peal of distant thunder. He urged the stallion as fast as he dared, and searched for shelter. The tops of the trees were already bending, and the moist smell of rain was in the abruptly humid air. He disliked being in the midst of so many towering giants, each one capable of attracting a bolt from above. Scattered drops began to fall, and just when he resolved himself to taking shelter at the base of a trunk, he spied the cliff.

To the north, barely visible above the forest, was a high outcropping of rock. It ran from east to west and was crowned with pine trees.

Thankful to find any sanctuary at all, Nate made for the cliff. His arms were feeling the effects of the sustained strain of holding Sitting Bear on the stallion while leading the spare animals, and he looked forward to taking a break.

The forest went almost to the cliff wall. Nate paused at the edge of a narrow strip of grass bordering the base to pick where he would make his stand. More and more rain descended every second, and he blinked as drops splattered on his brow.

To the east, perhaps 50 feet away, was a spacious opening. Nate rode to it, and smiled at discovering a cavern 20 feet high and the same distance wide that extended back into shadowy recesses. He lost no time in dismounting and taking the horses inside. As he gently deposited the Crow on the dusty floor, the storm unleashed its full fury.

Lightning crackled nonstop. The attendant thunder rumbled continuously. Like the yowling of a pack of wolves, the wind howled tremendously loud. The sky became an inky canvas.

Nate knelt and watched the trees dancing as if alive. He hoped the lodge would be able to withstand the savage onslaught, and wished he'd reached it first.

Sitting Bear groaned.

A bigger problem prsented itself. What was he going to do after he got the Crow home? The warrior would be in no condition to hunt or defend his family for days, probably weeks. Nate debated whether he should stick around, and the mere thought provoked anxiety. He simply couldn't stay away from his wife for that long.

Winona would worry herself sick. There had to be an alternative, but what?

A brilliant flash lit up the cavern when a nearby tree was struck, and the resultant thunderclap startled the horses.

Nate rose and soothed them, holding onto the reins and speaking calmly. In a couple of minutes they quieted and he returned to Sitting Bear.

Gradually the frequency of the lightning strikes abated, but the rain and the wind persisted.

The prospect of spending more than an hour in the cavern annoyed him. He wanted to reach the lodge as soon as possible, and he was inclined to ride out before the storm ended completely. Such exposure, though, would aggravate Sitting Bear's condition, and he resigned himself to staying put for the time being.

With nothing better to do, Nate ruminated on his future. In a couple of weeks Shakespeare would help him set out beaver traps and teach him the tricks of the trade. The idea of becoming a full-fledged trapper, of relying on his wits and strength to provide his livelihood, appealed to him. He'd learned how to be largely independent since leaving civilization, and the more he learned the better he felt. No longer did he depend on the market and the mercantile for everything under the sun. He could feed and clothe himself. He was his own man, and the feeling of self-reliance was the greatest he'd ever known.

Nate felt sorry for all the people back East who had no idea what they were missing. They went about their humdrum lives, day in and day out, totally reliant on others for their well-being. He would never allow himself to slip into such a deplorable state again, not even—

A scratching noise from the right interrupted his musing.

Twisting, Nate tensed as he laid eyes on a bulky, squat form moving toward him. He rose, leveling the Hawken, unable to identify the creature until a streak of lightning briefly illuminated his surroundings. With the flaring glow came recognition, and with recognition apprehension. The last thing he wanted to do was tangle with a beast that rivaled the grizzly in ferocity.

Coming toward him was a dreaded wolverine.

Chapter Ten

Roughly bearlike in shape, wolverines were considerably smaller than bruins, with the males reaching four feet in length, standing a foot and a half high at the shoulders, and weighing between 40 and 50 pounds when in their prime. But when compared pound for pound with every other mammal on the continent, wolverines rated as the most powerful in existence.

Nate had heard tales galore about the prowess of the gluttons, as they were commonly called. Wolverines had been known to drive panthers and grizzlies from their kills, and one trapper had observed a wolverine bring down a full-grown moose trapped in heavy snow. They were notorious for following trap lines and either eating the bait or consuming the animals that had been caught. They also raided cabins, and in the process they would deposit their musk on everything they didn't eat.

The indistinct form flowed nearer, then halted and loudly sniffed the air.

Of all the luck! Nate thought, and cocked the rifle. He didn't know if the creature was entering or leaving the cavern. All he cared about was that it departed, and did so promptly. If the horses got its scent, there would be hell to pay.

Still sniffing, the wolverine took a few steps. Another lightning strike revealed its beady eyes were fixed on Sitting Bear.

Nate deduced the beast must smell the dried blood on the Crow's leggings. Knowing its appetite for any and all flesh, he feared he would have to fight it off. Once the shimmering glare from the heavenly bolt faded, all he could see was the carnivore's black form. If he had to fire in the dark, he couldn't guarantee he would hit it.

The wolverine suddenly growled.

"Go away!" Nate shouted in the hope the sound of his voice would drive the thing off.

Instead, the wolverine moved closer still.

"Go!" Nate bellowed.

Snarling deep in its throat, the beast charged.

Instantly Nate squeezed the trigger. He saw the wolverine jerk backwards and fall, and he thought for a second that he'd killed it. His mistake became apparent the next moment when the animal scrambled to its feet and attacked once more.

This time it bounded toward him.

One of the horses whinnied in terror as Nate drew his right pistol and extended his arm. He stood his ground, his lips compressed, until the wolverine was almost upon him, and then fired the flinklock at close range.

Again the animal was hit, and again it spun around and went down. As before, it heaved erect and leaped.

There was no opportunity to reload. Nate

released the pistol, seized the rifle by the barrel, and waited until the wolverine was almost at his very feet before he swung the Hawken like a club. The shock crashed into its skull, dazing it for a moment, and he grabbed at his left pistol to finish the animal off.

Yet another thunderbolt cast the cavern in a bright halo.

Nate could see the wolverine's upturned, feral visage, see its mouth wide and its tapered teeth poised to snap. Startled, he pointed the flintlock at its sloping brow and squeezed the trigger, the booming retort making his ears ring even more.

The ball penetrated the wolverine's head between its eyes, and the brute immediately went into convulsions. It thrashed about on the floor, pawing at the ground as its tail whipped in a circular motion.

Prepared to sell his life dearly should the beast renew its attack, Nate braced himself and raised the Hawken on high. He'd club it with his dying breath, if need be.

The terror of the woods uttered a short hiss, sprawled onto its stomach, and went limp.

Nate remained motionless for a full minute before he dared poke the creature with the rifle. After prodding it four times he smiled and vented a sigh of heartfelt relief. Another few inches and the wolverine would have had him.

Outside, the rain and the wind slackened, the downpour becoming a drizzle. Most of the lightning and thunder now occurred to the east.

The horses were fidgeting, so Nate went over and calmed them before attending to the reloading of his guns. He stepped to the cavern mouth and watched the storm clouds sailing rapidly in the direction of the lodge. To the west sunshine caused the soaked vegetation to glisten.

Eager to get going, Nate nevertheless delayed mounting until the rain completely stopped. When he headed out, he stuck to the clearer tracts between the trees to avoid brushing against the drenched limbs and being drenched to his skin. He looked back at the cavern only once, wondering if he should have skinned the wolverine, and decided it was too late to turn around.

The pristine forest seemed renewed by the rain, washed clean of all dirt and dust. Even the wildlife was invigorated. The birds came to life with renewed vitality, warbling or chirping songs in joyous abandon.

Mankind could learn a lot from Nature, Nate reflected. Animals knew how to live life to its fullest; they displayed a passionate zest for existence that most humans sorely lacked. Where men and women were prone to gripe about their lives and bemoan their fates, the animals simply accepted their place in the scheme of things and savored every moment.

Nate pushed the stallion faster than before. He was worried that Sitting Bear had not regained consciousness, and speculated the Crow's life would depend on Evening Star's ministrations. So it was that he smiled broadly when he glimpsed the meandering stream through the trees and shortly thereafter emerged from the woods. He glanced to the right and left, and off to the north stood the lodge, maybe a quarter of a mile distant. At last!

Bringing the stallion to a gallop, Nate covered the wet ground swiftly. Farther to the east was the storm. Thanks to the heavy downpour, the stream had expanded a foot on either side, the water rushing at twice its previous rate. He noticed a log floating downstream. Calmly perched on top, apparently enjoying the ride, was a chipmunk.

Nate expected to see the mother or the boys in the vicinity of the lodge, but none of them were in evidence. He also observed there was no smoke curling up from the top, which he deemed odd since the temperature had dropped a few degrees. Perhaps, he reasoned, they'd taken shelter inside when the storm approached and simply stayed there.

Unexpectedly, Sitting Bear mumbled a few words and stirred. His head snapped up and he looked around.

"It's all right," Nate said, unable to use sign language. "We'll be with your family in a bit."

The Crow spoke a single word, then sagged.

As yet no one had appeared.

"Evening Star! Strong Wolf!" Nate shouted. "Get out here!" He focused on the flap, anticipating it would open, and when he covered another 40 yards without anyone coming out he reined up, certain something was wrong. Even though the family couldn't speak English, they knew his voice. At the very least one of the boys would venture from the lodge to investigate.

Sitting Bear began muttering.

Nate scanned the woods and the field. Sparrows flitted about in the trees immediately behind the lodge, which indicated there was no one lurking in the forest. He looked at the field on the other side of the stream again, and realized with a start that his mare and pack animal were gone.

Stunned, Nate rode to the lodge and halted ten feet from the door. Only then did he see the slash marks in the buffalo skin and a broken bow lying in the dirt nearby. He quickly dismounted and lowered the Crow to the ground, then hefted the Hawken and advanced to the flap.

Something moved to his left.

Nate spun, his thumb on the hammer, and was horrified to see Strong Wolf crawling from the high weeds. The boy's face and shoulders were caked with blood. "No!" he cried, and ran to the youth, stopping a foot short when he laid eyes on top of the boy's head and discovered someone had scalped him. "No," he repeated weakly.

Strong Wolf had his neck craned so he could look up, an eloquent appeal mirrored in his eyes. He said a sentence in Crow, the words rasping in his throat, and coughed up crimson spittle.

Kneeling, Nate placed his hand on the youth's right shoulder. He saw a wide trail of blood extending back into the weeds and shuddered.

Gritting his teeth, Strong Wolf raised his right arm and pointed at the lodge.

Nate nodded and sprinted to the doorway. He opened the flap and ducked inside, the Hawken at the ready, prepared for anything. Or so he believed until he beheld the savagely butchered form of Red Hawk in the middle of the floor. The boy's hands had been hacked off and his eyes gouged out. His mouth hung wide, exposing the fact his tongue was gone. Nausea swamped Nate, forcing him to back from the lodge and gasp for fresh air. No matter how many times he witnessed the results of the atrocities Indians perpetrated against one another, he couldn't get used to such merciless slaughter.

A questioning voice diverted his morbid thoughts.

Nate swung around to find Sitting Bear trying

to sit and gazing about in bewildered anxiety. He walked to the warrior and signed for him to lay back down.

The Crow did so, then lifted his head. "Where is my family?"

"I do not know yet," Nate partly lied.

"They should be here."

"Rest. I will check on them."

"I should help," Sitting Bear said, pressing his palms on the grass.

"No," Nate responded. "You are in no condition to get up. Stay where you are and I will take care of everything."

Reluctantly, the Crow complied. His eyes closed and he breathed noisily.

Swiftly Nate returned to Stong Wolf, who had collapsed onto his forearms, and squatted.

The boy glanced at him and feebly manipulated his hands. "Is my brother dead?"

"Yes," Nate answered, sadness filling his soul.

"My mother and sister?"

"They were not in the teepee."

Strong Wolf gazed at his father. "What happened?"

"The Utes attacked us," Nate explained, eager to pose queries of his own. "What happened here?"

"More Utes," Strong Wolf responded, moving his arms with considerable effort.

"Let me roll you over," Nate proposed.

"No."

"You will be able to use your hands easier," Nate explained, and gingerly grasped the boy by the shoulders. Despite a frantic shake of Strong Wolf's head, he rolled the youth onto his back. And promptly wished he hadn't.

The young Crow had been gutted, his abdomen

sliced open from side to side, and his intestines dangled from the cavity.

Nate recoiled, aghast.

"I tried to spare you," Strong Wolf said, his hands gesturing sluggishly.

A sudden, red-hot rage made Nate tingle. He gazed into the boy's eyes and saw reflected a knowledge of the inevitable. Still, he had to try. "Do not move. I will make bandages."

"You would be wasting your time. I am dead."

Nate could only swallow. Hard.

"Will my father live?"

"I honestly cannot say."

Profound sorrow lined the youth's tender visage. "The Utes will have much to celebrate."

"Tell me what happened," Nate prompted.

Strong Wolf licked his lips and inhaled deeply. "They came just before the rain, a band of nine warriors. Red Hawk and I were practicing with our bows and saw the war party riding toward us from the southwest. I knew we could not protect our mother and sister from so many, so I sent him into the lodge to get them while I ran to your horses." He paused. "We would have returned them."

A peculiar lump had formed in Nate's throat.

"The Utes were faster than I thought, and they were on us before I could bring the horses. I saw Red Hawk push Mother and Laughing Eyes inside while he blocked the doorway and defended them. And then six of them attacked me. I put an arrow in one," Strong Wolf related proudly.

"Did you see what happened to your mother and sister?"

"No. I heard them screaming and the laughter of the Utes, who had left me for dead in the field after scalping me." Strong Wolf blinked, and there were tears in his eyes. "I wanted to help them, but could not."

"You did all any man could have done."

"I am not yet a man."

"You are in my eyes."

A smile creased the youth's lips. He abruptly arched his back, uttered a strangled whine, and died, his wide eyes fixed on the bright blue sky.

For a minute Nate didn't budge, too overcome with emotion. His mind seemed to be swirling like a tornado, and there was a bitter taste in his mouth. These had been decent, friendly people, people he'd grown to like, people he was proud to know. To have their lives so callously taken was the height of injustice. The boys' best years had been ahead of them, and now they were nothing more than mutilated corpses awaiting the embrace of the cold earth.

He stared into the distance, a fiery resolve solidifying within him, a grim determination to see those responsible punished. If he didn't seek retribution, no one else would. If nothing else, he could attempt to rescue Evening Star and Laughing Eyes and see them and Sitting Bear safely to their tribe.

Nate stood, his mind made up. One way or the other, the Utes were going to pay. Even if it cost him his own life.

Chapter Eleven

Nate was seated next to the fire, dozing off about midnight, when a firm hand nudged his left leg. He snapped awake, staring blankly at the interior of the lodge until gruesome memories of the events of the day returned in a rush.

Again someone nudged him.

Fully alert, Nate glanced down at the Crow warrior lying on his left. He smiled and used his hands to say, "How are you feeling?"

"A little better," Sitting Bear signed, and looked around. "Where is my family?"

Nate hesitated.

"Tell the truth," the warrior admonished.

Although loath to add to the man's misery, Nate complied. "Strong Wolf and Red Hawk are dead, killed by Utes."

"And my wife and daughter?"

"I wish I knew. I could not find their bodies, so I believe the Utes took them."

Sitting Bear closed his eyes and sighed.

Had he fallen asleep again? Nate wondered

hopefully.

The Crow looked up again, profound inner pain lining his countenance. "This has been the saddest day of my life. I have lost the boys who were the joy of my heart, and because of my wound I cannot go after the fish-eaters who have taken the rest of my family. What have I done to deserve such anguish?"

"You did nothing."

"I must have done something. All suffering is for a purpose."

Nate studied the warrior's face, amazed the man could be so calm after learning of the death of his sons. Or was Sitting Bear crying inside, where it hurt the most? "I will make you some stew to eat," he offered.

"There is another thing you must do."

"What?"

"Save Evening Star and Laughing Eyes. The Utes will take them to their village. You must intercept the band before then or my wife and daughter will be lost forever."

"I plan to go after them as soon as you recover enough to take care of yourself."

"Go now."

"I cannot."

"Why not?"

"Even if I wanted to, it would do no good. I cannot track at night."

Sitting Bear peered at the top of the lodge. "Stars. I did not notice them before." He stared at Nate. "Then you must go at first light."

"I will not leave you alone."

"Then take me with you."

"You must be delirious. You know you are in no condition to travel."

Exasperation flicked across the warrior's face.

"Surely you understand that my life is unimportant. You must save my wife and daughter and not worry about me. Leave enough jerked meat for me to get by and some water. I will be fine."

Nate frowned. "I am sorry. No."

Sitting Bear put his hands on the floor and endeavored to sit, but he only succeeded in rising to his elbows. He swayed, then sank down with a groan.

"See? You are too weak to fend for yourself. If I left you behind, it would be the same as killing you," Nate told him.

"Please go after them in the morning."

"No."

"I beg you."

"No," Nate signed emphatically. "Now rest while I prepare food."

The Crow's mouth compressed into a thin line.

Feeling supremely guilty, Nate devoted his attention to cooking a tasty bowl of stew using the remains of a rabbit he'd shot earlier for his own supper. Both the buffalo and buck meat had been stolen by the Utes.

As he heated the water he noticed a smudge of dirt on the back of his left hand, reminding him of the hour he'd spent digging graves and burying the two boys, and thinking about the grisly job turned his stomach. He remembered how full of vitality they had been, and he could well imagine the depth of Sitting Bear's love for them.

The warrior grunted.

Nate turned to discover the Crow sitting up, flushed from the effort. "You should not exert yourself," he advised.

"I must convince you I am well enough to take care of myself," Sitting Bear replied. "If not, I must take more drastic steps."

"What do you mean?"

Ignoring the question, the warrior examined the charred hole in his side. "Did you do this?"

"Yes. It was the only way I could think of to stop the bleeding."

"You did well." Sitting Bear gazed at the wall. "Those vermin even took our parfleches. All my wife's herbs were in one of them."

"I can collect more herbs tomorrow if you will describe the plants to me," Nate said.

"You will not be here tomorrow," Sitting Bear stubbornly insisted. "Not if you are truly my friend. I would do the same for you if the situation were reversed."

"I will think about it," Nate offered in the hope of having the subject changed.

The warrior smiled wanly. "Once you have done so, you will realize you must go after them."

Nate placed a few extra limbs on the fire to build up the flames. He gathered an armful of wood before settling down for the night, and he hoped it would be enough to last them until dawn.

"You must be very careful tracking the Utes," Sitting Bear mentioned, apparently taking Nate's departure for granted. "They are extremely clever. My people have fought them for many generations, yet we have not wiped them out yet."

"I do not intend to get my head shot off."

"The war party probably headed southeast toward their main hunting grounds. All Ute villages are in that direction. The nearest will be two or three days off. You must ride hard to overtake them," the Crow said. "Is your mare a good animal?"

"They stole my mare and pack animal."

Sitting Bear's mouth dropped. "Then how will you ever catch them?"

"We brought back the three horses belonging to the warriors who attacked us, remember?"

"No."

"You revived somewhat when we were riding back. I thought you would," Nate said. "One of the animals is a fine black stallion. I will use it."

"They will stay close to the stream for the first day, then take a trail that leads to the Green River."

Nate stirred the stew and tasted its temperature with his right index finger, then turned to the Crow. "There is something I do not understand."

"What?"

"I suspect the three Utes we fought were the ones who tried to sneak up on us last night. But where did the second group come from? And why did the larger party attack your family instead of us? If all of them had gone after us, we would never have stood a chance."

Sitting Bear suddenly pressed his hand to his temple. He swayed for a moment and sat down.

"Are you all right?"

"A little dizzy. It will pass," the warrior said. "As for your question, the four who crept up on the lodge must have been part of the larger war party. When you drove them off, they went back to their companions and told them what had happened. Then they watched our camp and saw us leave."

"We should never have gone."

The comment made Sitting Bear's face become a mask of sorrow. "I agree. The blame is all mine."

Nate realized his mistake and promptly urged, "Go on with what you were saying."

"In order for the warriors who were driven off to prove their courage, they came after us themselves. I wish all of them had done so."

Nate swept the lodge with his gaze. "Why did they leave your teepee standing?"

A faint hint of a smile curled Sitting Bear's mouth. "Indians rarely steal lodges. It is difficult for a war party to make an effective escape while dragging twelve or more poles the size of small trees and a heavy buffalo-hide cover."

Amazed that the man could joke in the midst of such tragedy, Nate grinned and tested the stew again. It still wasn't hot enough. He moved closer to the warrior. "Let me feel your forehead."

"Why?"

"To see if you have a fever."

"I am fine."

"I want to see for myself," Nate stressed, and placed his left palm above Sitting Bear's brow. For an instant he had the impression he'd touched a scorching coal. "You are burning up."

"I may have a slight fever," the Crow allowed.

"You must lie down and rest. If you overexert yourself, there could be serious complications. Trust me."

"Are you a healer?"

"No, but I know a little about medicine."

"White man's medicine."

"And what is wrong with our medicine?"

"I do not know exactly because I have never met a white medicine man, although I was told such do exist. But they must not be very skilled because whites are so unhealthy."

"We are not," Nate said.

"Then why is it so many white men get mouth

rot? My people never have problems with their teeth, yet in white men such a disgusting condition is quite common."

Nate had no answer for that one. Shakespeare had told him that tooth decay was unknown among the tribes.

"And if your medicine men do know what they are doing, then why do quite a number of white men suffer from a whirling brain?" Sitting Bear went on.

"I do not know," Nate admitted. When an Indian said someone's brain was in a whirl, it meant the person was insane.

"Our medicine men teach us valuable things like which foods are best and those we should avoid. They keep us healthy at all times, and that is why we live so much longer than you whites. In my village alone there are eleven men who have seen over one hundred winters go by, yet I have never heard of a white living that long."

"Few of us do."

Sitting Bear nodded. "Beause your medicine is wrong or weak or both. Perhaps your Great Chief should send white medicine men to us and we will train them properly."

"I will mention your idea to the Great Chief the next time I am in . . ." Nate paused because there was no hand gesture for Washington, D.C. He finished the statement using language the Crow would understand. " . . . the village where all our chiefs gather."

"Does this village have a name?"

"Yes, but it is unlike any name you know."

"Tell me."

Nate did so, employing English.

Clearly perplexed, Sitting Bear repeated it several times. "You are right. I have never heard such a strange name. What does it mean?"

"The city was named after our first Great Chief, the man who defeated the British and secured peace for us all."

Sitting Bear nodded. "You refer to the war between the redcoats and the tea-drinkers. Yes, I known all about it from a trapper." He stopped and pondered for a moment. "Is it true what he told me about the manner of fighting in that war?"

"What did he say?"

"That when both sides wanted to fight, they would march up to each other in straight rows, stop, and shoot until one side or the other had lost too many men to continue."

Nate grinned. "Some of the battles were fought in that way, yes."

"And they did not hide behind trees or rocks?"

"Not in those instances."

Sitting Bear shook his head slowly. "White men are so strange. I do not understand why the Great Mystery put them in this world."

"Some white men have wondered the same thing."

The warrior looked into Nate's eyes. "Please do not be offended by my remarks. They do not apply to you. Out of all the men I have known, you are one of the bravest. And in your inner spirit you are very much an Indian."

"Thank you," Nate responded, feeling self-conscious at being the subject of such blatant flattery.

"I mean every word, Grizzly Killer. You are a man who is at home in the wilderness. You will never leave it."

The assertion troubled Nate. He thought of his parents and friends and Adeline. Especially Adeline. "One day I might, just to visit those I love."

"But you will be back."

"How can you be so sure?"

"It is your nature," Sitting Bear signed.

Nate heard the stew boiling and turned to it. The tantalizing aroma of the rabbit filled the lodge. He stirred the stew, thinking about New York City. Maybe he wouldn't go back after all. The prospect of being away from Winona for a month or two was singularly unappealing. Perhaps it would be for the best if his family never heard from him again. They'd simply assume he'd been slain and go on with their lives after a period of mourning. Why stir them up by going back?

Some things were better left alone.

Chapter Twelve

Nate awakened to the cheerful sounds of chirping birds. He rolled onto his back, stretched, and sat up. Sunlight streamed in the open doorway, which puzzled him because he knew he'd shut the flap before retiring. He idly glanced at the fire and received a shock.

Sitting Bear was already awake and in the process of preparing the morning meal. He wore a clean pair of leggings and had washed the dried blood from his body. Arranged in his hair were the five eagle feathers obtained at such a terrible price. He looked around and smiled. "Time to greet the new day."

"What are you doing up?" Nate asked while sliding out from under his blanket.

"One of us had to make breakfast and you were sound asleep."

"That is not what I meant. You should be resting, taking it easy until your wound heals." Nate stood.

"I wanted to prove to you that I am capable of

taking care of myself so you will go after my wife and daughter," the warrior explained. "I have prepared a pouch containing lots of berries and wild onions. I also saddled the black stallion for you."

Nate glanced at the door. "Saddled him?"

"Yes. I found your saddle in the field where the Utes must have tossed it. They are not very fond of the kind white men use."

A rejoinder concerning Indian saddles was on the tip of Nate's tongue, but he kept his peace. Many Indians liked the simplicity of bareback riding, but there were those who used saddles that were constructed from rawhide and stuffed with grass or buffalo hair. While the Indians considered them comfortable, the whites genereally disdained them.

"So will you save Evening Star and Laughing Eyes?" Sitting Bear inquired anxiously.

Nate bent over to retrieve his rifle, giving himself time to weigh all the factors involved. His friend was mending much faster than he'd anticipated, and it certainly seemed as if Sitting Bear would fare all right on his own. There was also the fact that the sooner he started, the sooner he'd be reunited with Winona. Straightening, Nate nodded, tucked the Hawken under his arm, and used sign to say, "I will leave right away."

Raw relief was mirrored on the Crow's countenance. "You have made me the happiest man alive. But first you should eat. You will need all your strength to kill the fish-eaters."

Nate attended to his morning toilet, ate, and went out again to mount the stallion. Once in the saddle he glanced at the spot where he'd buried the butchered boys, keenly aware the same fate awaited him if he failed, then wheeled the horse. He looked at the doorway and saw Sitting Bear watching him.

"May the Great Mystery guide your footsteps."

Nate nodded and rode to the southeast, feeling the warm sun of his cheeks and a light breeze in his hair. The stream was at its former level, enabling him to cross easily, and soon he had settled into the flowing rhythm of the stallion. Thankfully, the horse didn't mind the saddle, leading him to surmise a previous owner had used an Indian version.

True to Sitting Bear's prediction, Nate found plenty of fresh tracks to indicate the war party had indeed healed the same way. Since the Utes had evidently ridden off just as the storm passed on, the prints of their animals were distinctly imbedded in the soil. He had no difficulty following them.

He worried about how he would save the mother and daughter once he caught up with the band. Nine Utes were formidable opposition. He'd have to improvise, to use his head. Above all, he had to ensure he spotted them before they saw him. The element of surprise was in his favor, the only advantage he possessed, and without it rescuing the Crows was a forlorn proposition.

The minutes went by swiftly, as did the terrain. Nate pushed the stallion, hoping to catch up with the war party before nightfall, encountering abundant wildlife everywhere. There were herds of elk and buffalo, squirrels chittering in the trees, ravens soaring on the air currents, and an occasional predator or two in the form of a wolf or a fox. As always, he felt as if he were traveling through a veritable paradise, a Garden of Eden where many of the animals simply stood and stared at him because they had not yet learned to fear the mere sight of a human being as did their bestial cousins back East.

He stopped at midday and rested on the bank of the stream while munching on a wild onion. Minnows darted about in the water, and an insect that resembled a thin spider swam from side to side on the surface. After consuming the snack he knelt and drank deeply, savoring the cold liquid.

Once in the saddle, Nate resumed his southeasterly journey. He estimated the Utes were no more than two or three hours ahead and moving much slower than he was. Apparently they believed themselves safe from reprisals. He was a bit surprised they hadn't waited for their three companions to catch up. But then, maybe the reason they were going so slowly was to give the trio an opportunity to do just that. Little did they know the threesome would never lift another scalp.

At one point he spied an enormous grizzly bear off to the east. The monster watched him go by, its kingly composure undisturbed, and did not display any aggression.

The stream wound through a series of low hills, then flowed into a wide valley. Antelope and deer filled their bellies on high grass. Ground squirrels scampered from his path. It took him an hour to traverse the valley. Beyond, the tracks took a course between two hills, and there lay a small plain hemmed by mountains. He reined up in surprise when he saw a column of smoke curling skyward on the far side.

Puzzled, Nate angled toward a stand of trees a few hundred yards to the right. The Utes must have stopped, but he couldn't understand why. Plenty of daylight remained, and it seemed unlikely the Indians would waste it without a good reason. He studied the position of the smoke and deduced the camp was almost three quarters of a mile away.

Off to the south five vultures circled high above the landscape, seeking carrion.

Nate rode into the trees, a cluster of cottonwoods, and dismounted. He secured the reins to a limb and ventured to the south edge where he could see the smoke unobstructed. Now what should he do? Trying to approach the camp when the sun was up qualified as certain suicide. The wise thing to do was wait until nightfall.

The whinny of a horse came from the north.

Startled, Nate pivoted and beheld a pair of Indians heading in the direction of the smoke. They were less than 50 yards off, both mounted and both armed with bows.

Utes!

Nate crouched and slid behind the trunk of a cottonwood. One of the Indian mounts whinnied again. He wondered if the animal had detected the airborne scent of the stallion, and he moved toward his horse to prevent it from answering. But he was too late.

The black stallion vented a neigh loud enough to rouse a hibernating bear.

Halting in midstride, Nate saw the warriors stop and look at the trees. Would they investigate or keep going? He hefted the Hawken and waited for their reaction, barely breathing.

The pair turned their steeds and rode straight toward the cottonwoods.

Nate hurried to the stallion, keeping as low as he could and using the boles for cover. He didn't want to tangle with the duo if a conflict could be avoided. Gunshots were bound to alert the rest of the Utes.

Fidgeting and tugging on the reins, the stallion had its eyes on the approaching horses.

Quickly Nate reached his animal and wrapped his left arm around its muzzle. He could see the Indians through the trees. Neither betrayed any hint of alarm. They appeared to be mainly curious. He began to guide the stallion to the west, moving slowly, hoping the shadows screened them from hostile eyes.

The taller of the warriors halted and made a motion as if he wanted to continue on to their camp. Responding in the Ute tongue, the second man kept coming.

Nate stopped within a yard from the last of the cottonwoods. He held the stallion still except for the twitching of its tail, and rubbed its neck to keep it calm.

The inquisitive Ute reined up near the trees and peered into the stand, leaning forward, his dark eyes narrowed. He scanned from right to left and back again.

This was the moment of truth, Nate realized. The stand was approximately 30 yards in diameter, and many of the cottonwoods were quite large. Plenty of underbrush further served to counceal him and his mount. The odds of escaping detection were excellent provided the stallion cooperated.

Evidently satisfied there was nothing to see, the Ute turned his steed.

Suddenly the big horse acted up, trying to pull from Nate's grasp. Its buttocks bumped a trunk.

Nate held on with all of his might. He saw the Ute twist and look back, and he was certain the warrior would ride into the stand to check things out. Instead, after a minute, the Ute rejoined his fellow tribesman and together they made to the southeast.

Relief washed over Nate and he expelled a long breath. He stayed where he was until the warriors were far away, then let go of the stallion. That had been too close! He'd have to be much more careful in the future or Evening Star and Laughing Eyes would never be rescued.

Deciding to remain in the stand until evening, Nate moved to the center, tied the stallion so it wouldn't get any ideas about wondering off, and sat down with his back to the trunk. He devoted himself to formulating a strategy for dealing with the war party. When the time came to snatch the mother and daughter, a diversion might enable him to pull it off without a hitch. What kind of diversion, though? He formulated and discarded various ideas, absently listening to the sounds of insects and the songs of the birds. After a while his eyelids began to droop, and before he knew it he was asleep.

A sharp noise brought Nate rudely awake, and he glanced up in consternation when he realized darkness had descended. How long had he slept? He stood, amazed to see faint stars through the branches, and looked westward where hues of red, orange, and pink rimmed the horizon. The sun had set within the past half hour, he guessed.

The stallion shifted, one of its hooves cracking a twig with a pronounced snap.

Now Nate knew what had wakened him. He undid the reins, climbed on board, and rode out of the cottonwoods, bearing in the direction of the Ute encampment. A flickering ghost of light marked the exact location. He shook his head to clear his mind of lingering sluggishness, and surveyed the plain in case there were warriors ahead.

The war party, as it turned out, had made camp at the base of a densely wooded slope on the east side of the narrow stream. There was plenty of water, plenty of game, and the forest gave them a convenient avenue of retreat should they be attacked by a superior force.

Nate perceived there were actually two fires, not one, spaced ten yards apart, and he distinguished figures moving around the camp. He slanted to the right, riding toward the woods bordering the plain. The same forest that the Utes would use as an avenue of escape was also their weak spot. Moving slowly as not to create enough noise to give himself away, he gained the cover of the woods without mishap. The steadily gathering gloom compelled him to cautiously pick his way among the trees until he reached the slope to the rear of the band. After tying the stallion yet again at a sufficient distance from the enemy to ensure they couldn't hear it should the horse neigh, he crept through the vegetation toward the fires.

Laughter and boisterous conversation arose, contrasting with the deathly stillness of the forest. Nate bent over at the waist as he covered the final 20 yards, advancing from trunk to trunk and thicket to thicket. Less than eight feet from the end of the woods he flattened and crawled to a cluster of high weeds at the very limit. Inching his right hand foward, he gingerly parted the stalks and leaves.

Both fires were only 25 feet off. To the right were the tethered horses, including the mare and the pack animal. Five Utes were seated around the fire on the left. Four warriors were sitting near the one opposite. Laughing Eyes sat on the ground close to them, watching her mother serve food to the band.

Nate congratulated himself on his cleverness. Perhaps a diversion wouldn't be needed, after all. If he waited long enough, the Utes were bound to go to sleep. He learned from Shakespeare that Indians rarely posted guards at night unless they were certain of being attacked.

A strapping warrior unexpectedly stood and walked directly toward him.

Chapter Thirteen

Nate froze, not knowing what to do, afraid to so much as blink. Panic seized him, and for a moment he believed the Ute must have spotted him. Only when he observed the warrior hitch at the leggings he wore did comprehension dawn. He relaxed slightly, his left hand holding the rifle firmly.

Whistling softly, the Ute glanced over his shoulder and made a comment that caused the others to laugh. He paused, studying the trees, and finally stepped to the right and disappeared behind a towering pine.

Straining his ears, Nate detected the splattering of urine on the ground. He dared not turn his head, and didn't until the warrior emerged and moved back to the campfire.

Another Ute barked a command at Evening Star, who promptly went over to him.

Nate saw one of the warriors wearing a crude rawhide bandage, and realized it must be the Indian Strong Wolf had wounded. The man was in a bad way, doubled over and holding his left side, sitting almost on top of the flames. A chest wound, Nate guessed, and probably close to the heart.

Evening Star was busily cutting meat from a cooked haunch, her despondent features reflecting the misery in her soul.

From the aroma Nate's nostrils detected, he knew the band was eating part of the buffalo he'd slain, and he wryly wished the meat would give them all indigestion. A lean Ute sporting four eagle feathers in his hair rose and went to the horses, returning moments later bearing a parfleche stolen from Sitting Bear's lodge. Nate recognized it as the one in which Evening Star stored her herbs and medicines from the decorative beadwork on the pouch.

The lean warrior knelt alongside his wounded fellow, then snapped a sentence at the Crow woman.

Obediently, Evening Star ceased working on the meat and hurried off. The parfleche was shoved into her hands, and a curt gesture from the Ute signified she should tend to the one who had been shot.

Nate scowled in anger. The war party was using her to do every chore imaginable, reducing her to the status of a slave. He thought about the nine or ten hours of night remaining and his scowl deepened. Would they abuse her in *that* manner too?

Evening Star opened her bag and took out some herbs. Next she removed the injured warrior's bandages, then proceeded to administer treatment.

A deep admiration for her courage caused Nate to think of his own wife, who had demonstrated her own resourcefulness more than once. He unconsciously compared them to Adeline Van Buren, imagining how the socialite would behave under the same circumstances, and almost laughed aloud. Adeline would have been in hysterics by now, pleading with her captors to let her go and offering them all the wealth her father owned.

Nate rested his chin on his forearms and bided his time. The Utes talked and talked. After nursing the wounded warrior and feeding the others, Evening Star was permitted to take her daughter in her arms and sit off a ways. Four of the Utes retired relatively early, curling up in their robes and falling asleep.

A northwesterly breeze kicked up, fanning the flames and carrying glowing red sparks aloft.

The hours dragged by. Nate was impatient for the remainder to doze off, and finally all did but two. This pair was engaged in an earnest dialogue and gave no indication of stopping soon. Evening Star had been given a blanket, and she was lying on her back with Laughing Eyes at her side.

To the west a wolf howled.

Nate speculated the time must be after midnight, and he wondered if the talkative twosome intended to stay awake all night. He felt stiff from lying on the ground for so long, and he keenly desired to stretch his legs.

A minute later the last of the war party lay down to sleep.

Nervous expectation revitalized Nate. He waited a reasonable length of time to guarantee the Utes were all slumbering, then eased backwards, twisted, and crawled to the right, keeping to the edge of the woods until he was directly to the rear of the horses. Now came the perilous part. His gaze riveted on the Utes, he inched from the vegetation and slid to the animals, expecting at any second that one of the war party would awaken, spot him, and shriek a warning to the others.

A few of the horses heard him and glanced back, but none snorted or reared.

Nate reached the mare and slowly rose, his knees bent, stooped over, and stepped to her neck. He rubbed her behind the ears and whispered softly, letting her know there was no reason to be skittish. The Utes had tied all of the animals to a pair of logs, evidently hauled from the forest for that very purpose, to guarantee the horses wouldn't stray away during the night. He moved to the log and quickly untied the mare, then did the same with his pack animal. Gripping the reins of both, he led them into the trees at a snail's pace, and when he had put a good 15 yards behind them he went faster, taking the two horses to where he'd left the stallion. He secured both and hastened back.

The Utes were still sleeping soundly.

Exercising the same care as before, Nate crawled to the horses again. Earlier he'd seen a rope lying next to one of the logs, and he now used it to prepare a little surprise for the Indians. Going from horse to horse, he looped the rope around the front legs of each animal, then securely knotted the end to the log. That done, he crept to the Crows.

Mother and daughter were sound asleep. In the flickering light from the fading fire tear streaks were visible on Evening Star's cheeks. She had her left arm draped protectively over Laughing Eyes.

Nate crouched, then hesitated. All around were sleeping Utes, and any loud noise would bring them to their feet in a rush. He gently placed his right hand on the mother's shoulder and squeezed.

Evening Star's eyes snapped open and she looked up. Astonishment caused her to gape until she had recovered sufficiently to smile broadly.

Nate pressed a finger to his lips, and was gratified when she nodded to indicate her understanding. He held the Hawken in both hands and covered the band while Evening Star lifted her daughter.

A nearby Ute tossed in his sleep and mumbled for a bit.

Motioning for the mother to precede him, Nate gestured at the trees and waited until she went ten feet before he followed. The rescue had turned out to be much easier than he'd anticipated, and he wondered if the Utes didn't have an unjustified reputation as fierce fighters.

At that instant, with Evening Star just reaching the shelter of the woods, a muscular warrior lying close to the nearest fire abruptly sat up and gazed about him in drowsy curiosity, as if he wasn't quite sure why he had woken up. His gaze alighted on Nate and he blinked in disbelief.

Backpedaling, Nate trained the rifle on the Ute and cocked the hammer. He still had a few feet to go to the forest when the Indian leapt erect, whipped out a knife, and vented a strident whoop. Nate shot him.

The rest of the war party awakened immediately, the warriors scrambling to their feet and voicing bewildered exclamations.

Spinning, Nate took a bound and plunged into the woods. Evening Star was waiting for him, and he grasped her elbow and propelled her in the direction of the horses.

Shouts and bellows of rage arose in the encampment.

Nate repeatedly looked back as he ran, searching for the telltale silhouettes of pursuers, certain the band would be after them any second.

In confirmation, four warriors materialized at the edge of the woods, their forms backlit by the firelight. They peered into the murky woods, and one of them called out and pointed. All four leaped forward.

Nate prodded Evening Star. She understood and pumped her legs harder, clasping Laughing Eyes to her bosom, tearing loose from occasional limbs that snatched at her buckskin dress.

The Utes voiced shrill shrieks, a veritable pack of frenzied wolves closing in for the kill.

Keeping pace with the Crow woman, Nate marveled at her fleetness. She ran like a terrified doe, leaping logs and adroitly skirting trunks and dense bushes. He glimpsed Laughing Eyes awake and staring at him, her eyes wide. Incredibly, the girl didn't cry or scream.

A minute went by.

The vague shapes of the horses appeared in the darkness.

Nate glanced back, thinking they would get away without further incident, and discovered that one of the Utes had outstripped his companions and was now less than 15 feet off. The warrior held a tomahawk in his right hand.

Nate had a choice to make. Either he confronted the Ute now and gave the Crows time to reach the horses, or he waited until they were at the animals and exposed mother and daughter to the wrath of the warrior. There really wasn't a choice at all. He halted and whirled, drawing the right flintlock.

Roaring in triumph, the Ute raised the tomahawk overhead and came straight at him.

In a flash Nate extended his arm and squeezed off a shot. The ball hit the Indian squarely in the center of his chest, and he flipped backwards and sprawled in the weeds. Not bothering to verify the kill, Nate turned, and was surprised to find Evening Star had stopped to wait for him. "Go!" he urged, well aware she couldn't understand him.

Now that he was safe, the woman resumed her flight and came to the horses. She paused and looked at Nate, apparently awaiting instructions.

Nate indicated the mare, awkwardly took Laughing Eyes into his arms, and waited for Evening Star to mount. He handed the girl up and stepped to the stallion.

Out of nowhere streaked an arrow to thud into a tree a couple of feet away.

Hastily wedging the flintlock under his belt, Nate seized the reins and swung into the saddle. He grabbed the lead for the pack animal, wheeled the big black, and made off to the northwest. Instead of sticking to the forest, he intended to cut directly across the plain. The level ground would be easier to traverse, and the Utes might not perceive the strategy until it was too late.

Yelling erupted to their rear.

Nate led the Crows rapidly through the trees to the grassland and galloped from cover without a second thought. He slanted toward the distant stand of cottonwoods and glanced to the right.

A raucous commotion was taking place in the Ute encampment. Evidently one of the warriors had tried to give chase on a horse and discovered the animals were tied together. Some of the band were staring into the forest and talking excitedly. Not one was paying attention to the plain.

Yet.

Nate kept the stallion next to the mare. He was uncomfortable having only one gun still loaded, and wished to reach the stand quickly so he could attend to the Hawken and the expended pistol. After that, his next priority would be to locate a safe hiding place where they could stay until morning.

Evening Star glanced at him and grinned. She said a single word in Crow.

Although Nate didn't know the term, he intuitively knew she'd thanked him for saving the two of them. He concentrated on the ground ahead, alert for pale dirt mounds that betokened the presence of animals burrows. Many a horse had stumbled in an unseen badger or prairie dog hole and broken its leg, and for such an accident to occur at that moment would have the direst of consequences.

They made good time, and in due course the stand loomed out of the murky night, appearing as a single, gigantic black mass.

Nate slowed and entered the trees, proceeding until he came to a small clearing, where he climbed down.

The Crows were right on his tail. Evening Star reined up, then performed sign language, moving her hands slowly so he could read them without difficulty. "I thank you for saving us from a life of misery."

Nate stepped up to the mare. "We are not safe yet."

"Why do we stop now?"

"I must reload."

Evening Star gazed around at the cottonwoods. "Where is my husband? He should be with you."

"Sitting Bear was wounded by other Utes. He would have come if he could."

"Where is he now?"

"At your lodge. He begged me to leave him and try to save you."

About to motion in response, Evening Star stiffened and cocked her head.

At the same moment Nate heard the sounds too.

The unmistakable drumming of hooves drawing swiftly nearer.

Chapter Fourteen

There was no time to reload. Nate remounted and led the way to the east. He couldn't imagine how the Utes had found them so quickly, but he did know the band would expect him to take a northwesterly direction, the shortest route back. If he swung eastward for a few miles, he would elude them. Hopefully.

The approaching horses drew abreast of the stand, then went past.

Nate could see the Utes, four in all, riding hard toward the gap between the two hills. He realized the war party had no idea where to find them. The quartet were probably going to guard the gap as a preventative measure, nothing more. Stopping, he waited until the Indians were out of sight, then dropped to the ground and loaded first the Hawken, then the pistol.

Distant yells came from the encampment.

Once back in the saddle, Nate continued to the east. He was briefly worried when they emerged from the sanctuary of the trees onto the open plain, where they could easily be spotted, but their ride to the base of a wide mountain was uneventful. He turned to the north, hoping to locate a different gap or pass. In half a mile they found a gorge that cut sharply to the right, and acting on a hunch he entered it.

The walls of the gorge were 40 feet apart, sheer precipices rearing on high. A few dwarf trees were scattered along the gravel bottom and large boulders were everywhere.

Nate prayed he hadn't taken them into a dead end. Ten minutes later, when they came to an incline on the left, he eagerly rode to the top. Before them stretched a seemingly limitless expanse of forest.

Satisfied that they had escaped, Nate decided to stay on the rim until morning. He communicated his desire to Evening Star, and after the horses were secure they found a comfortable spot under a spreading canyon maple. Laughing Eyes sat in her mother's lap, staring at the country below. He shifted to face them. "I am sorry we cannot use a fire."

"I understand," Evening Star assured him.

"We will wait until daylight, then leave."

"You need not stop on our account."

"It is not safe to travel at night, as you well know," Nate noted. "What difference can four or five more hours make?"

"The Utes will not rest until they recapture us."

"I doubt you have anything to worry about. They will not find us now."

Evening Star did not respond.

Nate leaned against the trunk and let the tension drain from his body. All in all, he'd handled himself well. Shakespeare would be proud. His stomach growled, reminding him of the onions and berries in his pouch, and he wondered if the others were hungry. "Would you like something to eat?"

"No. The Utes let us eat earlier."

Nate went to the stallion and retrieved the pouch, then settled down and munched contentedly on the food. The escapade had taught him a valuable lesson in self-reliance. He could, when the necessity arose, hold his own against some of the toughest warriors in the West. Where before his heart pumped faster at the mere mention of the Utes, now he recognized they were no worse than any other tribe. All the Utes had going for them was an unjustified reputation.

Word of mouth, he determined, had a lot to do with the status of individual men or entire tribes. Embellished by drink or imagination, tales concerning the likes of Jim Bridger, Joseph Walker, and Shakespeare McNair tended to give those mountain men an exaggerated aspect, and the same held true for the Utes and the Blackfeet. For years everyone had been saying those two tribes were the terrors of the Rockies, and now the claim was widely accepted as verified fact. Actually, the Utes were no worse than the Bloods and the Piegans, two lesser known tribes who also killed whites on sight.

Nate listened to animal noises carried by the cool wind. Wolves were particularly active at night, and their howls ranged far and wide. Owls hooted regularly. Now and then a panther would scream like a woman being tortured. And ominous, deep growls sounded from somewhere farther up the gorge.

Evening Star was intently studying Nate. The little girl had reclined on her back, her head on her mother's leg.

"Is something wrong?"

"No," Evening Star answered. "But I wonder about something. May I ask you a question?"

"Go ahead."

"Why did you risk your life to save ours? We hardly know you."

"Your family fed me, sheltered me, treated me as a friend. I could not stand by and let you be abducted."

The woman nodded. "You are an honorable man, Grizzly Killer. You will become great if you do not die first."

Nate smiled and took a bite of onion. In her own way, Evening Star was almost as attractive as Winona. Almost, but not quite. She possessed a calm, stately bearing he admired. Like most Indian women, she was earthy and self-disciplined, the exact opposite of her civilized white sisters in the States. What was it about civilization, he mused, that produced men and women who were overly dependent on the society in which they lived? The longer he lived in the wild, the more convinced he became that too much so-called culture tended to breed physical and moral weaklings.

"You must miss your wife," Evening Star signed.

A frown curled Nate's lip. "With all my heart."

"She is very fortunate to have such a brave husband."

"Sitting Bear is also brave. You should have seen him fight the Utes."

"Did he get the feathers he wanted?"

"Yes."

The Crow sighed and gazed at a small pine tree swaying in the wind. "Then the worst is yet to come."

"What do you mean?" Nate inquired.

"Once he heals, he will try to steal enough horses from the Arapahos to make up for those that were stolen. It will be very dangerous, yet he insists on going alone."

"I could go with him."

Evening Star smiled. "Thank you. But we both know he is too proud. He will never permit you to accompany him. This is something he must do by himself." She paused. "If only my sons were alive. He might have consented to take them."

Nate suddenly lost his appetite. "I am extremely sorry about your boys. They were a credit to their parents and would have grown to be mighty warriors."

The quiet night was abruptly shattered by the crack of a gun from the direction of the plain.

"It must be the Utes," Evening Star declared.

"Why would they fire a shot?" Nate remarked.

"It could be a signal."

"Perhaps," Nate conceded. "But I doubt it has anything to do with us. They cannot possibly know where we are."

"Never underestimate them. They are excellent trackers. By daylight they could pick up our trail."

"By daylight we will be on our way to your lodge. They will never catch up."

"You have much confidence for one so young."

Nate chuckled. "I wish I did."

"Never underestimate yourself," Evening Star said, grinning, and looked at him. "There is another question I would like to ask. A trapper once told me incredible stories about white women and I have often wondered if he spoke the truth. You must know their customs well."

"I know a little about women," Nate said, then added a quote from his mentor, Shakespeare.

"Any man who claims he knows all there is to know is a liar."

Evening Star laughed lightly. "Women find men equally as difficult to understand."

"Even Indian women?"

"Did you think we would be different? Women are women." Evening Star began to tenderly stroke her daughter's hair. "This trapper wanted me to believe that many white women do not marry until they are twenty winters or older. Did he tell the truth?"

"Yes. Some white women marry young, but the trend seems to be for them to marry older and older all the time."

Evening Star shook her head in amazement. "But why do they wait so long and waste so many of their best child-bearing years?"

Nate was about to answer that it simply was the fashion, but there wasn't an equivalent sign gesture. Instead, he shrugged.

"Very mystifying," said Evening Star. "Indian women would not think of waiting twenty winters to marry. As soon as a girl becomes a woman, she is eligible for marriage. Most have a husband by the time they are sixteen."

"How does a girl become a woman?" Nate naively asked.

Evening Star reacted as if surprised by the query. "When she bleeds for the first time."

"Bleeds?" Nate repeated, and then comprehended her meaning. Extremely embarrassed, he pretended to be interested in the eastern horizon, and even made a casual, if inane, comment. "The stars are very bright tonight."

"Yes," the Crow woman replied.

"I do not think I have ever seen them this bright."

"You must not look at the night sky very often."

Taking another bite of onion, Nate saw a brilliant, thin streak of light shoot across the heavens from west to east. A meteor always enthralled him. As a child, he'd always wanted to chase one down and find where it crashed. Meteors served as reminders of the vast, unknown realms existing out among the stars. Many an idle hour had been spent dreaming about the other planets in the solar system: Mercury, Venus, Mars, Jupiter, Saturn, and Uranus.

In a way, his early fascination with the heavens had carried over into his adult life. From his childhood fascination with the mysteries of the universe grew his later fascination with the mysteries awaiting anyone who ventured beyond the Mississippi River in the Great American Desert, as the expanse between the Mississippi and the Pacific Ocean was so frequently called. The unknown held an irresistible allure, a siren call that had beckoned him into the winderness.

More brave souls were answering that call every year. The numbers of trappers and traders was growing rapidly. Shakespeare believed that one day there would be as many people in the West as there were in the East, but Nate was skeptical. For one thing, the Plains and the Rockies were inhabited by dozens of Indian tribes who weren't about to pack up and leave just because the white man wanted to move in. If there ever came a time when the whites did want the land for themselves, there would be hell to pay.

Besides, from what he'd seen, there was no reason the whites and the Indians couldn't live together in harmony. There was enough living space for everyone, and there would never be a shortage of game. The immense herds of buffaloes alone fed millions, and there was little chance of the bison ever dying out.

Nate hoped that he'd never see the day when the current way of life came to an end. There were those, like Shakespeare, who maintained it would, who believed that whites were too greedy and too arrogant to leave well enough alone. There were also those who asserted the U.S. had a right to expand westward to the shores of the Pacific, if need be. So far, their voices were in the minority.

He would be the first to admit that times were changing, though. Why, only a few years ago, Colonel John Stevens, a veteran of the Revolution, had constructed a steam wagon on his estate, a contraption powered by steam and capable of carrying passengers. One day, some claimed, steam-powered devices would replace horses.

About the same time, in Quincy, Massachusetts, a man named Bryant had opened an enterprise he called the Granite Railway. It consisted of horse-drawn wagons that hauled heavy loads effortlessly along miles of hardwood tracks. More such railways were expected to spring up in the years ahead.

The world never stood still, Nate reflected. Change seemed to be the natural order of things, which didn't bode well for the Indians or his peace of mind. All he wanted out of life was the opportunity to live it as he saw fit, without interference from anyone else. And in that respect civilization and the wilderness had something in common. There were always those who took delights in oppressing others, whether it be a tyrannical employer in New York City, or murderous Utes in the Rockies.

Nate glanced at Evening Star and saw she was lying on her back, Laughing Eyes beside her, asleep. He closed his own eyes and let his thoughts drift, savoring the tranquility and hoping it would last.

But it didn't.

Chapter Fifteen

A faint trace of light tinged the eastern horizon when Nate awoke. He blinked a few times before he recalled where he was and the circumstances that had brought him to the top of the gorge. Rising, he stretched and went to relieve himself, then returned and gently shook the Crow woman.

Evening Star came awake instantly and glanced up. She nodded and went about rousing her daughter.

"Do you want food?" Nate asked.

"We will wait until midday," Evening Star responded.

"I can shoot something for breakfast."

"No. We should leave before the Utes come. But thank you for the offer."

"The Utes are not coming," Nate assured her, and headed for the horses. He halted when he heard a peculiar soft patter arising in the gorge. It couldn't be, he told himself, and ran to the rim to listen. Amplified by the rock walls, soft and inaudible at times but nonetheless recognizable, was the dull thud of horse hooves striking the gravel floor. He whirled and motioned for Evening Star to mount.

"The Utes?"

Nate frowned. "You were right."

"You killed two of the war party. They will chase us until they do the same to you and recapture us, or until all of them are dead."

So much for the Utes having an exaggerated reputation, Nate reflected, and quickly climbed onto the stallion. Once the mother and daughter were on the mare, he lead the pack animal off to the northwest, entering a verdant forest carpeted with pine needles. He reasoned that the Utes must have been tracking them all night since the band was already in the gorge. Once the war party found the spot where they had slept, the Indians would pick up the pace in the expectation of catching them soon.

Nate rode as fast as he dared, constantly avoiding trees and boulders, and whenever he came to a knoll or hill he would look back to see if there was sign of pursuit. Gradually the sun climbed into the sky, bringing the woodland to life, and with it came a steady rise in temperature.

Two hours after the sun rose Nate was perspiring freely. The day promised to be very warm, which meant they must locate water if they intended to push their animals to the limit. But although he scoured the terrain ceaselessly, none of the precious liquid was to be found.

In four hours the ground slanted downward into a broad valley, and in the center a small lake sparkled invitingly. Nate pointed at it and smiled, and Evening Star nodded happily. They pressed on until they broke from cover and saw the shore ahead, then galloped to the water's edge.

A flock of ducks was disturbed by their arrival, and across the lake a herd of deer moved warily off into the undergrowth.

Nate let the horses and the Crows slake their thirst first. When it was his turn, he dropped to his hands and knees and drank until he couldn't hold another drop. He straightened, smacked his lips, and wiped the back of his sleeve across his mouth.

"Do you think it is safe to stop for a while?" Evening Star inquired.

Turning, Nate surveyed the woods and hills they'd traversed. "There is no sign of the Utes yet. Yes, we can rest for a spell."

"I saw raspberry bushes over there," Evening Star signed, and pointed to the south. "If you will watch Laughing Eyes, I will collect them."

"Go ahead."

The Crow spoke a few stern words to her daughter, then ran off. Laughing Eyes gazed up at him, nervousness mirrored in her young eyes.

"You are safe with me," Nate promised her.

An uncomfortable silence ensued. The girl seemed transformed to stone, her gaze locked on his face.

Self-conscious under the child's scrutiny, Nate tried to initiate a conversation. "You are very mature for your age. I hope my own children turn out like you."

Laughing Eyes did not reply.

"Soon we will have you back with your father. Would you like that?"

At last the girl responded, her hands moving tentatively. "Yes."

"He will be very happy to see you," Nate predicted.

"I will be very sad."

"Why?"

"Because both my brothers are dead. I loved them with all my heart, and now I can never play with them again."

"They were good boys," Nate acknowledged sorrowfully.

"I hope my mother and father have another son one day so I can have a brother again."

"Maybe they will."

Silence descended once more. Nate didn't know what else to say. No amount of soothing words would alleviate the girl's suffering, and he'd rather keep quiet than remind her of the calamity. He squatted and splashed water on his throat and the back of his neck, then stood and watched their back trail.

Evening Star returned within minutes, her forearms cupped to her stomach and brimming with luscious red raspberries. She deposited them on the grass and smiled. "I can get more if you want."

"I am not very hungry," Nate said. "The two of you eat your fill." He stood guard while they crammed berries into their mouths, grinning as juice dribbled down Laughing Eye's pointed chin. Every now and then he bent down and grabbed a few berries for himself, and it was as he straightened for the fifth time that he saw the tendrils of dust rising approximately a quarter of a mile away. Shoving the raspberries in his mouth, he glanced at Evening Star. "The Utes."

She looked and stood. "We must leave immediately."

In a minute they were mounted and riding along the western shore of the lake. Nate cut into the trees when they came to a rocky stretch of ground that would make their tracks harder to read, then resumed their original northwesterly bearing, driving the horses even harder than before, sweating more than previously as the temperature climbed higher.

When they arrived at the north end of the valley they ascended a hill and paused to gaze at the lake. Visible on the west shore were seven riders.

The sight spurred Nate onward with a vengeance. Despite his best efforts, the war party would catch them by nightfall unless he came up with a ruse to throw the Utes off the scent. But what? How could he lose men who had demonstrated the ability to track at night? Doubling back was out of the question; it would put them behind the band and increase the jeopardy. A mile or two of solid stone underfoot would do the trick, but the woodland soil was essentially soft except for small tracks here and there. He toyed with the notion of an ambush to even the odds, and pondered whether he could prevail on the Crow to ride ahead without him.

Evening Star rode up alongside the stallion. Her daughter now sat behind her, arms looped about her waist. She caught Nate's attention and motioned while holding the reins. "There is a trick the Crows use to fool the Utes that might help us."

"What trick?"

"If we drag a limb behind us, our tracks will be erased. An excellent tracker would still be able to follow, but it would slow him down."

"It is a great idea," Nate signed, and reined up. He swiftly jumped down and used his knife to chop a thin, long branch sporting an abundance of leaves from a cottonwood. Next came the matter of a rope, which they didn't have.

Evening Star slid to the ground. "Give me your knife," she said, and extended her right hand.

Puzzled, Nate complied, and stared after her as she walked into the brush until she was out of sight. He smiled up at Laughing Eyes, who sat stiffly on the mare, and waited anxiously for the woman to return.

When Evening Star did step out, her dress was several inches shorter. She'd cut a continuous strip off the bottom hem of her dress, producing a tough buckskin strand ten feet in length. She beamed as he gave it to him.

Nate tied one end of the makeshift rope to the base of the branch, wrapped the other end around his left hand, and climbed into the saddle. "You will have to take the pack animal," he advised Evening Star.

She mounted the mare, took the lead, and rode forward.

Following on the pack animal's heels, Nate sat sideways so he could guide the path of the branch and ensure their prints were completely obliterated. He found that by moving his hand from side to side, the branch moved in a corresponding manner and effectively wiped the earth clean. Their deeper tracks were still imbedded in the soil, but even those were covered with a layer of needles, bits of vegetation, and dirt.

For half an hour they continued in such a manner, until the leaves on the branch were worn off by the friction and Nate had to halt to prepare a second limb. In no time they were on the move.

The blistering afternoon sun arced across the sky, and the shadows in the forest lengthened. Many small animals darted from their path and larger ones regarded them in curiosity. All went well until they came to a severely steep bald mountain.

Nate saw it first and realized the drawbacks it posed. Not only was the slope at an angle that would drastically slow the horses down, but the absence of trees and brush meant they would be visible for miles, exposed to the Utes. They might as well paint a sign announcing where they were. Rather than be foolish, they had to go around.

Evening Star bore to the left.

For no logical reason Nate felt inclined to bear to the right, but since she had already turned he acquiesced to her decision. The going became difficult, with numerous large boulders blocking the route, although the trees thinned out, which compensated somewhat. When the leaves on the second branch rubbed off, Nate reeled in the buckskin and placed it in his ammo pouch to use later. They'd traveled about two miles while covering their trail, and he figured that was enough to slow up the war party.

As they swung around the mountain a new vista unraveled before their eyes, a series of a dozen or so hills, each higher than the one before, most densely forested.

Nate was elated. There would be plenty of game and undoubtedly water, and with night approaching they needed both. If he constructed a lean-to, he could justify the risk of building a fire. A troubling notion occurred to him, giving him second thoughts. What if the Utes tracked them into the night? If so, the band would overtake them in the early hours of the morning before the sun rose. He had to weigh the benefits of stopping with the possible consequences.

Shortly they completed skirting the bald mountain and rode onto the nearest hill, where again a cushion of pine needles and leaves deadened the footfalls of their animals.

Nate decided to take the lead, and had started to swing around the other horses when the wilderness demonstrated once again why a person couldn't let down his guard for an instant. He heard loud barks off to the left and glanced in that direction.

Speeding toward them was a pack of wolves.

Chapter Sixteen

There were ten big gray wolves in all, their powerful forms flowing over the ground in rhythmic bounds, their reddish-pink tongues hanging out of their mouths, their sturdy teeth exposed. Standing close to three feet high at the shoulders and over six feet in length, they packed upwards of 130 pounds of sinew and muscle on their sleek frames. Individually, each wolf was formidable; together, they were terrors.

"Go!" Nate shouted at Evening Star, who had seen the pack and was already galloping away. He rode on her left side, intending to take the brunt of the assault if the wolves closed. All that he had ever learned about wolves came back to him in a twinkling; they were fast runners, tenacious hunters, and social animals who mated for life and were devoted to their offspring. Wolves normally avoided humans, although there were reports of attacks against trappers on record. Ordinarily hunting at night, they could be found abroad at any hour of the day if hunger drove them from their lairs.

The pack loped in pursuit, the leader 30 yards distant.

Should he fire to discourage them? Nate mused, and opted to hold off shooting until there was no alternative. A gunshot would give away their location to the Utes, and might serve to spark the band to intensify their efforts.

They crossed the crown and started down the opposite slope, the horses maintaining a steady gait. Evening Star rode easily, her daughter clinging tightly to her waist, proving that some Indian women were the equal of the men in horsemanship.

Nate noticed the wolves were not making a concerted attempt to overtake the horses, but were racing at a steady pace, and he reckoned the pack might be trying to tire the horses out before closing in. He scanned the countryside ahead and spied a creek that bisected the next hill halfway up.

Evening Star glanced back once as she neared the creek, her resolve transparent, all of her maternal instincts aroused by the potential threat to her child. She never bothered to slow down when she drew close to the bank. Undaunted, she plunged right in, the mare dutifully obedient to her prompting.

When Nate reached the bank, he halted. The wolves hadn't gained more than a yard or two, and now they cut back to a walk. The male leader suddenly stopped and sat on its haunches.

Unaware of this, Evening Star prodded the mare to the far bank 15 feet away, the water rising to the animal's chest, laboriously hauling the pack animal across.

All of the wolves had halted.

Nate realized the pack wasn't going to attack. The wolves must have given chase out of curiosity, not impelled by hunger. He'd heard about wolves that had trailed men for hours without displaying any hostility, which invariably mystified those nervous unfortunates who were the object of the wolves' attention. He rode across the creek and joined the woman and child. "I do not believe they will attack us," he signed.

"Apparently not," Evening Star replied, "but one never knows with wolves."

Nate gave a cheery wave at the pack, took the pack animal's lead from her, and began to head out. After the scare of the chase, his relief was all the more intense, and in the flush of relief he almost made a blunder. Jerking on the reins, he drew up short and glanced at the gently flowing water. The creek was ten feet across, and did not appear to be in any respect treacherous. He looked at his companions. "I have an idea. We should follow the creek for a few miles and slow the Utes down even more."

Evening Star seemed puzzled. "Along the bank? What good would that do?"

"Not along the bank. In the water."

Comprehension dawned and Evening Star smiled. "I should have thought of that."

Nate led off, moving to the middle of the flow, taking a northerly bearing. They would swing around to the northwest again later. He smiled at his cleverness, certain even the most proficient tracker in the world couldn't trail prints through water. The creek was crystal clear, and he could see every stone and pebble on the bottom as well as the many fish that flitted out of the stallion's path. He wished he could afford to take the time to catch a few for supper. Perhaps later, if all went well.

They pushed on until the sun touched the western horizon. The creek adhered to a generally northerly course the entire time, curving from time to time as it wound among the hills and mountains. Over a dozen times they startled big game drinking at the water's edge: buffalo, elk, deer, and a few black bear. Once they saw a panther that snarled at them before leaping off.

A cool breeze stroked Nate's brow and alleviated the heat. He spied a clearing up ahead on the left side and twisted in the saddle. "I propose to spend the night there," he told her, and indicated the spot.

"Good. Laughing Eyes needs rest badly."

"How are you holding up?"

"Well," Evening Star said, but the fatigue etched in her face belied her statement.

Nate gazed back along the winding watercourse. "Do you think the Utes have given up by now?"

"No."

"Why not? Between dragging the branch and following this creek, we are bound to have lost them."

"They will not give up because they are Utes."

"I still think we are safe."

"You thought that once before."

Having no retort for her astute observation, and troubled by the implications, Nate rode to the clearing and gladly climbed down. He tied the stallion and the pack horse to a tree, did the same with the mare, and walked into the trees to gather an armful of straight limbs for use in a lean-to.

"What are you doing?" Evening Star inquired when he emerged.

Nate dropped the load at his feet. "I will build a lean-to and a fire for tonight."

"Starting a fire is not wise. The Utes will see the smoke."

"Not if we build the fire *inside* the lean-to and keep the flames low. We will be able to cook and have enough warmth so we can sleep comfortably."

"But it is a great risk. If any of the smoke rises, the Utes will know where to find us."

Nate pointed at the little girl. "Do you want your child to go through another night without a hot meal and a comfortable place to sleep?"

Evening Star stared fondly at her offspring, and frowned. "No."

"Neither do I. I say we take the chance and build a fire, but I will forget all about the idea if you object."

"Go ahead."

With her helping him, Nate had a serviceable lean-to constructed before the sun dipped from sight. He rubbed his hands together, removing bits of bark and dirt, and gazed at the gradually darkening sky. "We will wait to build the fire until the sun is completely gone. That way, even if some smoke does escape, I doubt that the Utes will spot it. In the meantime, I must catch something for our meal."

"What will you catch? If you use your gun to kill game the Utes might hear."

Nate nodded at the creek. "I could catch fish for our meal."

"My people do not eat fish."

"I know, and under normal circumstances, I would not think of asking you to go against your beliefs. But the fish are handy and I can catch them without firing a shot." Nate glanced ar the child. "Laughing Eyes must be very hungry."

Evening Star looked at her daughter, her brow knit, the corners of her mouth curled downward as she wrestled with the dilemma of whether to violate the tribal taboo. At length she sighed and signed, "I would rather have my child eat than go hungry. If we must eat fish, we must."

"Are you sure?"

She locked her eyes on his. "My daughter is more important than our beliefs. I will live with the shame."

"All right. Stay on the bank and watch." Nate walked into the creek and moved slowly outward, bent at the waist, searching the bottom, trying to recall every aspect of the lessons Shakespeare had imparted in the finer art of fish catching. He saw a large whitefish swimming slowly toward him and crouched, oblivious of the water soaking his clothes and swirling about his legs. He slid his arms under the surface all the way to the shoulders, keeping his hands flat, the palms up, and waited expectantly. Fish were incredibly quick, and trying to hold onto their struggling, scaly bodies was like trying to hold onto a pig coated with grease—next to impossible. The secret to catching fish with bare hands was not to grip them, but to *flip* them.

The fish glided nearer.

Nate tensed, hoping the fish thought he was a rock, and when it started to swim over his hands he surged upward, clamping his fingers on the creature's slippery side as he swept his arms up and out. He couldn't quite believe his eyes when the fish sailed through the air and plopped onto the grass within a foot of the water. He'd done it! Elated, he dashed to the bank and scrambled out to prevent the fish from flopping back into the creek. He attempted to grab it but the fish popped from his grasp. Again and again he tried, each time with the same result. At last he succeeded in holding fast and glanced up in astonishment at hearing airy laughter.

Laughing Eyes was in hysterics. She spoke a few words to her mother between cackles.

"She says you are the funniest man alive," Evening Star translated, gazing at Nate affectionately.

"The fish are responsible for that."

Holding her sides, the girl laughed and laughed.

Evening Star chuckled. "Thank you," she signed, and gently touched his left cheek. "I was beginning to think she would never laugh again."

The comment caused Nate to recall the deaths of the boys, and brought to mind a revolting custom practiced by many of the Rocky Mountain tribes. Whenever a person lost a family member, the mourner engaged in an act of self-mutilation by hacking off part of a finger. His own wife had done so, and he now wondered if Evening Star would do the same.

"Is something wrong?" she inquired.

"No."

"What were you thinking about?"

Nate hesitated, then decided there was no reason to conceal the thought, although he rephrased it. "I am glad you did not cut off the tips of your fingers. You show good sense. The practice is barbaric and should be abolished by all Indians."

Evening Star's face clouded and she stared at her hands. "I am sorry you feel that way, because as soon as we return to the lodge I will slice off the tips of two fingers to mourn the passing of Strong Wolf and Red Hawk."

"Do you realize what you are doing?"

"Certainly. My people have always done this, since the days of the very first human beings. When a loved one dies, it is appropriate to express our grief in a fitting manner. By cutting off parts of our fingers, we prove the depth of our love and express our loss."

"Why not just cry your grief out?"

"Because crying does not show how deeply we loved those who died. People cry when a favorite horse is killed in a buffalo hunt, or when they have been injured and are in great pain. There is nothing special about crying. To demonstrate how special a loved one was, we must sacrifice a small part of ourselves."

"But why cut off a finger? Why not just jab yourself a few times with a knife or hold a burning coal in your palm?"

Evening Star shrugged. "It is our way. It has always been our way, and it always will be."

"I will never slice off part of my fingers," Nate vowed.

"Even if your wife were to die?"

"I would mourn her, yes, and I would miss her terribly, but I would not take a knife to my hand."

"If you become as we are, then you will."

Nate snorted at the idea. "I like the Indian way of life, but do not expect me to embrace every Indian custom. If Winona ever passes on, I will settle for crying many, many times."

"You never know," the woman said enigmatically.

"I know," Nate assured her. He went back into the creek, and in due course caught five more fine mountain whitefish.

Evening Star volunteered to clean the fish, but she grimaced as she hacked off the heads and removed the entrails.

The sun was gone by the time Nate got around to starting a fire in the lean-to. He carefully arranged the tinder and a circle of twigs and small branches in the middle of a ring of rocks, and once the flames took, he nursed it until he had a fair-sized fire going.

Stars filled the heavens and night enshrouded the land.

Evening Star handled the cooking. She rolled three large, flat stones into the heart of the flames, then removed them when they glowed red, using a stick to align them in a row. Placing a cleaned fish on each one, she hovered over the meal as the fish hissed and crackled.

Nate savored the tasty aroma. He walked to a pine tree and pried off sections of bark to use as plates, then returned. The girl was practically drooling on the fish, her eyes fixed hungrily on the sizzling morsels.

All in all, Nate decided, the day had gone well. They'd eluded the war party and had likely thrown the Utes off the scent. Although they'd swung wide of their original course, they would still be at the lodge by dark tomorrow. Once they arrived, he'd prevail on Sitting Bear to pack up the lodge and get the hell out of there.

Evening Star deftly flipped the fish over using twigs. A few stray wisps of smoke curled around the edges of the lean-to, but for the most part the smoke was blocked by the shelter and dissipated at ground level by the breeze.

Nate leaned back, feeling relaxed and content, and consequently he was unprepared for the loud whinnying of the stallion and the splashing sounds made by something or someone that was coming up the creek directly toward them.

Chapter Seventeen

Nate surged to his feet, the Hawken in his hands, and swung to the south in time to see a pair of Utes round the last curve at a gallop. At the sight of the lean-to they screeched and charged, one of the warriors waving a lance while the other nocked an arrow to a stout bow. Bewildered by their unexpected arrival, Nate took a second to recover from his shock.

Laughing Eyes threw her arms around her mother and whined pitiably.

The Ute with the bow took aim.

It was the thought of an arrow tearing into his chest that made Nate whip the rifle to his shoulder, take a hasty bead on the bowman, and fire. Simultaneously the Indian released the shaft, and both the ball and the arrow sped toward their respective targets at speeds too great for the eye to follow.

The ball took the warrior in the head and catapulted him from his mount. He fell into the creek with a splash.

A fraction of an instant later the arrow speared out of the night and streaked past Nate, narrowly missing his left side, to thud into the lean-to behind him. In order to protect the Crows better, he discarded the Hawken, drew both pistols, and ran to meet the second Ute head-on.

Throwing off a spray of water that seemed to sparkle in the moonlight, the warrior's horse made straight at Nate. The Ute arched his spine and drew back his lance, his features contorted in feral hatred.

Nate was almost to the bank when he pointed both flintlocks, cocked them, and stroked both triggers, the twin retorts booming as one, discharging small clouds of smoke, the recoil snapping his forearms upward.

Struck high in the chest by the balls just as he swept his arm forward, the Ute was lifted off his steed and sailed a good eight feet before he crashed into the water. His horse instantly swerved to the right and kept running until it disappeared in the blanket of darkness.

"Damn!" Nate swore, staring at the crumpled figures bobbing in the creek. Once again he'd misjudged the tenacity of the Utes. Their reputation for savagery, as he was learning to his sorrow, was, if anything, understated. He spun and marched back to the lean-to, where Evening Star and Laughing Eyes awaited him with tense expressions.

"The rest will be after us now," the mother signed. "Your shots have let them know where to find us."

Nate nodded and devoted himself to reloading all three guns, reflecting on their predicament as he did. The way he figured it, the Utes must have tracked them to the creek, at which point the band lost the trail, and then separated. Some of the warriors must have gone north along the watercourse, others south, and maybe a few had continued to the northwest just in case. If his calculations were correct, there were five warriors left and one of those was the one wounded by Strong Wolf.

"I will get the horses ready," Evening Star volunteered.

Nate glanced at the fish simmering on the stones and interrupted reloading to respond. "Eat first."

"We do not have time for food. The Utes are coming."

"For all we know they are miles in the other direction. It may take them a couple of hours to get here. And after all the trouble we've gone to preparing a decent meal, we are going to take a short time and enjoy the food," Nate said, and added for good measure. "Think of your daughter. She needs to eat to keep her strength up."

With obvious reluctance, Evening Star accepted his argument and knelt by the stones. She used her fingers to break the fish into bite-sized pieces and gave several to Laughing Eyes, then dug in herself.

Nate finished with the rifle and pistols and helped himself to a hot handful of delicious fish, his mouth watering at he took his first bite of the tasty, succulent meat. He was famished, and he consumed his fair share of the whitefish in no time. He even licked each of his fingers and his thumb when he was done, and smacked his lips in satisfaction. "The best fish I have ever eaten," he remarked.

"Fish *is* very tasty," Evening Star signed in amazement.

Laughing Eyes merely grinned from ear to ear, tiny bits of fish sticking to her chin.

"Now we can leave," Nate proposed.

"I will get the horses," Evening Star said, and walked off with the child in tow.

Nate put out the fire. He tore out a clump of long weeds, soaked them in the creek, and deposited the dripping vegetation on the flames, which sputtered and hissed and gave off lots of smoke. He tramped down hard repeatedly, stamping the fire out, and when there were no burning embers in evidence he moved to the horses.

Evening Star was already on the mare, Laughing Eyes behind her. She moved her arms slowly so he could read them in the gloom. "Will we go up the creek?"

"No. Since they know our approximate location, we might as well head directly for your lodge. If we ride all night we can be there by daylight."

"I like your plan. I am very worried about my husband."

Nate swung onto the stallion, took the lead to the packhorse in his left hand, and headed out, entering the dank, shadowy forest. Many of the big predators, like panthers and grizzlies, were more active at night, so he was extra alert as he rode on a beeline to the lodge. At least it was cool, which made the riding comfortable, and he liked the feel of the soft breeze on his face. After traveling for about half an hour they came to a clearing and he reined up to check his bearings, using the North Star as a guide.

Once Nate was convinced they were on the

right course, he pushed on as fast as the benighted conditions warranted, the Hawken resting across his thighs. The minutes became hours as they forged steadily onward, crossing hills and valleys, skirting the high peaks and the deep ravines, traversing several streams and passing another lake.

Nate listened for sounds of pursuit, but none materialized. Her periodically fought off bouts of drowsiness, and once almost dozed off in the saddle. The tip of a branch gouged him in the cheek, snapping him erect, and he shook his head vigorously to clear out the cobwebs.

Evening Star and Laughing Eyes rode silently, unable to communicate with him because of the gloom.

As the night wore on, the ride acquired a degree of monotony that Nate found oddly reassuring. Every mile they went without being attacked increased the likelihood they would reach Sitting Bear without further incident. He hoped the warrior was resting, as he'd suggested.

Occasionally an owl hooted in the trees. Wolves howled frequently. Crickets chirped all around them.

Nate kept scouring the countryside ahead for a landmark he might recognize, such as a familiar mountain, but the terrain was alien at night, an inky expanse stretching into infinity.

At one point, as they were passing through a particularly dense track of woodland, an ominous, throaty growl pierced the air from a thicket off to their right, and the entire thicket shook and rattled as if alive. Finally they heard a huge beast crash through the undergrowth, heading to the north.

Slowly the positions of the stars shifted

minutely as the night waned, and eventually a faint tinge of light graced the rim of sky to the east.

Nate was beginning to think he'd misjudged the bearing when they rode out of yet another stretch of forest, and there, not 15 yards in front of them, was the stream he'd followed to the southeast, the same stream that ran past Sitting Bear's lodge. He reined up in surprise, then looked at Evening Star, and they both beamed. Advancing to the bank, he scanned in both directions, and concluded they weren't more than two or three miles from the camp.

With a happy heart Nate turned to the northwest and hastened along the east bank. They had gone a mile when the stallion suddenly snorted and acted up, its ears pricked, its eyes on the trees to the west. Nate stopped and listened but heard no unusual sounds, so he urged the big black on.

Evening Star brought the mare alongside the stallion as they neared the vicinity of her home. Her daughter was slumped against her back, swaying with every step, asleep.

Nate thought of how delighted Sitting Bear would be to have his wife and daughter safely returned, a joyous reunion they would never forget, and complimented himself on a job well done. It felt good to have done something for others that would bring them such happiness, almost as if he'd contributed something meaningful to the scheme of existence. He'd never considered himself much of a philosopher, and had never attached much significance to his life, but at that moment he felt as if he'd justified his presence on the planet.

Dawn flushed the sky with striking hues of

pink, orange, and yellow by the time they drew close enough to spy the lodge. Smoke curled from the top and the front flap was open.

Evening Star laughed, reached back to wrap her left arm around Laughing Eyes, and broke into a gallop.

About to do the same, Nate abruptly changed his mind. The husband and wife would probably desire a few moments of privacy. He slowed up and absently gazed at the trees and the sky, enjoying the unfolding of a new day.

Halting near the teepees, Evening Star slid to the ground, took her daughter into her arms, and hastened inside, calling out as she did so.

Nate saw the other two horses he'd brought back munching on grass at the edge of the field near the trees, which assured him no Utes had been there since his departure.

Suddenly mother and daughter burst from the lodge and Evening Star motioned excitedly for him to come over.

Puzzled, Nate complied, sliding off the stallion almost at her feet. "What is it?" he asked.

"Sitting Bear is missing."

Nate glanced at the doorway. "He is not in there?"

"No," Evening Star said, and apprehensively scanned their surroundings.

"He has to be here somewhere," Nate assured her. "Maybe he went for a walk." Deep down, though, he doubted his own explanation, and he moved toward the stream while scouring the landscape for the warrior. Since the fire in the lodge was still going, Sitting Bear couldn't have gone very far. He probed the woods to the rear, then the field, and finally the stream.

Off the the left, partly concealed in thick weeds on the bank, was a prone form.

"Evening Star!" Nate called out, forgetting himself, and dashed to the water. There lay Sitting Bear, unconscious, his forearms dangling in the stream. Kneeling, Nate pulled the Crow higher and rolled him over. He felt as if he'd grabbed a burning torch in his hands.

In a twinkling Evening Star was there, examining her husband carefully, her countenance mirroring her anxiety. "He has an extremely high fever," she reported. "We must get him inside right away."

"Take my rifle," Nate signed, and gave the Hawken to her. He lifted the warrior and hurried into the lodge to deposit Sitting Bear near the fire. No sooner did he straighten up than his rifle was back in his hands and the woman was tending to her husband.

Laughing Eyes sat nearby, watching intently.

"Is there anything I can do?" Nate asked.

"Do you know how to recognize herbs?"

"No."

"Then watch my daughter while I get the medicine Sitting Bear needs," Evening Star suggested, and dashed out before he could respond.

Nate smiled encouragement at the child and took a seat. He noticed a stack of broken branches, and fed a few to the fingers of flame simply to keep busy. So much for his great plan to leave right away. If they tried to move Sitting Bear in his weakened state, the man would surely die. They were stuck there until the Crow recovered sufficiently to travel, which could take days and meant the Utes would easily overtake them.

The Utes.

He stared at the doorway, reflecting. If the war party was eliminated, so was the danger. But how could he hope to defeat five Utes by himself? So far he'd been lucky, and luck was a fickle ally to rely on. Despondent over the turn of events, he absently gazed at Sitting Bear and blinked in surprise.

The Crow's eyes were open.

Chapter Eighteen

Nate promptly moved closer and smiled at his friend. "Stay right where you are," he directed.

Sitting Bear licked his lips, his eyelids fluttering, then recovered enough to feebly move his hands. "Evening Star and Laughing Eyes."

"They are here safe and sound."

The warrior craned his neck with great effort and saw his daughter. Smiling broadly, he spoke a few words to her.

Voicing a cry of joy, the child scrambled to her father's side and placed her head on his chest. Tears poured down her cheeks and she uttered soft sobs. Sitting Bear tenderly patted her head, then glanced at Nate. "Are the Utes all dead?"

"Five still live."

"They will follow you here."

"I know."

"Do you know what must be done?"

"Yes."

"There might be another way. If you hide us in the forest, perhaps they will not find us and will leave."

"You know better."

A slight nod signified the Crow's acknowledgment, and he closed his eyes, sighed, and passed out.

Nate let Laughing Eyes stay with her father. He rose, grabbed his Hawken, and moved to the doorway, where he crouched and surveyed the terrain to the southeast. When the Utes came, they would likely come from that direction. He saw no sign of them, but that didn't mean the war party wasn't out there, maybe five miles off, maybe ten.

A robin landed near the flap, saw him, and took wing again.

He was like that bird, he told himself. He couldn't afford to sit still when there was a threat to his existence, and that of his new friends, lurking in the background. Either they fled, which they couldn't do given the circumstances, or they made a fight of it. Or one of them did.

Nate was still pondering the inevitable when Evening Star returned bearing a selection of plants. She immediately went to Sitting Bear, and Nate watched her for a minute before slipping quietly out and making for the stallion. There was no sense in trying to explain his decision. She might argue, try to get him to change his mind, when there could be no turning back. Her ministrations would keep her too busy to notice his absence for a while, and he could ride off unnoticed. He was almost to the horse when he heard the patter of rushing feet and a hand fell on his right shoulder. Calmly, unwilling to show how nervous he really was, he turned and smiled. "You should be with Sitting Bear."

"Where do you think you are going?" Evening Star demanded.

"You know where," Nate told her.

Her eyes darted to the southeast and back again. "We can run. Let me tend my husband, and in an hour we can head for our village."

Nate took the liberty of affectionately touching her cheek, and shook his head. "You know better. Take good care of him. If I am not back by tomorrow morning, you should make a travois and get him and your daughter out of here. Understand?"

Evening Star simply nodded. Her eyes conveyed her feelings more than words ever could. Turning, she ran back to the lodge and disappeared within.

An odd wave of raw emotion engulfed him, and Nate coughed as he walked to the stallion and swung up. Jerking on the reins, he wheeled the animal and rode toward his rendezvous with five of the fiercest fighters in the Rockies. He recalled a certain spot they'd passed the night before, a narrow opening between two steep hills, that would admirably serve his purpose if he could reach it before the band.

Although fatigue gnawed at his mind and body, Nate galloped into the midst of the mountains again, stopping only once after two hours to take a drink from the stream. By the third hour he'd arrived at the site, and sat in the saddle while determining the best place to make his stand.

The two hills were devoid of vegetation and covered with rocks and boulders. Between them was the opening, ten yards at the widest and 30 yards in length, rimmed by scattered, isolated trees, a mix of cottonwoods and pines. He turned to the right and rode into the shadowed shelter of a boulder as big as a house, then dismounted and let the reins drag on the ground. If he needed to make a quick getaway, he didn't want to bother with untying them.

Nate jogged to the opening and halted behind the trunk of a cottonwood. His gaze roved over all the trees and depressions, seeking an ideal ambush point. None were outstanding, but there were three pines growing close to each other on the left side that would suffice. He moved behind them, estimating the boulder to be ten yards off, and crouched.

Now let the Utes come!

After confirming all three guns were loaded, he leaned his back against the trunk and plotted strategy. He wasn't a skilled military man, so he must rely on cunning instead of firepower. Even if he killed three of the war party with his first three shots, which was unlikely, the rest would be on him before he could reload. How could he slow them down?

Nate suddenly remembered the buckskin rope Evening Star had made, and reached into his ammo pouch. It wasn't the strongest rope ever made, but it was thin enough and long enough to do the trick. Rising, he stepped closer to the boulder and selected two cottonwoods spaced approximately nine feet apart. He shimmied up one, tied the rope at a level corresponding to the height of a man on horseback, then climbed down and repeated the procedure on the second tree. Once on firm footing, he regarded his handiwork critically. Anyone going slowly was bound to notice the trap, so it was up to him to make certain the Utes had no time to admire the scenery.

He walked to the pines and knelt, adjusted the pistols under his belt, and lifted the rifle. All was in readiness. Now all he could do was wait.

A jay landed in the tree overhead, voiced its

shrill cry a few times, and flew off.

Nate thought about Winona. She must be very worried about him, and he wouldn't blame her if she gave him a scolding when he finally made it back to their cabin. Knowing her as he did, he knew she'd probably simply hug him until his ribs cracked and whisper in his ears how much she'd missed him. Never had he felt so loved, never so happy, as when they began their married life. He leaned against the tree, ruminating.

The sun rose higher and higher into the blue vault of the sky.

Nate's rumbling stomach reminded him of his acute hunger, but he refused to leave his post to find food. The discomfort helped to keep him awake and alert. If he ate, he'd become too drowsy to keep his eyes open. He'd never gone this long without sleep before, and he didn't know how much longer he could hold up.

By noon his eyelids were drooping, his chin sagging. He slapped his cheek repeatedly to no avail. Shaking his head vigorously did nothing to stem the overwhelming tide of weariness. Frustrated, he heaved to his feet and swung his arms from side to side. He listened to the birds and the whispering breeze.

Suddenly, from the southeast, came the whinny of a horse.

Nate froze and stared through the opening at the woods beyond. He thought he detected movement far back under the trees and he squatted, now in full possession of his faculties. It had to be the Utes!

Soon a rider appeared, then another and another, alternately passing through shadows and beams of golden sunlight, sitting loosely astride their mounts.

Scarcely breathing, Nate molded his body to the tree and peeked around the edge, exposing as little of himself as possible. Now that the band had finally arrived, it almost seemed like a dream, as if he were detached from the proceedings, an observer instead of a participant.

The first Ute carried a fusee, the second a bow, the third a lance. The third man was the same warrior wounded by Strong Wolf, still wearing the crude bandage and swaying precariously with every step his animal took. It seemed doubtful he'd live out the day.

Nate kept the Hawken pressed flush with his body. He saw the lead rider studying the ground, and entertained the hope of catching the man completely off guard. But as the Utes approached the gap, the foremost warrior paid less attention to the tracks he was following and more to the terrain ahead.

The second warrior looked over his shoulder, then halted and waited for the wounded man to catch up. They exchanged words, then rode on together.

An unexpected wave of dizziness assailed Nate, and he had to close his eyes to steady himself. The lack of sleep and food, plus the sustained strain of the flight, was taking its toll. Not now! he thought, and gazed at the Indians again.

When the lead rider reached the gap, he halted and intently scrutinized the hills and the trees for a few moments, as if he suspected something was wrong but couldn't put his finger on it. Holding the fusee in his left hand, he goaded his animal into the opening.

A strange, troubling thought entered Nate's mind: What if he was killed? Winona would never know what had happened to him. His body would lie where it fell, slowly rotting, or be consumed by scavengers. He envisioned his scalped form, partly eaten and stinking to high heaven, lying in the dirt, and felt bile rise in his throat. The image sparked a fleeting terror, and he hesitated.

Ten yards into the gap, the first Ute watched a pair of doves take flight from a cottonwood.

Nate almost panicked, almost whipped the rifle up and fired prematurely. Realizing the consequences of such rash action brought him to his senses. He had to be calm, to keep his wits about him at all times. Waiting was the key to success. Wait. Wait. Wait.

The lead Ute drew within 20 feet of the three pines. He shifted and looked at his companions.

In that instant when the warrior's attention was diverted, Nate raised the Hawken to his shoulder, cocked the hammer, and took careful aim.

Both the wounded Indian and the warrior with the bow spotted him and cried out in warning.

Swiveling, the lead rider instinctively started to bring the fusee to bear while simultaneously diving to the right.

Nate had to compensate, tracking the Ute's body, and he rushed his shot, squeezing the trigger while the warrior was in midair. At the same instant the Ute cut loose with the fusee, and a burning sensation lanced through Nate's right shoulder. He'd been hit! Stunned, he staggered backwards, then dropped to his knees behind another tree.

The first Ute was on the ground and scurrying on his hands and knees toward his friends, who had reined up and were taking cover.

Looking at his shoulder, Nate was horrified to

see a tear in the buckskin and blood seeping out. He fought to get a grip on his nerves and resisted an impulse to flee. Yes, he'd been hit, but he was still alive, still able to fight. He gingerly probed the tear and discovered he'd sustained a flesh wound, nothing more. The ball wasn't imbedded. Relieved, he looked toward the Utes in time to observe the lead rider crawl behind a waist-high bush.

There was no sign of the other two.

Nate pulled his head back, rested his forehead on the bole, and took stock. His carelessness had cost him dearly. Not only had he ruined the element of surprise, but apparently he'd missed. There were three Indians out there somewhere, eager to slit his throat.

Hold on a second.

Why were there only three?

Perplexed, Nate straightened and began reloading. There should be five Utes left out of the original nine. What could have happened to the other two? Were they en route to the Ute village for reinforcements? Or were they farther back along the trail?

A peculiar trilling noise arose to the southwest.

In the act of feeding powder down the barrel, Nate paused and scanned the gap. That sound had been like no bird he'd ever heard, and he wondered if the Utes were trying to circle past him. Working swiftly, he finished pouring the powder, wrapped a ball in a patch and wedged both into the barrel using his thumb, then shoved both all the way down with the detachable ramrod. After sliding the rod into its housing, he was ready.

All the wildlife in the immediate vicinity had fallen silent, and the breeze had died down.

Since the Utes knew where he was, Nate decided to head elsewhere. He flattened and made toward a pine ten feet away, and once its trunk sheltered him he rose cautiously to his knees and risked another look-see. Still no trace of the warriors. He looked toward the bush where the first man had vanished and detected a crimson smear on the grass. Maybe he hadn't missed, after all.

A twig snapped to the right.

Pivoting, Nate spied one of his foes moving behind a boulder, proving they were trying to hem him in. He flattened again and retreated even farther, until he was lying at the base of a forked cottonwood and peering between the two trunks. Easing the Hawken out, he scoured the opening and the facing slopes.

Come on!

Show yourselves!

One of the Indians did, the man carrying the bow. He was creeping around the bottom of the boulder on the right, an arrow set to fly, his attention on the last pine.

This time Nate was determined not to miss. He sighted on the warrior's head, and he was just about to fire when he heard onrushing footfalls to his left attended by a strident screech of savage fury.

Chapter Nineteen

In the instant Nate had to react, he squeezed off the shot and rolled to the right, not bothering to see whether he'd scored or not, flipping onto his back and reaching for his pistols.

The first Ute was almost on him. A ball had struck the warrior in the lelft side, gouging a deep furrow in his flesh, and he had discarded the fusee in favor of a tomahawk that he arced at Nate's chest.

Desperately throwing himself to the left, Nate narrowly evaded the weapon. The tomahawk bit into the earth within inches of his ribs. He swept both flintlocks up and out, certain of slaying his adversary before the Ute could swing again, only the warrior pounced instead of swinging, batting Nate's arms aside and landing on his chest.

Whooping lustily, the Ute raised the tomahawk for another blow.

There was no time to shoot. Nate elevated the right pistol and deftly deflected the tomahawk as it drove toward his face, then smashed the left flintlock into the man's cheek, sending him sprawling. Surging to his feet, he tried to extend both pistols and fire, but the warrior, still on the ground, kicked Nate's legs out from under him and he fell onto his back.

The tomahawk descended toward his face.

Nate rolled, and heard the thud as the sharpened edge hit the soil where his head had just been. He scrambled to his knees and twisted, and there was the warrior lunging at him, the tomahawk uplifted once more. In reflex he pointed the right pistol and sent a ball into his face.

Because of the angle, the shot took the Ute squarely in the throat and rocked him backwards. A red geyser gushed from his severed veins, but that didn't stop him from trying to wield the tomahawk yet one more time. Gurgling, he coiled to spring.

Firing from the hip, Nate delivered a ball to the warrior's forehead that slammed the man rearward. Discarding the right flintlock, he drew his knife, prepared to close if necessary.

The Ute wouldn't attack any more trappers. He was limp, on his back, his eyes wide and lifeless.

For a second Nate stared at his vanquished enemy, amazed he had triumphed, and then he remembered there were other warriors eager to take his scalp. He dropped down, stuck the one pistol under his belt and retrieved the other, then crawled to his rifle.

An unnatural silence gripped the wilderness.

Nate glanced at the boulder, and nearly shouted for joy at spying the bowman dead at its base. Two down and one to go, and that one was wounded! He set about reloading all three guns, starting with the Hawken, and he was tugging on the ramrod to extract it when the heavy pounding of hooves sounded and a defiant cry rent the air. Startled, he glanced up.

The third Ute intended to go out fighting. Despite his wound—or was it because of it?—the warrior had remounted and now galloped forward, the lance upraised, grim determination etching his visage.

Letting the rifle drop, Nate clutched the knife and stood, using the right fork for cover, aware that a misstep would cost his life. Neither of the cottonwood forks were wide enough to conceal him entirely; he'd have to dodge at the very instant the lance was hurled.

The Ute's eyes had a crazed aspect. He sneered and rode right up to the cottonwoods, apparently aware the rifle and pistols were expended.

Nate tensed, and saw the lance tip sweep at his head. He shifted, keeping the trunk between them, but he shifted too far and exposed himself on the other side. Again the lance stabbed out, and he barely skipped backwards out of range.

Laughing harshly, the warrior expertly maneuvered his horse so he could strike between the forks.

Nate darted to the right, racking his brain for a way to turn the tables. If he stayed where he was, eventually the Ute would connect. A knife was no match for a spear. There had to be a better way.

"Bastard!" the Ute barked, and struck.

So surprised was Nate at hearing English spoken by his foe, that he stood there for a fraction of a second in shock. The lance was within inches of his chest when he frantically twisted and glided to the right, the razor tip tearing through his buckskin shirt and slicing a furrow in his chest.

The warrior whooped.

And suddenly Nate knew what he had to do. All trace of fear was gone, supplanted by a firm resolve to win at all costs. He whirled and ran, but not at his top speed, and glanced over his right shoulder.

Predictably, the Ute took the bait, goading his mount around the cottonwood tree and giving chase.

"Fish-eater!" Nate yelled, his legs pumping, ignoring the intense stinging sensation in his chest, heading toward the boulder, deliberately holding back until the proper moment.

Elevating the lance, the warrior rapidly covered the ground. A grin betrayed his confidence. He thought he had the white man right where he wanted him.

Nate looked at the pair of trees, then at the Ute. It would be close. He ran faster, his heart thumping, his temples throbbing, caked with sweat. Just a few more feet! That was all he needed. The drumming hooves seemed to be almost on top of him when he passed under the buckskin rope, and he leaped to the right as he glanced at his enemy.

The Ute rode straight into the trap. Rabidly intent on throwing his lance into the hated white's back, he concentrated on his running quarry to the exclusion of all else. The makeshift rope caught him a few inches below the neck and lifted him clean off his steed to topple hard onto his back, the lance flying from his hand.

The thought of taking a prisoner or sparing the warrior never entered Nate's mind. He sprang, alighting on top of the Ute and plunging his knife into the man's chest in the same motion. Once, twice, three times he buried the butcher knife to the hilt, and with each blow the warrior bucked and hissed.

Abruptly, the Ute gasped, thrashed feebly, and expired.

Taking a deep breath, Nate slowly rose, his eyes on the warrior's. He'd won. He'd actually won. Oddly, he didn't feel elated, didn't feel pleased with himself. How could he when he'd just slain three men? Three more to add to the total. What *was* the total so far? He'd honestly forgotten.

Did it even matter?

He took several wobbly strides, the excitement making him giddy. At least Sitting Bear, Evening Star, and Laughing Eyes were safe. He'd repaid them for their kindness and generosity. All he had to do was see them safely to their village, and he could hasten to his cabin and the lovely woman he longed to embrace.

The war party was finished.

Or was it?

Nate recalled there were still two members of the band unaccounted for, and he adhered to his earlier reasoning that the others must be scouring the countryside elsewhere or on their way to their own village. Who *cared* where they were? It didn't matter in the slightest.

Or did it?

A chilling thought instantly sobered him and prompted him to stare to the northwest in alarm. What if—and the idea was almost too horrible to contemplate—what if the remaining pair wasn't somewhere along the back trail? What if they had taken a different route and were in *front* of him? What if they'd taken a shortcut to the

Crow camp while the others had followed the tracks? That way, the Utes would have been assured of catching all of them.

Dear Lord!

Could it be?

A terrible premonition seized him, and he dashed to his guns. He fumbled with the powder and the balls as he reloaded the flintlocks and the rifle, and then he was sprinting to the stallion and vaulting into the saddle.

Please let him be wrong!

He jerked on the reins and brought the big black to a gallop, riding recklessly, the rifle in his left hand, forgetting all about his wounds, thinking only of the family he'd grown to care for, to love as if they were his very own.

The terrain flashed by. He lost all track of time, all track of the ground covered, all track of everything except his burning desire to reach the lodge as quickly as possible. When the stallion flagged, he urged it on, knowing the animal needed rest just as he did, knowing it had been through so much already, knowing it might die if he kept pushing, but push he did. The precious lives of the three Crows were more important than that of a horse, more important than his own. He'd vowed to protect them, and protect them he would, with his dying breath if need be.

Deer fled at his approach. Elk snorted and melted into the shadows. Buffalo regarded him warily.

Nate hardly noticed. His chest stung, his shoulder ached, his thighs were sore, his back stiff, but he cared not at all. All that counted was reaching the lodge.

The stallion was breathing heavily, its chest flecked with foam, its nostrils flaring, when they finally broke from the last stretch of forest and saw the field ahead. Nate's own breath caught in his throat when he spied the strange horses near the teepee and spied two men moving about near the doorway. An uncontrollable rage gripped every fiber of his being, a fury surpassing all furies, and he saw the world through a reddish haze. "No!" he screamed, and swept onward.

Both Utes were on their mounts in a flash, and together they wheeled and rode to meet him. One carried a bow, the other a war club.

Nate never swerved, never deviated from his course as he bore down on the warriors. He saw the bowman notch a shaft, but paid no heed. The Ute bearing the war club raised it on high, but he ignored that. All that mattered was protecting the Crows. All that counted was making sure the Utes never killed another innocent person. Even when the bowman aimed and let the arrow fly, he kept on charging.

The shaft streaked through the air, a lethal blur that no man could evade.

Nate didn't bother trying. His blood boiling, all he cared about was reaching the Utes. He glimpsed the shaft as it whizzed past his face, nicking his left cheek and drawing blood, and then he was almost upon them, still galloping all out. The Hawken molded to his right shoulder, he took a bead on the archer's head, and fired. Without waiting to observe the result, he angled the stallion at the second warrior, ramming the big black into the Ute's mount and bowling it over. The impact nearly unseated him, and then he saw the warrior struggling to rise, the man's leg pinned under the downed animal. He tossed the rifle aside, drew his knife, and vaulted from the saddle.

The Ute looked up and tried to bring the war club into play.

Nate landed on the Indian's horse as it tried to rise, sliding over its back to slam onto the warrior. His left hand grasped his foe's wrist, preventing the war club from swinging, even as the Ute grabbed his knife hand. The horse reached its feet, leaving them free to grapple and roll from side to side as each man strived to prevail.

As he glared into Nate's eyes, the Ute's countenance was transformed by sheer hatred into a feral mask.

Nate's fury lent strength to his arms. He ripped his hand loose and sank the knife into the warrior's side, not once but again and again and again, stabbing long after the Ute had ceased moving, long after his hand was coated with blood and red dots covered his shirt, neck, and chin. Only when a drop of blood sprayed onto his upper lip did he stop, suddenly aware of what he was doing, and lower his arm.

Feeling a singular numbness in his limbs, Nate rose awkwardly and shuffled a few feet from the Ute. He stared at the archer and found him dead in the high weeds. Belatedly, the shock hit, a reaction to the incensed combat. For a minute he stood still, striving to recover his senses. And then he remembered the Crows.

Evening Star!

Spinning, Nate ran toward the lodge, his gaze taking in the open flap and the lack of activity, as well as the absence of smoke. Please let them be all right, he prayed. Please let them be bound or staked out or hiding in the forest, but please let them be alive above all else! He slowed ten feet away. "Sitting Bear! Evening Star! Where are you?"

There was no answer.

Nate had to force his legs to take the necessary step to the lodge, and he was trembling when he sank to his knees and looked inside. A whine escaped his lips. He closed his eyes and groaned. "Oh God," he said softly, and doubled over, his arms wrapped around his midriff. The tears, when they came, wouldn't stop, and for the longest while the only sound that arose from the Crow camp were great, choking sobs.

Epilogue

The beautiful Indian woman with the flowing tresses and the troubled dark eyes were strolling along the south shore of a lake high in the Rockies, near a quaint cabin, when she happened to look to the west and spotted the lone rider. Instantly her hand flew to her mouth and her heart fluttered. She watched, scarcely believing her eyes, then broke into a run and shouted one of the few English words she knew. "Shakespeare! Shakespeare!"

From out of the cabin came a grizzled mountain man wearing buckskins and a brown beaver hat. He stared at her in bewilderment, then addressed her in the Shoshone tongue. "What is it, Winona? A grizzly?"

Winona gestured and exclaimed happily, "Nate! Nate!"

Pivoting, the mountain man let out a yell of delight. He waited for her to reach him, then they ran to meet her husband. "What did I tell you?" Shakespeare said. "I knew he'd come back safe and sound."

"Nate!" Winona shouted.

The solitary rider was leading a string of six horses. He gave a little wave and rode faster. Both the man and the animals appeared tremendously fatigued. When he reined up, he slid from the mare and seemed to sag. Straightening, he tossed his rifle to Shakespeare and opened his arms wide to embrace Winona.

His eyes narrowing, the mountain man studied the younger man's face. "You had us a bit worried. Where the hell have you been?"

Hugging his wife close, Nate stared over her shoulder at his mentor. "Took me a little longer than I figured. Sorry."

Shakespeare noted the haggard aspect of his friend's features and detected—something—in Nate's eyes, something that hadn't been there before he left. "Are you all right?"

"Yes."

"Another day and I would have lit out after you."

Nate didn't respond. He closed his eyes and inhaled the sweet fragrance of Winona's hair.

"What happened?"

"I don't want to talk about it."

The curt reply made Shakespeare pause. "Whatever you want, Nate. I didn't mean to pry." He turned and walked toward the cabin.

"Wait."

Shakespeare halted and looked back. "What is it? I thought I'd give you some time to yourselves."

"Are you on good terms with the Crows?"

Mystified by the unusual question, Shakespeare nodded.

"Do you know their top chief?"

"Chief Long Hair? Yep. Know him well. Why?"

"Do you know where he has his village this time of year?"

"Sure. Up near the Wind River," Shakespeare said. "Do you mind telling me what all this is about?"

Nate whispered a few words into Winona's ear, then released her. He stepped to his pack animal and removed a number of thin items from a pouch.

"What are those?" Shakespeare inquired.

"Eagle feathers," Nate said, extending his arm and opening his hand to reveal five feathers.

"What in the world are you doing with those?"

"After I've rested up, I want you to take me to Chief Long Hair's village. These feathers are for him." Nate motioned at the extra horses he'd brought back. "So are they."

Bewildered, the mountain man scratched his head and nodded. "Okay. If that's what you want. But I don't understand."

"I'll explain later," Nate promised. He took Winona's hand and headed toward their home. "Right now there's another favor you can do for me."

"Anything. You know that."

"Go for a ride."

"A ride?" Shakespeare repeated, and gazed at Winona's back. "Oh. Sure. At least I understand this request."

"Thanks. You have no idea how much this means to me."

Chuckling, Shakespeare stepped to the mare and took her reins. "Don't worry about the horses. I'll tend to them, then go for my little ride." He started to lead the animals toward the meadow bordering the cabin. "Say, how long do you want me to be gone, anyway?"

Nate answered without turning around. "Two or three days would be nice."

AUTHOR'S NOTE

Most people are familiar with the fact that at one time there was in widespread use among American Indians a medium of communication known as sign language. Combining hand movements and arm gestures, this universal language enabled Indians from different tribes, who ordinarily spoke quite distinct languages, to converse freely and easily. In 1885 it was estimated there were 110,000 sign-talking Indians in the U.S. Since then, with so many Native Americans enjoying the presumed benefits of a modern education, there are few left who can converse in sign.

In frontier times, when the first white men went West, many of them learned this language and used it extensively in their dealings with the Indians. Not until you read the actual accounts of trappers and mountain men do you realize just how widely this was done.

Certain liberties have been taken in this book to accommodate modern sentence construction because the proper sign sequence might cause confusion. For instance, the question "How old are you?" translated into sign becomes: *Question-how-*

many-you-winter." Or take another example such as, "I feel very sad." In sign this becomes: *"I-heart-on-the-ground."* I hope historical purists will forgive me for conforming to current literary form.

Indian sign language is an effective, beautiful medium of expression, and it's unfortunate that sign is now relegated to the status of a relic from the past.